This is a work of fiction. Names, characters, places and incidents are either the product of the author's imagination or are used fictitiously.

WHORL
First publication: November 2016
Copyright 2016 by James Tarr

ISBN: 978-1539723783
Printed in the United States of America

WHORL

James Tarr

"Is Detroit going to turn things around? I could lie and tell you yes. But you know what? This city's screwed. The only place I've ever been that looks anything like Detroit does now? Chernobyl. I'm not being funny, that's the truth."

Anthony Bourdain
November 2013

PART I

THE ONE-PERCENTERS

"Out of every one hundred men, ten shouldn't even be there, eighty are just targets, nine are the real fighters, and we are lucky to have them, for they make the battle. Ah, but the one, one is a warrior, and he will bring the others back."

Heraclitus

CHAPTER ONE

David Anderson turned onto Third Street and pulled his beat-up Jeep Cherokee into the gravel parking lot. The lot was small, and enclosed by a rusty eight-foot chain link fence topped with menacingly shiny concertina wire. The electric gate was on rollers, but it was always left open. He doubted whether the motor would even work if they tried it, but they never really had any problems.

Technically the lot was under surveillance, but he'd seen the black and white picture the camera on the roof fed to the TV in the control room. It might as well have been one of those ultrasound pictures of a baby in the womb. They looked like moonscapes; he could never see the baby, and in the camera's fish-eye lens he couldn't even recognize his own car on the TV screen.

He climbed out of his car and stretched. The sun was just coming up over the buildings on Cass, and shadows still covered most of the ground around him. Outside the lot on one side was a building with impressive stonework that had probably been built in the twenties or thirties. It was now a blackened, windowless hulk that would look at home in a zombie movie.

The vacant lot on the other side sported knee-high grass that would be a foot taller in a month. The city used to do a better job of mowing the vacant property, but there was just so much of it, and so little tax money coming in anymore, that pretty much anybody who could get out of the city was gone. Too much space, not enough money, not enough people, and the ones who were left.....

Weeds grew along the fenceline, some of them nearly as tall as he was, and there were a few maple saplings growing in the corner. It was ironic; the closer Detroit got to death, the greener it became. In nature things usually worked the opposite way.

There was only one person on foot that he could see, a woman heading west down the sidewalk. Deathly skinny, from her stained, crumpled sweatshirt and jeans it was hard to tell if she had been in a fight or just up all night. She wasn't wearing a bra, he could see that, whether he wanted to or not. Mostly not. She took one look at him and his freshly laundered and pressed uniform shirt, and gun, and didn't bother to proposition him. Dave was still young enough that being that close to a hooker, even one who looked like she had several infectious diseases, gave him a little naughty thrill.

He waited for her to pass, then did a quick check for traffic. With hardly anybody living in the area the cars were few and far between, but in a city where the cops ran from one violent crime to the next speed limits were almost as big of a joke as stop signs. Street clear he headed across the street to the nondescript tan building. Two stories, concrete, with a single overhead door (closed) and a single pedestrian door. No company name or sign indicating what the business was, although all anybody had to do to find out was look into the fenced-off yard on the west side of the building. Or watch the trucks coming and going all day.

Ten foot chainlink around the yard, no rust on this fence, topped with overlapping coils of razor wire. Whoever came in last, unless they were in one of the new trucks, had to park in the outside yard. In the summer it wasn't bad, but in cold weather he usually had to scrape the ice and snow off himself. Though it was late May the early morning air was a little chilly, but he'd left his uniform jacket at home. It'd be eighty by noon, hotter inside the truck.

With his fingers touching the handle Dave looked up into the camera above the door. After a few seconds of nothing, he hit the doorbell and grabbed the handle again. Whoever was manning the controls finally spotted him and buzzed him in.

Inside the building resembled a warehouse more than anything, which made sense considering it was nothing more than a glorified garage attached to a big safe. The airy space echoed with the shouts of men and the revving of truck engines. Dave hurried up the gently sloping ramp just in case one of the scarier drivers was on his way out. There'd been a couple of close calls, on the ramp and in the loading area, but somehow nobody had been run over. Yet.

He punched in, then looked around for Aaron. He found him at the window, checking out their load. Everything was locked up overnight in the vault. Outside the vault was the office, with the pass-through window. All the messengers called the small room where they picked up and dropped off their cash the Fault Room, because if their load was ever found to be short, that's where it was discovered, and it was always their fault.

"I take it I'm driving today," Dave said as he watched Aaron counting the boxes of pennies on his steel cart. In the armored car business the messenger, and the messenger alone, was responsible for the money. He signed for the load in the morning, had to keep track of what he picked up or dropped off and get signatures for everything, and then turned whatever he had left into the vault at the end of the day. All the driver did was drive.

"Fuckin' Huntington," Aaron said, kicking one of the penny boxes. "I thought I was going to have a light load today, until I saw their twenty boxes of fucking pennies." Aaron, like most veteran messengers — the honest ones at least—had long ago stopped thinking of his cargo as money. To him it was just weight. Pounds, not dollars. Cash was good, he could do cash all day. Paper, paper, paper. It was the coin that killed you, especially around the holidays. Christ. First week of December, every day he had two hundred boxes of coins to deliver.

"Are you done bitching?" Joe asked through the window. "I want to finish checking you out before I die of old age. Huntington cash, one, for four hundred thou even." He hoisted the canvas bundle onto the steel shelf and shoved it toward Aaron, who spun it around so he could check the tag against his paperwork, then yanked it down onto the cart. All twenties inside, by the size of it.

Joe was nearly six foot six and slightly older than God, at least if you believed what he said. He practically had to fold himself in two to look out through the vault window. A few wispy white hairs dotted his age-spotted skull, and he reeked of tobacco. His yellow and usually bloodshot eyes were huge behind Roy Orbison-looking glasses. He wore his uniform pants in true geezer chic style, pulled up into his armpits, revealing white, droopy socks and legs as skinny as toothpicks and damn near the same color. His uniform shirt had last been white sometime during the Nixon administration.

"You're going to outlive all of us, you pissy bastard," Aaron said good-naturedly. He turned to Dave. "You'll never guess what we've got today," he said with a smile. It was a real smile, he seemed highly amused by something, but the look on his face would have scared most people away. Dave figured that was why Aaron had never been robbed -- he looked slightly insane.

Jet black hair, a little too long so it touched his collar, and a true '70s pornstar moustache that needed a trim. Bad teeth -- not horrible, but two years of braces would have done wonders for him. Of course, his mother had barely been able to pay the rent on the trailer when he was growing up, so braces were out of the question. So were regular visits to the dentist. Slightly buggy eyes, and an intense staring gaze that made Dave think of a serial killer. A real one, not a Hollywood archetype. One glare and even the freakiest-looking loiterer left the area when he was unloading the truck at a stop. Surprisingly Aaron wasn't ugly but rather handsome, in a bad-boy sort of way, and could be very charming. He did his best to bed every teller better looking than a Rottweiler, and had succeeded more often than he'd failed.

The two of them had never been robbed while working together. Dave figured it had to be because of the way they looked. Aaron glared at any male like he was wondering how their livers tasted, and Dave always paid attention and looked competent. "Short-haired college boy" is how he was usually described, with "suburban white boy" following a close second. Not only was he always wearing a clean, pressed uniform, whenever they were at a stop he actually scanned the area for possible threats. Not like some of the drivers the company had, that's for sure.

"I shudder to think," Dave said.

"A third man."

Technically, every truck, every day, should have a third man, a guard who would exit the truck and stand beside the messenger as he loaded his dolly, follow him wherever he went, but most customers didn't want to pay for the extra service.

"How do we rate?"

"New guy, you're supposed to train him," Joe said through the window.

"Christ. So am I driving?" Dave occasionally worked as a messenger, but because he was only part-time, and his schedule was the same every week, he usually worked with Aaron. Drivers weren't supposed to get out of the vehicle, but Dave always wore body armor under his uniform shirt, just in case. Aaron wore a vest and plate, every day, religiously.

"Yeah, I don't trust this monkey in traffic, but he'll do fine as a bullet catcher," Aaron said.

"Jesus, Aaron." Dave looked around to see who had heard him. "Where is he?"

"Out at the truck. We've got the Beast again today."

"Well, at least it runs." *Even though it doesn't have air conditioning, or a radio, or shocks*, he added silently.

"Runs, it's fucking *Christine*, that thing's never going to quit."

The vault door banged open, and one of the supervisors barreled out. "Jesus Reg!" Dave exclaimed, jumping out of the way just before the cart wheel would've run over his foot, undoubtedly breaking something. "What's your hurry?"

"Gotta be done by three, got Tigers tickets," Reg called back over his shoulder. His chunky legs pumped behind the cart, heavily laden with coin.

Dave left the fault room and stood looking for the truck. He spotted it near the back of the garage, and was pleased to see it'd been parked indoors overnight. The garage walls were painted grey over an odd shade of blue, except for the big patch at the back where Stuey'd run the coin truck through the cinderblocks. Drive, Reverse, whatever. Half again as long as the other trucks, the coin truck had a beefed-up suspension to handle its heavy load. Stuey and Jeff went back and forth to Ann Arbor every day with several tons of coin. The two of them were as unlikely a pair as Dave could've imagined, but had worked the run together for years without a hitch.

Jeff came rolling by on a forklift, sporting a full pallet of $1000 quarter bags from the coin vault. Instead of counting the coins they just weighed the bags, and the scales were accurate to within +/- one quarter. The forklift beeped loudly no matter which direction it was heading, forward or back, but still about once a year somebody managed to hit it with a truck. Its yellow skin was scraped and dented like it'd been mauled by a dinosaur.

Stuey was standing at the back end of his truck, watching as his partner raised the pallet up to the open door. He was a big black man, a heavy gut straining at the suspenders holding up his back-support belt. His "white" uniform shirt was uniformly grey, and his hair, always a bit too long, was spotted with grey to match. Dave had always thought Stuey looked a little like Don Cornelius of *Soul Train* fame, but the resemblance ended whenever Stuey opened his mouth.

"Ey bi' mannnn, whatcha at?" Stuey called out to Dave as he walked up. He had to shout to be heard over the forklift. "Lookin' sharp, lookin sharp, gotta sweet mama waitin' fo ya affa work t'day?" He cackled and looked to Jeff for a reaction. Jeff smiled but never looked away from the pallet as he threaded it through the doorway, and inch to spare on either side. Stuey's unique speech pattern had been termed *Alabama Marble-Mouth* by Aaron, a description which hardly did justice to the abuse Stuey heaped upon the English language.

"No, I'm all gussied up for you, you big teddy bear," Dave said with a grin. He quickly scooted around the back of the forklift -- Jeff was notorious for abrupt changes in direction -- and kept on toward his truck. Stuey cackled even more, and glanced up at Jeff, who was lowering the pallet onto the enclosed bed of the truck. Even with the heavy duty springs the truck bed sunk two inches under the weight of just one pallet.

"Teddy bear," Stuey said with a smile. "Heh heh heh."

Jeff was in his late forties, a chain smoker with sandy brown hair going grey and a handlebar moustache. He would've looked more at home in a string tie and cowboy hat, and still had some of the twang, even though he hadn't been back to Arkansas in twenty years. "Yeah, that's just what you are," he said drily, looking down at Stuey.

"Bi' black sessy teddy bear," Stuey rolled on with a smile. "Good fo *allll* the ladies, givvum some a dat Teddy Bear blacksnake, da ol' one-two, dey be smilin' like it's Christmas." His deep voice sounded like gravel down a metal chute, and his three-pack-a-day habit wasn't making it any clearer. Most people couldn't even understand him, which was just fine with Stuey. He liked to be left alone as much as possible.

Reg Coleman was throwing the heavy coin boxes into the back of his truck like a madman. It reminded Dave of news footage he'd seen of people frantically tossing sandbags onto the banks of a rapidly rising river. Pete, his regular driver, just stood out of the way, grinning. He gave a little wave to Dave as he passed. They were both part of the same sub-species at Absolute, white boys from the suburbs looking to get into law enforcement. Pete had his name on a couple of hiring lists, and would probably be working for one police department or another by the end of the year.

Dave reached "The Beast" and looked around for the third man. Nowhere to be found. What a surprise. One of the oldest trucks in the company, 1555 was also the biggest, second only to Stuey and Jeff's coin truck. Although the exterior had been recently painted, and the diamond-plate polished, the interior of it was as inviting as a turn-of-the-century jail cell. During winter the heater only worked when the truck was moving, and in summer the steel got so hot Dave couldn't lean his forearm against the door for more than a few seconds. Anything over eighty-five degrees outside and the truck turned into a rolling oven. Technically the air-conditioning worked, chugging out cool wisps of air so faint they were imperceptible six inches from the unit, but there really was no recourse. The tiny gunports wouldn't stay propped open when they drove, and armored car windows don't roll down.

Aaron arrived, pushing the cart. He tried the side door of the rear compartment and found it was open, and the two of them began transferring the cart's load into the back of the truck.

"I think I've been working here too long," Dave told Aaron.

"Why?"

"I just had a conversation with Stuey, and I understood every word he said."

"Jesus Christ. Get out, get out now, while you still can."

Squatting in the open doorway Dave looked up and saw who had to be their third man approaching. He looked barely sixteen, but by law had to be at least twenty-one since he carried a gun. The fat gave him a baby face, and a build like Santa. He looked nervous and eager to please. Dave tapped Aaron and nodded at their third. Aaron turned around.

"Where the hell have you been?"

A guilty look. "The bathroom."

"Well Christ, don't just unlock the truck and walk away, we're not delivering fucking milk you know."

"I--"

"Forget about it. This is Davey, my partner. He may look like a brainless college kid, but he knows what the fuck he's doing, which is more than I can say for most of the humps around here, so you listen to him."

"Gee, thanks," Dave said. He saw the kid was carrying one of the company guns, a battered Smith & Wesson M&P revolver that had probably been new during the Truman administration, in a cheap padded nylon holster. Probably loaded with the company ammo, too. He shook his head. Kid would be better off with a baseball bat.

"What's your name? Mo? That short for something?" Aaron asked.

The black kid squirmed. "Elmo," he said, looking at the floor.

"No shit? As in *'Tickle Me'*? Hey, don't knock it, at least it's a real fuckin' name, not like Ikea or something."

Dave blinked and shook his head in confusion. "Ikea?" They'd opened up a big store not too long ago in Canton.

"You want to bet money that there isn't a little girl born in Detroit the last few years that ain't been named Ikea?" Aaron challenged him. "I know someone at Wayne County, they can do a name search on the birth certificates. Fifty bucks on it? Hundred? No? How bout we limit it to the past two years?"

Dave shook his head. "I'm not taking that bet."

"Bout the best way to shout 'I'm stupid' to the world, you ask me, give your kid a fucked-up name."

Dave stared at his co-worker. "You're just a regular politician, aren't you?"

"Hey, I'm just a fuckin' observer."

"You'll have to forgive my partner, he was raised by wolves," Dave told the new kid, who wasn't sure what to make of their exchange.

"Taylor-tucky trailer trash, born and bred," Aaron said proudly. "Dave's gonna drive today," he told Mo. "You'll be my guard. They tell you what a guard's supposed to do?"

"But they said--"

"I don't give a fuck what they said. I'm the messenger on this run, which means I'm the boss once we get out that door. I tell you to sit on the hood and wave your cock at the hookers, you do it. Driving an armored car ain't like regular driving, and I'm not going to have you behind the wheel your first day out. Dave'll show you how it's done. Every run's different, but you'll get the idea. He's good. He can make this beast *dance*. Hell, you know he got this thing airborne once? Four feet of fucking daylight under the tires."

Aaron loved telling this story. Mo's mouth opened in awe and he stared at the truck towering above them.

"Not on purpose," Dave assured him, shaking his head.

Dave wrestled the big truck up onto the sidewalk in front of the ugly gray building and parked. They had eight feet of clearance between the truck and the building, with the driver's side of the truck flush with the curb. There was parking allowed on the street, but Aaron preferred it this way, and knowing his reasoning Dave wasn't sure he was wrong. Dave looked back through the steel mesh at Aaron, then back out the windows. As Mo went to open the passenger door and jump down Dave stopped him.

"I'll get out here," he told Mo. "You just stay in the cab."

"You sure? Why?"

"Because for one thing you were about to open that door, again, without looking around," Aaron chastised him from the back. "For another, this is a hot location."

"Hot? You mean, like robbery attempts?"

"Not so far, but between the cars and the foot traffic you need to keep your head on a swivel here. Vernor and Junction, baby, *estamos en el ghetto Mexicano*."

"What?"

Aaron just sighed. Most of the signs along Vernor were in both English and Spanish, and of the ones that were in only one language, most of those weren't English. It still wasn't as bad as Dearborn, though. No women dressed as ninjas walking around, all the signs looking like they'd been vandalized by scribbling toddlers.

"You see who's having lunch again?" Dave asked his partner with a jerk of his head.

Aaron glanced back over at the blue Michigan State Police Charger parked in front of the coney island across the street. Even after all these years they still only had one big red gumball light on the top. "Yeah, I saw 'em. Fucking ramp roosters, they practically live there."

"That's good, right? That the cops are there? So it scares away anybody thinking about robbing us?" Mo looked back and forth between the two of them. Dave let Aaron take it.

"Maybe," Aaron said. "As a general rule, though, cops get the fuck out of the area when they see us, *just in case* there's a robbery attempt. They don't want to get caught in the crossfire. That's why you probably won't see them come out and leave while we're sitting here. Our stop here is, what, ten, fifteen minutes? And we've seen an MSP car there probably two dozen times over the years. How many times have they finished lunch, walked out, and driven off while we've been parked here? Dave?"

"Never."

Aaron looked at the new guy. "Never. That, dude, is what they call a *statistical anemone*." He looked back at his partner. "You see anything?"

"Just that guy sitting in that piece of shit gray Chevy down there in front of the thrift shop, been there since we rolled up." There was a decent amount of foot traffic on the sidewalk on both sides of the street, but other than the occasional glances no one was paying the armored car much attention, or loitering close by.

"Yeah, I saw him." All the cars in this neighborhood were pieces of shit, although half of them were layered with extra chrome or gold or decals of the Virgin Mary on the back window or some such. Hadn't these people ever heard of stereotypes? Aaron's mouth spun up again. "What the hell is with all the 'In Loving Memory of Pablo' or whoever the fuck family member who died, commemorated by a big sticker on the back window of their car? What's in loving memory, the sticker? The back window? The car? Did they buy their shitty Buick with dead Pablo's life insurance benefits? I swear to God." He shook his head, then peered out the dirty windows to either side, studying the cars and pedestrians. "Okay," he said to Mo, "what's company policy if you're a driver and someone grabs your messenger, tells you to open up or they're going to shoot him?"

"Uh, um, I drive away."

"Why?"

"Why? Ummmm, I guess 'cuz they figure the dude only wants the cash, so if I drive away...."

"...they've got no one to bargain with, so they just get pissed off and walk away," Aaron finished for him. "It's a good theory, and it might even work part of the time. Maybe even most of the time." He leaned forward and his voice dropped an octave. "But when it doesn't, they'll put a bullet in your messenger's head because they're so pissed off, or because he's already seen their face, or because he already has some cash on him that he took out of the truck."

Mo didn't really have an answer for that. Aaron leaned even further forward.

"So what you need to do is work out with your messenger beforehand what he's okay with you doing. I don't care what company policy is, you ever drive off and leave me standing there with a gun to my head, you better hope I die, otherwise I'm coming for you." He looked at Dave as the new employee's eyes went wide and said cheerfully, "You ready?"

Dave popped the door and jumped down, and by the time he had the door shut again he had his pistol in his hand, per company policy. He kept it down along his leg, walked around the back of the truck, across the sidewalk, and stood against the building next to the front door, looking up and down the street.

A middle-aged man in dirty work clothes approached the bank. He registered the truck, then Dave in uniform standing next to the door, then the pistol in Dave's hand, but all he did was nod as he headed into the lobby. Just another day in Detroit.

Aaron popped the back door, lowered the dolly to the ground with a clank, jumped down, and began stacking boxes of coin. The tendency was to watch the messenger, but the trick was to fight your natural instincts and look away from the target. Dave checked out anybody on foot within fifty feet, any passing car, and even scanned the few second floor windows nearby, just looking for something out of the ordinary, some disruption in the natural pattern and flow.

"We good?" Aaron was finished with the coin and was about to start with the cash bags.

Dave's head kept moving. "So far." He glanced up at the cab of the truck and saw the new kid watching the two of them, instead of what he should have been, which was everything else. Moron. Nice enough, but not a whole lot going on upstairs.

Past the bank was the parking lot, then another narrow building that at the moment was vacant, and then an alley. Dave saw the squad car as it nosed out of the alley and paused halfway across the sidewalk.

It was a two man DPD squad car, and both officers were scanning the street. They saw him a second later and he stared back, expressionless, giving them a nod. There was a slight pause, and Dave saw they were taking in the scene— the truck, his and Aaron's uniforms, the dolly stacked with tan canvas cash bags, and the gun in Dave's hand. Then the driver gave him a slight nod in return, and pulled out— heading away from them. Quickly.

"Who dat white boy think he is, standing there with a gun in his hand in *my* city?" Aaron said with a smile, watching the squad car drive away. "We be the po-lice, ain't nobody else should have no guns. Ain't got no respect. Muthafuckin racist, dat's what dat shit is, whitey with a gun, just another perpetration by the man to keep a *brutha* down!" His voice kept getting louder. "Can you dig it? I said, *can you dig it?*"

Dave threw his free hand up in the air. "You know, just 'cause I'm standing here with a gun in my hand doesn't mean I want to get into a gunfight today."

"Relax," Aaron said dismissively. "Man, nobody has a sense of humor anymore. You can't even mention race without being called a racist. Archie Bunker'd get arrested for hate crimes."

"You need some help wheeling that thing in or something?" Dave asked him, glancing up and down the sidewalk. Maybe they'd be able to clear the stop without Aaron causing a race riot.

"Nah, I'm good," Aaron said cheerfully, his voice back to normal. Dave opened the lobby door for him, scanned the interior quickly, then stepped aside for his partner.

"You need to lighten up," Aaron told him as he pushed the heavily laden dolly by. "Have some fun. And I'll give you five bucks if you can figure out what movie I was quoting."

"Seriously? *The Warriors.* Try something hard next time."

"Shit."

Seven minutes later they came back out, Dave in front. He had to step out of the bank onto the sidewalk before he could check left and right, and when his partner didn't get jumped or shot Aaron followed him out with the dolly. He didn't need the dolly as the cash bag, even filled with $86,000, didn't weigh that much, but Aaron wasn't about to fill both his hands. Keep your gun hand free if at all possible.

Dave stood with his back to the front of the bank and swept the area with his eyes while Dave rolled the dolly toward the side of the van. The door could be opened by the driver, but neither of them heard a click.

"That moron listening to his iPod again?" Aaron asked.

"Looks like it." Mo hadn't even noticed them come out of the bank yet, he was bobbing his head and staring off down the street. The State Police cruiser was still parked in front of the Coney, the troopers nowhere in sight.

"Jesus, I'm going to shoot him myself before the day is out." He banged the door violently with the flat of his hand. "Pop the door!" he yelled.

Dave used the remote on the garage door but parked in his driveway out front. The Mustang was parked inside the garage on the left side, with about three feet between the car and the wall, which had a small, curtained window. Technically it was a two-and-a-half car garage, but preventing door dings on the 'Stang was a constant battle.

He went into the house through the garage, shutting the overhead door behind him. The canvas lunch bag he tossed onto the island in the kitchen, then hit the switches which flooded the kitchen with light.

The house was quiet, with a few dust motes floating in the air before him. Dave checked his watch and saw that it wasn't even four thirty yet—early day, but that was all for the better. Aaron had been about ready to kill the poor kid by the end of the day's run. He seemed nice, but actually paying attention to his surroundings seemed a little beyond Mo, which is not what you want in an armored car company employee.

"Nice kid, he'll probably be President of the United States some day, but he's not fucking driving for me again," Aaron told Joe back at the vault, never mind that Mo hadn't spent a minute behind the wheel of the truck. His lack of observational skills, an attention span, and his apparent addiction to his iPod had been enough.

"Somebody put you in charge when I went to go take a dump?" Joe asked him, peering through his thick glasses. Dave had just walked away as the arguing commenced.

He grabbed a plastic bottle of Diet Coke out of the refrigerator, took a swig, then headed upstairs to change. Gun, magazines, holster and magazine pouches came off the belt and went onto the bed. It was a big bed, King-size, and he'd made it before going to work. Black uniform belt got hung in the closet on a hook, shoes on the floor in the closet neatly lined up, and the uniform shirt and pants into the hamper.

A fresh pair of jeans came out of one dresser drawer, a black t-shirt out of another. He grabbed the brown reinforced leather belt off the hook in the closet, then the holster and Glock went back on his belt. The double magazine pouch he only carried when he was in uniform for Absolute, and he grabbed a single magazine carrier off the dresser and clipped in onto the belt on his left hip. The other spare mag and the double magazine carrier he left on top of the dresser.

The doors to the other bedrooms on the second floor were open but Dave didn't glance into them as he walked down the hallway and headed downstairs to the big kitchen. The kitchen cabinets were really dated. Had he noticed that before? They might have been original to the house, which was built in '78. Maybe he should paint them, or replace the doors. The appliances weren't that old. He stood there for a while, thinking, then noticed the noise, or lack therof. The house was really quiet when he was the only person there. A dog would be nice. He'd had a dog growing up, Lacey, but she'd died at the ripe old age of fourteen. But he couldn't get a dog. He was gone too much for a grown dog, never mind a puppy, with all that housetraining. And no fucking way he'd get a cat. Single guy with a cat? Might as well pierce his ears and start wearing pink shirts with popped collars.

No surveillance job tonight, or over the weekend for that matter, so he was on his own until Monday morning. He decided it wasn't too early to eat and dug around in the fridge to see what he had. The leftover pizza he'd save for Saturday....hmmmmmmm. Half a steak, already cooked, some lettuce.....simple enough. He heated the steak in the microwave while he chopped up some of the lettuce, added a few grape tomatoes and sliced onions. He sliced the steak into thin strips and laid it on the salad, then drenched the whole thing in Italian dressing.

This time of day there was nothing on TV but crappy local news or reality TV court shows. He didn't do reality TV. Ever. "I deal with losers, liars, and idiots all day at work, why would I want to watch them on TV?" he'd said to one of his co-workers recently, and meant it. Daytime TV seemed to be specifically designed to keep losers and morons entertained and distracted from their shitty lives. He grabbed the book he was currently reading, Hemingway's Green Hills of Africa, his Diet Coke, and sat down at the small kitchen table by the bay window. When he was done eating he left the book on the table, bookmark slid into place (not as good as For Whom the Bell Tolls, but not bad), rinsed the bowl out in the sink, and put it in the dishwasher. He stood in the big kitchen for a while, leaning against the counter, looking toward the window behind the table but not seeing anything, lost in thought. The house was completely still.

After a few minutes like that he took another swig of Diet Coke, then pulled the cardboard silhouette targets out from behind the couch and hung them on the nails on the mantel above the fireplace. As a kid he used to hang his stocking from them, but that was a long time ago....

He spaced the targets about a yard apart then went back into the kitchen. From the edge of the kitchen to the targets was eight yards exactly. Not as far as he would have liked, but he made do. He unloaded his Glock and placed both the magazine that was in it and the spare on his belt onto the counter, with the round he racked out of the chamber next to them. Then he triple-checked to make sure his pistol was empty. The corner drawer held the weighted dummy magazine and the electronic timer, which he hung on his back pocket.

The timer could be programmed for a random start, and had a par time function with a second beep programmable down to the tenth of a second. Dave checked the par time setting—one second even. Good enough to start. He hit the start button, relaxed his hands at his sides, and waited. Somewhere between three and five seconds later (closer to three this time) the timer beeped and he did a smooth draw of his pistol, getting the front sight settled evenly in the notch of the rear sight and centered on the chest of the center silhouette target, his finger lightly on the trigger, just as the timer beeped a second time.

"Slow *and* sloppy," he muttered to himself. He needed to work on his reloads and shooting on the move, but he started every practice session with the basics, beginning with the flat-footed draw. He took a deep breath, hit the button again, and let his arms hang naturally.

An hour later, his right shoulder and forearm sore and aching, he put the timer and faux magazine away. The spare magazine went back into the carrier on his hip, and he reloaded his Glock and put it back in the kydex holster on his right hip. Glocks, with their polymer frames, weren't heavy to begin with. Carrying it every day he didn't even notice the weight anymore.

Dave checked his watch. Shit, still barely six o'clock. He peered out the window again, then used his phone to check the weather report, to see if there was any rain rolling in. Nope.

Only a few streets in the square mile subdivision in which his house was located were straight, to deter non-residents from cutting through the neighborhood. Well-maintained sidewalks lined both sides of every street, and as long as there wasn't snow on the ground they were great to jog on.

His four mile route kept him mostly inside his subdivision and the next one over, with only a brief stretch on a main road. He did a Figure 8 or the infinity symbol depending on how you looked at it. If he was just jogging and not working on his sprinting he normally did eight-minute miles, and much preferred to do them on pavement as opposed to a treadmill. Treadmills didn't work the back of your legs nearly as much. The early evening weather was mild, and in a t-shirt and shorts he didn't break a sweat until he'd done the first mile.

Back at the house he kicked off his shoes and pulled the small Kahr 9mm out of the holster inside the front of his waistband and set it on the coffee table in the family room so he could stretch. He wasn't very flexible, and not likely to ever become so, but knew that if he didn't stretch regularly his chances of injury rose with physical activity. The little pocket auto had a polymer frame and a stainless steel slide and wasn't likely to rust from his sweat, but he still made sure to wipe it down after every run.

Dave grabbed the remote and scanned the programming guide on the TV to see what was on, then flipped over to HBO. They were doing a Godfather marathon in honor of Pacino's birthday, the original and parts 2 and 3 all in a row. Part 3 was mediocre at best, but the first two......it was going to be a good night.

Dave jerked awake and sat up on the couch, not sure why. Something had woke him up, but what? The TV was still on, some Adam Sandler movie, and Dave grabbed the remote and hit Mute. He grabbed the Kahr off the table and stood up, checking his watch. After three-thirty in the morning. Late.

The garage door opened and Gina came in as loud as a car crash in her swishy nylon jacket and high heels on the kitchen floor. She looked at Dave rubbing the sleep from his eyes.

"You're here late," he said. He checked his watch again, wondering if he'd read it right half-asleep.

Gina set her big purse on the kitchen counter and looked at what he was wearing, with the TV on behind him. "I was hanging out with Tiffany and Kelly after work. You fall asleep watching TV?" she asked with a smile. She watched him set the gun down as she took off the white thigh-length jacket and hung it over one of the kitchen chairs. Underneath she was in an orange thong bikini above the red shoes, which had four inch heels. How she could drive in those he had no idea.

"Apparently," he said as she stalked over to him in her tall heels. He could smell the alcohol on her, and the marijuana, when she was six feet away. He blinked a few more times to get his head clear.

"I am so fucking horny," she told him, wrapping her arms around his neck. In the heels she was almost as tall as him, and her chest put his to shame. He wondered if the money he'd spent on health club dues over the years was more or less than what she'd paid her surgeon. She definitely had more to show for it. They kissed, and her tongue was all over his. The taste of alcohol on her was strong. Driving had probably been a very bad decision on her part. He grabbed her curvy ass with both hands and gave both cheeks a quick squeeze.

"I'm a little grungy," he told her. "I went jogging in these clothes, and didn't shower."

She bent her head to the crook of his neck and inhaled deeply. Anyone watching would have seen her nipples harden inside the bikini top. "Perfect," she murmured in his ear, and undid the drawstring of his shorts.

CHAPTER TWO

They'd done all the prep work and surveillance that they could, but the day of the thing they always arrived early and got eyes on. The Suburban was parked in a lot across 8 Mile, and they had a good view across the eight lanes of traffic and the grassy median.

Not a lot of cars in the lot they were watching, and the normal amount of traffic on 8 Mile for 11:30 on a Saturday morning. Wilson had shotgun, and looked up and down the border with Detroit through the tinted windows. Nothing looked out of sorts, and there was nothing unusual on the scanner. Not that the lack of concerned radio traffic meant anything, there were always ways for units to keep in touch that didn't involve police channels.

"Fuck, let's *go*," Eddie said from the backseat, squirming. The tension in the car was palpable. Wilson ignored him, as did everyone else. They all had their heads on swivels.

"Anybody got anything?" Wilson finally said.

"Ain't shit," Eddie said.

"I got nuthin, Top," Parker said. Gabe, behind the wheel, just shook his head.

Wilson took a deep breath. "Okay, let's do this. Everybody remember what you're supposed to do, where you're supposed to be. Commo check."

There was a rustling as everybody put their headset mikes over their heads and switched them on. Thirty seconds later they'd verified everybody's equipment was working, and Wilson took another deep breath. His heart was hammering in his chest. Getting too old for this shit.

"Hoods," he told everybody, and pulled the balaclava over his head.

"You know it!" Eddie said.

Gabe, now looking like a bulky ninja behind the wheel, checked to make sure traffic was clear and then pulled out onto 8 Mile. He angled across all four westbound lanes, hit the Michigan left around the median, and waited for a break in the eastbound traffic. When he had one he powered the Suburban across all the lanes, into the lot, and under the jutting roof.

The valet was in a polo shirt with the club logo on it, and he had almost reached the driver's door when Parker popped open the back door and shoved the AK in his face.

"Shut up and fucking turn around," Parker growled.

"Shit!" the kid said, and froze. Parker was a big man, and muscled the kid, who looked like he was a college student, around to face the club's door. As he marched the kid toward the entrance, one hand clamped around the back of his neck and the AK pointing past his shoulder, Wilson and Eddie closed in behind.

Parker had the kid open the door and they went in quickly. It was dark inside the club, and the shit music was blasting away. Kid Rock, of course.

The bouncer just inside the front door didn't make a peep at the sight of the guns and was swept before them as they hit the main room. Parker shoved the valet away from him and moved left as Wilson and Eddie arrowed ahead.

"Everybody get the fuck down!" Wilson yelled out into the big room, straining to be heard over the country rock. Holy shit did he hate this music. He brandished the AK on its sling, grabbed a man at a nearby booth and pulled him out of it by his shirtfront and threw him on the floor. "This is a fucking robbery. Get on the floor and shut the fuck up."

"Floor! Floor! On the floor!" he heard Parker and Eddie yelling behind him. He kept along the right wall, along the bar, and at muzzle point put about half a dozen customers and dancers on the floor.

The skinny tattooed bartender looked like she didn't know where to go. To get out from behind the bar she would have had to walk away from the man with the gun, and that didn't feel like the best idea to her.

"Climb over," Wilson told her, gesturing with the AK. He then stopped and shouldered the rifle, pointing it at the heart of the man he knew was the floor manager as he stood up from a bar stool. About five ten, with a blonde ponytail, the guy was a serious body builder and probably ran two-fifty, all of it muscle. "We going to have a problem?" Wilson asked him.

"Nope," Shane replied. His hands went up. He was staring at the end of the rifle, and noticing just how steady it was. He had a .380 in his pocket, but one small pistol against three guys with AKs and body armor who looked like they knew what they were doing was a losing proposition. If they were just there to rob the place, fine, they'd never know he had a gun. If they decided to start capping people, that was something different. That happened, he was going down shooting.

"Walk ahead of me," Wilson told him. Shane turned and moved, and Wilson stayed two steps behind him, just out of reach, the AK leveled at his back. *Jesus, this redneck was as wide as he was tall.*

Parker pointed his AK across the room at the DJ in his little elevated booth. "Shut that shit off and get down here!"

he shouted. Kid Rock cut off in mid-sentence, and the dancers still frozen on the stages started climbing down awkwardly in their high heels.

Parker stayed by the door and Eddie moved halfway down the bar to cover the middle of the room as Wilson headed for the back.

"Get the fuck out there!" Wilson yelled at the dancers, waitresses, and "shot girls" he encountered cowering in the hallway, one of them still holding the tray of Jell-O shots. *Bunch of skinny white bitches with fake tans, none of them with titties unless they bought 'em, and not one sister.* They sounded like screaming seagulls as they ran past him toward the stage where Eddie was shoving a big drunk guy off a chair onto the floor. Drunk before noon on Saturday. Nice.

Shane stopped in front of the office door. Black steel, it had an electronic eye in the center, and a keypad off to one side. "Open it," Wilson told him.

". . . I said get the fuck down! Hey!" Eddie shouted behind him, and the sound of the AK going off was huge. Wilson spun around and immediately saw that the big guy was either too stupid to know what he was supposed to do or too drunk, or he actually might have been trying to put up a fight. Eddie had fired a warning shot into the air, and as Wilson laid eyes on him he saw his partner buttstroke the fatass in the face. He went down then, moaning and bleeding.

"Roo? You got it?" Wilson yelled at him, spinning his head back and forth, keeping an eye on the strip club Hercules in front of him as well as his partner. Eddie had been a bit twitchy lately, and a warning shot was a bullshit amateur move. Now, however, was not the time to lecture him.

"Yeah," Eddie yelled back. He kicked the man, hard, then backed away and swung his AK around the room. The dancers were crying and wailing like they were trying out for an opera.

Wilson turned back to the assistant manager in front of him, and pressed the muzzle of the AK into the back of his neck. "I've got a key right here that can open that door," he said threateningly.

"Yeah yeah yeah," Shane said quickly, and punched his code into the keypad.

"Shut the fuck up!" he heard Eddie yell at the dancers.

"Everybody empty your pockets, and don't make me ask twice," Parker shouted around the club, as the office door swung open. "Cash, cell phones, watches and wallets." Wilson shoved the big man inside. Mr. Utley was in the office, sitting behind the desk, his hands up.

Wilson pointed the AK at the chubby guy behind the desk, wondering just how much his suit cost. Probably thousands of dollars. Well, the guy was worth millions.

"Open the safe," Wilson told him. He gestured at the bodybuilder with the hand not on the pistol grip of the AK. "On the floor." Shane went down without protest.

Utley nodded slowly. "Not a problem," he said, at least pretending to be calm. "We just opened though, you're not going to get much."

"Don't bullshit me," Wilson warned him. "I know you got all your receipts and cash from Friday still. You hold out on me and shit's going to get real painful."

Utley nodded again. "Fair enough. I did hit the alarm, though," he informed the big man standing in his office. Dressed all in black like a SWAT cop, body armor and spare magazines for the rifle bundled around his chest, he took up a lot of space in the small room. Wearing some sort of face mask that left an oval for his eyes, and gloves, he could see the guy was black, but that was it.

"Well then, you'd best be quick about it," Wilson told him. "Bullet holes won't make this place any classier."

Detective John George parked his unmarked unit at the curb on 8 Mile and got out, after first checking the side mirror to make sure no passing car took off his door. Hell, it had happened — not to him, thank God.

On the sidewalk he looked at the club, then looked past it and back behind him. Not near an intersection, no banks nearby, mostly just parking lots...he didn't see any place within two hundred yards which might have a working security camera that covered the club or its parking lot. Par for the course.

COCONUTS. He'd been to a bachelor party here years before, he was pretty sure, although the strip clubs sort of blended together in his head. He wasn't a strip club guy anyway — it was like going out to eat when you're hungry, but only being allowed to smell the food, not eat it. An exercise in self-frustration, far as he was concerned. His life was full of frustration, he didn't need to add any more.

The lot was blocked by a marked unit, with a uniform standing next to it looking bored. George made sure his badge was visible as he walked by the officer but didn't say anything. He was too damn tired, and this was supposed to be his day off.

There had to be a good thirty people inside the club, maybe more, including half a dozen uniforms just standing around eyeballing the strippers, most of whom hadn't bothered to put on any more clothes. At least they'd corralled all the strippers into one corner, out of the way. They did not look happy, like a bunch of wet cats. Actually, they had the same look that he saw on his daughter's face, more often than not. Teenage girls were horrible. Shit, who was he kidding? He'd rather be working than at home, his wife in one ear and his daughter in the other, stereo bitching

"Okay, Rodriguez, what do we have?" He called out to one of the detectives assigned to the task force.

"Same crew," Manny told him. "Unless we have a copycat four man team, using all the same gear." Two other detectives, Bill Jordan and Ronda Sykes, closed in, waiting for their orders.

"Okay, anybody taken any statements yet?"

"Just started," Sykes told him.

"What was their ride? Same green Tahoe?"

Jordan shook his head. "Black Suburban."

"Shit," George said. "Probably stolen. Well, Bill, once we get the time they rolled in nailed down as tight as possible, I want you to go up and down 8 Mile as far as you have to, see if anybody's security camera caught that thing driving by. Bank, party store, gas station, I don't care. I want a plate."

"Wouldn't that be nice."

George looked around, and up, but the ceiling was painted black. "They got cameras in here?" Yep, there they were. "Anyone take a look at the video?"

"Not yet, Ringo," Ronda told him. "The owner says all the cameras are working, though, so the whole thing should have been caught on tape. Or CD, or whatever they're recorded on."

"Where are they, in the office? Get in there and sit on them. Right now. I don't want anything getting *accidentally* erased." He waited until she started off. "Anybody know if they were wearing ski masks?"

Jordan looked at his notebook. "I've got two told me ski masks, some others said ninja hoods."

"Shit, let's get these witnesses separated before they start polluting each other's stories. Bill, get those uniforms working on that instead of staring at their tits. We got an owner or a manager?"

"Owner is Craig Utley, he was in his office at the time, and he's still back there as far as I know. Been waiting on you, figured you'd want the honors. Floor manager's that dude right there." He pointed.

"Holy steroids, Batman. Okay, I'm going to talk to him, then the owner. Let me know if you get anything."

George had the guy by maybe an inch or two, but he outweighed the detective by twenty pounds, all of it muscle. Not that George had much muscle of his own....too much coffee, and fast food, and piloting a desk for too many years. He couldn't even remember the last time he'd worked out. And now balding, too, goddammit. Where had the years gone?

"I'm Detective George, the lead on this case," he said to the ponytailed Hulk. "You're the floor manager?"

"Yes sir."

"What's your name?" He dug out his notebook and a pen.

"Shane McDonald. This the same crew that hit The Princess' Diary and Goldfinger's?"

George shook his head. "I don't know. You hear from anybody at the other clubs about what happened when they were hit?"

The big man nodded. "Sure. When the Diary got hit the floor manager Rudy called me up and gave me the low down. I don't know anybody at Goldfinger's, but from what Rudy told me it sure seems like the same crew. Very professional. Body armor, AKs, spare mags, balaclavas, the works."

George looked up from his notebook. "You sound like you know a thing or two about it." How many people even knew what a balaclava was?

Shane smiled. "I know what a fucking AK looks like. Marine Corps. I did two tours in Iraq. These guys knew how to wear their gear, handle their weapons, and work the room. They were moving as a team, they were no gangbangers. Well....."

"What?'

The manager shrugged his huge shoulders. "Well, one of them fired a shot into the ceiling, a warning shot. One of the customers was a little slow to move, get down on the floor. That guy, over there." He pointed out a man getting attended to by one of the fire fighters, looked like he'd been hit in the face with something big and hard.

"And?' The warning shot might mean something. This was the first robbery out of the three where anybody had fired a shot. Or needed to, maybe. At least he knew now this crew wasn't running around with toy guns, or those damn airsoft things that looked just like the real thing.

"And nothing. I didn't see him when he fired the shot, but when I looked over I saw him hit the guy, then it was pretty much over."

"Ummm," George was thinking as he scribbled furiously on his pad. He had a number of questions for the man, and wasn't sure which one to hit first. Where was the shooter standing, what direction was his rifle pointing, how—"Why weren't you looking at him?" he asked the beefy manager. "Guy comes into your club with a rifle, I'd think you'd be looking at him."

"One of the other ones, the leader I think, was walking me back toward Mr. Utley's office. I had an AK pointed at my head and was looking at the office door when he fired."

"Did he shoot straight up? Or—"

"He called him Roo."

"What?"

"The guy who had me, was holding onto me when the other guy fired the shot, he looked back over at him and said, 'Roo, you got it?'"

George lowered his notepad. "'Roo'? Not who, or you, or Lou?"

"No, man, he was the length of a rifle away from me, and I've got good ears. Music was shut off at that point. He called the guy Roo."

Roo? Roo? Shit. He stood there and thought hard for several seconds. "You give your statement to anybody else yet? Any of the uniforms?"

Shane shook his head. "No sir, you're the first person I've talked to."

Oh, boy, this one might have blown wide open, but nobody's going to be happy about it, he thought. "You think this other one, the one who called the other perp 'Roo', was the leader? Tell me about him."

CHAPTER THREE

Mickey checked the menu. His eyes went to the prices first. After all, this was Georgetown, where he was once offered the option to rent a 650 square foot one bedroom apartment for a mere three thousand dollars a month. Unbelievable. Then again, all of D.C. was like that....at least the areas it was safe to walk in. Woodbridge, where he lived with Ben, was ten miles outside the Beltway and still expensive as shit.

"It's not too expensive, is it?" Kimberly asked him.

He shook his head. "No, it's not bad. Besides, I'm celebrating."

Mickey's roommate shook his head. "You're doing this wrong," Ben observed. "Don't you know you're supposed to be upset and miserable when you break up with your girlfriend? Especially if she's hot."

"The fact that I'm not, that I actually feel relieved, tells me that I made the right decision," Mickey said. Just saying it out loud felt huge to him. And it felt right. If anyone had told him a year ago he'd be happy about breaking up with Rachel, who looked like a runway model and shaved everything, he'd have told them they were nuts.

"You look happy," Kim said to him, nodding.

"At least the two of you won't be fighting through dinner," Ben said with a smirk, then winced as his girlfriend punched him in the shoulder. "What? You didn't like her anyway."

"Don't say that," she told Ben, giving him a dirty look. She turned back to Mickey. "So what's the official reason for the breakup?"

"Heck, I don't know if there's just one reason. We were just wrong for each other. She said a lot of things during that last fight, most of which...I don't even know what she was talking about. She was upset that I liked my job. Like I shouldn't be happy with my job?" He took a sip from his water glass. "I've been thinking about it. I think the real reason we broke up is because she figured out she couldn't turn me into a different person."

"Women always want to change guys," Ben said, shaking his head. "Bitches."

Mickey laughed, he always did when Ben tried to go gangsta, and Ben winced as Kimberly gave his arm another shot. "You're fine just how and who you are," she assured him.

"Whether I am or not, this is who I am," he told her. It was something he'd figured out during the fight with Rachel. She just hadn't liked who he was. Or, at a minimum, she couldn't be happy with him as he was. He had a sneaking suspicion she wouldn't be happy with anyone. Kimberly and Ben, on the other hand, seemed to be truly happy with each other.

"Who'd she want to change you into?" Ben asked. "Brad Pitt? You work for the freaking FBI."

"I don't know, and I don't care," Mickey said. "And...yeah, I work for the FBI, but I'm not an agent. Something she liked to point out. She seemed very aware of it."

"It's not always about looks, or sex," Kimberly told her boyfriend.

Ben rolled his eyes. "Maybe not for girls."

Their waiter returned with their drinks, and Mickey took a long pull from his Sam Adams. "Are you ready to order?" the waiter asked. He was a slender young man, maybe the same age as Ben and Mickey. Mickey idly wondered how the guy had ended up a waiter. Was he a student late to graduating, just doing this for money, or had his plans for a career, for the future, not worked out? Maybe the young man had never had any plans for the future, which was how he'd ended up as a waiter at a crowded Georgetown bistro. Mickey'd had a good idea what he wanted to do before he graduated high school, and at age twenty-five he was doing it.

"New York strip," Mickey announced proudly. Ben looked down at the menu, saw the price of the steak, and squinched his eyes.

"Hell, make that two. Might as well celebrate with you. She had a great ass, but I'm glad you're free of that miserable bitch."

Mickey and Ben were eating their salads when Ben said, with his mouth full of croutons, "Maybe Rachel ditched you because you don't have a real job."

"What?"

Ben shrugged, and continued with affected innocence, "I mean, you guys down there just make shit up as you go, sort of like weathermen."

"By 'down there' I'm assuming you mean the FBI Lab?" Mickey said, raising his eyebrows. Kimberly just rolled her eyes and stayed out of it. This wasn't the first time they'd had this discussion.

"I don't know," Ben said. "Is that what they call it? Because I don't know how they can even really call it a lab. I mean, *I* work in a laboratory...."

"Here we go," Mickey said with a sigh. Ben worked as a chemist for the FDA in downtown D.C. Their apartment in Woodbridge was almost exactly halfway between D.C.

and Quantico. Mickey wiggled his fingers in a "come on" gesture at Ben. "Okay, let me have it."

"I mean," his roommate continued with a shrug, "normally people who work in a lab are scientists, and scientists work with absolutes. They do work using the scientific method, and part of that method is reproducible results. Mix two chemicals, get a reaction. Every time you do it, provided the proportions of the chemicals are the same, same conditions, you should get the exact same reaction."

"Which exact part of my job are you attacking this time?" Mickey asked politely.

Ben smiled smugly. "There are so many aspects to it open to criticism, but let's go with fingerprints."

Mickey sighed. He worked as a Fingerprint Examiner in the FBI's Latent Print Operations Unit, although he was low man on the totem pole. In fact, he was still a probationary employee, had only been on the job nine months, but he really enjoyed the work. It paid pretty well, and as it was a government job he was guaranteed pay raises every year. And it wasn't as if he was doing unskilled labor, he had a freaking Bachelor's Degree, with Honors, in Forensic Science from Purdue, and was working on his Masters at George Washington University, or "GW" as everyone around D.C. called it.

He had the scientific background to do the job—and then some—as soon as he got out of college, but getting hired by the FBI wasn't as easy as working at McDonald's. There was the yard-long application, the fingerprinting, the background check, the interview, the polygraph.....it had taken him over a year from application to first day on the job. Which seemed totally ridiculous to him, but he'd since learned that was common. His uncle.....he wanted to know why the hell Mickey hadn't just applied to the Bureau to become an agent. Uncle Mark was a recently retired FBI Special Agent himself, and the fact that Mickey wanted to work for the FBI, but not as an agent, just didn't compute.

Mark wanted someone, anyone in the family to follow in his footsteps, and Mickey was his best bet—heck, Mickey was his only bet, nobody else in the family wanted anything to do with law enforcement.

Mickey loved forensics, it was interesting as hell, but he didn't want to chase guys or shoot guns, he just wanted to work in a lab. Blood spatter analysis was gross, DNA was interesting at a very technical level, testing substances to find out if they were actually the drugs they looked and smelled like was so boring and easy a monkey could do it, and tool mark comparison put him to sleep. But fingerprints….he loved fingerprints.

As he was still relatively new to the job they had him running civil—as in non-criminal—prints through the database. Why? Because nobody else wanted to do it. Usually they were part of background checks for concealed weapons permits around the country, or for employment purposes. It was surprising just how many professions required fingerprinting. He'd also run the prints of some unidentified bodies which had been drowning victims of Hurricane Sandy. The LPOU was part of the FBI's Laboratory Division, which was a heck of a lot bigger than he would have expected before he got the job.

Before he was hired, he assumed he'd be working in the J. Edgar Hoover Building in D.C. but the FBI Lab was actually located at the Marine Corps base in Quantico, along with the FBI Academy. He worked in a big and relatively new office building, and soon learned how lucky he was not to have to work at the Hoover Building. Regular trips there quickly revealed that the place was a dump, well past its prime and starting to come apart at the seams. Even the GAO, the Government Accounting Office, had recommended the building be destroyed. As much money as the government was throwing around to anyone who asked for it, you'd think they could spare some to get the FBI a new headquarters, but so far no such luck.

As big as it was, it was still the freaking FBI Crime Lab. There were hundreds of applicants for every position that opened up, maybe thousands. Mickey had the right degree, but he was pretty sure Uncle Mark had put in a good word for him. And Mark still had hopes that once Mickey saw how wonderful the FBI was that he'd want to join up as an agent. To that end he'd taken Mickey shooting, and given him his FBI-issued Kevlar vest, as he'd retired to the middle-of-nowhere Indiana and wouldn't need it. Mickey had taken it, not wanting to say no, but what the hell was he going to do with a bulletproof vest?

Mickey'd been fascinated by fingerprints ever since he was a little kid and saw a blown-up photograph of one at a local museum. He could stare at them for hours, at their intricacies and patterns. Loops, arches, tented arches, whorls.....especially whorls. Plain, accidental, peacock's eye, central pocket loop whorls.... His favorite—and he knew it was weird to have a favorite type of fingerprint pattern—was the double loop whorl. It looked so much like the Yin/Yang symbol that he wondered if that was how the Chinese philosopher, or whoever it was, dreamed up the famous design—by staring at one of his fingertips.

"And what's wrong with friction ridge impressions?" he asked Ben, using the technical term. What people knew as "fingerprints" were actually the patterns of minute ridge formations on the fingertips.

"Nothing," Ben admitted. "They make great party gifts, and all you need is paper and ink—and fingerprints—to make some more. I've got friction ridges, you've got friction ridges, everybody's got some. It's just the voodoo you use to compare them—"

"Voodoo?" Mickey couldn't let that one slide.

"Sure. What do you call it? It's not a science. It'd be complimentary to call it a pseudoscience. What do they call psychology, a 'soft science'? Nice term. Probably a psychologist came up with it, trying not to hurt anybody's feelings. How exactly do you compare prints, to find out if they belong to a criminal?"

"We run them through the computer, the Integrated Automated Fingerprint Identification System. 55 million prints on file. The computer runs them through our database, and spits out maybe a dozen possible matches. The possibles are ranked with a percentage, likelihood of a match, and then we, me, one of us there goes through and, starting with the most likely one, compares the print with the possible."

"And the computer doesn't actually look at the print, right, it looks at a map of the 'points of comparison'? Where the ridges split, or arch, or whatever."

"Right. Bifurcations, where a ridge splits into two, trifurcations where one splits into three, or the spot where a ridge tops an arch, or the center of a loop or a whorl."

"And does the computer decide where the points of comparison are on the print? Or is there human input? How are the points of comparison of a print entered into the database?"

"By a latent print examiner."

"But does your computer pick the points of comparison, all by itself, or is there some human input? Some human discretion?"

Mickey saw where his roommate was going with this, but found himself unable to shut him down. "There is human input on the points of comparison," he said grudgingly.

Ben beamed. "So a human picks what he feels are the important points of the print, and tells the computer. And that's just the first step in the process. Ever heard the phrase, 'garbage in, garbage out'? And you're actually not comparing the prints themselves when you make an ID, you're comparing the points of comparison. How backward is that? And how do we know no two prints are alike? Just because somebody says so? Just because the odds against it are so high? Does that even sound like science to you? Do you know the odds against a specific sperm reaching an egg? And yet it happens, all the time."

"Really? At dinner?" Kimberly said to him. She sat back and smiled at the two of them as they continued to go at it. It was funny, the two of them were so much alike that some people thought they had to be brothers. They were both dark-haired and skinny, and smart, that was how they were similar. Really smart.

She'd had dumb boyfriends before. She'd been pretty enough in high school to date a few jocks, and didn't regret it, because it had been a learning experience. While they looked good, and had a lot of repetitive motion capabilities in the bedroom, there wasn't a whole lot of *there* there. Ben and Michael weren't quite geeks or nerds, but they were tiptoeing along the razor's edge. Smart guys maybe weren't as pretty, but they were *smart*. Smart meant they could talk about things other than sports and reality TV, and had real jobs. Real jobs meant careers, and earning potential.

A few of her more idiotic girlfriends still occasionally asked her, "What do you see in him? He's such a geek." Kimberly was quick to point out they were the ones dating bartenders, or retail 'sales associates', cute guys who had little to no future.

"And even the computer can't say whether or not the print is a match, that has to be done by an individual examiner," Ben said, making his points in the air with his fork. "How many times have members of the FBI Lab testified in court to a fingerprint identification of a suspect that later has turned out to be completely wrong?" he asked Mickey.

"Um, I don't know." Which was a true, if not quite complete answer.

"Yeah, right. I've got three words for you. Brandon Mayfield."

"That's three words?" Kimberly said.

"Oh, geez," Mickey said.

"I'm just saying, one of your high-falutin' FBI agents testified that he was involved in the Madrid train bombings in 2004. What was the phrase the agent used? Oh, yeah, a '100 percent positive match'. One hundred. Not ninety-eight, not ninety-nine, but one hundred. And the actual fact was it wasn't Mayfield's fingerprint at all. How many millions of dollars did the FBI have to pay out for that debacle? I mean, in addition to the formal apology they issued."

"Do you do research or something so you can give me more shit?" Mickey asked his roommate. "I mean, come on, give me a break."

"But you know that it happened. You're right, I did look it up. The Department of Justice report on that train wreck said that the error was caused by a 'misapplication of methodology'. Which I'm pretty sure means that you guys were just making shit up. And that's far from the only time it's happened."

Mickey had to nod. In addition to Mayfield, every member of the lab quickly learned the name of former Special Agent Dr. Frederick Whitehurst, the biggest whistleblower in the history of the Bureau. He'd been Supervisory Special Agent at the lab, and his testimony on scientific misconduct at the lab affecting as many as ten thousand cases had resulted in dozens, if not hundreds of overturned convictions.

Ben sat back. "If identifying fingerprints was a science, how can that be? You shouldn't call it the FBI Crime Lab, you should call it Fantasy Land."

"We've had some problems, but all that's in the past," Mickey said. He shook his head. "You're such a dick sometimes. Remind me, why am I your friend?"

CHAPTER FOUR

Aaron stood by the fence smoking, just staring out at the street. He was early, the truck wasn't ready, and Dave wasn't even there yet, so there was nothing for him to do but wait. Just past seven A.M, the sounds of the city were fainter than the repetitive banging sounds echoing out of the service bay behind him. Trash twisted along the curbs from a light breeze, fast food wrappers mostly. He heard her before he saw her, coming down the sidewalk in front of the building. She saw him standing inside the truck yard, hesitated a second, and then angled toward him.

"How you doing?" she asked him.

Aaron just smiled around the Marlboro. "Not bad."

She eyed the uniform shirt, then the trucks in the yard behind him and the building. "You just starting, or getting off, or looking for something to do?"

Aaron pulled the Marlboro out and let the smoke curl around his face. "No thanks, officer, I don't think I want to go to jail today." She might as well have been wearing a badge for all the red flags she was throwing up. And they had nothing to do with the time of day, a lot of the local hookers were busy taking care of executives on their way downtown before a busy day of work. The GM Headquarters was only a few miles away.

Her eyebrows went up. "What makes you think I'm a cop?" she asked him. "I'm not a cop, I'm just looking to party."

Aaron squinted at her, then stepped close to the fence. With exaggerated care he looked first one way up the street, then another, then back at her. He spoke quietly. "Look," he told her, "you're obviously new at this, so let me help you. First thing, your hair is washed, or at least looks clean and brushed. You've got all your teeth, too, although I know you can't do anything about that. But your jeans, seriously? You've got a crease in your jeans. You actually look like someone I'd want to have sex with, which for damn sure means you're a cop. You're in the Cass Corridor, not pretending to be an escort in Windsor. You've got to blend with your environment. Your sergeant's not doing his job if he didn't tell you that, and if you're miked up I hope he heard me." He stuck the cigarette back in his mouth and waited. He hadn't seen the covering cars, but knew they had to be out there somewhere.

The woman stood there for a few moments, not saying anything. Then, a rueful smile growing on her face, she said, "Thanks," and, after a second's hesitation, moved off down the sidewalk.

"Anytime." Aaron moved his head close to the chainlink and watched her walk away. Her jeans were just as tight as he'd thought. He tossed his cigarette away and headed back toward the metallic banging sounds, which weren't getting any quieter. The mechanics they had working here were morons.

Dave ran into Aaron just leaving the vault, pulling a cash cart. "Guess who we've got again today?" Aaron asked his partner.

"Who?"

"Slo-Mo."

"Who?"

Aaron made a face. "The kid, Elmo, the borderline tard."

Dave looked around. Aaron never cared who heard him, but it was always a good idea to watch and listen for incoming. "Hey, give him a break, he's trying," Dave said, trying to be nice.

Aaron thought for a second. "You know, I think you're right. Which is kinda sad." They reached the Beast and Aaron slowed down the coin-heavy cart with his body.

"At least he's nice. I know a few really smart people who are dicks. Hell, half the population of the country has below average intelligence," Dave reminded him.

"Yeah, and you know what the problem with that is?"

"What?"

"Even 'average' is pretty damn stupid. You're driving," Aaron told him pointedly.

The incline wasn't steep enough to downshift but the truck lost a few mph by the time it crested the small hill. There were vacant lots to either side with random piles of assorted dumped trash, some of it starting to get overgrown with weeds. Off in the distance the ruins of Tiger Stadium were visible, as was I-75.

Dave took a left when the street ended, and two big pheasants broke from cover. They ran a short distance, then began walking along the curb.

"Again!" Aaron exclaimed from the box behind him. "Every fucking time we come to Brinks. I swear to God I'm going to have you stop one of these days so I can shoot one."

"Your ten millimeter isn't exactly a good pheasant gun," Dave told him.

"I've got a shotgun." The truck rolled past the pheasants, which ignored it. Dave could just imagine what the truck would smell like with a pheasant hanging in the back all day. Aaron was bad enough.

"Why would you shoot a bird?" Elmo asked them.

"It's not a bird, it's a pheasant," Dave told him. "And the same reason people kill chickens. They're delicious."

In the Brinks parking lot Aaron hopped out and walked into the office. He was back a few seconds later.

"Guardian's in there now, but we're next," he told Dave.

"Fine." Dave pulled the truck over to the far end of the lot and backed against the fence, facing one of two overhead doors, both of which were closed. He took a long swig of his Diet Coke, knowing he'd have access to a bathroom soon.

"So how long you going to be doing this shit?" Aaron asked him, stretching out in the captain's chair some enterprising soul had installed in the back of the rig. No one knew where it had come from, probably a custom van that someone had totaled. It even had cupholders.

Dave looked back at him through the metal mesh. "What? Don't you love this job?"

"Fuck you, college boy. I was looking for a job when I found this one, but it wasn't the one I was looking for. How long's it take to get into the F.B.I., anyway?"

"Depends on the year, and the government budgeting. Application process takes months, at least. But you've got to be twenty-five before they'll hire you, so I couldn't apply right out of college. They've got my application, but whether they've even looked at it yet I couldn't tell you."

"If you were a black Chinese handicapped lesbian transsexual you'd probably already be an agent," Aaron told him.

"A black Chinese lesbian, what was it? ...handicapped transsexual, with an accounting degree, yeah," Dave corrected his partner. "But I've got a couple of letters of recommendation from FBI agents, so hopefully that will move me up on the list."

"Door's going up," Elmo told them.

Dave grabbed the radio handset. "1555 heading into Brinks."

"Roger that, 1555," he heard Deano reply. "Remind Aaron he's there for business." Dave smiled

"Fuck you too," Aaron said to radio.

They watched the red Guardian truck back out of the building and turn around. Dave waved at the other driver and headed into the cage.

Brinks didn't allow the truck crews of other companies access to the inside of their building, but rather had an internal truck cage. Any transfers were done inside the cage. Aaron waited until the door rolled down behind them before hopping out of the back with his clipboard. The cage was that, an actual metal cage inside the Brinks truck garage. They had five feet of room on either side and over twice that in front and back of the truck. Dave shut the truck off and hopped out, Brinks being one of the few stops on their route where he had that luxury.

The entire back wall of the cage was removable, but most of the time traffic used a pedestrian door secured with a magnetic lock. A Brinks employee he recognized but whose name he couldn't remember stood on the other side of the door, which was constructed of dark, rough-looking steel slats, like something out of Mad Max Beyond Thunderdome. Two men enter.....

"You guys have anything for us?" he asked them.

"Two small bags," Aaron told him. "But I think you've got a lot of coin for us."

"I'll go get Arlene," he told them, and headed off.

Arlene was the vault manager and showed up a minute later pulling a flat metal cart piled with the loose coin bags Brinks favored, although there was one solitary box of pennies. Thirty-eight years old, she was five foot four in her work boots, and in her bulky coveralls looked like she weighed all of a hundred and thirty pounds. In fact she weight one hundred and ten, all of it lean muscle, and outworked everyone else in the vault, including the high school kids.

At the door, she waved a hand over her head, and the magnetic lock before her buzzed open. "Hey Dave, how ya been?" she asked him. Her hair was a natural strawberry blonde and teased up big.

"Good," he told her.

"I've got two for you," Aaron said, holding up two small sealed canvass bags and his clipboard.

"I'll show you mine if you show me yours," Arlene told him with a smile.

Aaron looked at the cart behind her. "I was hoping to get my hands on your box today," he told her.

"Not until you sign on the dotted line," she told him with a smirk, and they exchanged clipboards.

"You two," Dave said, shaking his head. He looked up from one surveillance camera to another. "Those things have sound?"

"No," Arlene said, and leaned forward to give her boyfriend a kiss. Aaron came away grinning. "You coming over later?" she asked him.

Aaron grabbed the heavy cart and pulled it toward the side door of the truck. "Oh, yeah. I'll have another deposit for you tonight."

"Promises, promises."

"You know you two sound like a couple of high schoolers who have never been laid," Dave told them. They were always like that, and some days it was worse than others.

"Sounds like someone's jealous," Arlene said to him with a laugh, then she headed back out the door with her two bags.

"Here, make yourself useful, help me load these bags of quarters into the back," Aaron told Mo, pulling the metal cart to the rear of the truck. Dave wandered back there with them, but there wasn't really room for him to help out.

Aaron climbed in the side door, then popped open the rear. "Hand them up," he told Mo.

"Hey, have you guys ever had to shoot anybody?" Mo asked

Aaron and Dave exchanged a glance. "You mean driving around for Absolute?" Aaron said. "No, and you know why? Because we fucking pay attention. We look around. Most of these guys that have these robbery attempts, that have to shoot people, it's because they're not paying attention. They're giving the bad guys the opportunity."

"Why's the hammer cocked on your gun?" Elmo asked Aaron. "Isn't that dangerous?"

"Oh boy," muttered Dave.

"Of course it's dangerous, it's a fucking gun," Aaron said. "But the cocked hammer doesn't make it dangerous. This is a Colt Delta Elite ten millimeter. Stainless steel. It's a 1911—that's the kind of pistol it is. With a 1911, if the hammer's not cocked, the gun won't fire. Period. You could bang on it with a hammer and it wouldn't go off, because it's got two safeties. Look at Davey's Glock there. No cocked hammer, looks boring, but the fact is that it's cocked on the inside. Mine looks scarier, but it's actually safer."

Aaron had it more or less right, Dave thought. He looked down at his Glock 35.

"You ever had to pull your gun?" Elmo asked Aaron.

Aaron smiled big and jumped down from the back of the truck. He pulled his Colt out of its holster, popped the magazine, and racked the round out of the chamber. He then reholstered the unloaded pistol and looked at Mo, who'd been watching him.

"Want to see something cool?" he asked the young kid.

"Su—" Mo started to say, and then he was staring at the muzzle of Aaron's unloaded pistol. "Holy shit!" he said. Aaron had drawn his gun so fast that Mo hadn't even seen it.

"He is fast," Dave agreed with a nod. "Hitting anything further than ten feet away, though, that's something he's not so good at." Dave had competed alongside professional shooters, and Aaron's draw was as fast as any he'd seen. He'd taken Aaron to a few "action" pistol competitions, and his partner had held his own, but USPSA-type matches involved a lot more than just fast draws at targets spitting distance away.

"Kiss my ass," Aaron said with a smile, reloading his pistol. "Anyway, anyone tries to rob us, they're not going to be across the street, they're going to be on our ass. Okay, Elmo, push the cart back to the door it came through, then everybody climb aboard, time to blow this pop stand." He stuck his Colt back in its holster and climbed in through the back door.

"Where to next?" Mo asked them when they were clear of the building and heading out.

"Downtown," Aaron told him. "The Comerica main vault. Five to drop off, none to pick up, and still it'll take an hour. That's why Wednesdays suck."

Heading downtown, Aaron yelled to Dave over the roar of the Beast's diesel engine, "So, when are you going to take your 'Stang racing? You never race it."

Dave laughed. "And I'm not going to. Racing will totally trash it."

Aaron sat forward in his captain's chair. "Then why the hell did you have me put all that stuff on it? You've got what, two hundred horsepower over factory?"

"Because I like going fast," Dave told him with a smile. "Hey, did I tell you, I upgraded the tires and suspension and brakes to handle the new horsepower?"

"Yep, and again, what the fuck for if you're not going to race it?" To Aaron a fast car you didn't race was like having a hot girlfriend you didn't bang—it immediately put you under homo suspicion.

"Leave me alone and go look at the pictures of your birthday present on your phone," Dave said with a smile.

Aaron's face broke out into a wide grin. "Yeah, that was awesome."

"What'd you get him?" Elmo asked him. "A hooker?"

Dave had paid most of Aaron's course fee three months earlier when they'd attended a 2-day precision driving course at Skip Barber's Racing School at Lime Rock Park, Connecticut. While the techniques they practiced didn't have a lot of pertinence when Dave was driving the Beast, it helped him a lot when he was following people doing the PI work. Plus, he was able to write the entire course fee and travel costs off on his taxes.

"Tranny hooker," Dave told the new guy.

Aaron laughed. "Screw you. We went to Skip Barber's Racing School," he told Elmo.

"Who?"

"Never mind."

"You have a Mustang?" Mo asked Dave.

"Yep."

"What year?"

"It's two years old," Dave told him. "A GT."

"What color is it?" Mo asked him. "Do you park it in the lot? I haven't seen it."

"No, I drive an older Cherokee down here," Dave explained. "That 'Stang would get stolen in a week."

Mo looked from Dave to Aaron, then back at Dave. "You have two cars? How much do you guys make?"

Dave heard the laugh from Aaron in the back. "Not that much," Aaron straightened the new guy out.

"I got a bit of an inheritance," Dave explained.

"Oh, cool," Mo said, bopping his head.

Dave looked out the windshield. "No," he said quietly. "Not so much."

It was leaving the Comerica vault and heading east that they ran into the traffic jam.

"What the fuck?" Aaron said from in back. "There an accident or something? There's never traffic like this, this time of day."

"I don't know, I can't see anything," Dave told him.

"Can you get us out of this?"

They were in a sea of cars. "By the time I have an opening, we're going to be at our turn anyway," Dave said.

After five minutes, and a quarter mile, they could see what the problem was. Everyone was slowing down to stare at the protesters in front of the courthouse. There were at least a hundred people, some of them with signs, TV crews, somebody with a bullhorn...."What the hell is this shit?" Aaron asked, his face pressed against the mesh partition so he could see out the windshield better.

"I don't know...." Dave said. "No, wait, did the trial start? The one with the two cops? Has to be. That's why it's such a circus over there, Jesse Jackson was supposed to show up."

"That's where the cops shot the unarmed pregnant lady, right?" Mo asked them.

"She wasn't unarmed, she had a knife and stabbed one of them in the arm," Dave told him.

"I never heard that," Mo said.

"And she was only like six weeks pregnant, there's a good chance even *she* didn't know she was pregnant," Aaron said through the mesh. "It was the coroner who ended up telling everybody. Didn't her mother once let slip that even she didn't know her daughter was pregnant? Now she's talking about how they were sitting down picking out baby names. Total bullshit."

"Then why are they on trial?" Mo asked him, showing some argument.

"Fuck if I know," Aaron told him. "Jesse Jackson and all his type have been getting everybody in Detroit riled up, saying it's racial because she was black, and one of the cops who shot her is white. But his partner is black, or half black, or something. Trying to turn it into the next Rodney King. I can't turn on the TV without seeing her mother's stupid face on TV."

Dave had observed that the dead woman's mother was hard to avoid. She had made all the local news shows, and started around the national daytime shows, talking to all the usual suspects. She hadn't struck him as being especially....intellectual, but she sure was entertaining to watch, if you liked train wrecks.

"And that's another thing," Aaron said. He was on a roll now. "Just how fucking stupid do you have to be to name your daughter Felanie? Honestly. I mean, really, fucking *Felanie*?"

"Felanie Washington," Dave muttered to himself. "Sounds like she should be a senator's daughter."

"And you gave me shit about 'Ikea'," Aaron reminded him.

"What's wrong with it?" Mo asked Aaron.

Aaron just blinked at him through the steel mesh, then said, "Hey Mo, you know what's better than winning the Special Olympics?" He didn't wait for an answer. "Not being retarded." Then he looked at Dave, who was smiling. "I gotta get out of this fucking city, man," he told Dave. "The inmates are running the goddamn asylum. Head out west."

"'I say we take off and nuke the entire site from orbit,'" Dave said with a smile.

Aaron smiled back. "Only way to be sure," he said with a nod. "God I love that fucking movie."

"I grew up in Arizona. Still have that place out there," Dave reminded him. "You're welcome to use it any time."

"Yeah, that's a nice spread," Aaron remarked. He'd vacationed there with Dave for a few days the year before. "Desert, that's what I need. Sand, cactus, and no people." He threw a glance at their oblivious third, who was back to looking out the window at the crowd and bopping his head to music only he could hear. "Who's the Sheriff somewhere in Arizona, Shotgun Joe? Guy who arrests illegal aliens even though the feds tell him not to, makes his prisoners wear pink clothes, keeps suing the federal government?"

"Shotgun John Osterman. Tohono County Sheriff, that's where my place is."

"What's wrong with Detroit?" Mo asked them, jumping back into the conversation.

"Have you ever been anywhere else?" Aaron asked him. "Chicago, Des Moines, Lincoln, Nebraska? Anywhere? Trust me, if you'd been anywhere else, you wouldn't be asking that question."

"Detroit's not so bad."

"Fifty thousand wild dogs roaming the streets, that's what the news said last week. It's the largest city in the country to ever declare bankruptcy!" Aaron practically exploded from the back. "It looks like *I Am Legend* out there."

"Detroit didn't do that, the dude, the financial guy appointed by the governor filed bankruptcy," Elmo said.

"And it's a good damn thing," Aaron argued. "Detroit's been bankrupt for thirty years, it's about time the adults stepped in and tried to do something about it. Made it official. Goddamn Detroit City Council is a circus act."

Elmo mumbled something then, and it might have gone unheard if the armored car wasn't a bare-walled steel box idling in stopped traffic. Aaron sat forward.

"Racist?" he said. "I'm not a racist. Do you even know what a racist is? It's not somebody who can use his eyes and see there's a difference between how people look or act. Racism is saying that some people are better or worse than others, specifically because of their race. I don't think black people are stupid, I think stupid people are stupid. I don't hate black people, I hate stupid people. I hate lazy people. I hate liars. These days you can't even speak the truth without being called a racist, which is Big Brother censorship bullshit."

Aaron huffed. "You want some truth?" He scowled and shook his head. "Detroit is seventy percent black. The blacks have been running this city for decades. There wasn't a white mayor for forty years, and look what happened in those forty years. It's so bad Detroit has lost two-thirds of its population; forget 'white flight', even the blacks are leaving this sinking ship. You don't like the way the city is, then fucking *do* something about it. Stop shouting 'racism' and claiming that it's 'the man' keeping you down. In this city, *you're* 'the man', and *I'm* a minority." He gestured around the back of the armored car. "I guess that's why I'm riding in the back of the fucking bus."

Dave looked back at Aaron through the mesh window. "Rosa Parks was twice as tough as you'll ever be."

Aaron nodded and sat back in the captain's chair. "Ain't that the truth. Ain't that the fucking truth." And he stared out the window at the cars.

Elmo looked back and forth between the two of them, trying to figure out if they were making some sort of joke, but it sure looked to him like they were serious. Which left him seriously confused.

CHAPTER FIVE

Detective John George got off the Southfield Freeway at the Grand River/Fenkell exit. He had to wait through three lights to get through the intersection. The Southfield Freeway met with both Grand River Avenue and Fenkell at that point, and the confused jumble of corners looked a little like the Star of David when seen from above. The Omega Grill, a Coney island, sat at one of the corners, and was always busy. South of that on the corner of Fenkell was a Chase bank built like an oversize pillbox. When he finally cleared the traffic cobweb he headed westbound on Fenkell.

Should he? Just a drive by, just a look. It was on his way. He knew he shouldn't, he should stay as far away as possible. But it was a hell of a thing, what he'd set in motion. All because of one word, that might have been misheard. Everything else fit, though, that was the problem.

George shook his head and took a left down Glastonbury into Rosedale Park. The neighborhood had actually been named a "historic community" or some such a few years back, and as Detroit neighborhoods went it was one of the nicer ones. The houses, mostly two story red brick, were big and had character. They'd been built, for the most part, in the thirties and forties, when some of the men who laid brick were real artists. All the streets featured grassy and landscaped medians, although the medians stopped and started in no discernible pattern. Where there weren't medians, the front lawns of the houses were big, much bigger than the back yards.

Glancing to either side as he slowly cruised down the street, George saw that the houses all had detached garages to the rear, added almost as afterthoughts. Well, who could have known eighty years ago just how many cars there would be in this country? Well, Henry Ford probably, but back when Rosedale Park was being built, Detroit had a well used public transportation system, and only the very well-off owned cars. Now everybody owned one, or three. In fact, he believed that was one of the reasons the traffic in the Detroit area was never as bad as it got on the east coast or Chicago. The roads and cities had been built up around the automobile as the main method of transportation. George had been to Boston, and he didn't know how anybody got anywhere. If he had to move there, he'd probably ride a bicycle to work.

The residents of Glastonbury Avenue—most of them, anyway—still cared about their houses, and did the maintenance and mowed the lawn and trimmed the hedges. Daylilies were blooming, and rosebushes. In fact, there were nicely trimmed bushes and flowerbeds in the medians. Idly he wondered who took care of the medians, which had been freshly mowed. Considering the state the city's finances were in, his bet was on the locals taking care of it themselves.

Neighborhood Watch signs were everywhere, for what good they did. In the first block south of Fenkell he only saw one empty house, and there were no vacant lots. The neighborhood actually reminded him a lot of one of the Grosse Pointes, the very expensive very white very small suburbs located to the east of Detroit on Lake St. Clair. Except....the houses in the Pointes sold for hundreds of thousands of dollars, and didn't have wrought iron grates over their windows and doors. The same thing couldn't be said for Rosedale Park. These same houses in one of the Pointes would cost two, maybe four times as much. The Detroit housing market was in the shitter.

He'd read recently that the average cost of a house in Detroit was $15,000. Some days driving through certain neighborhoods he could believe it, but other days he shuddered at what that meant for the city. Goodbye tax base. Not for the first time he wondered whether his pension would be more fiction than fact.

Nearing the end of the second block he slowed down, and his eyes scanned the area. Not a lot of cars parked on the street, and nothing big—no vans, no repair trucks, nothing like that. The house was on the corner of Eaton and Glastonbury. Dark red brick, two stories, white trim, in pretty good shape. Nothing to see, he told himself. Keep on moving. Instead, George came to a complete stop at the stop sign, then turned right.

The house's garage was set at the rear of the yard with the short driveway running out onto Eaton. It had peeling wooden siding and looked a little rickety. There were two cars parked in front of the garage, a Charger and an Explorer, and several more vehicles parked on Eaton.

George rolled slowly by the house and he could see the whole back yard, as only a black wrought-iron fence ran along the sidewalk on Eaton. He wasn't expecting to see a handful of people hanging out on the concrete patio behind the house, but there they were, and a few glanced his way. Shit. Before he realized what he was doing he pulled to the curb and hopped out of the car.

"Verlander's in over his head this season. He just doesn't seem to know what he's doing."

Paul Wilson stopped scrubbing the grill long enough to look over his shoulder at Randy Parker. "The fuck you talking about? He pitched seven no-hit innings yesterday, they destroyed the Jays eleven to one." Wilson had on a Detroit Tigers baseball cap, and had even worn it on raids a few times before the lieutenant had seen it and chewed his ass. He'd been a fan ever since he was a kid, when his father used to take him down to Tiger Stadium. They'd buy hotdogs and sit in the bleachers and talk about catching home runs. Wilson had come close a few times, but he'd never gotten a home run ball. The best, though, the absolute best was his father managing somehow to get them two tickets to Game 4 of the '84 World Series. Tigers versus the San Diego Padres, and he'd just turned twelve years old. The game itself wasn't that exciting—it was over in the 3rd inning, not that the Padres knew it, and the Tigers would go on to clinch the Series in Game 5. How his father managed to get them he'd never say, but that day had been almost magical. Now Tasia was thirteen, older than he'd been at that game, and Tiger Stadium was history. Where the hell had the time gone?

Parker took a slug out of his Budweiser bottle. "One good game doesn't mean shit. He's been wild all season, yesterday he just found a little control."

Wilson looked over at their third. "Roo, back me up here. You hear what he's saying?"

Eddie "Kangaroo" Mitchell looked over at his DPD SWAT teammates. "Baseball? The fuck I know about baseball? You want to talk about OchoCinco or LeBron or something, I'm in, but not that slow-ass cracker game."

"I look like a cracker to you?" Parker said, his eyebrows going up. "'Austin Jackson' sound white? Prince Fielder lookin' a bit pale these days? Maybe you need your eyes checked."

"Whatever," Eddie said with a quick wave of his hand. He finished his beer and reached for another. "Fall asleep watchin' that shit."

"You see his wife, Chanel?" Wilson asked Parker. "She's pale. Normally I don't like that much cream in the coffee, but she fine."

"Fielder's wife? That sister's hot, but she be nuts," Parker said. "Going all vegetarian and shit. Man need to eat meat. Can't hit no home runs eatin' fucking celery."

Wilson tossed a handful of burgers on the grill and listened to the sizzle. He had a few hot dogs as well, but they took less time to cook, so he'd wait to put them on until he flipped the burgers. The grill was new and looked it, all polished stainless steel and chrome. He had it parked right outside the glass-walled enclosed porch off the back of his house. The porch was too cold to sit in in the winter, but the rest of the year it was pretty nice. They'd put up vertical blinds for a little privacy, but most of the time left them open. Closing the blinds cut too much light, turned the porch into a cave.

"Top, you know this dude?" Parker asked him. Wilson looked at Randy, then swung his head the other direction to see a white guy in a suit walking across the street towards them. He looked familiar, but it took him a second to place him.

"Ringo?" Wilson said in surprise. "The fuck man, what are you doing here? Haven't seen you since...shit, I don't know." He peered at the man. Last thing he'd heard, Ringo was a detective on the east side.

John George smiled and paused on the sidewalk outside the wrought-iron fence. "I thought that was you, Paul. As I was rolling through the neighborhood I thought I remembered that you lived over here, but it wasn't until I was driving by and saw you that I recognized the house."

"It's been a while," Wilson admitted. He looked at the detective. "You working on a weekend? Thought you were stationed on the east side."

George put his hands on the fence and nodded. "I'm in the Eastern precinct, but the family's out of town and I've got a bunch of cases stacked up."

"Same here." Wilson gestured at the men sitting behind him. "This is Eddie Mitchell and Randy Parker, they're on the team with me. Boys, this is Detective John George. He and I went through the academy together, then worked the Sixth Precinct for a few years, sometimes in the same car. My man Ringo."

"I know Eddie," George said, nodding at the man. "He was in the Academy with us, remember? How you doin', Roo?"

"Shit, that's right," Wilson said. He'd hadn't gotten to know Eddie until he'd transferred out of the Sixth Precinct. In the academy he'd just been another face.

"'Sup?" Eddie said, then sucked hard at his beer. He squinted at the detective. "They never said, how you get the nickname Ringo?"

"My name's Jonathan, John Paul George." He smiled self-consciously.

"Yeah, and?"

Both his SWAT teammates turned to look at Eddie. "Really dude?" Parker said incredulously.

"So what are you doing on this end of the city?" Wilson asked him. He watched George as he answered.

"Caught a rape case, the victim's sister also used to date the perp. Talked to her once at the station, but I thought maybe banging on her door might make her remember a few things. She still seemed sweet on the asshole, even though he busted up her sister. Lives around the block on Stahelin. Emily Green. Know her? Just off of Lyndon."

Wilson shook his head. "Don't know anybody on that block."

"Don't worry about it." George looked around the patio. "Just guys this weekend? Where's your wife and daughters? It's daughters, right? Two?"

"Thirteen and eight. They're with their mother visiting family in Tennessee."

"So you got some quiet time, nice. Okay, sorry for bothering you, but it was good to see you. Guys." He gave a little wave to the two other men, then trotted back to his unmarked detective's ride and headed off down the street.

"Ain't nobody gonna tell me how he got the name Ringo?" Eddie complained a minute later.

"You never hear of the motherfuckin' Beatles?" Parker said in wonder.

"Why would I listen to that shit?"

"Top," Parker called out to Wilson. "Smells like the burgers are burning. You want to check that?"

"Yeah, hold on," Wilson said. He had a fast wi-fi connection, and could work his thumbs pretty fast on his iPhone. The online phone directory did show an Emily Green living right down the street on Stahelin. Still, that had been weird. Ringo showing up like that, out of the blue, after how many years? Wilson knew he was on the task force handling the club heists. And Ringo had to know he knew. Could the detective know something, have something? They hadn't left any evidence, he was sure of it. Hell, if they'd left any evidence, it wouldn't have been one detective driving by, it would have been a raid team knocking down the door with a ram. Some lily-white SWAT team from out in the suburbs or something, maybe feds. Nah, he was just being paranoid.

"Top?" Parker said again. "Shit's on fire there."

George climbed back into his department car. He wanted to sit there and think, but he knew he had eyes on him, so he started it up and pulled away. After the conversation with Paul Wilson he felt like going home and thinking for about an hour, and maybe drinking half a dozen beers, but instead he turned left at the next corner and found

Emily Green's house. He didn't think she would or could tell him anything useful, but she was the sister to a rape victim.

She was home, and let him in. He didn't have much to ask, and she had even less to say, so he was back out on the porch less than ten minutes later. He looked up to see a silver Durango doubleparked next to his department ride. As he stepped slowly down off the porch, the driver's window of the Durango slid down. A white male in his thirties, in a polo shirt, was behind the wheel, and he just gave George a dirty look. As George started walking across the street, he could just start to see the logo on the man's shirt.

"How bout you and me have a little talk, Ringo," the FBI agent said.

"You do realize that we're in the middle of an investigation here, don't you? I mean, aren't you the one who came to us? Are you trying to spook him? What the fuck."

George was sitting in the passenger seat of the Durango in the parking lot of a McDonald's on Grand River, his sedan parked the next spot over. The FBI Agent, who'd showed George ID that identified him as Special Agent Abil Safie, was not happy.

George didn't blame him; he wasn't happy either. Eleven days earlier he'd knocked on his lieutenant's door and stuck his head in. "Lou? I need to take you to lunch today."

Lieutenant Fred "Freddie Mercury" Avila looked up from his desk. "Ringo, that's great, I appreciate it, but you would not believe—"

"No, Lou," George said firmly. "I need to take you to lunch."

The lieutenant looked at him, saw the look on his face. "Yeah? Shit."

They ended up at Fishbone's in Greektown. After ordering, Avila took a sip of his water, smoothed his tie, and crossed his hands. "Okay, why are we here?"

"It's about the crew hitting the strip clubs."

"Yeah? Where are you on that?"

"Honestly? Nowhere. They've used three different vehicles for four scores. We've recovered two out of the three, and they were stolen. Interiors soaked with bleach, so even if there was any trace evidence, hair, skin cells, the bleach killed it. Three black males go inside, and a fourth man stays in the getaway car—haven't been able to get a description on him yet. These guys are professionals, and know how to handle themselves. The last takedown gave us the most physical evidence in that the one guy fired his rifle into the ceiling. We recovered the slug, but it was so mangled we'll never be able to match it to a rifle. We recovered the case as well; steel case commercial Wolf ammo. Very common. No print on it. Firearms and Toolmarks should be able to match it to a rifle using the extractor marks, if and when we ever find a rifle to match it to. But even so…"

"All we've done is place the rifle at the scene," the lieutenant said, nodding. "Okay, so….?"

"Bouncer at Coconuts was a real good witness, solid. Did a couple of tours in Iraq with the Marines, looks like it would take a lot to shake him. He specifically heard one of the crew call the guy who fired a round into the ceiling 'Roo'."

"Roo?" Avila tried to make sense of that.

"Yeah. Line was, 'Roo, you got this?' This 'Roo' had just buttstroked one of the customers and fired a round into the ceiling."

"Right, I remember," the lieutenant said. "But I don't remember that line in your report."

George pursed his lips. "You don't have my full report yet. So you're covered."

Avila cocked his head. "Why do I need to be covered?"

"I went through the academy with Edward Mitchell. His nickname was Kangaroo. Roo. Right now he's on the SWAT team. Shit, I mean SRT." Special Response Team? He couldn't quite remember what the initials stood for, but it still meant SWAT. Hell, the A&E channel called their show about the DPD's SRT team *Detroit SWAT*.

The lieutenant looked like he was going to be sick. "I know we're not here just because somebody said something that might have sounded like somebody's nickname, back in the day." He smoothed his tie again, nervous habit.

"No, and my hope was, what I was trying to do was put this to bed without causing any problems. We've already taken enough black eyes."

"Yeah."

"So I talked to Ben Broussard. He's a Sergeant on the team, handles operations and logistics. We spent almost five years together in the same car."

"Didn't you take a bullet for him?"

"My vest did, back in the day. I don't recommend it, it really fucking hurts. So yeah, we're tight. I asked him for the SRT schedule for the last two months. I didn't tell him why, and told him not to ask."

"What if he'd been one of the guys..."

George shook his head. "Some guys you know, some you don't, some guys you're never sure of. I know Ben. Broussard is all about being the Good Guy. He couldn't start pulling heists, it would wreck him. He's straight, and he knows I'm straight, so he handed it over no questions asked."

"Okay, and?"

"And Eddie Mitchell was off during all four of the strip club heists. He was not working."

"Oh God." The lieutenant put his head down on the table and banged it gently, then sat back up. "He's all over that fucking TV show, he's practically the face of 'Detroit SWAT'. What the hell's his nickname on the show? Not Roo."

"'Chainsaw'."

"Right. Shit."

"So I crosschecked the work schedule of everybody else in SRT against the robberies. Four other guys were off during every robbery."

"Four?" the lieutenant said incredulously. He'd been hoping Mitchell had maybe been working with some friends, that he'd started running with a bad crowd outside of work. Childhood friends who'd ended up as gangbangers or something. Not this.

"I was able to eliminate one guy, Ted Brown. He's been off because he's actually on medical leave, he fell off a roof and got busted up real bad. But that leaves three other guys. Three members of SRT, plus Eddie Mitchell, all of whom were *not* working every time one of those strip clubs was hit."

Avila took a deep breath. Then another. "Who."

"Paul Wilson, Randy Parker, and Gabriel Kilpatrick. I actually went through the academy with both Wilson and Mitchell. That's one reason I wanted to get this out there. How many guys that graduated with us are still with the department, all these years later? If they're dirty, I don't want anybody to think I knew and didn't say anything."

Avila shook his head. "Wilson I might know. The others....they black?" He didn't give a shit about their races other than the fact that the three guys who had been doing the robberies had been identified as black males. George nodded.

"Shit."

"We've got nothing right now, simply circumstantial shit that wouldn't hold up in a junior high school court. And I still hope to God I'm wrong, that's it's just a weird coincidence. The next step is to start trying to build a case.

Pull financials, to start with. We don't have nearly enough for a search warrant or wiretaps, much less surveillance. But...I can't do that, we can't do that. Shouldn't. Not something this big, that involves so many officers. Not me, not us, not even Internal Affairs. Am I wrong?"

Avila looked him in the eye. "Ringo, you are one damn fine detective, and right now I really fucking hate you for it." He sighed. "No, we're not going to be able to do this ourselves. Somebody's going to have to call the FBI, but I'll be damned if it's going to be me. This has gotta go upstairs." He pulled out his cell phone.

Since the Chief of Police had contacted the FBI, Ringo hadn't heard a word. He and his team had continued to investigate leads in the strip club robberies, because to do otherwise would have raised red flags, but they were no closer to solving the cases.

"I just wanted to get a feel for him," George told the FBI agent as they sat in his Durango. "I haven't seen him for a few years, but we went through the academy together, and spent a lot of time riding around in a car. I know I was the one who called you, but it's been bugging me, you know? I only meant to do a drive-by, I didn't know they'd be sitting out there. Once they saw me, I thought it'd be weird if I didn't stop and say hi. I didn't say anything about this. We just bullshitted."

Safie knew exactly what had been said in the back yard, he'd been listening through the whole episode. "I heard what you said." Dumbass. Well, the detective hadn't torpedoed their investigation, but maybe his visit would spook the SWAT cops into doing something stupid. Right now all their investigation had turned up was circumstantial evidence, and not much of that. No huge purchases by any one of the suspects, although most of them seemed to be two paychecks away from bankruptcy.

Wilson spent all of his off duty time with his family. Mitchell practically lived at strip clubs, Parker had been to three Tigers games in the past week, and all Kilpatrick seemed to want to do was work out and play blackjack at the casinos. The FBI had nothing tying them directly to the robberies….but then again they hadn't turned up any evidence that cleared them, either. "And?"

George sighed. "And he feels dirty."

"Feeling dirty doesn't do shit for us."

"Yeah. Hey, where are your guys? Looked for a vehicle, but didn't see one. You in a house somewhere?"

Safie just gave him a dirty look in response. "Don't go near Wilson or anybody involved with this case again or I'll have you arrested for interfering with a federal investigation, we clear *Ringo*?"

"And people say the FBI are officious pricks who don't play well with others," George said, shaking his head. He got out of the Durango, back into his own vehicle, and took off.

Al Safie sat in his car and thought for a few minutes. He'd watched the impromptu meeting on a widescreen TV sitting a block away from the action, and the image of Wilson tapping on his iPhone stuck in his mind for some reason. There was something there.

PART II

NO SHAME

From infancy on, we are all spies; the shame is not this but that the secrets to be discovered are so paltry and few.

John Updike

CHAPTER SIX

Traffic wasn't bad heading in to work, but then Mickey had it easy — living in Woodbridge, he drove away from D.C. during morning rush hour, and toward it in the evening — the exact opposite of most everybody else.

That's not to say traffic was good — east coast traffic just plain sucked, all day every day, second verse same as the first. But, most days he was able to travel in sizable fractions of the speed limit on I-95. Not like those poor bastards in the northbound lanes, bumper to bumper and just crawling along. Like Ben, who had to work in D.C. Well, actually, Ben did have a car, but he almost never drove it all the way in to work. The drive took too long and parking fees were highway robbery. Ben, like a lot of D.C. employees, used the Metro. He parked at the Franconia-Springfield station and rode the rail in to work. Not driving saved him at least half an hour of travel time each way.

Mickey exited I-95 at Russell Road and headed west. When he'd first started working at the FBI lab, he'd been surprised at how much green there was so close to D.C. There were huge parks everywhere, plus the lab was on the Marine Corps Base at Quantico, which was ninety-five percent forest. There was a wall of trees to either side as Russell curved this way and that, and ahead he saw a large office building on the left. Among other things it housed the Air Force Office of Special Investigations. If he kept following the road around the curve to the right he reached the entrance to the base. Some days there were only a few cars and he was able to zip right in, other days the line— lines, actually, there were three lanes to get in—stretched for hundreds of yards. He knew sometimes the delays were due to heightened security, and more than once he'd seen the Marines bring in their dogs to sniff cars.

He always made sure to have his FBI ID out ahead of time—Federal Bureau of Investigation employee Michael Mitchell. It still seemed a little surreal to him, having FBI ID. The baby-faced Marine guards checked his ID as well as the stickers on his vehicle, and then he was waved through with a polite, "Have a good day, sir." Having Marines be so polite to him every morning just seemed wrong. He could see some days they were fighting back the impulse to salute him ingrained into them in boot camp. These were the kids— kids, because most of them looked younger than him—who fought America's wars. Shit, he should be saluting *them*.

Past the checkpoint Russell Road became MCB 1. He followed its winding path for just over a mile and saw the Marine Corps Information Center. Behind it was the Marine Corps Association building. Just past them MCB 2 ran off to the left. Apart from the occasional isolated building, there still wasn't anything but trees to either side of the road. He wasn't exactly sure how big the base was, but it seemed huge. He'd only ever driven on a small section of it. Half a mile beyond the intersection with MCB 2 Mickey turned left onto MCB 4 and headed into the FBI complex.

He left early every day in part because there was no way to know how bad traffic was going to be on I-95, or how long the stack-up of cars would stretch at the Marine checkpoint. But he also left early because he loved his job.

Mickey worked with some true-blue, third-generation, FBI-runs-in-my-blood-and-they'll-bury-me-with-my-badge types, but that wasn't him. He worked for the FBI because he loved forensics, fingerprints especially, and the FBI was *it*. There was nobody bigger. When you wanted, when you *needed* evidence in a crime handled, when life or death was on the line, when only the finest techniques and the latest technology in the world would do, you went to the FBI. The lab did as much or more work for police departments around the country, examining their evidence, as it did for its own investigations. The FBI even did work for some foreign governments.

But….if there was somebody bigger or better than the FBI, he'd be working there, because it was the job that was important to him, not the Bureau. However, he knew better than to actually say that out loud. A lot of the lab employees treated their employer like a hometown sports team, and anybody that didn't love it better shut the hell up. FBI agents took the "team player" thing to a whole new level. Mickey wasn't much of a team guy, but he liked his job, a lot. If all the other techs in the lab wanted to mistake his love for forensics for love of the FBI, he wasn't going to correct them.

Ben's criticism of the lab bothered him more than he would admit in part because he knew, to some extent, it was accurate. They'd had some problems, with Lab staff acting as agents for the prosecution first and scientists second, which was completely contrary to what they were supposed to be doing. You didn't take a side with science—the facts were the facts, the evidence was the evidence. Once you brought it to light, you let it speak for itself. It was finding it, winnowing the information from the scraps of prints he sometimes had to deal with, which was the fascinating part of the job.

While he loved everything to do with fingerprints, the whole world of forensics fascinated him, and to get where he was he'd had to learn a hell of a lot of chemistry and math. Not that he used much of either; the closest thing he got to chemistry was the rare occasion where he would help a senior tech use superglue vapors to bring up the print on an object that didn't lend itself to traditional printing techniques. Ninhydrin, diazafluorenone, vacuum metal deposition, ethyl cyanoacrylate polymerization....modern techniques for revealing and retrieving fingerprints were amazing.

Mickey parked in the mostly empty lot and headed toward the building, then stopped as a black helicopter roared over the two new buildings next to the lab used for training intelligence analysts. It startled him, and he looked up to see guys hanging out both sides of the helicopter in raid gear. HRT — The FBI's elite Hostage Rescue Team, doing more training.

Mickey watched the bird turn stand on its side as it executed a sharply banked turn, then roar back toward HRT's nearby training area. Right before it dipped out of sight Mickey saw thick ropes unspool from the sides of the chopper as the agents prepared to "fastrope" — a term he'd learned — to the ground. He checked his watch. They were at it early that morning; never a dull day at Quantico.

It was a beautiful morning, with a blue sky and a few wispy clouds reflected in the lights of the big Lab building. The J. Edgar Hoover building in D.C. — *that* looked like a lab. Actually, it looked more like a prison, but that was another opinion he kept to himself. The FBI lab at Quantico...it looked like an upscale office building designed by IKEA. Both inside and out. The exterior was all glass, and indoors was none of the drab colors or stuffiness you'd expect from either a laboratory environment or a government office. There were windows everywhere, letting in a lot of light, and all the cabinets were clad in blonde wood. The first time he'd seen the inside of the place he thought it looked very alpine, like Carl Sagan channeling a ski lodge.

With over 500 employees at the lab, FBI agents running in and out on cases, plus forensic scientists from around the world constantly visiting, the guys running security in the lobby didn't know everyone's name, but familiar faces got a nod and a smile. Coming in as early as he did, avoiding the rush, Mickey's face was more familiar than most new employees to the uniformed guards, and he returned a wave before heading to the elevators.

Once at his desk, he powered up his computer and checked to see if he had any work emails. He knew what he'd be doing at least for the next day—the FBI was in the process of hiring another batch of agents, and it was his job to run the prints of the applicants through the system. Most of the time it was very boring work—scan the prints, run them through the database to see if there was a match, and if the computer spit out a possible with a high likelihood of a match, he then had to compare the two. There were a number of different databases, but he was only checking the criminal database, as many of the applicants had prints in the federal system due to jobs in law enforcement or the military. You wouldn't think someone with a criminal record would be stupid enough to apply for a job with the largest federal law enforcement agency in the country, but he was learning to never underestimate the stupidity of some people.

A lot of the veteran lab employees worked odd hours, helping agents with rush cases, but Mickey for the most part was a 9-to-5 guy. He really wanted to move up to examining evidence from important criminal cases, but knew he had to do the grunt work first. Every organization did things a certain way, and the federal government was set in its ways and slow to change. It was also weird.

The FBI got a respectable chunk of the multi-trillion dollar U.S. budget every year, and yet they wouldn't buy their employees coffee, or water, or anything else. There was a small break room near their work area, and on the counter was their coffee club's Keurig coffee machine. The lab employees had discovered the convenience of Keurig one-cup coffee makers, and even though it was more expensive per cup, the savings on filters and wasted coffee probably made it a wash—but everybody got what they wanted. He'd bought into the use of this one, with the warning from his co-workers that its presence in the lab was somehow a violation of the FBI workplace rules. Stupid. It was overlooked by management, but they could change their mind at anytime.

There were three carousels of K-cups, the single serving plastic coffee containers, and he spun through them looking for something that looked tasty. He finally settled on a dark French roast, then grabbed the containers of sugar and powdered creamer while he waited.

Mickey was a bit of a coffee snob, and at home would only drink coffee lightened with half-n-half, or better yet heavy whipping cream. There was a full-size refrigerator in the kitchen, but bringing his personal cream to the lab offices just hadn't worked out. Whether it was half-n-half or heavy cream, somebody else (or probably several somebodies) kept using it. It frustrated him to no end.

He'd begun marking the waxed paper containers DO NOT USE in heavy black marker, but that hadn't worked. As large as the lab complex was, it was subdivided according to task, and their office area was only home to a couple dozen people at most. It didn't take much effort to figure out that the cream or half-n-half belonged to the new kid, which meant it was self-serve—or at least that's how it seemed to him. As a last resort he'd brought in some cream in a labelless plastic container, onto which he wrote URINE SPECIMEN. "Who the hell put a urine specimen into a food refrigerator!" Fortney, their group supervisor, roared not half an hour later across the work area. A lot of the techs working in the Latent Print unit of the lab had great senses of humor, but Fortney, an FBI Special Agent assigned to the lab, was not one of them.

Mickey had just sighed, then explained, and from that day forward submitted to the indignity of having to use the bulk powdered creamer in his coffee. The irony was not lost on him as he sat in the middle of the FBI lab. Trust them to process the evidence for a high-profile capital crime? Sure. Trust them not to steal your cream for their own coffee? Not a fucking chance.

"Good morning Mickey! You have a good weekend?" Brenda was two hundred pounds of red-headed Irish enthusiasm each and every morning, and he knew to keep still when they both were in the narrow room because she changed speed and direction without warning. Mickey was one of the few people who regularly beat her into the office.

"Yep. How 'bout you?" He pulled his cup out of the coffee maker and began adding cream and sugar.

"My little sister came in from out-of-town and we did the tourist thing all weekend. You know, I've lived here five years and never been to any of the monuments? Too busy working I guess. Here, look." She pulled out her smartphone and flicked her finger back and forth a few times, then shoved the phone under his nose. Mickey looked at a self-shot of Brenda and another redhead in front of the Lincoln Memorial. Her "little" sister looked even heavier than Brenda.

"I did all that stuff with my parents when I was a kid," Mickey said. "Good thing, 'cause it seems like I'm always too busy to do it now. How old's your sister?"

"Thirty. Three years younger than me."

"What's she do for a living?"

"She's a stripper," Brenda said, as she pulled her lunch out of her massive purse and stuck it in the refrigerator. She had a neutral expression on her face as she turned back, but could only hold it for a few seconds before she burst out laughing.

"Oh, you should have seen the look on your face!" she giggled. "That was priceless. No, she's in sales, a farm equipment company in Pennsylvania." The thought of seeing Brenda, much less her bigger little sister, in a g-string

86

and gyrating on a pole, had been a bit disturbing. Mickey pushed through it. "How's Larry doing? He hang out with you guys too or was it just a girls' weekend?" Larry was her boyfriend who did some sort of construction work.

"He likes Marcie, but took the opportunity to do some fishing with his buddies this weekend. What are you doing today? Still the Special Agent application prints?"

"Yep. All day and then some." He wasn't sure how many FBI agents there were across the country, but he knew it was thousands, and they were always retiring. It was rare that the FBI Academy didn't run several new classes a year, and for every new agent there were hundreds if not thousands of applicants who made it to the fingerprint and background check stage of the hiring process.

"Booooring," she said. "I've got a bunch of prints and partials from that plane crash last week. Trying to identify bodies....and body parts. Putting the right arms with the.....left arms. And the right bodies. Doing that with Dave and Shelly."

"Ick."

"I feel for the families. Some of those bodies…did you see the pictures? Looked like a bomb went off. Hell, at the speed they hit, it was practically like a bomb. They're doing the DNA tests down the hall on the bits and pieces."

"And people say fingerprints are boring. DNA is so much worse. It's like….I don't know, watching stock market results in super slo mo."

She laughed. "See you on the flip side." She was gone with a wave.

Brenda was so bouncy and hyper that Mickey wondered how she'd ever found herself in a job that required sitting still in front of a computer and lab equipment for long stretches of the day, but she seemed to be one of the better techs in the lab. Coffee in hand, he headed out to his desk. Time to get to work.

The cafeteria was a necessity. Nobody wanted to pack their own lunch every day, but due to the lab's location on the Marine Corps base heading out to eat would only have been a possibility if they'd been allowed 90 minutes for lunch. As necessary as it was, the FBI had spared none of the taxpayer's expense when designing the menu. Or at least that's what Mickey told his friends. Truth was the lowest bidder had won the contract for the cafeteria, and the result was ugly. But at least the mediocre food was expensive. The inflated east coast/D.C prices had unfortunately made their way onto the menu, but if you wanted to eat something other than what came out of a brown bag it was the only option. He'd heard the cafeteria at the nearby FBI Academy wasn't any better.

Coming back to his desk after lunch, a little stuffed from too much sticky pasta, Mickey first checked for new emails, then headed over to check the latest print results at the terminal connected to the scanner. He got a little thrill when he saw there were actually some returns on the prints — high percentage matches. "Sweet," he muttered. But when he sat down and started to review what he had, the results didn't make any sense. "Wait, two....?" He tried to skim what he had, and saw that wasn't going to cut it. Taking a deep breath, he waded in.

"Sir, I've got a very agitated young man out here from Latent Prints who says he needs to speak with you. He says it's an emergency."

Boone Stephenson, the Director of the FBI's Laboratory Division, looked over his half glasses at Maggie, his secretary. She'd been his secretary for six years, and they knew each other as well as any man and woman who'd never had sex could.

"Agitated? And young?"

Maggie smiled. "He seems very earnest."

"Yes, I'm sure, but about what?"

"Something about fingerprints." She waved a hand.

"Well, that would have been my first guess." He sighed, and checked his watch. Almost four o'clock. "Okay, show him in, but if he's still in here in five minutes throw me a rope."

"You got it." She popped out, and a few seconds later Stephenson saw a slender young man walk through his doorway carrying a large stack of folders. He looked excited, almost scared.

"Sir, I appreciate your seeing me," Mickey told the Director. He'd met Stephenson before, even spoken to him the day he'd started in the lab, but since then he'd only been a face at the podium or in the halls. He was sweating, and his heart was hammering in his chest.

"Appreciate it quickly, I've got a busy day," Boone said, not unkindly. "Who are you?"

"Mickey—uhh, Michael Mitchell, sir. I've been here almost ten months."

"Yes, but I meant 'Who are you?' more in the sense of, 'What do you do here?'"

"Oh. I'm in the Latent Print unit sir. And that's why I'm here." When he saw Stephenson waiting patiently for him to go on, he did. "For the past few days I've been running the fingerprints of FBI Special Agent applicants through the criminal database. I think they're getting ready to hire another big batch of agents."

Stephenson nodded. No shortage of money for federal agencies under this administration.

"Well, when I got back from lunch, I saw I had a hit. A match. Two, actually."

"Two applicants came back with criminal records?" It shouldn't surprise him, it seemed like people were getting stupider by the day.

"No, sir, it was two matches on the same set of prints."

"You've lost me."

"This applicant, his right thumb, a plain whorl, came back at a 97% match to Juan Alfredo Rodriguez, and his left middle finger, which is a tented arch, came back at a 98% match to Jerome Beiers."

That got Boone's attention. He sat up a little straighter. "And I'm assuming that the person applying for a position as a Special Agent has indicated that he is neither Jerome Beiers or Juan whoever."

"Right. The applicant in question is David Anderson, of Troy, Michigan. I've got his whole hiring packet."

"No aliases listed for him? Wait, why did you pull his hiring packet? And why are we having this conversation? Shouldn't I be having this conversation with your group supervisor?"

"Sir, honestly, I didn't tell my supervisor initially because I thought I had screwed up. Anything over a 95% match on the computer and it's pretty much a lock, but we always compare the prints ourselves to double-check. Final verification is always done by a properly trained examiner. I re-ran the prints through the computer. And got the same results."

"Who took the prints?"

Stephenson didn't know that? "Sir, all applicant prints are taken at the local FBI office. In this case, Detroit." Pretty much because the FBI didn't trust anybody else to do it right.

"And are these Live Scan or ink-and-paper?"

"Ink and paper."

"Why not Live Scan? Since we're doing them ourselves. Quicker, easier, no ink smudges, scan 'em and they go straight into the computer."

Mickey had asked that question himself less than a month before. "With the Live Scan system, the field office has to send in the print digitally. If someone, either at their end or at ours, makes a mistake in how the prints are addressed or sorted, they could end up in the criminal records, the CJIS system. It's apparently happened more than once, and nothing will screw up your job application with the FBI quicker than getting your prints entered as that of a criminal simply because someone pressed the wrong button on a keyboard. So all the Special Agent applicant prints are still being done with ink and paper."

"Were the submitted prints smudged?"

"No sir. Whoever did these in the Detroit office, ummmm, looks like Special Agent Hoff, he's a pro. There are no smears, no smudges, no light or dark spots, these exemplars are nearly textbook perfect."

"Okay, so what you're telling me is that there's a screw-up somewhere. It happens. More that I'd care to admit. I'm still not sure why you thought this was an emergency."

"Sir, I'm a mediocre driver and I can't carry a tune, but when it comes to prints I'm good. I'm damn good. I know what I'm looking at. I double-checked them. Hell, I quadruple checked them. I went over the prints at every magnification I could, using my eyes, not a program. I matched twenty-eight points of comparison on David Anderson's right thumb to the print taken from Juan Rodriguez. As you know that is far more than what we need to consider it a perfect match. I matched thirty-three points on Anderson's left middle finger to the print taken from Jerome Beiers."

Boone frowned and leaned forward. "Are you saying he's got multiple identities?"

"No sir." Mickey spread out all the files in front of his boss, and pointed as he explained. "Juan Alfredo Rodriguez, born January 13th, 1936 in Mexico City, Mexico. He was arrested in 1982 by us, the FBI, for wire fraud. He was three months from release in 1987 when he died of a heart attack, in federal prison. David Anderson's right thumb print is not a match to Rodriguez's right thumb, it is a match to Rodriguez's *left ring finger.* Jerome Beiers is thirty-eight years old, Jewish, obese, six inches shorter than Anderson, and currently living in Newark. He has eight months left on his probation. Four years ago he was convicted of embezzlement from his law firm. The print on David Anderson's left middle finger matches the print taken from Beiers' *right ring finger.* As you can see from the photos, none of the men looks anything like the other."

The head of the FBI didn't say anything. His eyes were darting back and forth over the files. "What about Anderson himself?"

"David Matthew Anderson is twenty-five years old. Graduate of Michigan State University, degree with honors in Criminal Justice. Initial background check shows he's never been arrested. Parents dead, no siblings. He has two very glowing recommendation letters from FBI agents in his hiring packet, plus one from the Chief of the Warren, Michigan police department, and because of that it appears he has been fast-tracked."

The young tech had printed out samples of the fingerprint matches, and Stephenson could see from the photos in the file that none of the three looked like they could even be related, but that wasn't enough. It wasn't nearly good enough. "Where's the nearest AFIS terminal?" he asked Mickey.

Forty-five minutes later Boone Stephenson leaned back from the hi-def monitor and rubbed his aching eyes. The door behind them was closed—Boone had closed it ten minutes after sitting down, when he started seeing things he didn't want to see. "This can't be the first time he's been printed. He works for an armored car company for Christ's sake. *We've* probably run his prints before." He was trying to find something, anything, that would take away from what he'd just seen with his own eyes. He glanced down at the files in front of him, but they were no help.

"I don't know what to tell you sir. He has a concealed weapons permit as well. I'm guessing that if anybody got an AFIS match before, they looked at the age of the person at the other end of the match, maybe just looked at the photos, and automatically discarded it as a...I don't know, false positive."

"Who's your supervisor over there?" Boone asked him.

"Frank Fortney, sir."

"And what did he have to say about this?"

"Nothing, sir, I didn't say anything to him. I didn't say anything to anybody, I've just been working on it all afternoon. Like I said, at first I was afraid I'd screwed up. Now I'm afraid I didn't."

"You know it's impossible, right?"

"What's that, sir?"

"Two people can't have the same prints."

Mickey sighed. He'd been thinking about just that for several hours. "I know that's what we say. But, really, there's no way to prove that. There are tens of millions of people living in this country alone who have never been printed, so how do we know that their prints don't match somebody? We've always said no two prints are alike because we've never found any. Because nature almost never makes identical copies of anything. Because the chances against it are astronomical. Just like we say that no two snowflakes are the same—it's an unprovable hypothesis." He scratched his head. "I think it was Francis Galton, Charles Darwin's cousin, back in the 1890s, who declared the odds of two people having the same fingerprint were one in sixty-four *billion*. But then I came to work today."

"Do you know how....." Boone searched for the right word. Nothing seemed sufficient for what he needed to say. "....important this is?"

"Yes sir, I think I do."

"Okay, tell me." Boone turned in his chair and stared at the young man.

"We've just discovered that fingerprints are not individualistic. One person has, for all intents and purposes, fingerprints which are identical to those belonging to *two* other people. If that's the case, who knows how many other matches there are out there in the world? This completely turns the science of fingerprinting on its ear. Uh, so to speak."

Boone regarded the young man for three long beats. "You're talking about the science side of it....but the science doesn't happen in a vacuum. People are fingerprinted for very specific reasons. Mostly for *a* very specific reason. People are fingerprinted because it is an undisputable technique to uniquely identify them. More crimes have been solved with fingerprint evidence than for any other reason, short of actual confessions. If the general public finds out that two people can have the same fingerprints...what do you think will happen?"

"I...hadn't really thought about that sir."

Boone nodded. "Yes, I see that."

"Sir, what do you mean *if* they find out? If Anderson's prints match two other people, what are the chances that he's the only person like this in the world?"

"People have been getting fingerprinted for over a hundred years, and there's never been a match before. Maybe Anderson is the exception to the rule."

"Actually, sir, I've been thinking about that, and I wonder. Anderson had to have been printed before, but somehow whoever ran his prints either didn't find the match or discounted it. Maybe the reverse has happened as well—people getting blamed or arrested for something because of fingerprints, and yet they insist they're innocent. Who's to say they aren't, and the fingerprints belong to someone else?"

"Mr. Mitchell," Boone said to him very seriously, "that's the very thing I want you to think about. Go home now," for he could see on the clock above the door that it was after 5 p.m., "and think about the ramifications of releasing this discovery to the public. Think very hard on it. Come and see me tomorrow morning in my office, and we'll talk. Between now and then, don't talk to anyone about it. Not your wife, your girlfriend, your priest, not Fortney, no one. That's an order. Are we clear?"

"Yes sir."

"Good. Go home and think about what this means to you, to your career, to the Bureau, to law enforcement in general. Go ahead and close the door behind you. I'll take care of these." He waved his hand over the files on the desk. Boone also needed to clear the terminal so there was no immediate evidence of their activity.

"Okay. Good night, sir."

"Good night."

After the door closed Boone put his head in his hands. "Oh sweet Jesus," he whispered.

CHAPTER SEVEN

Dave pulled up in front of the doors and waited. A few seconds later one of the bouncers, Quentin, stuck his head out and waved at him, then disappeared back inside. Dave yawned and blinked. The dashboard clock read 2:44 a.m. He had to get up in three hours to head out on a surveillance, and knowing Gina, he wouldn't be getting any more sleep tonight. It was a good thing he'd crashed early, and already gotten five hours of sleep.

The door of the club opened and Gina came practically skipping out, big purse in hand. She had on white tights, high heels, but had nothing on above the waist but her orange bikini top. "Hey Sweetie!" she said, swinging open the door. "Thanks for picking me up."

"Yeah." Her Acura was at the dealer for a problem with the passenger side window motor. He glanced over as she sat down in the seat. Didn't look like she had anything on underneath the tights.

"Aww, is baby sweepy?" She leaned over the center console and gave him a wet kiss, pushing her tits against his arm. She tasted of whiskey, and smelled of cigarettes, although she didn't smoke. He knew a lot of the noise about the dangers of second-hand cigarette smoke was bullshit, but most non-smokers weren't working a stripper pole, breathing heavily in a dense cloud of smoke every night.

"Buckle up," he told her, trying not to smile. He looked to his left coming out of the parking lot, but at that hour of the morning there was only one set of headlights visible, far down the eastbound lanes of 8 Mile. "I should be done by about noon today, short day, so I can take you to pick up your car then."

"Okay."

He drove across the four eastbound lanes and hit the boulevard turnaround. There was nobody in sight in the westbound lanes, so he coasted through the Stop sign in second gear. He'd just shifted the Mustang into third when he saw the red and blue lights in his rearview.

Shit, he thought to himself. He signaled, then angled across the lanes and turned into a parking lot. He couldn't see anything in his mirrors other than the flashing lights even before the cop turned on the spotlight and aimed it at his side mirror to illuminate the inside of the Mustang.

"This is such bullshit," Gina grumbled. "Why are they stopping us?

"Shhh," he said. Even without him running the stop sign, he knew that a black Mustang coming out of Detroit at that hour of the night *was* probable cause. By the time the cop walked up to his door he had the car shut off, the window down, and his hands on the steering wheel, his driver license and CPL in one of them.

"License, registration, and proof of insurance," Dave heard over his left shoulder.

"Yes sir. I've got a CPL," he told the officer. Michigan law required a person with a Concealed Pistol License to tell a law enforcement officer immediately if he was armed. Dave took his hand off the steering wheel and held his cards out for the officer. He glanced over his shoulder, but the officer was just a silhouette behind a bright flashlight.

"Are you armed?" the officer asked, taking the cards from Dave's hand.

I wouldn't tell you about my CPL if I wasn't, Dave thought, but only said, "Yes sir."

"Where is it?"

"On my right hip."

The cop swung his flashlight beam around inside the already well lit car. "Okay, just keep your hands on the—" the flashlight beam paused on the cards in the officer's hand, then swung up to Dave's face. "Cobb? Hey, man, how you doing?"

Dave turned and looked at the officer, and squinted past the flashlight beam. The officer lowered the flashlight and leaned down so Dave could better see his face. The face was familiar, but it wasn't until he checked out the officer's nameplate that it clicked. "Drake? What's up? Good to see you. You're looking good." He glanced out the windshield. *That's right, Warren bordered Detroit along this stretch of 8 Mile.*

Drake smiled, and peered into the car past Dave. "What are you doing out this late?" *Holy shit, who the hell was this in the passenger seat? A hooker?*

"This is my girlfriend, Gina," Dave said, sticking a thumb at her. "She works at Goldfinger's. Her car's in the shop, so I had to pick her up after work."

"Hiya doin'?" the cop said to Gina, giving her a very detailed examination. "You a hostess?"

"Dancer," she told the dark-haired officer. *He looked like most cops to her—bulky and mean, maybe a little stupid.*

Drake raised his eyebrows at Dave, and Dave just smiled. "What have you been up to?" the cop asked him. Dave saw his eyes flick over to Gina's big bikini-clad tits in the seat next to him. *They were like eye magnets, most guys could hardly bear to look away. They made her a lot of money.*

"Waiting to get into the FBI. Had to wait until I was twenty-five to apply. Been working as a P.I. and for an armored car company while I waited."

"That's right, I remember that you wanted to do the fed stuff. You ever decide to come work for us, we'd be happy to have you."

"I appreciate that, but I'm not much for being a slave to the radio. Although if I remember, it can get exciting some days...."

"Shit. We're still talking about that. Hell of a day."

"How's Kennedy?"

"He's good, he's real good. He's a sergeant now, and getting close to retirement, but I don't think he'll quit any time soon. Gonna have college to pay for pretty soon. I'll tell him I ran into you." He handed back Dave's driver license and CPL. "Nice ride."

"Yeah, I'd always wanted one, and I came into some money, so..."

"Oh, yeah, shit, I heard about that. I'm sorry. Man, you never know, right?"

"Life's short," Dave agreed. "Date a stripper."

Drake stared at him for a second, then burst out into laughter. "Life's short, date a stripper!" he repeated. "That's awesome, Cobb. I'm gonna get that on a shirt. You stay safe, okay? And good luck with the feebies. I'll tell everyone I saw you." He bent down farther and looked at Gina. "Nice meeting you ma'am. You take care of this guy. Cobb makes the rest of us look like pussies." He tapped the roof of the Mustang twice, then headed back to his cruiser.

"What was he talking about?" Gina said.

Dave just shook his head as he started up the Mustang. "Nothing. Don't worry about it."

"Why does he call you Cobb?"

"It's just a stupid nickname."

She made a face. "I swear, sometimes I feel like I don't know anything about you at all." She sat back in her seat, then looked at him. "Did you get an inheritance or something?"

Mickey hadn't been able to sleep for shit. Not because he thought he was in trouble, but he'd been flying on adrenaline the first time he'd barged upstairs and demanded to see the Director of the Lab. With a whole night to think about their conversation, about going back to speak to the Director concerning something so important, he was a nervous wreck.

"I can't believe I just marched right up there," Mickey mumbled to himself for about the eighth time as he drove in to work even earlier than usual. But what should he have done? Gone to his supervisor? Frank Fortney was a blowhard who was a Yes Man first and a Bureau Kool-Aid drinker second. Actual forensic investigations ranked about tenth on Fortney's personal priority list.

Too late for self-recriminations now. And besides, the impromptu meeting with the Director hadn't gone badly. The man was smart, had seen the importance of Mickey's discovery right away

"Where'd you disappear to yesterday afternoon?" Brenda asked as she came swirling into the kitchen. Mickey checked his watch. Only a little after seven a.m., and he was already on his third cup of coffee, but hadn't done a bit of work. Couldn't focus. He was planning on heading up to speak to the Director at 9 a.m., but the morning dragged on ahead of him interminably.

"Got pulled off on a side project. Very hush hush. It involves Elvis," he told her conspiratorially.

"Awesome. Tell him I said hi."

Mickey was standing in front of the Director's secretary exactly at nine a.m. "Michael Mitchell, to see the Director," he told her quietly. He hoped she couldn't see how sweaty he was.

The woman nodded, stood up, and gestured for him to follow. Apparently the Director had told her to expect Mickey. "Sir?" she said, standing in Stephenson's doorway.

Stephenson looked up from some papers. To Mickey's eye he looked tired. "Thank you Maggie," he told her, then stood up. Stephenson walked over to the doorway. "No calls," he told his secretary, and closed the door behind Mickey. Stephenson headed back to his seat, distractedly pointing Mickey to the chair in front of his desk.

"Okay, son, talk to me," Stephenson said. "You look like you've had a long night. What are you thinking?"

Mickey took a deep breath. "Sir, I really don't think the importance of this can be underestimated. To the world of forensics, I mean. It's a complete paradigm shift, at least when it comes to fingerprinting as a means of identification."

Boone was nodding, but inside he felt cold. Everything that the young fingerprint examiner was saying was true....if the public found out about his discovery. If they didn't, then nothing changed. It was honestly that simple. "I asked you to think about the big picture on this, how your discovery will affect....nearly everything we do. And you tell me that it will be a paradigm shift?"

"Yes sir." That was clearly obvious, surely the Director could see that?

"Hmm. Let me tell you what will happen from a practical viewpoint," the Director told Mickey. "If the FBI announces that we have discovered fingerprints are no longer a reliable way to unquestioningly identify an individual, every person who has been convicted of a crime in this country, where fingerprints were simply even submitted as evidence in their trial, will ask for a mistrial. And they'll get it. We're talking hundreds of thousands of felons, if I had to guess. And that's just in this country. Around the world, I can't even imagine what the reaction will be. But this news could result in literally millions of hardened criminals being set free."

"Yes sir, at least in the short term, until they can get new trials."

Stephenson stared at him. "New trials? Do you know how backlogged our court system already is? It's already overwhelmed, everywhere. To arrange thousands, tens of thousands of new trials? You're talking a process that would take at least a decade, if not two. Cost hundreds of millions of dollars. Maybe billions."

"Yes sir, like I said, in the short term, I know, it will be quite a mess. But at the end, I believe we'll come out the stronger for it. And who knows, maybe one or two of those men in prison right now actually is innocent. Like I mentioned yesterday, I can't believe Anderson is the only person in this world of six billion people whose fingerprints match somebody else."

"I can see you're a scientist," the Lab Director said to him slowly. "I can't fault your logic." He frowned, leaned back in his chair and crossed his arms. "What would you say if I ordered you to keep this secret, if I told you that telling anyone would violate the terms of your employment?"

Mickey frowned as well. "Sir....it doesn't. This is a general scientific discovery, not classified information from an intelligence briefing. It does not violate any of the non-disclosure agreements I've signed."

Stephenson nodded quickly. "Okay. I wanted—I needed to ask you, to see exactly how you felt. The science...that's more important to you than anything, isn't it?"

"Sir, that's why I'm here."

"I'm glad to hear. Okay, Mr. Mitchell, you tell me what you think we—I—the Bureau—should do."

"I think half-measures just won't do with this one, sir. I'd recommend a press conference. Get all the facts out there. Not releasing Mr. Anderson's name, of course, just stating the facts that the FBI lab has determined that it is possible, however unlikely, that two people can share a fingerprint."

"And if releasing the facts of this discovery to the public results in tens of thousands of dangerous felons being released from prison to await new trials? Bad, truly evil people?"

Mickey was pretty sure he was being tested, so he was completely honest even though it made him sound a little naïve. "Sir, I have faith in our justice system. In the short term this might—well, it will cause a lot of problems, but we're stronger than that."

"'We'?"

"The justice system. America."

Stephenson laid his hands flat on his desk. He paused long enough to take two breaths, then said, "Whatever plans you might have had for this evening, you should cancel them. We have a six o'clock appointment with Director Gonh."

Mickey blinked. A meeting with the FBI Director himself. That only made sense, a discovery as important as this, but knowing it was important, and hearing you had an appointment with the Director of the FBI, were two different things.

Stephenson looked him in the eye and said very firmly, "Until we talk to the Director, and until he schedules this press conference, you are to say nothing to no one about any of this, are we clear? Not a word. You made the discovery, but there's a right way and a wrong way to do this. I'm sure you'll be standing up there next to the Director when he makes his statement to the press, but *he's* the guy who has to make the announcement, understand? You do not want to be the guy who pisses off the Director by stealing his thunder. Not a soul. Do we understand each other?"

Mickey was so startled by the image of him standing next to the Director of the FBI while camera flashes strobed and reporters yelled questions that he almost forgot to respond. "Uh, yes sir! Perfectly."

Stephenson nodded sharply. "Good. I'm not sure where we're actually going to meet the Director, he's a very busy man, but be ready at five o'clock to take a ride. I will call you this afternoon when I have more details. What's your extension?"

Mickey went about his work the rest of the day on autopilot, almost in a daze. He'd only been with the Bureau nine months, and this kind of thing....this was a once-in-a-lifetime event. Hell, once in ten lifetimes. It was surreal. Stephenson didn't have to worry about him telling anybody, he could hardly believe it himself. He was afraid that if he told somebody, he'd wake up from the dream, he'd fall through the looking-glass and find himself back on planet Earth.

He tried to shake it off, tried to focus on his job, running the prints of more FBI Special Agent applicants, but after what he'd discovered that could hardly capture his attention. Mickey looked through the stack of files on his desk absently, wanting to look at Anderson's file again, then realized Director Stephenson had it.

What a crazy world. Maybe if one of the other fingerprint techs in the unit had been the one to run Anderson's prints, they never would have discovered the truth. Or they would have just shrugged off the match. Matches. And what would happen if Anderson got printed again, for whatever reason? Chances are the prints would come right back to the FBI, to be run against their database. The FBI was the final word on fingerprint matches in so many ways, but there wasn't really anybody checking their work, not really. Mickey looked up from his musings to see Frank Fortney standing in his doorway and looking out over the cubicles. Looking at Mickey. Not sure whether to smile or nod or what, Mickey nervously bent his head back down.

He was busily typing up a report when his phone rang, and he picked it up without thinking. "Mitchell."

"Mr. Mitchell, our meeting has been moved back due to a conflict," Director Stephenson told him. "Meet me in the downstairs parking garage at eight p.m. I'll have a car."

"Uh, yes sir," he said, heart beating a little faster. That was all Stephenson had to say to him, and hung up without another word. Mickey put his receiver back down, and stared at it for a good minute. Then he checked his watch. Then looked back at the phone.

Shit. He was thinking too much, that was the problem. Too much imagination. Maybe if he was more of a team player, more of a Bureau man.....

He finished his report, then looked at his coffee cup. There was just enough cold coffee in it to cover the bottom. He splashed it on his shirt, then stood up and walked to Fortney's office. He knocked, and his supervisor looked up from his computer.

With a disgusted look on his face, Mickey pointed at the coffee stain on his white shirt. "I'm having one of those days. Okay if I take off a little early today? I can put in for some PTO if you want, I've got a bunch saved up."

Fortney glanced at the clock on the wall, above a framed portrait of the President. Just after four p.m. "Nah, don't worry about it. I've had those days too. I've got to leave early today myself. Just make sure you log off your computer, and I'll see you tomorrow. Um, Mitchell?"

"Yes sir?"

"How old are you now?"

"Twenty-five."

Fortney nodded. "Have you ever thought about applying to the Bureau as an agent? You do a good job, you're smart, and you're a conscientious worker. I'm glad

I've got you in my group, but there's a lot of room for advancement with the FBI."

"Thank you," Mickey said, trying not to sound too surprised. "I have thought about it....but I know that even if I wanted to come straight back to the lab I couldn't. I'd have to do at least a couple years at a field office, and right now I like what I'm doing too much."

Fortney laughed. "Well hell, if you like working here so much I'm not going to tell you to leave, but you keep it in mind, okay? The FBI's big, lots of places to go and things to do as a Special Agent, especially with your skills and background. There's no place else that you could go and have the same opportunity that you do here."

Ben came into the apartment as Mickey was getting ready to leave. He was surprised to see Mickey, normally the lab rat wasn't back until close to six. Ben had cut work early because he had a date with his girlfriend, which meant, after dealing with traffic, he'd arrived home at an hour that would be considered normal for any American who didn't have to deal with Beltway traffic.

"You're home early. What, are you leaving already?"

"Yeah, I've got a meeting. For work. Tonight."

"You okay?" Mickey looked a little stressed out.

Mickey stopped, then turned to his roommate. "Ben, you know all those conspiracy movies you love to watch? All the spy novels you read/? I've been thinking about them today. You know, everybody involved in a conspiracy seems to end up dead or in prison." When he was leaving Quantico there were agents training at what sounded like at least one of the nearby shooting ranges, and waves of gunfire were echoing off the front of the Lab. It hadn't helped his state of mind.

"What? Hey, why are you all dressed up?" He eyed Mickey's fresh shirt and tie, and the suitcoat in his hand. "You got a date?"

Mickey got off the elevator and looked around the parking garage, then checked his watch. Nine thirty exactly. Stephenson had called him again at seven o'clock to tell him the meeting had been pushed back again, which hadn't made Mickey any less nervous. By that time he'd been alone at his desk for over an hour; even the hardest working person in their group long departed for home. Fortney had been gone by the time Mickey had returned to the office in his fresh clothes.

The FBI Lab building itself wasn't very old at all, which meant that neither was the underground parking garage; instead of a dimly lit, cramped structure, it was open, and well lit. The garage was reserved for supervisors and the Bureau's pool cars, and Mickey would have to have a lot more years on the job before he was allowed to park down there, although this wasn't his first visit. Normally it was pretty packed with cars, but at this hour of the night there weren't a lot of vehicles visible.

He heard the sound of tires on concrete echoing off the walls, but couldn't tell from which direction. Mickey looked around, then watched a big Lincoln pull around the corner and stop at the curb in front of him. The rear window behind the driver, a bored agent Mickey didn't recognize, slid down. "Hop on in," Lab Director Stephenson told him from the far side of the back seat. He was barely visible in the dim interior. "I got us a driver tonight."

Mickey opened the door and climbed in behind the driver. He felt very uncomfortable, but did his best to hide his unease as the window slid back up and the driver pulled away. "Hopefully traffic won't be so bad this hour of the night, but you never know," Stephenson told him amicably.

He eyed Mickey's suit coat and tie but didn't say anything. The driver stayed silent. The radio was on in the front seat, very low, tuned to a news channel.

As they pulled up the ramp and exited the underground structure the setting sun was turning the sky orange. Mickey glanced at the Director, who was busy texting on his phone, then at the back of the driver's head. As they got on the road to head off the military base, he leaned back into the leather seat and tried to relax.

They rolled north up I-95 as the sun set to their left, traffic thick but moving steadily. Ten minutes into the trip, the driver, who at that point hadn't said a word, informed them, "Bad accident on 395 past the Beltway. Going to have to take the long way in."

Stephenson looked up from his phone, on which he'd been checking his email. He shook his head, then looked at Mickey. "The traffic in this town, I swear." He then went back to his phone.

The Lincoln got on the Capitol Beltway heading northeast, and they circled around Washington D.C. to the south. The driver got off at an exit Mickey didn't catch, although he had the vague sense that they were to the southeast of the center of D.C. Wasn't Anacostia somewhere around here? There were some bad neighborhoods in D.C., and Anacostia was supposed to be the worst.

As they got off the interstate Mickey looked around. Even in the growing dark he could see that they were driving through a depressed area, with a lot of the businesses on the road they were passing shuttered and dark. He hoped the doors of the Lincoln were locked. He glanced at his door, then across the back seat to the Director's door, but it was too dark for him to see whether or not they were locked. He caught the Director looking at him. Stephenson forced a smile. "Shouldn't be long now, I don't think," he said to Mickey, but the driver was the one who answered.

"No sir."

Stephenson flashed a smile at him, then went back to his phone, which was lighting up his face in the growing darkness of the car. Mickey stared at him, then back out the windows. They'd gotten off the freeway on a major surface street, two lanes in each direction, but now they were on a narrower road, and, if possible, in a worse neighborhood. Then the driver made another turn, and Mickey saw they were heading into a decrepit industrial area. Vacant lots, old newspapers blown up against sagging chain link fences. No activity, and hardly any lights.

"We're not going to see the Director, are we?" Mickey said, staring at Stephenson. Then he grabbed at his door handle, tried to open it. Nothing happened.

Instead of trying to stop Mickey, Stephenson reached behind himself, and came out with something dark in his hand. There was a flash, and a thunderclap, and Mickey felt something smash into his chest. He realized that the Director of the FBI Lab had just shot him.

Forgetting about his door, Mickey lunged for the man, grabbing for his gun. Stephenson grunted in surprise and found his gun hand wedged between their two bodies. It was too dark in the car to see anything, and the young man fought blindly, grabbing at Stephenson's shoulders. Stephenson elbowed him away far enough to get his gun pointed correctly, and pulled the trigger. The inside of the Lincoln pulsed like a disco at the gunshots. Two, three, four, five bullets to his midsection, and still the young man clung to him. Boone shoved him away, against the far door, and saw Mitchell weakly working at the door. Then somehow he got the locked door open, and was falling backward out of it even as the Lincoln was still moving.

Surprised, Stephenson shoved his gun forward one handed and fired again, then Mitchell was gone, the open door empty. The car stopped with a jerk, and the open door bounced and almost closed. Stephenson pushed it back open and stuck his head out. Mitchell was crumpled facedown in the middle of the street, not moving.

"What the fuck was that? I thought you wanted me to do it," Boone heard the driver say angrily, from seemingly far away. Idly the Director of the FBI Lab wondered if he'd permanently damaged his hearing by firing so many times in such an enclosed space. He stared out at Mitchell. Still, not a twitch. He had to be dead. How many times had he shot him? Five, six? At point blank range, he'd practically had his gun in the kid's belly. No way he could survive that. Boone felt something on his hand and looked down. There was a dark smear across his palm. Blood on the car door.

"We've got to get out of here, the door was open for that last shot. Cops roll out on gunfire even in this neighborhood." Boone looked at the man, trying to process the situation. He wasn't a driver, per se, he was a man who had been recommended to him when he'd reached out for someone with....special skills. The Bureau was a big place, and Stephenson had been there a long time. He didn't know any....what was the popular term? Operators, yes...but he knew people who knew people. And the Bureau was good at cleaning up its messes. Marsh, they'd called this man, even though he hadn't introduced himself when he'd showed up in the Lincoln two hours before.

Without waiting for a response, Marsh accelerated from the crime scene, and the open door swung shut. Stephenson stared out the back window at the body on the pavement. It was just a misshapen lump, melting into the asphalt as they drove away, fading into the background glare of the distant city lights until it was gone. Problem solved.

CHAPTER EIGHT

Banging on the steel security mesh hurt his knuckles, and hardly made any noise. Dave paused, then pounded on the door again with his palm. He looked up and down the street from the small porch, but nothing was moving. There was the distant sound of traffic, and birds tweeting.

The house was old, and the wooden door on the other side of the steel mesh security door looked solid, but the morning was quiet. He heard a faint noise in the house before a woman abruptly asked him, "What you want?"

"I work for a lawyer, I'm trying to track down a witness to a car accident. There a David Gregory who lives here?"

The thick wooden door swung inward, but Dave could barely see the woman in the dark interior through the steel mesh. There were security grates over all the first floor windows as well, he felt like he was at some third world castle. "No," the woman told him. "He move, he don't live here no more."

"I don't know if this one, living here, is the right David Gregory or not," Dave said to her silhouette. "Accident was on 7 Mile last year. I've got a check, a witness fee from the law firm for him, but the address they had for him was bad. This one came up when I searched for him though." Whenever there was money on the table, memories improved, phone calls were made, things happened.

"He was rentin' the house afore me," the woman told him, taking half a step closer to the door. She sounded like she was in her twenties, but looked a lot older. "Don't know where he moved off to."

"Do you have a phone number for your landlord?" Dave asked her. "Maybe he has a forwarding address or a phone number for Mr. Gregory."

"Landlord said he took off owing five hunnert fiddy dollar, didn't leave no forwardin address, shit. But I'll take the check," she said, laughing. "How much is it?"

"Not much," Dave told her grudgingly. "But I guess some's better than none, right? How long ago did he move out?"

"I been staying here three weeks, so before dat," she told Dave, taking another step forward. She was pretty short, but apparently she had confidence in her security door; either that, or Dave looked honest. She had nothing to fear from him, Dave didn't think he would have been able to breach the door's thick steel hinges with a shotgun.

"All right, well thanks anyway," Dave told her. He started to head off the porch.

"You need a witness, I'll say whatever you want, the check big enough," she called to him.

"I appreciate that," Dave said with a wave, heading back to his Cherokee, parked on the far side of the street. He didn't grab the walkie talkie until he'd driven out of sight. "Moved out three or four weeks ago," he said after he keyed the radio.

"Crap," his boss replied over the air. He heard John sigh. "All right, follow me out of here to the parking lot, let's figure out what we're going to do."

They'd spent the entire morning on surveillance, waiting for Mr. Gregory to do something contrary to his work comp injury, but apparently they'd just been wasting their time. The Chrysler Intrepid registered to him was nowhere to be seen, but there had been a detached garage behind the house, door closed.

"We ran him for driver's license and vehicles, right?" Dave said to his boss when they were parked door to door in the parking lot of a vacant grocery store on 7 Mile Road.

"Yeah, yesterday," John said. "Both came back to this address. But you know how it is, half the people in this city don't change their addresses until it's time to renew their license."

"If then. You want to call the adjuster, see if she's got a more current address?"

John frowned and shook his head. "I just got this case three days ago, if Michelle has a more current address that's on her. I'm hungry, you want breakfast? I'm buying."

"Like I'd say no to free food?" Dave looked around, then back at John sitting in his big SUV. "We gonna eat around here?"

"Follow me up to 8 Mile, there's a McDonald's about a mile down."

The two vehicles headed out, and four minutes later were pulling into the lot of a McDonald's on 8 Mile Road, the border between Detroit and the northern suburbs. Behind it was a small strip mall. Above them was a huge billboard advertising a local lawyer who'd had so much work done she looked like an aged porn star. Big blonde hair and even bigger red lips.

John pulled into a parking spot, and Dave pulled up behind his vehicle but didn't get out, instead just rolling down the passenger window. "Hey, what about that?" he asked John, pointing. In the strip mall was a Comcast Cable bill payment center, in-between a check cashing place and a tae kwon do studio that looked out of business. "Maybe we can get lucky."

John looked over and saw the bill payment center. "They won't tell you shit, you know how many times I've tried? Not them, Consumer's Energy, Detroit Edison—hell, DTE is the worst, they want to see a subpoena before they'll even tell you what time it is."

"You want to bet breakfast on it?" Dave asked him.

"Well, I was going to treat anyway, but you're on," John said, and got back into his car. They drove into the adjoining parking lot and got out. John followed Dave inside, where there was only one customer standing in front of the armored glass. John hung back as his young employee approached a short woman sitting at a window.

"Hi," Dave said, with a big smile. "I'm trying to track down my buddy, who lives in the area. I know he had Comcast but he moved. I'm just wondering if you can tell me when he moved, or if he gave you a contact phone number, or forwarding address? His cell's disconnected." He kept the smile going, and turned up the wattage and charm as far as it would go. The young woman was maybe his age, with medium length brown hair short on one side and spiked long on the other.

"I'm sorry, Sir, but we can't give out any personal information on our customers."

"Is he a customer then?" he asked innocently. She hadn't looked anything up on the computer, but maybe....

"I'm sorry, sir, I can't help you."

"Not even a phone number? Can you check, maybe he's not even a customer any more? Then you wouldn't be breaking the rules, right?" Smile, smile.

She frowned, but she didn't seem angry. "I'm sorry, sir, there's no way I can—oh my God, is that a Hong Kong Cavaliers shirt?"

Dave looked down at the t-shirt he had on under the open and untucked button-down shirt. He spread his covering shirt open enough for her to see the t-shirt, but not his gun. "Yep."

"Where did you get that?" she asked eagerly.

114

"The internet. You can find just about everything you can think of." He paused, and looked at her, at the makeup, the multiple earrings, at the faint streaks of color in her hair. "I've got a Weyland/Yutani 'Building Better Worlds' shirt at home as well. Do you know what…"

"Of course I do, I'm a huge geek," she gushed. "I go to all the cons. Went to San Diego last year."

"I've never made it out there. What's your favorite show?"

"There can be only one…." She said, then her mouth twisted into a sideways smile. "And that's Malcolm Reynolds."

Dave nodded. "It's a little warm for a coat," he told her seriously. "But when I wear one it's gorram brown."

She blinked, then squinted. "What are you doing, really? You're not looking for a buddy."

Dave smiled, chagrinned. "Private investigator," he told her.

Her eyes went a little wide. "Really? Cool." She looked left and right, then leaned forward slightly. "Hold on a second."

A minute later, Dave was walking out with the claimant's new address where Comcast was providing service, and the girl behind the counter had one of his cards, and promised to call.

John waited until they were in the parking lot heading for their cars before he said, "What the fuck just happened in there? I felt like I was having a stroke, I couldn't understand a thing you were saying."

"You're not a sci-fi fan?" Dave asked him.

"Was that what you were talking about?"

Dave smiled as he climbed into his Jeep and started it up. John made a face as he heard the music blasting out of the speakers.

"What the hell are you listening to?"

Dave checked his iPod display. "This is Bitch Slap Sister," he said.

"Is this the kind of music you listen to when you're on surveillance?" John asked him, still making a face at the sounds coming out of the young man's car.

"Mostly. I like Tool, Alien Death Hammer, Taint, Flint Eastwood, Eminem, Asian Dawn, music like that."

"Asian Dawn? Well, I haven't heard of any of them but Eminem, but after hearing *that* I'm not sure I'd call it music."

"Okay, Grampa, what are you listening to?"

John opened up the door of his SUV and hit a button on the dash. A CD ejected into his hand. "Dire Straits, *Brothers In Arms*," he said, reading the label.

"CDs?" Dave said. "You're still listening to CDs? You need to get an iPod. It's the twenty-first century."

"I don't want an iPod," John told him. "All of my music and songs mashed together. I want my music....compartmentalized. I don't want to listen to one song from this group and one song by someone else, I listen to albums all the way through. Like they were intended to be listened to. That's how it was when I started listening to music on records, LPs and 45s. And don't say how old I am, I'm not that old. Things just change. Look at Detroit in the last few years. You're probably too young to even remember Boblo, or the downtown Hudson's, or what real Vernor's tasted like. Or the Heidelberg Project."

"What's that?"

"Depends who you ask. It was either art, or the graffiti of a nutjob, or the artistic graffiti of a nutjob. Polka dots," he said finally, by way of explanation. "Lots and lots of polka dots."

Dave stared at him. "Sometimes I have no idea what the hell you're talking about."

Dave took the opportunity of the early day to get in a long workout. Full upper and lower body, he hit the weights heavy for two hours, until every muscle he had was shaking. He tried to lift five or six days a week, and run three or four times a week. Was he in world class physical condition? No, but he was in good shape. He wasn't exactly sure how hard the FBI Academy was going to be, physically, but his plan was to not be the weak link in his Academy class. Once he actually got accepted to the Academy, actually had a start date, then he'd ramp up his workouts—longer runs, maybe some cross-training.

Craving carbs after all that lifting he hit Burger King for early dinner, then headed up to the Forum to catch a late afternoon showing of the latest Iron Man movie. It wasn't as good as the first one, but sequels rarely were.

It was still before nine when he pulled the Mustang into his garage. He didn't have to get up until five to head out on David Gregory's new address (the adjuster had his current address in the file, she'd screwed up and given them his former residence....once again), so he set up his targets and practiced his draws, reloads, and shooting on the move.

Even cold, he could draw and fire and hit a six inch target seven yards away in under a second, every time. A quick draw had never been his problem, but winning matches was about more than just fast shooting. For an hour, the only sound in the big empty house was his Glock going in and out of the holster, the click of the trigger, and the electronic beep of his timer.

Jerome Beiers turned in off Passaic Avenue and found the parking lot was full. Dammit. He didn't want to park on the street. Not just because he hated walking, hated any kind of exercise, but because the lot was well lit. Well, shit, it wasn't like anyone was going to steal *his* car.

He circled the block and finally found a parking spot at the very rear of the lot. He turned the key off. After a few seconds, the battered Chevy Beretta stopped rattling and the engine died with a wheeze. He hated the car, and direly missed his Lexus, but it was all he could afford when he got out of prison. It was a bullshit car, just like his conviction had been bullshit, but things were looking up. He was making some moves.

He slammed the door hard, as it was starting to rust and needed some convincing, then sauntered across the lot towards the brightly lit façade of the diner. The Taps Diner was considered the best in the area, maybe the best diner in the world if the people of New Jersey and East Newark had anything to say about it. He couldn't afford to eat there every night after work, but the nights he didn't get the red velvet pancakes---which were to die for—he just got coffee. The coffee was good, the food was excellent, but they weren't the only reasons he loved Taps.

"Hey, your boyfriend's back," Nancy said to Lori as she grabbed an order.

The young blonde turned around. "Who?" The veteran waitress nodded her head in the direction of Beiers, just sitting down at a table. Lori stuck out her tongue at Nancy and made a gagging sound.

"He's just like I like my creepers, short, sweaty, hairy, and fat," she said. She saw him already looking around the restaurant for her—or rather, her tits. She took a deep breath, then headed over. Better to get it over with quick, like pulling a Band-Aid off a scab.

"Hi, Jerome. If it's Thursday, it must be just coffee, right?"

He smiled greasily up at her.....well, most of the way up, and said, "No, you know what? Can I get some pancakes, the red velvet pancakes? I know it's late and you close at one tonight." Friday and Saturday they were open until four a.m., but every other night they were only open until one. Considering Jerome worked at the copy center until midnight—that is, if he could get out of the damn place on time—that often didn't leave him enough time to get more than a cup of coffee.

"Shouldn't be a problem," she told him. "Coffee too?"

'Um...." He was doing the math in his head. He was barely making more than minimum wage at the twenty-four hour copy center, a far cry from his $100K salary before the arrest. "No, just water," he told her big tits. They had to be real, at her age, especially how they moved when she walked. And her ass, mmm. He bit his lip watching her walk away.

"You hear that knocking sound? It's him banging against the underside of the table watching you walk away," Nancy whispered to her as she got back with the order.

"Oh, ick. You're just gross," Lori told her, as Nancy turned away, laughing.

The food wasn't that expensive at Taps, especially for what the customers got, but it was busy all the time, so the tips added up. Lori was attending community college three days a week and working around her classes, but she just couldn't seem to get away from working nights...and nights were where the creepers like Jerome showed up. She tended to the rest of her customers, trying not to think of how he stared at her practically every second. At least he'd never asked her out, or followed her after work or anything like that. She wondered if he still lived in the basement of his mom's house, a middleaged loser, staying up late to perv on underage girls across the internet.

She got him his pancakes by twelve thirty, and as she slid the plate onto the table glanced out the window. The lot was usually pretty well lit, and the managers walked the girls out to their cars, but still she was glad she'd parked close to the building. The rear of the parking lot was pretty dark, had been for almost a week, ever since one of the light poles had been hit by a drunk. God only knew how long it would take to get that fixed. Freakin' Newark.

For as infatuated as he seemed with her various body parts Jerome's warmth seemed to fail him when it came time to leave a tip. He never left more than fifteen percent, and most of the time it was closer to ten. A lot of it in change. Whatever. At least he didn't hang around for hours. He came in, stared at her tits and ogled her ass, drank his coffee or ate his pancakes, breathing loud through his open mouth the whole time, then he'd leave. Probably to go home to his smelly basement and jerk on himself while thinking of her, but as long as he went home to do it she didn't care. Although it was disgusting to think of him doing that. Ew.

Lori was delivering drinks to another booth when Beiers got up to leave, and he watched her bend over with a smile on his face. He counted out her tip carefully — if she wanted to make more money she should have had a better job, he wasn't going to be an enabler of ignorance — then headed out to his car. As he walked toward the back of the lot he saw how dark it was. He hadn't realized it was that poorly lit when he'd parked back there, probably because he'd been looking at the brightly-lit diner. He got even more nervous when he saw a guy walking toward him as he got close to his car.

The guy had on a dark baseball cap and was coming in off the side street, hands in the pockets of his jacket. Jerome stopped nervously and stared at him. White guy, didn't look like a punk, but he was in darker clothes, and you never knew...

"Hey buddy," the stranger said to him, tilting his head so he could see Jerome from under his baseball cap, "the diner still open? How late they open?"

Jerome glanced at his watch, then over his shoulder at the diner. "They close in —" he began to say, turning back to the man, when he felt a sharp pain in his chest, and was suddenly out of breath. Jerome was confused; somehow he'd fallen down, and was on his back on the asphalt next to his car. How'd that happen? He opened his mouth to say something—he wasn't sure what—but no sound would come out. It was like an elephant was standing on his chest. He looked down, and saw something…what was that? A handle?

Beiers gurgled and twitched as Marsh pulled the gardener's pruners from his pocket and grabbed Beiers' right hand. The fat man grunted as Marsh separated Beiers' ring finger from the others, applied the pruners to the first knuckle, and squeezed smartly. Beiers jerked and keened as the thick blade severed his finger with a wet crunch. Without a pause Marsh stepped away from the body and walked back toward the dark side street, leaving Beiers twitching in the parking lot. The entire incident had taken ten seconds.

Would he live? Maybe. The knife had a six inch blade and Marsh had hit his diaphragm perfectly, anglng up toward his heart….but the human body was elastic. He was pretty sure he'd felt Beiers' heart beating against the blade of the knife, but it didn't matter. He no longer had anything of interest to them, and there were no fingerprints on the knife he'd left stuck in the man, so if he lived or not was irrelevant.

Marsh reached the end of the block without incident, turned the corner, and headed toward his rental car, on which he'd switched the plates. He was in and driving away ten seconds later. Thirty seconds after that he was driving over the Passaic River, and he threw Beiers' finger out the window toward the dark water. He kept driving with the window down, and peeled off the fake moustache, tossed it, the clear glasses which changed the shape of his face, tossed them out the window, and finally tossed the gloves, slowly, one at a time, when there were no oncoming cars to see. He might have some of Beiers' blood on his clothing or shoes, but he'd take care of them once he was safely out of New Jersey.

CHAPTER NINE

Dave was sitting on the couch with Gina, eating pizza for dinner and watching TV, when his cell phone rang. He glanced away from Castle, which had been a compromise—she'd wanted to watch one of the Kardashian train wrecks, he wanted to catch a Law & Order. The number on his phone was local, but he didn't recognize it. 313 area code, which meant Detroit.

"Hello?"

"Jackass."

It took him a second to place the voice, which was resonant but not quite deep. "Hey, Hollywood! What are you doing? Are you local?"

Dave heard Taran Butler sigh on the other end of the phone. "Hotel phone. The battery died on my iPhone, it's charging now."

"What are you doing in Detroit?"

"Working on a Michael Bay monstrosity. A gigantic turd of a zombie movie. I've been in town all week, we've been filming downtown among the ruins and filth."

Dave had met Butler two years previous at the United States Practical Shooting Association's National Championships, where the best pistol shots in the country, and the world, vied for the combat-type pistol shooting title. Butler was a professional shooter based in Simi Valley

California, who had made a name for himself not just winning matches but working as a 'technical advisor' for movies. He was one of the people directors hired to make sure actors looked like they knew what they were doing when they were handling guns. The past few years he'd spent a lot of time in front of cameras and behind the scenes of the History Channel show *Top Shot*. He and Dave had hit it off, and kept in touch. They saw each other a few times a year at major pistol matches as well.

"Is it that bad?"

"I don't know, maybe not. Don't tell anyone I said that. You never know what the camera's looking at, or what the movie's actually going to look like after they put in the special effects. What do I know? I thought *Public Enemies* was going to be a huge hit."

"Who are you working with? Are you the lead or backup or part of a team?"

"Harry Humphries. This thing's bigger than Ben Hur, they've got everybody and their mother's brother here telling the stupid actors not to stick the guns in their mouth, don't look down the barrel and pull the trigger. Human idiots, it's so irritating. Got to work with Mark Wahlberg some, he's the hero on this one."

"Cool. How's he to work with?"

"Not bad. He listens when you tell him stuff, and cares about trying to do it right. His brother Donnie's in it too. Donnie did Band of Brothers, so he knows not to scratch his nose with his gun. But we're doing crowd scenes, military versus zombies, and it's been a nightmare. Sixteen, eighteen hour days."

"Poor baby. I bet you're only making, what, twenty grand a day?"

"Dude, nobody makes twenty grand a day doing this. Well, maybe Marky-Mark. I was making that much money, I'd have naked sprites sucking on my toes right now."

"Don't you have a friend goes by the name Poptart Sprinkle?" Dave said with a smile. He'd met her. She was very nice.

"Whatever, she's just a friend. Pervert. Listen Gunfighter, we wrapped early today, and my flight doesn't leave until tomorrow night. There anything to do around here? I'm stuck downtown, and I can't see *nada* from my hotel. You maybe want to catch a flick or something tomorrow?" There were very things more entertaining in the world than watching a movie with Taran Butler. Especially if he was in the mood to start imitating the actors. He could do a perfect Arnold Schwarzenegger.

"Dude, I can't, I'm shooting the Sectional tomorrow, the State Championship."

"Oh." Taran sounded seriously disappointed.

"Hey, why don't you shoot it with me?" Dave said. "That'd be cool."

"I don't have any gear with me," Taran said.

"You can borrow my spare gun and gear. I've got everything you need."

"I don't know. What is it?"

"A Glock 35. I've got an extra rig, magazines, ammo, all of it."

"What kind of rig?"

"Blade-Tech holster and magazine pouches."

"I don't like using somebody else's gay gun." Even though he usually competed with a custom high-capacity 1911, Dave knew Taran could shoot Glocks well. Very well.

"Dude, it's one of your guns. You customized it. Or one of your people did, it's a TTI Custom. Stippled grip, trigger job, your sights with the fiber optic front. I've got two of them. You built my rifle and shotgun too, don't you remember?"

"No. What kind of shotgun?"

"Beretta M2. I swear, you have the memory of a goldfish. Come on, shoot with me."

"You think they'll let me in?"

"I'll get you in, don't worry about it. You can shoot with me, I'm on the Super Squad, such as it is." Most of the national championships for the shooting sports were attended by professional shooters, but amateur average shooters were welcome as well. To keep the pressure as fair and even on the pro shooters as possible, they were usually squadded together over the three or four days needed to complete a major match. The squad filled by the pro shooters was nicknamed the Super Squad, or the God Squad.

"Do I know anybody on it? Other than you?"

"No, I don't think so. Come on, let's do it. I'm not taking no for an answer."

He heard Taran sigh. "I don't have a ride, you're going to have to pick me up at the hotel."

"So what else is new?"

"I told you you should come to the match," Dave said to his girlfriend when he got off the phone. "Now you really have to. You can meet Taran, he's kind of a celebrity. He trains all the actors in Hollywood how to shoot, or at least look like they know how to shoot."

"Yeah. Like who?"

"You remember *Collateral*? That movie where Tom Cruise played the hit man? Do you remember that scene in the alley, the quickdraw? *'Yo, Homie, that my briefcase?'*"

"Yeah. It was fast, but it wasn't that fast."

"You're just saying that because you've seen me practicing my draw. Trust me, it was fast, and that's the kind of stuff Taran does, even though half the time he doesn't get the credit for it." It was especially impressive considering the crappy pistol, an HK USP, Cruise had been saddled with for most of the movie. Poor ergonomics, and worse trigger. "You can't teach it unless you can demonstrate it."

In fact, Taran had told Dave one day that Tom Cruise had been the best student he'd ever seen. "That guy was a machine," he'd admitted. "He practiced for hours every day, until he got it perfect." Taran had been visiting with Tom Cruise's trainer, Mic Gould, during pre-production of *Collateral*, and that's how he'd met Michael Mann, and got hired to work on Mann's movie *Public Enemies* with Johnny Depp and Stephen Lang.

Gina was no stranger to celebrities, she saw a few local and the occasional national famous faces drop by the strip club, but you never knew where or when you might catch that big break. Plus, Taran was from California, and worked in TV and movies. "Sure, why not," she said. "But I'm not getting up early with you when you go pick him up at the hotel. I'll meet you there." Her bodyclock was on strip club time.

"Okay, but don't forget eyes and ears."

"What?"

"Ear protection and eye protection." He reminded her, "It's a shooting match. That means there will be shooting."

Al Safie was sitting at the back of his Durango in the gravel parking lot, putting on his Salomon cleats, when Dave parked his Mustang next to him. Safie recognized the kid's ride, and was going to give him a friendly greeting, then he recognized the guy climbing out of the Mustang's passenger seat. What the hell?

"You fucker," he called out to Dave. "Thanks a lot. We're all going to be shooting for second place now."

Dave smiled at the guy he knew was an FBI agent as Taran grinned apologetically. "I'm sorry, I couldn't hear you over that loud whining sound. You want to repeat that? Maybe you can arrest him, then he won't be able to shoot," he called out over his shoulder.

"Smartass," Safie grumbled. There was going to be a lot of competition at this match. It was going to be tough even before Anderson brought in a ringer, and any slipup, no matter how slight, would probably bump him down a slot or two in the standings.

"Randy," Dave said to the guy handling the registration, "I found Frank Stallone wandering around downtown, homeless, you think you could fit him in on my squad?"

Randy looked up from the pile of injury release forms and saw Dave. "Hey Gunfighter," he said with a smile. He looked over Dave's shoulder and saw Butler in his brightly colored professional shooting jersey. Plastered across his chest and back, around his sleeves and shoulder were all the names of his sponsors, and he looked a bit like a NASCAR driver. A NASCAR driver with hair that.... shit, he *did* look a bit like Frank Stallone. Taran had a big mane of glossy black hair, like an extra from *Saturday Night Fever*. "What? Hey, uh, Taran. Wow, uh, sure, we can fit you in. Cool!"

Dave looked at Taran. "Told ya," he said with a smile. "It's like getting to play golf with Tiger Woods."

Shooters at USPSA were classed according to ability, and while only one person could win the overall title, everyone hoped to win their "Class". Dave had just earned a Master Class ranking. There were two other Master Class shooters on the squad, Al Safie and Brian Caffrey, and competition would be fierce among them. Caffrey worked in a tool and die shop. Taran Butler was a Grand Master in USPSA and nearly in a class by himself at a State Championship.

"Check out the snapdragon," Taran said. He and Dave had put on their pistol belts and were talking to the other members of the squad while waiting for the shooters' meeting to start. They all looked up and Dave saw his girlfriend walking across the parking lot toward them in a tight tank top, short shorts, and pink tennis shoes. She'd remembered eye protection, in the form of giant sunglasses that would have made Kim Kardashian jealous.

"Wow," Brian murmured.

She was aware of all the stares and ignored them even as she soaked in the attention. There didn't seem to be a lot of other women at the range, but that was fine with her. She stopped next to Dave with an extra bounce and said, "Hi honey."

"You're with him?" Taran said, the look of surprise on his face priceless. "What are you doing hanging around with this sack lunch?"

"Gina, Taran, Taran, Gina," Dave said, then introduced her to everybody else on the squad as well.

"That's just not fair," Brian muttered.

"What?" Gina said.

"Bringing a hot chick to the range."

She just smiled. "Why not?"

Brian looked at Dave. "You've never explained the point system to her?"

Dave smiled. "No, she doesn't come to a lot of matches."

"Okay, well here it is," Brian said to her, doing his best not to talk to her chest. Jesus. "First off, this is a major match, and winning or losing is usually as much about focus as it is shooting ability. Speaking as a heterosexual male, it's always harder to focus when there's a hot chick around. Always. And then there's the point system."

"The point system?"

"Let's take your average girl. Say she's a seven out of ten. Since most of the people you'll see at the range shooting are guys, any woman who shows up and is interested in guns, and in shooting, automatically moves up at least a point."

"Two," somebody else said.

"If she shoots," Brian continued, "she automatically moves up another point. So a 7 that comes to the range and straps on a gun automatically gets bumped up to a 9. You," and he looked her over, "just walking down the street, you'd be a nine, maybe a nine and a half. At the range, on a hot day, in those clothes, when we've got a major match going on? You're a twelve. Your boyfriend's a real asshole." He flashed Dave an evil look that also had a twinge of jealousy in it.

"I'll take any advantage I can get, perceived or real," Dave said with a grin.

"Only a nine and a half?" Gina said with a twinkle in her eye.

Brian shrugged. "I don't believe in perfection. You could have a hideous birthmark or something."

"I dance at Goldfinger's five nights a week," she told him. "My stage name's Krembrulay. You could come down and look for yourself."

Brian stared at her for a second, then looked at Dave. "I hate you."

Dave laughed and smiled. He moved a step closer to Gina and murmured in her ear, "You're not wearing a bra, are you?" It wasn't really a question.

Her only response was a smile.

The state championship consisted of nine separate and different shooting exercises called stages. Most of the targets were cardboard silhouettes, although there were a number of falling steel targets as well. Competitors began each stage in the mandated starting position, which could be standing with their loaded handgun holstered or sitting in a chair with their pistol unloaded in a nearby drawer. Every stage was different.

Upon the start signal from an electronic timer which actually heard the shots, the shooter had to engage the paper targets with at least two shots each, and engage the steel targets until they fell down. Accuracy, Power, and Speed were the words to live by in "action" pistol shooting, and Dave liked to say it was the shooting sports' equivalent of running with scissors.

Two hours later they'd already shot three out of the nine stages, and the match was moving along quickly, but Gina was obviously getting bored.

"How long is this match going to last?" she asked Dave.

"We've got nine stages, and we've shot three in just over two hours. What with the boxed lunches they're going to be bringing out, I'm guessing that it will be another five hours or so."

"Oh God." While the shooting was somewhat interesting, there just wasn't a lot of it. Dave's first stage had been what he'd called a "speed shoot", where he'd stood in one spot, drew his pistol, and shot four paper targets and two pieces of steel. It had taken him maybe three seconds. Then she'd had to wait forty-five minutes before he'd done anything else. *Boooooring.*

Dave caught the knowing smile Taran threw his way. "If you're bored, why don't you ask Taran about the time Jennifer Garner shot him in the nuts," Dave suggested. Taran had worked with all the principals of *The Kingdom*, and Dave was sure that was the main reason why the climactic running gun battle in the movie was so epicly awesome.

"You know Jennifer Garner?" Gina gushed.

"So are most of the guys shooting here today cops?" Gina asked after lunch, while they were waiting for the shooting to start back up.

"Oh, no," Brian told her. "We've got what, eighty people shooting the match? How many are cops or in law enforcement Gunfighter, four, five?"

Dave looked around. "Something like that." He thought out loud, and pointed each out in turn. "Downriver cop, he's a corrections officer, and somebody here is with Oakland County. Plus we've got this jack-booted thug with us," he said with a twinkle in his eye, pointing at Al Safie. Safie held up a hand like his name had been called. Dave looked at his girlfriend. "Most cops aren't much interested in shooting, and really aren't very good shots," he told her.

"No," she said, assuming he was just messing with her.

"I'm serious," he insisted.

She looked at the guy sitting with them, Al, who they'd told her was an FBI agent. He'd been staring at her tits all day, but she didn't mind. That's why she'd paid all that money for them. You've got to spend money to make money. "Is he telling me the truth?"

"I wish I could say he wasn't, but that's pretty much the case," Al admitted. "I think it's a little better with the FBI, but I spent six months last year running the range, and most of our agents only shoot when they're required to qualify with their weapons."

Brian jumped in. "Compare that to the average recreational shooter, who heads to the range, what, once or twice a month? And forget practical shooters, we're on another level entirely." Dave nodded, he had to agree. His dryfire practice alone was five or six hours a week.

Safie went on. "I try to get them interested in shooting, come to some of the local matches here, but nobody's taken me up on it." He'd actually almost been shot twice by accident during annual quals by a couple of agents who had no grasp of muzzle awareness or how to keep their finger off the trigger.

"It ain't that tough to pass most department pistol qualifications," Brian added. "There's a reason for that."

This didn't make any sense to her. "But don't they...I mean, they carry a gun every day—"

Brian shook his head. "They carry a gun, but what do they do? Cops do paperwork every day, and drive cars. They're great at paperwork and driving. And arresting idiots and wrestling with drunks. Shooting? Shit, chances are if they have to shoot somebody, they did something wrong, weren't paying attention. Most cops never have to pull their gun their whole career, right? What's the saying?"

Dave said, "*Cops do paperwork, shooters shoot.*" He looked at Taran. "Haven't you worked with a lot of high-speed military spec-ops types? Aren't those the guys who are doing a lot of the technical advising in Hollywood? Retired SEALs and Delta? How good are they?"

"Yeah, I've hung around with a lot of the ninja deathstalkers," Taran admitted. "A few of them are awesome shots. Most of them are okay shots. Not great, but okay. Mediocre. But they're mediocre shots crawling over glass carrying backpacks filled with snakes. Shooting people across the room doesn't take a lot of skill, it just takes a lot of balls. Especially if they're shooting back." He nodded at Dave.

"Hey, were you in on the arrest of that DPD SWAT team?" Dave asked Al Safie. It had been all over the news for the past week. Freaking Detroit Police Department SWAT team members doing armed robberies of strip clubs. Only in Detroit. He figured they'd end up in jail with the former mayor who'd been convicted of corruption, or racketeering, or bribery...something like that. Maybe all of that. There'd been so many trials it was hard to keep track exactly what the mayor had been convicted of, versus what he'd just been charged with. "I bet that was scary as hell, considering most of the assholes you go up against don't know how to shoot."

"I can't really talk about it," Safie told them, but he'd been face to face with Paul Wilson when they'd arrested him. They'd simply knocked on his front door and told him he was under arrest. His wife and daughters were home, and Wilson had been pissed about being arrested in front of them, but he'd gone quietly, without incident. Hell, that's why they arrested him at his house with his wife and kids—less chance of him doing something stupid like pulling a gun. Although, just in case, they'd had agents all around the house.

All the other arrests had gone smoothly as well, except for Edward Mitchell. He'd been at his apartment, alone, and blown his top when the agents told him why they were there. Mitchell had gotten in a couple of punches before they'd dog-piled him into a bookcase, and then it was over but for the swearing.

Safie had spent more than half of his twelve years with the Bureau in various sandy shitholes of the world working on multi-jurisdictional anti-terrorism task forces. Thanks to a very interesting family life, he was fluent in both Arabic and Chaldean, which was actually an evolved version of Aramaic, and his language skills had made him very highly prized.

When he wasn't in Iraq, or Yemen, he still found himself getting dragged into the same kind of cases, what with the huge Arabic population in Dearborn. It was actually kind of refreshing, getting to arrest good-ol'-fashioned Americans for a change.

"I'll take that as a yes," Dave said with a smile. It was that kind of cool shit that had made him want to join the FBI in the first place.

"You say California's fucked up, but at least we're not arresting our own SWAT teams," Butler said. There was suddenly a lot of activity around them. It looked like it was time to start back up, and Dave was first up after lunch.

Dave waved his hand as the Range Officer called out, "Next shooter!" He stepped into the start position, which was heels against the paint marks on one of the boards. The shooting area, the area that he had to stay within while engaging targets, was marked off by long wood slats nailed into the ground. For this stage it was a bit of a simulated hallway, and he'd have to advance down the hallway, engaging various targets through ports in the walls. There were a few tough shots, but mostly after the buzzer went off it would be balls to the wall at max speed, as all the targets were close.

"Shooter, do you understand the course of fire?" the RO asked him. Dave had known the RO for years, but range commands, at a big match, were codified and very formal. Dave nodded. "Then make ready."

As Dave loaded and reholstered his pistol, the RO looked back at the people walking by, coming back from lunch. "Line's going hot!" he warned them, and those few people who didn't have their hearing protection in place quickly reached for it.

"So, did you win?" Gina asked Butler as they were carrying their gear back to Dave's car. The weather had been nice, and even with the stress of it being the state championship they were barely dusty or sweaty. Action shooting was not an endurance sport, but it was stressful.

"I don't know. It took me a couple stages to get used to the gun. I haven't shot a Glock in a while."

"Please," Dave said, making a face. "Let's dump this stuff, then go back and check. They'll probably have the final results posted in just a few minutes." After a shooter shot a stage, his score was entered into a Nook or Kindle that had a scoring program, and then the totals were uploaded into the Match Director's computer. It was a lot faster than doing everything by hand.

"Hey, meat lover, you gonna be able to give me a ride to the airport?" Taran asked him as they walked back. "My flight leaves in like three hours."

"What were you going to do if I said no? Way to plan ahead, Hollywood. Yeah, don't worry about it."

From the crowd it looked like half the shooters were sticking around to see where they'd placed. "All right, I've got the finals now, I've just got to print out the different divisions and then I'll post them on the wall," Randy said from inside the small shed where he was working over his computer.

"Divisions?" Gina said.

"Competitors are separated based on what kind of gun they're using," Dave told her. "Revolvers only hold six shots and are slower to reload than Glocks, or anything else, so they're in a separate division. Taran usually shoots a really expensive custom 1911, and those are in a separate division from Glocks too. Usually." He actually could have gone into a lot more detail, but knew how long her attention span was when it came to a subject that wasn't shoes.

"All right, stand back and I'll post these on the Wailing Wall," Randy said, stepping into view with several sheets of paper. He stapled them onto the notice board on the side of the building, and the shooters clustered around. Butler had won Overall by two percent, and won his division, beating the second place finisher by fifteen percent. Dave saw he had come in third, with 84.59% of Taran's score.

"I knew you beat me, but I was hoping to do better than eighty-four percent," he said. "You beat me with my own damn gun."

"That's good, dude, you should be happy. How long have you been shooting this sport, a couple of years? And you're already a Master class shooter, and getting better. Don't worry about it. I've been doing this for twenty years. That Glock's pretty gonzo. How much did I charge you for it? Probably not enough."

"Nice finish, dude," Al Safie said to Dave, smacking him on the back. The FBI agent had finished second, beating Dave by a mere .23%. "You almost got me." A few other shooters standing nearby congratulated Dave as well.

A shooter Dave vaguely recognized moved away from the score sheets with a dark look on his face, grumbling. "Gumball circus shooting," he said to a friend. "Shooting like that would get you killed in the real world. No tactics, no cover, nothing. That's why I usually only shoot IDPA." It sounded like sour grapes. The man looked to be pushing fifty, and wearing an older GI Colt .45 in a leather hip holster.

The International Defensive Pistol Association had been founded by disgruntled USPSA members who'd thought the sport had drifted too far from its self-defense roots. Whereas USPSA was all about speed with accuracy, IDPA focused intently on use of cover, drawing the pistol from underneath a concealment garment, and re-enacting realistic self-defense shooting scenarios.

As far as Dave was concerned IDPA did everything it could to slow people down, including using a scoring system that unrealistically favored accuracy over speed. IDPA and USPSA were the two most common action shooting sports in the country, but they attracted two very different types of shooters. Dave didn't have a problem with IDPA shooters.....as long as they didn't badmouth his sport.

"In the *real world*," Dave said to the guy, "hitting the other guy first seems to me to be pretty tactical. As long as you're hitting what you're aiming at, whoever's fastest wins. IDPA does everything it can to slow you down." The inside joke was that IDPA really stood for *I Don't Practice Anymore*. "You guys are all wrapped up in stupid rules like never dropping mags with ammo in them on the ground. There's no rules in a gunfight."

The guy stared at Dave. "You don't know what you're talking about, kid," he spat. "The hell you know about shooting someone?" He looked to his buddy for backup, but his friend was a regular shooter, and knew Dave. He wasn't saying anything, and had an *Uh-Oh* look on his face.

Dave became aware that several people standing around them had tuned into the conversation, and gotten quiet. He probably wasn't going to say anything in response, but before he'd even made up his mind one way or the other Taran pointed at Dave and said loudly to the guy, "Jackass, how do you think he got the nickname *Gunfighter*?"

CHAPTER TEN

What surprised him was not so much the roll call room itself, which looked like most every classroom he'd ever stepped foot in (albeit a bit smaller), but the number of officers that turned out for each shift.

Warren was the third most populous city in Michigan, behind Detroit and Grand Rapids, with over 175,000 residents. Those numbers went way up during the day, when workers streamed in to the Chrysler plant on Mound Road, the huge GM Tech Center, U.S. Army TACOM, or any number of smaller factories and businesses. And yet, looking around the room, there were maybe a dozen officers getting ready to hit the road. Sure, there was the command staff, a couple sergeants, a lieutenant, an evidence tech, and any number of plainclothes officers working on interdepartmental drug or auto crime task forces, but hitting the streets? A dozen uniformed officers for afternoon shift for a city six miles square (minus the small chunk in the center that was Center Line); a city which had a six mile long border with Detroit, the infamous 8 Mile Road.

Since he didn't have to "suit up" in the locker room, Dave waited for the officers in the roll call room. At the back of it, actually; cops were no different than kids in school — everybody had their preferred seats, and woe to any baby-faced college intern who sat in one.

Afternoon shift started at 3 p.m. and ran til 11. Currently the department was a little tight with the overtime, so the officers who wanted the extra money (or time off, as they could burn the accumulated hours as comp time as well) had to be a little creative. Pulling over a drunk driver half an hour before shift end was the preferred way to get a guaranteed hour of overtime (for which they were credited time and a half). Arresting officers were required to complete the processing, it couldn't be passed off to officers coming on duty. Between the in-house breathalyzer, prisoner intake, and report writing, that was an hour, easy.

At about twenty before the hour officers started shuffling into the room, some of them toting oversize containers filled with coffee or Mountain Dew. A lot of the officers seemed addicted to Red Bull or Monster energy drinks. Afternoon shift was the preferred home of the younger officers, as that was where the action was. They had the lowest seniority and probably would have gotten stuck on that shift anyway, so the twice annual shift pick usually worked out to everyone's satisfaction.

Dave was a week and two days from the end of his five week internship, which counted for a four-credit class for his junior year at Michigan State. The first week had been both boring and interesting, sitting at the front desk answering the phones and listening to the officers interact with the residents who came in to make reports. Auto accidents where both people were able to drive away from the scene, petty thefts (mostly bicycles and power yard tools stolen out of unlocked garages), and random interpersonal problems usually involving neighbors or relatives.

The second week he'd ridden around with the evidence tech, which had been really cool. He'd seen two dead bodies (both geezers who'd croaked naturally), helped with a scene investigation at a fatal accident involving a motorcycle, and watched the officer as he dusted for prints at a local party store that had been broken into overnight.

The thieves had stolen tens of thousands of dollars worth of scratch-off lottery tickets, which were apparently a common target—who knew?

Week three had been riding around with a uniformed officer on day shift. He'd spent the whole week riding with Officer Jim Stone. They'd handled a lot of car accidents, residential burglar alarms (all false), a few family fights, one missing teenager, and a stolen car report.

His last week was scheduled with the Detective Division, and he wasn't sure whether that was going to be boring or interesting, but before that happened he had to get through his week-long ride-along on afternoon shift. Three days down, two to go, all of them riding with veteran officer "Wild" Bill Kennedy.

Dave still wasn't sure why they called him Wild Bill. Grumpy Bill seemed a lot more accurate....maybe Asshole Bill. Dave wondered why Kennedy had agreed to him riding along with him for the week, because he sure didn't seem to be enjoying it.

Officer Stone had been much more laid back and easygoing than Kennedy. He also apparently could go an entire eight hour shift without having to take a piss. He joked that his wife called him "Camel Kidneys". Dave had learned to pace his Diet Coke consumption accordingly on day shift, but Kennedy made frequent stops. That was the only thing Dave enjoyed more riding with Kennedy than with Stone.

Kennedy clumped into the room and dropped into a seat at one of the back tables, and then Dave moved forward and sat down next to him. Kennedy had a big round head and was balding. His hair looked like it might have been red, once, but now was the color of dust. He wore glasses and had a barrel chest above a sizeable gut made even bulkier by the addition of body armor. The Warren Police wore black uniforms, but at least with Kennedy, black wasn't slimming.

"Afternoon, sir," Dave said. Kennedy grunted in reply and pulled out his pocket-sized spiral notebook.

Everyone seemed to pile out of the locker room at the same time, and the roll call room filled up quickly.

Sergeant White stood at the front of the room behind the small wheeled podium and waited. To Dave, White had the build—and bushy moustache—of a 1970s football player.

White waited a few minutes, then said to the shuffling officers, "Everybody done playing grabass? Williams?"

"Sorry Sarge."

White looked down at his notes. "Not a whole lot going on today. Looks like day shift has been quiet. Just a reminder that Roseville has been seeing some increase in gang activity of some sort, graffiti, couple of fights, so keep an eye out those of you on the east side of the city."

"They wouldn't know what the hell to do if they had an actual gang problem," Drake scoffed from the second row. He'd hired on with Warren after doing three years with the Detroit Police Department. "Bunch of spoiled bored teenagers who've watched too many movies."

"Well," White responded drily, "on more than one occasion I have asked the Mayor to outlaw teenagers, but until he puts that ordinance into effect you'll just have to deal with them. And they're not out there singing West Side Story. Car assignments......Adam 10 is Drake, we've got Team Jacob in Boy-40...." the Sergeant said with a smile.

There were some hoots, and Williams in the front row flipped the bird to everyone behind him. There had been some references to "Team Jacob" in the weeks prior, and Dave had finally figured out that both Williams and his usual partner were named Jacob.

White read off the names of the rest of the officers, and their assignments. Two two-man cars, the rest were singles. Dave didn't count as an officer, so Kennedy's unit was considered a single-man unit—callsign Frank 10. The

Warren PD divided the city into zones, A through H, with A, B, C, and D bordering Detroit. Police used name designators (Adam, Boy, Charlie, David) instead of the military ones when calling out license plates, but Dave could tell which of the cops had military experience as they'd sometimes slip and revert back to the Whiskey-Tango-Foxtrot system. -10 cars were single man cars working a single zone. -20 cars were two man cars working a single zone, and -40 cars were two man cars working two zones. Two man cars always worked the south end of the city, on the Detroit border.

"There have been some reports of wild dogs roaming the south end, and a little girl was bit a few days ago. The Mayor has specifically asked us to watch out for any loose dogs, and if we see one to immediately call in animal control."

"So animal control is working past five o'clock today?" somebody in the back of the room called out.

White looked up. "No. Okay, bunch of vacation checks today."

White proceeded to read off several addresses of homes where the residents were out of town and had requested the police do occasional drive-bys. Everyone agreed the drive-bys were nearly worthless apart from the good PR with the citizens, but that didn't mean someday somebody wouldn't chance upon someone walking out of a front door with a TV.....

Kennedy wrote down all the addresses, not just of the houses in their zone, because you never knew. Frank ran north from Ten Mile Road to Twelve Mile Road, from Van Dyke Avenue east to Hayes. Frank was rather small and far enough from Detroit that Kennedy usually drifted beyond the borders and "poached" tickets and drunk drivers and radio calls where he could, just to stay busy.

White looked around the room. "Uh…Peterson. You've had a couple days off, so just let me remind you and everybody else that the crew doing the bank robberies in the area is still out there. FBI thinks the same crew has done six banks over the last two months, and two of those have been in our city. They did a Huntington in Troy right by Oakland Mall last week, pistol-whipped a lady real bad. Nobody's been killed yet, but we've got two or three black male suspects going in each time, in Halloween masks, all of them with handguns.

"If you remember, they fired a shot into the floor at their first or second robbery, so we know at least one of the guns is real. Driver waiting in a car outside, and they've used at least two different cars, a black Chrysler 300 and a silver Chevy sedan, maybe a Monte Carlo or Impala. Security cameras caught the plate on the Chrysler once, but it came back stolen. Last bank they hit in Warren was the Comerica at Twelve and Mound almost three weeks ago. They're not pros, they've just watched too many movies and have been lucky so far. Things are going to go bad sooner rather than later if we don't shut these guys down."

"FBI have a catchy name for the crew yet?" Stone called out. "Bruthas in Arms, maybe?" Stone looked around the room, saw Dave watching him, and winked. Dave had to smile.

"What about The Dark Knights?" someone else offered.

"Boyz II Men?" someone said quietly.

"I don't care if you call them Barbershop Quartet, I want these guys," White said. "I don't know if the FBI is working any leads or not, as they don't tell us shit and never have, but if any of you gets bracelets on one of these shitbags, I'm buying the beer. You should have the info sheet, but if not, come see me. Okay, that's it, stay safe."

Dave tagged along as Kennedy collected his car keys and a shotgun from the armory, a fresh disc from the Sergeant, then they headed into the underground parking garage. Kennedy opened the trunk and, after checking out there were no surprises in it, deposited his small bag there.

He loaded the blank DVD into the trunk-mounted recorder for the video camera bolted to the roof next to the rearview mirror, then clipped the mike to his uniform and somehow found space on his belt for the battery pack. Kennedy then thoroughly checked out the back seat, making sure there was nothing left there from the prior shift—Dave had learned that every officer at one point or another had found a weapon or drugs wedged down between the seat back and cushion by a suspect taken in on the previous shift.

Dave just stood out of the way and watched. He'd volunteered to help search the car, or look over the exterior for damage (which would then be noted on a checklist), but Kennedy didn't want his help. "It's my ass, not yours, if you don't spot something, so if it's all the same to you I'll do it myself," Kennedy had said to him.

Today's car was a much-abused Ford Crown Vic. They seemed to get a different car every day, and most of the Crown Vics were camera cars, although not all the PD's cars had cameras. There didn't seem to be any rhyme or reason to how the camera cars were distributed around the city, or whether they were assigned to one or two man units. Dave liked the looks (and performance) of the newer Dodge Charger cruisers, but once you stuffed a computer, radio, and shotgun mount into the front seat, there wasn't a whole lot of room left for a passenger in either car. Kennedy loaded the shotgun and then locked it into the floor mount next to the radio and behind the computer. The officer punched in his password into the laptop computer which gave them a digital readout of their radio runs, then grabbed the mike. "Radio, Frank 10, radio check."

"Frank 10, loud and clear," their dispatch responded. "Stand by for a run holding over from day shift."

"Already?" Dave said.

"Probably a bullshit call, which is why day shift didn't bother with it," Kennedy said. With the computer angled so the driver could see it Dave could hardly read the lines that popped up on the screen. Kennedy hummed for a second, then said, "Yeah. Welfare check. Senior citizen not answering their phone, called in by a family member who can't get hold of them."

Kennedy picked up the mike again. "Radio, Frank 10, show us en route."

"Frank 10, ten-four."

"What do you think it could be?" Dave asked.

Kennedy shrugged. "Could be nothing, or the lady could be dead in her bed of natural causes. Ninety-eight percent of these calls are one of those two."

"And the other two percent?"

"The other two percent is why you have cops," Kennedy said. He put the cruiser into gear and backed out of the parking space.

"Are we rolling straight there?"

"No," Kennedy told him gruffly, "first we're heading to my house, because I left my fucking cell phone sitting on the dining room table."

"Oh."

Dave didn't know what to expect, what kind of houses cops lived in, but Kennedy lived in a red brick ranch with a white-sided second story addition just off 13 Mile, slightly north of their designated patrol area. There was a detached two-car garage behind the house, and a movable basketball net off to one side. It looked like every other house on the block.

Dave opened his mouth to ask the officer if he had kids, but then thought better of it. Between the basketball hoop and the small boy's bike tucked in behind the house, the answer was pretty obvious. He got enough black looks from the chunky cop without asking questions he knew were borderline stupid. He followed the cop through the front door and into the dim house.

Kennedy grabbed the phone off the table, and kept on going toward the back. "Gotta hit the head, hold on a minute," he told the kid.

Not knowing what to do, and getting the feeling that sitting down to wait wasn't the right move, Dave just wandered around in slow motion, ending up near the fireplace. He was staring at a photo on the mantel when Kennedy reappeared, his gunbelt creaking.

"Who's this?" he asked.

"My wife," Kennedy said.

"No, I mean, who's the guy?" Dave asked him.

Kennedy stopped, and stared at him. "That's me," he said curtly.

"That's you?" Dave said in confusion. He leaned closer and studied the guy in the photo. The guy in the photo was young, had a trim waist, and was obviously a serious weightlifter. He was shaped like a V. No glasses, and all his hair, but after squinting for a bit, Dave could see the resemblance between the guy in the photo and the cop six feet away giving him the stink eye. "Oh," he said lamely.

"Shit, I guess it doesn't look like me, not anymore," Kennedy admitted. Back then, right after joining the department, he'd been all twisted steel and sex appeal. Now, twelve years and two kids later...his wife didn't look the same either, but at least she still had all her hair.

"Come on, let's go see if this old lady is dead or what."

Heading south in the cruiser Dave tried to find a comfortable position for his left leg. If he let it relax, the outside of his knee rubbed against the sharp corner of the clamp locked around the shotgun receiver and barrel. Just to the left of that was the control box for the lights, siren, PA, and shotgun lock. He remembered what Kennedy had said to him that first day they'd been in the car together.

Kennedy had pointed at one of the buttons on the control box. "That unlocks the shotgun," he told Dave.

"There's four in the tube, but the chamber's empty. You ever shoot a shotgun?"

"Yeah. I own a Remington 870 like that one."

"That's nice. I don't care." He jabbed his finger at the box. "Don't ever fucking touch that button, until it's time to touch that button," he nearly growled. "You understand me?"

"Yes sir." Officer Jim Stone had said just about the same thing to him the first day they'd ridden together....he'd just said it in a much nicer way.

Dave observed that Kennedy, like a lot of cops, drove his cruiser like he was mad at it. Sharp turns, sudden decelerations, and violent use of the gas pedal were the norm, even when they weren't heading to a call. And then there were all the curbs they drove over, which sounded like blacksmith hammers against the bottom of the car. The amount of abuse the cars took astounded him. He made a mental note to never buy a used police car.

The address they arrived at was a small ranch constructed of off-white brick that, like most of Warren's neighborhoods, had sprung up in the post-World War II boom. Kennedy parked on the street in front of the neighboring house and heaved himself out of the car. Dave had already learned to never park in front of the address you were going to, or stand in front of the door you were knocking on, in case there was somebody inside in a shooting mood.

There was no sign of life at the house, and no vehicle visible, although the door of the detached garage in back was closed. Dave stood off the porch, halfway between the front door and the driveway, as Kennedy tried the screen door, found it was unlocked, and pounded on the front door with his big fist.

"Police! Hello, police!" He waited about ten seconds, but there was no response. "Police!" he yelled again, banging even harder. He tried the front door, but it was locked.

Dave watched as Kennedy stepped to his left and looked into the big bay window on the front of the house. He cupped his hands around his eyes and peered inside, then knocked on the glass. "Ma'am. Ma'am! Police! Ma'am!" He knocked harder and harder on the glass, until Dave was sure it was going to crack. Kennedy apparently had the same concern, because he then started waving his arm up and down. "Ma'am! Ma'am!" Then, more quietly, "Jesus, finally."

Kennedy walked back over to the front door, which opened a few seconds later. Dave saw a frail-looking white haired lady looking up at Kennedy. "Can I help you officer?" she asked in a tremulous voice.

"Yes, ma'am, are you okay?"

"What?"

"Are you okay?" Kennedy asked her. "Your daughter couldn't get hold of you and she was worried."

"What? I can't—oh, I'm sorry, the batteries in my hearing aids must be dead, I can't hear a darn thing. Hold on a minute, can you?"

The old woman shuffled away from the door out of sight, and Kennedy turned to look at his ride-along intern. He had a "told you so" look on his face. Dave just smiled.

Ten minutes later they were back in the cruiser. The nice old lady had, with shaking hands, finally gotten new batteries into her hearing aids, then called her daughter on the phone to let her know she was okay. She'd then forced some oatmeal raisin cookies on them for their trouble. Dave had taken one only after Kennedy had accepted one off the silver, doilied tray.

"We're technically not supposed to accept gifts," Kennedy told him when they were in the car. "But not taking a cookie would have been rude. Stick this somewhere, will you?" He handed Dave his aluminum clipboard. Dave heard and felt a few hard things moving about and clicking inside. He cracked the bottom and looked inside to see a few driver licenses sliding about. Officers were supposed to confiscate them from anyone they arrested for drunk driving (in Michigan legal parlance Operating Under the Influence of Liquor—OUIL) and then destroy them, but he'd seen they were always forgetting to cut up the licenses.

Dave nodded, and glanced at Kennedy's gut. Actually, he was amazed at the amount of crap the cops had to carry on their belts—pistol, spare magazines, radio, handcuffs, Taser, pepper spray, and the ASP, which was an extendable steel baton. They almost needed to be fat, just so they had enough room on their waist to fit all the shit they were required to carry around.

Seeing as Kennedy appeared to be in a good mood, Dave asked him, "What about the discounts you guys get at restaurants?"

Kennedy just looked at him for a few seconds, and Dave was afraid he'd pissed him off again, but then the cop nodded. "You're right. Lot of guys won't eat at a place that won't give them a discount, and a lot of places give us discounts because they figure we're providing security. Who's going to rob a place with cop cars in the parking lot? They also figure if something happens, they get broken into at night, the owner gets pulled over for speeding, they'll get special treatment. And they're not wrong. I'm not saying it's right, but that's just the way it is." Dave appreciated the cop being straight with him, and nodded.

"All right, let's go see if we can find some actual police work to do," Kennedy said. He put the car into gear, pulled away from the curb, then got on the radio and cleared them from the call.

Ten minutes later they were cruising on Ten Mile when Kennedy got a call on his cell phone. He pulled it from his shirt pocket (there wasn't an inch to spare on his belt) and swiped his thumb across the screen. "Yeah?"

Dave wondered how he could even focus on whatever was being said to him, between the police radio chatter, car radio blasting classic rock, and driving.

"Ten Mile, near Hoover," Kennedy said. "Okay, see you in two."

Dave had learned not to ask questions if he didn't have to, so he just sat quietly in his seat as Kennedy piloted the cruiser to a large parking lot and parked across the lines far from the building. A minute later Peterson rolled up in his cruiser, and the two cops parked door to door facing each other.

"Forgot I owed you this, or I would have given it to you at roll," the other officer said, and handed Kennedy a couple of twenties.

"No sweat," Kennedy said, sticking the cash in his shirt pocket. "You got anything happening?"

Peterson shook his head. He was thinner, with rapidly receding black hair, and showed bright white teeth when he smiled. "Carload of Democrats running north with expired tabs, thought it might be something, but the driver had renewed his registration. He just hadn't gotten around to putting the new tab on his plate, and he had a car full of women he was taking shopping. Looked miserable, poor bastard. Hey, did you catch the game this morning?"

"Game? What game?" Kennedy asked him.

"The World Cup, man, are you kidding me?"

"Soccer?" Kennedy said incredulously. "What kind of metrosexual douchebag watches soccer?" he asked. He turned his head to look at Dave, and Dave caught the wink. Kennedy then turned back to Peterson. "Buncha lawn fairies flitting about."

Peterson's eyebrows went up, and he pushed himself up in his car so he could see deeper into Kennedy's. "Looks like you could use a little more flitting..." he said in a gay man's voice, then let up on his brake and started to pull away.

"Was that a fat joke? Did you just make a fat joke?" Kennedy yelled after the departing car, sounding like he was mad, but when he pulled his head back in the window Dave saw he was smiling.

Dave thought about it for about a minute, then asked Kennedy, "How did he know they were Democrats?"

"What?"

"In the car, that he stopped. He said they were all Democrats. How did he know? Is that on a driver's license when you pull it up on your computer?"

They rolled up to a red light, and Kennedy took the opportunity to look at the kid in the passenger seat. Was he fucking with him? From the look on his face, apparently not.

"Ninety-five percent of all blacks vote Democrat," Kennedy told him.

Dave's eyebrows when up. "Oh," he said, finally understanding. He sat for another minute, then said. "I don't understand it though. I mean, I believe your numbers, although I didn't think it was that high. But, seriously, it doesn't make any sense. Blacks are in much worse shape now, financially and culturally, than they were when FDR was in office. What has voting Democrat done for them?"

"Good to see that college education is paying off," Kennedy said. "No, it doesn't make any sense, but people don't make any sense. And you know what I call that?" he asked the young man.

"No, what?"

"Job security."

Half an hour later, on Van Dyke Avenue, moving south past the GM Tech Center. Kennedy pointed through the windshield. "Can you tell what month that tab is?"

Dave looked over at the small license plate sticker, indicating which month the vehicle's registration expired. He saw DEC. "December," he said.

"Are you sure? Shit, I need new glasses, it looks like February to me." They rolled through the light at 12 Mile.

Kennedy glanced over at the young kid in the passenger seat. "So, what do you think about the job, kid? Think it's for you?"

Dave wasn't expecting the question, and he hesitated in answering. "It's....it's not what I expected," he admitted. "You're such a slave to the radio, and so much of what you have to deal with is....."

"What?" Kennedy didn't look or seem angry, just interested in his answer.

"Bullshit," Dave told him. "Car crashes, old ladies who can't hear the phone ringing, husbands and wives fighting, traffic tickets, runaway kids. I mean, I'd rather do this than work in a factory, but I think I'd much rather do something where I could—" he almost said, 'use my brain', but thought better of it at the last second. "Do some investigating. Work cases." The chatter on the police radio was nearly constant, with other units calling in license plates for traffic stops or arriving at or clearing calls. At first it had been horribly distracting for Dave, and carrying on conversations in the car with Officer Stone that first week had been really tough, with the radio a constant distraction in the background, until he ultimately decided to tune the radio chatter out.

"What, like homicide?"

"No, not really. More....federal, I guess. I'd love to be part of the FBI task force working on these bank robbers. Secret Service, working counterfeiting cases. DEA, doing drug cases. Something like that."

"We've got detectives, we've got undercover guys working drug cases," Kennedy pointed out.

"Yeah, but....." Dave finally shrugged. "I guess I've always wanted to go federal, like FBI. But I wanted to do this internship, just in case I really liked it, or liked it more than I thought I would."

"I got news for you, you're going to have to deal with bullshit no matter who you're working for, just the flavor changes. How old are you?"

"Twenty, almost twenty-one," Dave told him.

"I remember when I was your age. Job's not for everybody," Kennedy admitted. "Me, I like working the town I live in. I live here, my parents live here, my kids go to the schools, it keeps me motivated to do the job right." They cruised over "the ditch", which is what all the Warren cops called I-696. The six lane, 70-mph freeway ran east-west and was below street level. Some stretches of 696 had steep grass embankments on either side, but at Van Dyke the walls were vertical concrete.

"I get that," Dave told him. "I just don't—

"Radio, all units, clear the air, stand by," jumped out of the radio.

"What's that?" Dave said. The female dispatcher had sounded a little tense.

"Shut up,"

The radio burst back into life. "All units, hold-up alarm at Michigan National Bank, 4860 14 Mile. Trying to make contact via a land line. Units responding?"

Before the dispatcher had even read out the entire address Kennedy had the car floored, and Dave held onto the door handle as the cop slewed the cruiser around two slow moving cars. If he'd thought the officer had been driving aggressively before, that was nothing compared to how he started driving after the call went out.

"George 10 is fifteen seconds away," Dave heard.

"Aren't we heading the wrong way?" Dave asked. They were heading south, and the bank was north and a little west of them.

"Red light, don't fight, make a right," Kennedy growled through clenched teeth.

"What?"

Kennedy didn't answer and instead hit the lights and siren, then turned up the police radio. Cars ahead of them hit their brakes and moved to the side, and when they moved too slowly, Kennedy passed them using the center left turn lane. He took the corner at 10 Mile with squealing tires and headed west, engine roaring.

"Radio, George 10, just talked to the bank manager in the parking lot, suspects just fled the scene in a silver sedan."

"George 10, you're saying this was an attempted robbery?"

"Ten four, good alarm, multiple black male suspects with guns, they got some cash, then got spooked and took off. Couldn't be more than two minutes ago."

"Right turns are easier, almost everybody turns right," Kennedy said to Dave over the roaring engine. "If they did that and they're heading back to Detroit there's a real good chance they're heading southbound on Mound right now."

Dave could see the medians of Mound road up ahead. It was a boulevard most of the way through Warren, with the wide medians plain grassy mounds, at their apex about three feet above pavement level. He wondered if the mounds on Mound were just coincidence. At 10 Mile, Mound was three lanes on either side of the median.

"Radio, Bravo 40, we're southbound on Mound from Twelve behind a silver Monte Carlo, multiple people inside." Dave recognized the voice belonging to Bravo 40 as belonging to Jacob Williams. Team Jacob. In the background of the call Dave could hear the siren behind Williams, and his partner on the PA shouting, 'Pull over!'"

There was a two second pause, then Williams was back on the mike, sounding only slightly more animated. "Dispatch, Bravo 40, be advised they have fired at us, they are shooting out the windows." Dave remembered that both Williams and his partner had done time in Iraq.

"Hold on to your shit, kid, this is why they give us body armor and guns," Kennedy told him, then grabbed the mike and they flew toward 10 Mile Road's intersection with Mound. The intersection was rather open, with a gas station at one corner, and a few other businesses, but no residences. "Frank 10 is holding at 10 Mile and Mound."

"David 40 is two minutes away."

Dave earlier had deliberately been tuning out the radio traffic, but it seemed to him as if a lot of the cops had been on calls of one sort or another when dispatch hit the air with the robbery call.

"You gonna get in trouble for bringing me into this?" Dave asked him.

"A whole shitload, especially if you get killed," Kennedy responded. He sounded completely serious.

At Mound Road the road planners who'd designed I-696 decided to shake things up a bit, and instead of having Mound cross over the freeway, Mound crossed under. The freeway also angled a little southward at that spot, and was just half a mile north of 10 Mile. Kennedy pulled into the big intersection, then drove northbound in the southbound lanes through a few cars which scattered in slow motion. Kennedy stopped a hundred feet north of 10 Mile and turned broadside to oncoming traffic, turning the driver's side of the cruiser toward the oncoming threat. Dave looked past Kennedy's chest down the gentle slope, under the freeway bridge, but didn't see anything.

"Anything happens, keep your head down, and stay in the car," Kennedy told him loudly, trying to be heard over their siren.

"Think they're going to stop?" Dave asked him. The car had filled with the smell of overheated brake pads.

"Oh, we're not going to leave it up to them," Kennedy replied.

"DPD has been alerted, they've got units rolling," dispatch said tersely, assuming this chase, like so many others, would continue southbound.

"Charlie 10's clearing my scene, I'm one minute out," they heard.

Dave heard them before he saw the two cars, Bravo 40's siren and two roaring engines. They appeared underneath the overpass, the silver Monte Carlo in the center lane, weaving back and forth, the cruiser with its flashing lights right on its ass.

The Chevy headed straight up the incline toward them at what to Dave seemed an incredible speed. Kennedy had his foot on the brake but the car in gear, ready to floor it to get out of the way if he needed to. The bad guys would stop or they'd fly by him, trying to get back across the border into Detroit.

"I'll tell you right now, this is going to end down in Detroit, with a crash and them bailing out of the car," Kennedy said to no one in particular.

The two cars seemed like they were almost on top of them, and Dave thought they were going to get rammed. Finally, at the last minute, the getaway driver seemed to notice their squad car broadside across the road, blocking half the lanes. He locked up the brakes in a panic and started swerving across all three lanes. Bravo-40 was too close, and when the driver of the Monte Carlo hit the brakes and slowed down, the cruiser moved past the rear bumper of the sedan. The two cars connected at seventy miles an hour, and then suddenly both of them were slewing out of control, almost on top of Kennedy's cruiser.

"Fuck!" he cursed, and floored his own cruiser to get out of the way, but the Monte Carlo was like a pinball, and Dave saw the front of the car heading straight at them through Kennedy's window.

There was a huge crunch, like God crushing a beer can, and the air sparkled with flying glass. The world spun and Dave felt his head rebound off the headrest, and saw through the tilting, spiderwebbed windshield in front of him a cop car sailing past airborne, sideways and upside down.

They came to a rest with a rubber chirping jerk, and Dave couldn't move for a second, too stunned at what had happened. What had happened? He looked over, and saw Officer Kennedy slumped against the door, which looked misshapen. The cop was making some garbled sounds, and moving erratically.

The impact with the fleeing car had spun them completely around once, and they were again facing the median in the middle of Mound Road. Sitting atop the grassy median, fifty feet from them, was something that hadn't been there before: the silver Monte Carlo, with major front end damage. There were huge gouges in the turf from where the car had slid sideways to its current resting place. Dave could see movement, people inside the car, and steam spraying out from under the hood.

Where the hell was Bravo 40? He felt stupid from the blow to his head, but then saw the other police car, sixty feet away at his two o'clock. The other cop car was upside down and looked like it had rolled several times. It was half on the grassy median and half on the concrete pavement. Bravo 40 was facing him, and its windshield was completely spiderwebbed and crushed from the impact. He couldn't see any signs of life.

"Sir. Sir. Kennedy! Bill!" Dave yelled at him, and got a groan in response, but that was it.

Dave instinctively ducked at a sound he didn't at first recognize, then retroactively felt the pieces of glass hitting his face. He looked through the damaged windshield in time to see the man in the front passenger seat of the Monte Carlo fire another shot in their direction. The second bullet whanged off the roof of their cruiser.

"Bill!" Dave almost screamed. He grabbed the cop by the arm and chest and shook him, but the only thing that happened was Kennedy's head fell forward, and Dave saw all the blood running down the left side of his head. Oh, shit.

Dave watched as the shooter climbed out of the Monte Carlo and start his way, firing three more shots as he advanced across the grass toward them. Dave could hear the bullets thudding into the car. Behind the advancing bank robber, Dave heard the getaway driver try to start the Monte Carlo. The starter turned and turned, but the engine wouldn't catch. He heard yelling from inside the Monte Carlo, but for some reason it sounded very faint.

"Fuck! Fuck! Bill!" Dave yelled, without result. Then it felt as if a switch flipped in his head, and he ripped off his own seatbelt, which was restricting him. He then grabbed at the shotgun, but it was locked in the clamp.

He yanked and yanked at the gun, but the aluminum clamp held it tight, and he nearly burst into tears. He glanced out the windshield and saw the shooter had halved the distance to them. The man was tall and skinny and he fired another shot in their direction, cursing at them. The pistol in his hand looked huge. Dave heard the bullet hit glass and a thump, and Kennedy groaned.

"GODDAMMIT!" Dave screamed in frustration, then saw the button to unlock the shotgun clamp.

"No, don't worry about me," Dave waved off the Warren firefighter running at him with his medical kit. "I'm fine. Help Kennedy!" He could feel the blood trickling down his face, and his hands tingled, but he wasn't in pain.

Dave backed away from their cruiser and looked around. Jim Stone, Charlie-10, was there, on one knee, half inside the upside-down Bravo-40, talking to the officers inside, and he waved the firefighter over. Two more firefighters were crowded into Kennedy's window, working on him—the window was gone, but the door wouldn't open. One let go of whatever he was holding and ran around the front of the car, then ducked inside the open front passenger door. His bulky coat blocked Dave's view of Kennedy.

Drake, half of David-40, had his shotgun in his hands and was standing on the grassy median by the Monte Carlo. He was angry as hell and kept squeezing the shotgun stock, his knuckles turning white, but at the same time he looked like he wasn't sure what to do.

The air smelled of gasoline and overheated rubber and radiator fluid. His hearing was still messed up, things just didn't sound right. Dave wandered back to the rear of the fire engine and sat on the bumper, staring at the scene. Cars with lights and sirens converged from every direction. Within three minutes every road officer on duty was at the scene, the hell with the rest of the city, clustered around the cars.

Several cop cars with strange markings roared up from the south, and Dave saw them met by an officer. With some yelling and waving hands, he had them slew their cars to better block off Mound, and Dave saw they were Detroit Police Department units. Two more fire engines arrived, and the paramedic-trained officers crawled half inside Bravo-40 to work on the officers still in there. It was hard to tell through the trashed windshield, but it appeared they were still hanging suspended from their seatbelts

After a while, he looked down at himself. His hands were covered with Kennedy's blood, some of it nearly dry. What was still wet was amazingly red. It was all over his shirt and tie, too. It looked like he'd wiped bloody hands on his shirt, even though he didn't remember doing it. He could smell blood, and taste tire rubber, and burning brake pads. The flashing red and blue lights made everything pulse in the fading afternoon light.

Booted feet appeared, and he looked up to see Jim Stone. The officer looked at him with concern. "Dude, are you okay? What the fuck happened?"

"I fucked up," Dave said, his voice quivering. "I fucked up. The guy kept shooting, and he hit Kennedy. I couldn't get the shotgun out, I panicked and forgot about the lock, and then I missed....."

Just then Drake appeared out of nowhere, his face red, the shotgun still in his hands. "You what? What did you do, you little prick? If Kennedy took a bullet because of your chickenshit ass —" he came at Dave, letting go of the shotgun with one hand to grab for the tie at Dave's throat. Two other officers nearby heard him raging and looked over, but didn't move to intervene. Everybody's blood was high.

Stone wedged himself between the two of them and pushed Drake back. "Cool your shit! Back off!"

"I'm sorry! I'm sorry," Dave said to him. "Is he going to be okay?" He looked over, but none of the injured officers were visible behind the firefighters working on them. There was quite a crowd gathering. Mound Road traffic in both directions was forced into U-turns, and all the cars were just crawling along, the drivers gawking.

"I'm going to fucking kill you if he's not! Wild Bill..." Drake's voice tapered off, then he lunged forward again. He was bigger than Stone, and pushed him back almost to Dave, still sitting on the diamond-plate bumper.

"What the fuck is going on here?" Sergeant White appeared and shoved Drake backward. "Drake, go secure the suspect vehicle," he spat.

Drake turned to him, his face red, but the sergeant got right in his face, moustache bristling. "Get your shit together and make sure there's nobody hiding in the fucking trunk or something. And put the shotgun away."

Drake shot Dave another look between Stone and Sergeant White, then stomped off. White looked at Dave, then tapped Stone in the center of his body armor. "Have the paramedics look at him, then get him out of here. Take him back to the station." The sergeant then looked pointedly at Dave. "And shut up," he told him fiercely.

"Sit here, don't move, and don't talk to anybody," Stone had told him, depositing him into the back corner of the empty roll call room.

The police station was practically a ghost town, everybody was still on scene, or at the hospital. One of the firefighters had looked him over, and saw some of the cuts in his forehead from flying glass were pretty deep. Stone had driven him to Bi-County Hospital where one of the doctors had stitched up the cuts in his head. One stitch for one of the cuts, two stitches for the other. He'd picked a few pieces of glass out of his hair, checked out his hands which had now started to hurt, and given him a handful of ibuprofen. His neck felt weird too.

Dave didn't feel any pain from the cuts even before the ER doc had given him the shot to numb his forehead. Stone was standing by the door when they heard a loud commotion outside that passed by. He looked at Dave. "Stay here," he said. Dave didn't have much choice, at the moment the doctor was threading one of his cuts closed. Stone was back in a minute.

"Was that him? Was that Kennedy they brought in?"

Stone shook his head. "Team Jacob."

"They okay?"

"I think they'll be okay. They got banged up bad, car rolled a couple of times. The paramedics brought them in here on back boards until they can x-ray their necks and backs, but they should be okay. Nothing more serious than some torn muscles, hopefully."

"What about Kennedy?"

Stone shook his head. "I don't know." The cop looked like he wanted to say more, but he pressed his lips together and just stared at the young man, then shook his head. "We'll find out. He got anything other than a couple of cuts, doc?" he asked the man sewing up Dave's head.

"Not that I see," said the skinny doctor. "You didn't hit your head, did you?" he asked Dave.

"No, I don't think so," Dave said.

In the back of the roll call room, Dave checked his watch. How long had he been sitting there? It felt like hours....it *had* been hours, it was almost nine o'clock, and the accident had happened about four-fifteen. Every so often he would hear someone walk down the hall, the squawk of a radio, but he had no idea what was going on. He assumed they were doing some sort of CSI stuff at the scene, but how long would that take? He had no problem sitting there however long they wanted him to, but it would have been nice for them to let him know how Kennedy was doing. Last he'd seen him, the big man had been pale from blood loss.

Dave had been able to wash his hands, but he was still wearing the same blood-stained shirt and tie. It would have been nice to be able to change, even though he didn't have a spare shirt at the station. Weren't they supposed to take it for evidence, or something?

He jerked roughly as his pocket rang. "Shit!" He pulled his cell phone out and looked to see who was calling. "Hi Mom."

"Dave? Are you okay?"

"What?"

"Are you okay? There's this big story about Warren on the news, bank robbers and the police and ambulances, and I wanted to make sure you were okay."

Dave smiled. "Yes, mom, I'm okay."

He heard her sigh. "I knew you would be," she told him. "I told your father they wouldn't let a college student just riding along get close to anything bad that was happening."

"I.....think I'm going to be late, though," he told her.

"Are you okay? You sound tired."

He smiled to the empty room. "Lot of stuff going on here mom. I'll talk to you later, okay? Tell dad I'm fine."

"I will. Okay, be safe, love you."

"Love you too." He stuck the phone back in his pocket and slouched in the chair. He was bored, and yet he was jittery, still. He'd heard the word flashback, before, but he really knew what it meant, now. He kept seeing the Monte Carlo coming at them in slow motion, the flying glass, the gun, the blood. No shakes for him though, not yet, no throwing up. He wasn't sure if that was normal or not. Talk about a huge adrenaline dump, though....wow. It had been like caffeine mixed with God.

Stone showed up about forty five minutes later and thumped into the chair next to Dave. He had a Pepsi in his hand, and had a bottle of Diet Coke for Dave.

"How's Kennedy? You hear anything?'

Stone shook his head. "Still in surgery, last I heard. I don't think it's too bad, but, you know...surgery."

"What about the bank robbers, the guy I hit? Are they talking to them?"

Stone turned and gave him a strange look. "What?" Dave said. Just then the cop's cell phone rang, and Stone grabbed it out of his breast pocket.

"Hey, yeah? No, he's still in surgery. I don't know. No. No, they were DRT. No, all of them. Kennedy? No, I don't think so. No, it was just him and his ridealong. I was first unit responding, and it was all over by the time I got there. I don't know man, we're still in keep-your-mouth-shut mode, and I don't know what the hell to think. He's sitting right next to me, I'm the babysitter. Brass? I haven't heard anything from anyone for a couple of hours, I've been securing the scene for the Evidence Techs, talking to command, and doing my report. I'm guessing they'll have some news on Kennedy and Team Jacob at midnight roll call. No, their cruiser rolled a couple of times, doing about eighty miles an hour. Yeah, they were wearing seatbelts, and the airbags went off, but you should have seen their cruiser, looks like Godzilla sat on it. They ended up upside down.

Yeah, no shit it's a circus, they called half of day shift back in to cover, where were you?" Stone paused. "Yeah, as soon as I hear something, I'll give you a call. Good thoughts, man."

Stone shut off his phone and pocketed it. He looked at Dave, but didn't say anything, just took another sip of his Pepsi.

Officers started trickling into the roll call room a few minutes later. Dave checked his watch—just barely after ten, roll call wouldn't be for another forty-five minutes. Maybe everyone was showing up early, or being called in early?

The room filled up slowly, a few officers asking Stone questions, but he didn't have any answers for them. Dave got a few looks from the midnight shift officers, some of whom might not have known who he was.

"Radio, all units," Stone's radio crackled. "Command has asked all officers going off duty to meet in the roll call room at twenty-two thirty hours."

By ten thirty the roll call room was packed. All the seats were filled, and a dozen officers were standing along the walls. All of afternoon shift, minus a few officers pulling overtime duty securing the scene, half of the recalled day shift, plus all of the officers about to head out. Dave also saw close to ten guys he recognized as officers in their street clothes, probably coming in just to get the news, and in case they were needed. The department was two hundred and fifty officers, but he'd seen they were a family of sorts as well.

Dave got a lot of heated looks from some of the cops, and Drake still looked like he wanted to kill him. But he also got a lot of stares as well, calculating looks he couldn't figure out. He was hot, and his hands were sweating as the cops talked among themselves, but the room was much quieter than it should have been with that many bodies in it.

Finally, Sergeant White entered the room, followed by an older man Dave recognized as the Chief of Police, and a blonde woman he knew was Lieutenant Younks, even though he'd never met her — her portrait was up on a wall in one of the hallways. White and Younks were carrying a folding table, on which were two computers and two flatscreen monitors.

The Chief stepped up to the small podium while White and Younks were messing with the computer. "I know the first thing on all of your minds are your fellow officers, and I'm glad to be able to tell you that everyone is fine," he told them.

There was a collective sigh around the room. The Chief went on. "Bill Kennedy is out of surgery and listed in serious condition at Bi-County. He lost a lot of blood from a gunshot wound to his neck, and took two rounds to his vest. He has a broken arm and several cracked ribs, and maybe a concussion, but the doctors don't think there's anything to worry about. They are 'cautiously optimistic'."

"Tough motherfucker," someone in the back of the room muttered.

"Jake Williams and Jacob Pulaski were both banged up when their cruiser rolled what looks to be at least three times. It may be a few days before we know the extent of their injuries, but they all appear to be mostly soft tissue from getting tossed about. Williams might have a broken hand, and Pulaski probably has a cracked collarbone, and I'd be surprised if they don't both have bad whiplash, but that might be it. Air bags and seat belts save lives, people, remember that — the trooper helping us with the accident reconstruction thinks they were doing at least seventy when they flipped."

"Go Team Jacob," somebody said.

Dave noticed two men in suits had appeared at the rear of the roll call room, standing quietly in the back. They looked like cops, but he didn't recognize them. Both of them glanced over at him, then went back to watching the Chief.

"The FBI," the Chief said, then nodded toward the two men at the back of the room, "tells us that the four men involved in the bank robbery today appear to be the same individuals responsible for half a dozen or so other bank robberies in the area." Many of the cops turned around to check out the feds. The FBI agents nodded cordially back. "We will be working closely with them to clean this up, and I expect full cooperation from everyone here, or I will have your ass. Is that understood?"

"Yes sir," the room replied, almost in unison.

The Chief looked down at the podium, then back at White and Younks. The two screens were lit up with blurred images. "Are you ready?"

"Yes sir," White told him.

"Are they synced?"

"Yes," Younks said. "Two seconds, let's go full screen on this," she told White.

While they were doing that, the Chief turned back around. "For those of you not aware, Kennedy had a ride-along with him today. Mr. David Anderson, a college student, who's sitting in back there." He nodded his head and most of the cops in the room turned to look at him. Most of the looks were not friendly. "Some of you may have heard there were a few....poorly worded comments made immediately after the incident, in the heat of the moment. They seem to have upset a few people." He ran a hand over his head, which was covered by a rapidly thinning layer of grey.

"Both Frank-10, Kennedy's car, and Bravo-40 were camera cars," the Chief told the assembled officers. "Both I and my staff have reviewed the video footage from those cameras. Bear in mind, we still have to complete a full investigation of this incident, in conjunction with the FBI, and we are following proper evidentiary and chain-of-custody procedures with these videos. However, after watching the video from the cameras we think it might be a good idea to show you the footage, just so everyone knows what happened. The FBI, by the way, has seen this footage."

He turned to the officers behind him. Both Younks and White were poised over computer keyboards. "Your show." He moved out of the way and stood against the side wall.

"Ready?" White asked. He looked at the room. "Get closer guys, you're going to want to watch this." The expression on his face was unreadable.

Chairs scraped on the floor as the officers got up and moved forward, crowding the front of the room. They shuffled and pushed, and finally ended up in three rows, sitting, leaning, and standing.

Younks nodded. "I've got the feed from Frank-10, Kennedy's unit, on my screen," she told the assembled officers. "The other monitor is the feed from Team Jacob's camera. The cameras should be synced...." She peered at the timecodes on the two video displays, then nodded.

Stone had stood up and moved toward the front of the room. Dave couldn't see anything, and didn't want to get close to the press of officers. After a moment of indecision, he stood on top of one of the tables so he could see.

"You ready? On three. One, two, three." On three, both Younks and White hit the buttons that started the videos playing.

The left screen looked almost like a still show, just a view of the raised grassy median of Mound. The tinny sound of sirens filled the roll call room, and it was the right screen that caught the eyes of everyone in the room. The rear of a silver Monte Carlo was visible just beyond the front bumper of Bravo-40, swooping back and forth across the lanes at what looked to be a high rate of speed.

"These assholes are starting to piss me off," Williams could be heard saying on the video, shouting over the sound of their siren. That got a few laughs from the officers watching.

"Anything happens, keep your head down, and stay in the car," Kennedy could be heard saying on the other video.

"Think they're going to stop?" Dave heard himself saying.

"Oh, we're not going to leave it up to them," Kennedy replied.

Bravo-40 flew down the slope toward I-696, the digital speed limit readout on the video display quickly climbing toward triple digits. The driver of the Monte decided to try to outrun the cruiser and stopped slaloming, but it just didn't have enough horsepower. The cruiser stayed right on its ass as they went under the overpass in the center lane. The room filled with the sound of roaring engines and sirens.

"Bump him?" Pulaski yelled on the video.

"Too fast," Williams yelled back. "He's going to lose it if he tries to take a corner!"

"I'll tell you right now, this is going to end down in Detroit, with a crash and them bailing out of the car," Dave heard Kennedy repeat.

Beyond the Monte Carlo, Dave could see Frank-10 sideways across the road up ahead, growing larger with frightening speed. Bravo-40 was right on the Monte Carlo's ass when the driver decided to start weaving from side to side, then apparently saw the cruiser slung across the road sideways. Their brake lights flared, Bravo-40 started to shoot past them, then in the corner of the video everyone could see the front corner of the Monte come back around.

There was a huge crunch, a squeal, the video feed from Bravo-40 spun sideways, and then suddenly there was blue sky and green spinning and no sound but the roaring engine and wailing siren. "Fuuuck!" somebody in the car yelled. The car hit with a huge crunch then, and rolled sideways, over and over and over. The view from the camera was a maelstrom of spinning debris and sparkling glass bits. There was no way to make sense of it.

While the view on the right screen was still spinning, Dave heard Kennedy yell "Fuck!", and then the view out their front windshield spun with the sound of a huge crunch. At the time he'd been too dazed, but he realized watching the video feed that the impact of the Monte Carlo had spun their cruiser around 360 degrees, until they were back facing the median through a now cracked windshield.

"Holy shit," one of the cops watching observed.

The crunching spinning thuds finally stopped from Bravo-40, and the camera looked out a windshield that looked like a festival of snowflakes. "Okay, stop here," Younks called out. Both the sergeant and the lieutenant hit the stop buttons on their computer video players.

"Their car's upside down now, I need to flip the monitor," Sergeant White said.

"That's was three rotations," one of the officers watching said. "One in the air, two on the ground."

"How did they not die?" someone in the room asked.

"Who t-boned Frank-10?"

"The Monte," White said. "Check out the front end damage. That's why Kennedy's arm and ribs were busted up, they hit his door almost straight on at about fifty."

"Fuck."

"Okay, it's a little hard to tell with the damage to the windshield, but Bravo-40's camera is now pointed almost directly at Frank-10. But most of the action you'll see here," Younks said, tapping the screen with the frozen image of the Monte Carlo on it. The camera from Kennedy's car. Dave didn't want to watch, he was soaking in sweat just watching it all again, but he couldn't look away.

"Ready?" She and White hit Play simultaneously.

Steam began roiling out from underneath the Monte Carlo's accordioned hood from a ruptured radiator. There were a few seconds where nothing happened, then Dave heard a groan. He didn't know if it came from him or Kennedy, but then he saw the passenger door of the Monte Carlo open and a tall black male kick his leg out. He looked around for a second, dazed, then focused on the one cop car in the area still on its tires.

"Sir. Sir. Kennedy! Bill!" Dave heard himself yelling, and there was a groan.

The man looking toward their cruiser raised his hand and Dave saw a gun in it. He fired, and the windshield in front of the camera shuddered. He took another second to aim, and fired again. On camera the sound of the bullet skipping off the cruiser's sheet metal sounded eerie.

"Bill!" Dave heard himself scream, and the cruiser started rocking. He knew he was shaking Kennedy at that point, but all the camera saw was the guy with the gun walking unsteadily in their direction, firing over and over. The camera caught the sounds of the bullets thudding into the car.

Behind the man advancing toward them the driver of the Monte could be seen trying to start the car, but it was having none of that.

"Fuck! Fuck! Bill!" Dave heard himself yell. The man with the gun was getting closer and closer, and suddenly he also appeared on the frosted view of Bravo-40s camera, twenty feet in front of Kennedy's car. The area in front of Kennedy's cruiser was a bit blurry from damaged glass, but the officers watching had a clear view of the passenger side of Frank-10. They could see Dave struggling inside.

The view from Frank-10s camera was shaking back and forth, and Dave knew that was because he was yanking with all his might at the shotgun, forgetting it was electronically locked in place. The guy with the pistol looked like he was right in front of the car as he fired another shot, which was followed by a groan from Kennedy.

"GODDAMMIT!" Dave heard himself scream. Then he got the shotgun unlocked, and everything slowed down.

There wasn't a lot of room inside the cruiser, but he managed to get the stock up to his shoulder and aim it through the cracked windshield at the guy who was at the corner of the car, coming toward Kennedy. He could see Dave as well, and fired at him. The bullet went through the windshield and passed between Dave and Kennedy. Dave pulled the trigger on the shotgun, and nothing happened. He held the shotgun in his hands stupidly, frozen for half a second, then remembered that the chamber was empty.

"Motherfucker!" he yelled at himself and racked the pump as the robber with the pistol reached Kennedy's window and stretched his hand out, the pistol pointed at the officer's head.

Dave shoved the shotgun across Kennedy one-handed and pulled the trigger. The gun boomed and bucked upward, and when it came down the guy was nowhere to be seen. At the time Dave had no idea if he'd hit the bank robber, but on the video he'd just seen the man's head literally explode from the load of buckshot fired at contact distance. He went straight down out of sight. The room of cops was silent.

Not knowing if he'd hit the robber or not Dave tugged at his door handle, and finally got out of the cruiser. He racked the empty shell out of the Remington and put it up to his shoulder. He started to move around to the other side of the car to check the gunman when another shot rang out and he jerked so badly he almost fell down. At the time he hadn't known where the hell it had come from. On the video they'd all watched another guy in a red shirt climb out of the back seat of the Monte with a revolver and take a shot at Dave.

Dave spun and fired at red shirt as he climbed out of the Monte, but the guy kept coming. Red shirt was a big dude and he was yelling as he charged at Dave.

Dave worked the pump of the shotgun and fired again. At the time, he thought he'd missed the slowly running man, but in the video he saw the red shirt puff out as the pellets hit it. They might as well have been spitballs for all the effect they had, however, as he kept coming, firing again and again.

Working the pump again, Dave fired a third time, and at the time he'd thought for sure he'd hit Red Shirt, but the guy just stopped, stood there, screamed, "Fuck you!" and fired again.

The bullet hissed past his head. Dave worked the pump again, pulled the trigger, and *click*. Only four shells in the shotgun, he was out of ammo. The terror he felt at that moment shook him to his core even now, just watching the replay. With a primal scream Dave charged the big man, who got off two more shots before Dave reached him.

Holding the shotgun by the barrel in both hands like a club, Dave ducked under the pistol and slammed the shotgun across the guy's big gut. As the man whoofed and bent over, Dave stepped past him and put all of his strength into a backhand while venting a huge scream. The sound of the walnut buttstock cracking across the back of the man's head was plainly audible on the video. Someone in the audience said, "Holy shit." The man went down on his face, and Dave fell to his knees, panting.

He stayed on hands and knees for three breaths, then pushed himself to his feet and hurried over to Kennedy's side of the car to see what had happened to the first gunman. Dave barely had a chance to register the sight of the body on the pavement when more bullets began whizzing by him and thudding into the car.

"Shit!" He dropped down to his knees next to the bowed-in side of the cruiser as the popping sounds continued. Dave risked a glance over the hood of the cruiser and saw the driver was still trying to start the Monte, but there'd been another person in the back seat of the car. He was trying to climb out while shooting at Dave with a silver automatic.

"Bill! Bill! Fuck!" With a grunt, Dave shoved his upper body in through Kennedy's door and grabbed at the cop's holstered Glock. He remembered that it was in a security holster, and desperately tried to remember how to unlock one of those. With one hand holding the seat belt out of the way he wrapped his hand around the frame of the Glock, and his fingers found a tab. He pushed it in and felt a click. There was another tab under his thumb, and he pushed that. But the pistol wouldn't come out of the holster. In the background could be heard sirens, getting closer and closer.

"Come on!" he screamed. Wait, there was something else he was supposed to do, push or twist or — the Glock 22 came free, and Dave fell backward out of the car. He landed on the body of the first gunman, then rolled and came up facing the Monte Carlo, Glock in a good two handed grip.

"Get this fucking thing started!" he heard from inside the Monte Carlo, and the man half out of the car and half in the front passenger seat turned and looked at Dave again. "S'up, bitch?" he yelled at Dave tauntingly, and fired again. "You want some a this?" He held the gun sideways and fired again, and Dave heard the round skip off the pavement next to him.

In Bravo-40s camera Dave was just visible in front of the cruiser, a fractured form on one knee. The Glock 22 has a 15-round magazine, and Dave emptied it as fast as he could pull the trigger. The last shooter jumped at the first shot, then slumped back into the open doorway of the car as a bullet visibly hit him in the chest. Dave fired and fired, bullets blowing out windows and punching holes in the sheet metal around the bank robber, but hitting him as well. The man fell backward, and dropped the pistol to the grass. On the video Dave saw the driver behind him slump forward, but when he'd been shooting he'd been too focused on the third shooter, he'd never realized he'd hit the driver as well.

Slide now locked back on the empty pistol, Dave dropped it onto the hood of their cruiser and jumped to

Kennedy's aid. There was blood all down the side of his face and neck. "Hang on! Hang on!" he heard himself saying, as Stone screeched up in Charlie-10. Terrified he was going to accidentally choke out Kennedy, Dave tentatively put pressure on the bullet wound on the left side of his neck. According to the time code on the videos, the entire incident from crash to Charlie-10 arriving had taken 59 seconds.

Dave climbed down off the table as White and Younks paused the video playback. He looked up to see every eye on the room on him. He was shaking uncontrollably.

"I'm sorry, I fucked up," he told them. "I couldn't get the shotgun out, I forgot about the lock. Forgot there wasn't one chambered. I couldn't hit that guy, couldn't hit him with a shotgun, and missed half the shots with the Glock." Dave looked down, and shook his head. He knew he might as well forget a career in law enforcement.

"Son, is that blood on your shirt?" the Chief asked him. "Didn't someone give you another shirt to wear?"

Dave looked up. "No sir."

The Chief looked around the room. "Anybody have a t-shirt he can borrow?"

"I do, sir," Drake said, standing up. He headed toward the locker room, and as he passed Dave he nodded. Dave blinked, confused. Something wasn't right, he wasn't getting something that was going on.

"Mr. Anderson," Sergeant White said to him. "I've been at the crash scene all day while the techs have been gathering evidence and taking photos. You didn't miss a fucking thing with that shotgun, that asshole took three loads of double-ought buck and kept coming. Dead on his feet, probably, but he kept coming."

"Until you scored the home run on his head," someone said.

"And cracked the bat," someone else added.

"You shoot Kennedy's Glock better than he does," someone else quipped, and the room erupted in laughter. Suddenly the group of cops surrounded him, all smiles and nods, loud laughter and quiet, appraising looks. Dave still didn't get it. It felt like he was having an out-of-body experience.

"I don't understand," Dave said to them. "I fucked up, I got Kennedy shot."

"Dude," Officer Jim Stone said to him gently, "*they* shot Kennedy. And he's going to be fine. You..." he took a deep breath, and touched Dave on the shoulder. "Jesus, kid, you went into a gunfight without a fucking gun and put four assholes in the ground. Empty gun and no Kevlar, and you charged a dude twice your size who was shooting at you. I was on scene and saw his head, I thought someone hit him with a car."

Dave blinked at that. "They're all dead?" he asked stupidly. He'd wanted to watch the video in part because he didn't remember some of what happened.

"What's your name kid? David? Try fucking *Goliath*," someone else said. "Holy shit."

"Try Babe Ruth," another officer said. "No, wait, fuck him, someone from Detroit—Ty Cobb."

"But, I..." Dave said. His legs suddenly felt like they were going to go out on him, and his hands started shaking. He half fell, half sat in a chair.

The Sergeant pushed through the crowd of officers, which began to disperse. "You have someone you can call, your parents, a girlfriend?" Sergeant White asked him. "Maybe you shouldn't drive home. You didn't know they were dead?" He looked around at what officers still remained. "Everybody hit the road. Any updates on Kennedy or Team Jacob's condition and I'll have dispatch send them out."

"I was.....too busy trying not to get killed. I thought maybe the one guy......"

The Chief of Police walked up. "Don't talk about this case to anyone other than our investigators," the Chief told him. "Especially the media. They are not your friends. And let me explain something to you—while you did a good thing, and our department is in your debt, you probably don't want to get your face or your name out there any more than it has to be, talking to the press. Every one of those men you killed have families, friends. They may learn your name, but they don't have to know your face."

"Also, while I'm sure we'll clear you, you can expect to get sued civilly by every one of their families. I doubt you've got any money, at your age, so they'll sue the department. Deeper pockets."

"What's new?" said Sergeant White.

"Sued?" Dave said.

"Maybe even your parents, if they can. Not sure of the law on that. You're going to need a lawyer."

Officer Drake reappeared, holding a t-shirt in his hand. "Here kid. Sorry I got in your face." He seemed embarrassed.

"Go home, get some rest. Come in tomorrow whenever you want, and give a statement to our detectives," Lieutenant Younks told him. "You look exhausted. And....we've got a department grief counselor, if you need to talk to someone. I'd guess you're still pretty jacked up, haven't had time to process everything, but you killed four people. Bad guys doing bad things, but still. If you need to talk to someone she's pretty good."

"Thank you." Dave sat there in the chair, t-shirt in hand, blinking.

"Stone, can you see that he gets home?"

Jim Stone nodded, then pulled his phone out of his pocket and hit redial and he walked toward the back of the room. "Dude, the brass rolled out the camera car video for the whole shift. Saw the whole thing. You're not going to believe it...."

The two men in suits walked up from the rear of the room, and the lead man held out his hand to Dave. Dave took it automatically. "We could use a few guys like you," he told Dave, and pulled out a business card. "You ever thought of joining the FBI?"

CHAPTER ELEVEN

Marsh had more information about this target than was the usual. Normally, a white kid like him coming into a Detroit neighborhood like this meant drugs, but he knew that wasn't the case this time.

Every target, every location presented its own set of problems. He'd done very minimal surveillance on the target's residence, minimal for two reasons. The first was that the target was no stranger to surveillance techniques, and might notice the vehicle right away. The second was the location. The target's residence was situated in a decent neighborhood, and unless Marsh rolled up in the middle of the night there was a chance a neighbor might see the car, or see him get out. Getting into the house quietly shouldn't be a problem, and it didn't look like he owned a dog or cat, but the kid owned guns and might know how to use them. There was always the house, but checking out all his options was how Marsh had stayed free and clear after eight years of doing freelance blackwork.

Traffic had been only moderate that morning, so he was able to keep the target's Cherokee in sight with a very loose tail. The neighborhood the kid had parked in was deep in Detroit, so it was obvious he was working. He'd parked, and presumably he was in the car, somewhere in the back behind the tint. Marsh had only done one drive-by, then parked almost three blocks down and climbed into the rear of his own vehicle, which that day was a black Chevy TrailBlazer.

It was a long street that was made to seem narrow by the tall houses packed tightly together on either side. Most of the houses were clad in light colored wood or aluminum siding that had seen better days, and were so close together there was barely room enough to walk between them. The houses had porches high off the ground, five or six steps up, and sharp angles on their roofs. Those houses which had garages had them located in back, on an alley.

Back maybe in the fifties it had probably been a very busy, very nice neighborhood. Now it wasn't busy, or nice. Marsh had been in place since just before seven a.m., and in close to two hours he had only seen one person leave for work, one car pulling out halfway between his SUV and the target's vehicle. He was amazed. What the hell did all the people that lived on this street do for a living? Sure, some of them probably worked afternoon shift, or maybe midnights, but there were a good forty houses between his car and the target's. A few of the houses were boarded up or obviously abandoned, but most of them seemed to be occupied. From the number of cars on the street there had to be people living to either side of them, but he saw no sign of them until just after nine, when movement to his right caught his eye.

A teenage boy, who looked maybe fourteen or fifteen, came out of a house and sat on the top step. He was in a Pistons jersey and baggy athletic shorts, and was wearing tennis shoes that looked expensive, although Marsh had no clue about that.

The boy glanced at Marsh's vehicle, then nonchalantly glanced up the street first one way and then the other. There were a number of cars nearby, but Marsh had to admit the TrailBlazer he'd stolen for the day was nicer than most of the cars on the street. It was either that, or the kid knew the cars belonging to everybody who lived on the street, and was curious about the Chevy.

The kid kept sitting on the porch, not really looking at anything, and after a few minutes looked over his shoulder into the house and shook his head. Marsh was parked in front of the house next door, and couldn't see who the kid had looked at.

Marsh glanced quickly down the street, and used his binos to eye the target's vehicle. It was on the opposite side of the street, maybe two hundred yards down. Marsh couldn't see him in there, but he knew he was there. He had to be. Where the hell else was he going to go in this neighborhood? There'd been a pack of wild dogs trotting down the sidewalk twenty minutes ago, for fuck's sake. Like a goddamn Third World country.

Okay, not *quite* Third World. Marsh had spent a lot of time in the Third World, it was where he'd learned his trade. Detroit was not nearly as bad as the Third World. No death squads, shanty towns, cholera, sharia law. However, you always hear stories, and he'd heard stories about how bad Detroit was. He didn't believe them, because stories were stories, they weren't reality. But when he'd arrived in the area he'd spent two days just driving around Detroit and the surrounding suburbs, learning the streets, the cities, and damned if the stories about Detroit weren't true.

There were bad, truly shitty areas in every big city. Some parts of Chicago and New York were like Baghdad. But even for all their bad neighborhoods, Chicago and New York were busy, populated, alive. People lived there, people who lived, lost, loved, and died. Driving around Detroit, he was shocked to see whole neighborhoods of the city gone. Vacant land. Huge parts of the city were just dead. And the rest of it, like this street, weren't doing much better. The people that lived on this street just didn't seem to be doing much living.

Movement caught his eye. Something had fallen — or been tossed — out the open second story window of the house where the kid was sitting. Had that window been open before? He couldn't remember. He also couldn't see whatever had been tossed out, it was lying in grass that was a week past needing to be cut.

Marsh stayed motionless in the car, and knew he was invisible behind the tint as long as he didn't move. The kid stayed on the step, just sitting there like he didn't have a care in the world. After a few minutes he looked up and down the street again, then lazily stood up and sauntered down the steps to the lawn.

He angled right for whatever had fallen or been tossed to the lawn, and bent down quickly to pick it up. He then walked straight for Marsh's vehicle.

Marsh hissed quietly, and drew his pistol as the kid got to within a few feet of the car. It was something new he'd picked up for this job, a Springfield Armory XDM. He liked it because it had the same grip angle as a Colt 1911, something he was very familiar with, and a decent trigger. Plus, the magazines were crazy — they held 19 rounds of 9mm. The only thing he didn't like about it was the two-tone finish. The stainless steel slide was a little fancy for him, but you worked with what tools you had. The teen stood next to the rear passenger door, inches from Marsh. His hands came up, and Marsh saw that what he had, the object that had been tossed out of the window, was a long flathead screwdriver.

The teen raised the screwdriver, and just as he was about to wedge it between the window and the door frame Marsh lifted his Springfield and knocked three times against the glass, right in front of the teen's face. The boy was close enough to see the gun through the tinted glass. His eyes went huge and he jumped back, dropping the screwdriver.

"Oh!" he nearly shouted. "Yeah. My fault. Uhh..." he stared at the window, through which he couldn't really see anything, then abruptly turned and nearly ran back into the house. Marsh nearly bit his lip to stop from laughing. Jesus, was that funny. The look in that kid's eyes......he'd nearly shit himself.

He glanced down the street at his target's vehicle, then back at the house into which the teen had escaped. "Shit," he muttered. He couldn't stay parked there, there was no telling who or what was going to come out of the house next. The target probably hadn't seen anything, but he hadn't stayed alive this long by taking unnecessary chances.

Marsh casually slid back into the front seat, Springfield still in hand. There was no movement at the house, and he didn't think there would be, but the quickest draw was one where your gun was already in your hand. He looked around, double-checked, then set the Springfield down on the passenger seat. Only after he'd pulled away from the curb did he reholster the pistol.

Dave rubbed his face, grunted, and checked his watch. Okay, that was eight hours, and nothing. He shut Rush Limbaugh off in mid-sentence and called John while keeping an eye on the claimant's house. Five foot four, two hundred and fifty pounds, and surprise, surprise, she had back problems. And knee problems. But apparently no problem getting to snacks.

"Yeah?" The answer was a short and harsh bark.

"Wow, you okay?"

He heard his boss sigh. "Yeah, sorry, just been on the phone for the last half hour with my wife, sorry, ex-wife, talking about divorce shit. Next time I think about getting married I'm just going to find a woman who hates me and buy her a house. Whaddaya got going on?"

"Nothing. Her car is here, and she came out onto the porch to get the mail about three hours ago, but that's been it. I'm at the eight hour mark now."

"You get video?"

"About half a second, the box is on the house right next to the front door, she was heading back in before the camera switched on." Dave had a good view of the front porch of the house, but once you factored in reaction time, how long it took to turn on the camera, and however long it took to actually start recording once you hit the Record button....

"Yeah, go ahead and kill it. I'll call the adjuster and see if I can talk her into another day on this one."

"Maybe if she's got any upcoming medical or legal appointments? That would get her out of the house, and then maybe she'll run some errands either before or after." He heard John sigh again, and realized that he probably wasn't telling him anything he didn't already know. John had been a P.I. for years, and a fed before that.

"We'll see. What are you doing next for me?" Dave could hear papers rustling over the phone.

"Half a day Thursday morning on Victor. That's all I've got right now."

"All right. I'll call you when something else comes in."

Dave hung up, checked his watch again, and glanced at the black leather...well, black fake leather folder on the seat next to him. He had a couple of subpoenas to serve, and it was early enough...... The Cherokee started up with only a slight hesitation even after running the radio for six hours (courtesy of the new battery he'd installed last winter), and headed out.

He didn't do a lot of process serving, but there were two law firms who had his number when they needed papers served. His first stop was a law firm in Southfield he'd never heard of, tucked in on the third floor of a black office building on Northwestern Highway. The receptionist was a blonde who was a little too skinny for his taste.

"Can I help you?" she asked him. Just from her tone and expression he could tell she thought she was a lot hotter than she was.

"Yeah, I've got a Notice of Hearing," Dave told her, holding it up with a half-apologetic smile. He found it was always more successful to go in with a smile than an attitude.

The blonde eyed the paperwork in his hand with a slight look of distaste. "Well, I'm sorry, I'm not authorized to take delivery of any legal documents, and none of the partners are currently in the office at this time. Perhaps if you could come back tomorrow..."

So that's how she wanted to play it? Dave just gave her an even bigger smile. "Well, whether you're authorized or not, I'm serving it on you," he looked down at her nameplate on the desk, "Rhianna, unless there's someone else here you'd prefer to see receive the service. Subpoena's addressed to the firm, so any employee will do."

She frowned at him, waited two beats, then picked up her phone. "Mr. Sebastian? I have a process server out here with a subpoena for the firm. Should I....?" Dave couldn't hear the other end of the conversation, but from the twitch of her lips he knew what the verdict was. "Yes sir, sorry to bother you."

"I can take it," she told him, not so feisty as before, and as she looked up at him Dave took a picture of her with his phone.

"Just so I have a record of who I served," he told her, leaving the Notice on the counter for her to grab. He checked his watch again as he headed down the stairs to his car. Evening and weekends were the best time to serve people at home, and it was still a little early, but he decided to try anyway since he was already out. It would be nearly five o'clock before he got to the trailer park where his target lived.

Fifteen minutes out his phone rang and he checked the caller ID before answering. "What's up?"

"You still out doing secret spy shit?" Aaron asked him. From the background noise it sounded like his partner was driving home from work.

"Serving papers," Dave told him. "To a trailer park, actually. Maybe one of your relatives."

"We're not all related. Listen, I'm taking the fastback up to MIS this weekend. Why don't you bring your 'Stang, we can do a little racing?"

"That thing's a classic, you're going to beat it up racing."

"What's the use of having a fast car if you're not going to drive it fast? Why do you think I never go to the Woodward Dream Cruise.? Six hundred horse and I'm going to sit in traffic, all day, doing two miles an hour, just so people can look at my car? I don't fucking think so."

"Driving fast is one thing, racing is another. You're going to blow out that pretty new engine of yours."

Aaron laughed. "Not before I kick a few asses. So? You coming?"

"Nah."

He heard Aaron growl in frustration. "Why the hell did you have me do all that work on your 'Stang if you're not going to race it? Haven't we had this conversation before?"

"Yes, but you don't listen. I just wanted my car to be all that it could be. All that horsepower's nice to have. Besides, you didn't add any nitrous or supercharger or anything, you just got rid of all the factory bullshit robbing power from the engine so the hippies can sleep well at night. Mostly."

"Fine, pussy. See you on Friday?"

"Not if I see you first."

Whether it was officially called a trailer park or a manufactured home community, his destination was not the nicest such he'd ever seen, but it was a lot newer and cleaner than some of the trailer parks he'd served papers or done surveillance in, which included the crappy park on the south side of Warren where Marshall Mathers spent some time growing up. Shit, Dave had spent more time in the worst neighborhoods of Detroit than Eminem could ever hope to dream of or rap about. They were so bad that he actually didn't have any problem with those residents—when they saw his white face in that kind of neighborhood, they just assumed he was a cop. And cops always had guns, and backup, so he was left alone. Any cops driving by assumed he was a fed, which was pretty funny. It was in the middle class neighborhoods where he always had the most trouble with local cops. When there's no crime to keep you busy, why not screw with the PI....

Most of the trailers were double-wides with car ports. While some of them were landscaped and still looked brand new, a majority of them showed signs of age and disrepair. He found his address in the back corner of the park.

The trailer was off-white and double wide with a sagging car port, under which was parked a rusting Impala with bad rear springs. Dave parked on the street out front and walked up to the front door, the PPO stuck in his back pocket.

The front door was open, but a storm door with a Plexiglas window showed him the front room was empty. He pressed the doorbell with a thumb, but when there was no answering sound from within the trailer he knocked on the aluminum door with his knuckles. It rattled loudly in the frame. .

He was up to Five Mississippi in his head when a woman walked into view. She was about thirty, with black hair, wearing a low-cut green blouse that matched the eyeshadow filling the entire space between her eyebrows and lashes. The blouse revealed a tattoo in the middle of her chest, two cherries hanging from their stems. *Classy.*

"Yeah?" She stopped several feet back from the door, a suspicious look on her face.

"Miranda Richardson? I have some paperwork for you from Oakland County." He pulled it out of his back pocket and held it up for her to see.

The woman shook her head. "She's not here right now."

Dave just smiled. "Well, ma'am, you match the description I was given of Miranda Richardson, so unless you can show me a picture ID that proves you're not her, or you can peel that tattoo off, I'm going to assume I've got the right person."

She shook her head again, now getting angry. "I'm not taking that. What is it, anyway?"

"Do you know a Brad Meisner? Were you aware that he went to the Oakland County Courthouse and obtained a Personal Protection Order against you?" PPOs were Michigan's version of restraining orders, and the way the system was set up the judge only had to have one person's side of the story to issue them. Most of them, in his experience, were a waste of the court's time and paper, but not all.

"That fucker," she spat. "I'm still not taking it."

"Ma'am," Dave told her nicely, "I don't need to hand it to you for you to be served." Everyone seemed to be under the impression he had to wrestle them to the ground and stuff the paperwork into their hand before they were legally 'served'.

"I'm not opening the door," she told him.

"You don't need to," Dave informed her. "I can leave it out here if you'd like, on the porch. Do you know how to file for an appeal hearing?"

"Fuck off," she spat at him. Behind her he saw a toddler staggering across the floor in a sagging diaper. Dave gave the toddler a wave as he stepped off the small porch, setting the PPO down on the concrete.

188

"Thank you!" he called back to her cheerfully. Nothing pissed them off more than being cheerful. In his car he noted the license plate on the car before driving out of sight. He paused in the clubhouse's parking lot and filled out the date and time on the Proof of Service form, and in his own Service notebook jotted down a description of her as well as the car, in case she claimed she was never served and violated the order. It had happened more than once.

"Done," he said to himself. Two served, forty bucks apiece to him, which meant eighty bucks in his pocket for not much more than two hours' worth of work, including the time he'd taken to pick them up from the lawyer's office. He'd have to stop and get the Proofs of Service notarized before mailing them out, but otherwise he was done for the day. He had time for a quick workout, then dinner, and maybe a late movie. Gina would be coming over after work, she always did on Fridays, but he didn't expect her until well after two a.m. Still, he needed to remember to shower after working out. You never knew when Gina would show up with an extra girl or two in tow.

CHAPTER TWELVE

"Downriver" wasn't on any map of southeastern Michigan, but that didn't make it any less real. To Detroiters, "Downriver" meant any of the numerous suburbs located immediately south of the city, "down" the Detroit River. As a rule they were middle- to lower-income bedroom communities with a lot of blue collar workers, and once almost every worker in the area was tied in some way to the Big 3: GM, Ford, and Chrysler.

Back when the auto industry was booming everybody in and around Detroit was doing just fine, but in this modern market it was every man for himself. Auto plant jobs were once nearly guaranteed for life, but that was history, and as the Big 3 had suffered repeated hits their Tier 1 suppliers had almost all declared bankruptcy or reorganized.

Local tool and die shops were filled with guys who had learned their trades in the auto industry, even if they no longer made anything having to do with cars. The domestic auto industry had never completely died, but Dave thought it had sure undergone a series of controlled demolitions. There always would be fewer Toyotas and Hondas on the streets of Detroit than in other major cities in the country, in part because of the huge employee discounts the Big 3 gave out, but Detroit would probably never go back to the way it had been, no matter how many bailouts the government offered. The genie was out of the bottle.

Traffic hadn't been bad for a holiday weekend, and he'd been able to do better than the speed limit the whole way down I-75 into Downriver. He exited at Eureka Road and headed west into Taylor. Some of the residents of Taylor were perfectly happy with the nickname Taylor-tucky, even though many of the people who used it weren't trying to be funny. As Aaron liked to say, "Shit, I do like guns, God, NASCAR, and wearing wife beaters, so if that makes me white trash, sign me and Kid Rock up." The driveway entrance Dave was looking for was just past Telegraph Road.

The trailer park was old enough that the management company didn't try to pretty it up by calling it a "manufactured housing community". Dave wasn't sure how old it actually was, maybe thirty or forty years just from the looks of the sign at the entrance. Not all the trailers in the park were that old, however, and even though a few of them sagged a bit there was more an air of disrepair about the place than danger. Most of the residents were old, or poor, or old and poor. He knew from personal experience it wasn't the trailer parks where retirees tended to settle that saw a lot of visits from the cops.

Dave was just starting to realize that most people viewed the world through eyes that had been colored by their own experiences — because he'd started doing it. Lately, as he'd been driving around the city and the suburbs, he'd been seeing two types of neighborhoods — those he'd done surveillance in, and those he hadn't. In the three years or so that he'd been working part time for John, he'd done surveillance all over the Detroit area and a few places out in Michigan farm country. He'd hunkered down in at least two dozen trailer parks over the years, and in Taylor at least a few times, but he was pretty sure he'd never done surveillance in this trailer park. Although they all tended to blend together in his memory. He remembered houses and trailers he'd watched, and cars he'd followed, better than he remembered the claimants' names.

The concrete parking pad at Aaron's trailer was taken up by his Mustang and Arlene's ancient pink Geo Tracker, which everyone called the BarbieMobile. Past the cars parked on a brown patch of grass was Arlene's other car, a green Ford Taurus that sat on one flat tire. Dave parked on the narrow street in front of the house, hoping nobody flew around the curve and tagged his bumper.

He climbed the steps and banged on the storm door, and as he waited he looked over his shoulder down at the Taurus. The front end of the sedan was crumpled in slightly, but apart from the flat tire the vehicle looked driveable.

"Hey, dude, come on in!" Aaron said, holding the door open for him. "You haven't been down here in a while, glad you could make it." A Marlboro was wedged into the corner of his mouth, bobbing with every word, and the smoke curled around his head. Even though they had the day off, Aaron was wearing his uniform work shirt, untucked over blue jeans.

"Fourth of July, where Americans started a long tradition of kicking ass and taking names," Dave said. He knew that Americans had actually been in combat for over a year before the Declaration of Independence was signed on July 4th, 1776, but nobody celebrated April 19th, 1775. Well, almost nobody.

"Damn straight," Aaron said, hoisting a big glass of something red and slushy. Aaron rarely drank, but the Fourth was one of those exceptions. "Can I get you something to drink, margarita? Arlene makes a killer strawberry margarita." Aaron headed back toward the double-wide's small kitchen.

"Whatever you've got," Dave told him. "Hey Arlene, something smells good." She was in the kitchen cooking something, and gave him a wave.

"My family's spaghetti recipe," Aaron told him. "She's just stirring it for me, I don't let anybody else make it."

While he waited Dave eyed the amazingly long orangish-brown shag carpet in the front room of the trailer. He thought they'd stopped making carpet like that in 1980. Maybe they had. The front room of the trailer was surprisingly big. Some double-wide trailers were over 1400 square feet, he'd read somewhere. Aaron had room for a ratty L-shaped couch, a La-Z-Boy recliner, a coffee table, and a big screen TV on a pedestal, and there was still room on the floor to wrestle. Past the kitchen was a full bathroom, and two bedrooms.

A brown blur came rushing at Dave from the back room, and he turned a hip to protect his groin as Aaron's dog slammed into him. "Hi Peanut," Dave said with a laugh. He reached down and rubbed the dog behind the ears. About forty pounds, Peanut was a pound rescue of indeterminate lineage. Tail wagging fiercely, Peanut did three circles around Dave, then ran back to Aaron's mother, who was rolling herself into view down the back hallway.

"Couldn't find anywhere else to go, or nobody'd who take you?" Aaron's mother asked Dave, then cackled. She had a thick cigarette hanging from her mouth as she rolled her wheelchair into the kitchen. After a second Dave realized the cigarette wasn't thick, her face was just very narrow. She'd lost a lot of weight since he'd seen her last, fighting a desperate holding action against some sort of nasty leukemia. Aaron's mother was wearing a graying sleeveless shift, and her arms were scary skinny, with very prominent blue veins.

"It was very nice of you to invite me, Freda" Dave assured her.

She just waved dismissively at him. "Somebody got my whiskey sour?" she half yelled. "I've got too much blood in my alcohol system." And she cackled again.

"Here mama," Arlene said, handing her a tall glass.

Freda hoisted the glass and took a long draw. "You got yourself a girl, Davey?" she asked him. "Someone to cook your dinner and be there when you get home?"

"Yeah," he said. He didn't really want to talk about Gina.

"Leave him alone about his old lady, ma," Aaron said. "You want your cashews?"

"Nah, they're giving me phlegm," she complained. She cocked an eye at Dave. "You don't mind if I smoke, do you? I'm trying to give my cancer cancer."

He laughed hard at that. "It's your house, you do whatever the hell you want. At least until they make smoking in your own home illegal."

"Ain't that the fucking truth," she grumbled, and took another drink, the glass shaking a little in her knuckly hands.

Dave looked around the trailer. The front half of it, including the big room he was standing in, was covered in dark imitation wood paneling. The Christmas lights were still up; Aaron had used a staple gun to run them around the room just below the ceiling, and he'd never taken them down. Either that, or he'd put up the same lights for the Fourth. He thought about telling Aaron that if they were up he might as well turn them on, but decided to hold his tongue.

"Here you go," Aaron said, handing Dave a huge frozen margarita. "It's pretty strong, so if you have more than one you might think about sleeping here."

"Thanks for the warning."

"All right, I got to get back to my sauce."

Dave hung back, sipping his strawberry margarita — which was strong as hell — and watching Aaron and Arlene in the kitchen. Aaron was fussing over the sauce, and put the noodles on to boil, while Arlene put garlic bread in the oven and started cutting greens for a salad.

"Aren't we supposed to have hot dogs and hamburgers for the Fourth?" Dave said.

"Not if you're Italian," Aaron told him. "Abruzzo ain't fucking Irish. Besides, this is better. You ever have my spaghetti before?"

"You've told me about it about a hundred times, driving around the city," Dave said. "Does that count?"

"You're gonna love it," Aaron assured him.

"It's very good," Arlene said. She walked past Dave. "Ma, you need anything? Refill on your whiskey sour? Oh, shit, better grab her cigarette." Dave looked over, and saw Aaron's mother had fallen asleep in the wheelchair, a cigarette burning between her skeletal fingers. Arlene plucked it out delicately, then grabbed the tilting drink.

"How 'bout you?" Arlene asked Dave, lowering her voice slightly. "Need a refill?"

"Hell, I'm a lightweight," he admitted. "This one's going to put me on the floor, and I shouldn't be drinking at all since I'm carrying."

"I'll protect you," Aaron said with a grin over his shoulder. He reached back and pulled up the tail of his uniform shirt, showing Dave his Colt in an inside-the-waistband holster.

"Both of us armed and drunk?" Dave said with a smile. "In a trailer park. What could go wrong?"

Aaron's spaghetti was very good, with a lot of basil and fresh tomatoes. He woke his mother up to eat with them, although she didn't have much of an appetite. "It's her recipe," Aaron told Dave. "She's the one taught me how to cook."

"I'm going to have to run all the way home to work off that garlic bread," Dave said. It tasted like Arlene had soaked the bread in melted butter before putting half an inch of grated parmesan mixed with fresh cut garlic on top. She'd eaten as much as any of them, but he'd heard about her hummingbird metabolism from Aaron.

"All the bread and noodles soak up the alcohol," Aaron said. He hoisted the half-empty glass of margarita sitting in front of him. It was his second, which he'd had with dinner. "I think I'm less drunk now than when I sat down."

"You two lightweights are like a couple of princesses," Freda told them. "I'm half dead and I can outdrink you."

"You're too ornery to be half dead," Dave told her. "I'm guessing a quarter dead at most." That got her laughing so hard she almost started coughing.

After dinner they watched some TV. Freda watched Wheel of Fortune and Jeopardy with near religious fervor, and never missed a night. Watching Jeopardy with her and Aaron was a competitive sport—whoever could spit out the answer (or rather the question) first did. Dave played along, and to his surprise found that all four of them were rather evenly matched.

"How the hell do you know so much about French furniture?" he asked Arlene.

"I lived in France."

"Really? When? For how long?"

"I lived my whole life there," she told him.

At Dave's confused look, Aaron told him, "She believes in reincarnation, and that in her previous life she lived in France. In what, the 1700s?"

"Late 1700s," Arlene corrected him.

Aaron shrugged. "I used to call bullshit, but she just knows too much weird stuff that she shouldn't. Considering nobody knows what the hell a soul is, who's to say it can't come back in a different body?"

Freda made it almost all the way through Jeopardy before falling asleep again. "I'll put her to bed," Arlene said quietly to Aaron and Dave. "You guys keep talking."

"Let's head outside and get some air, I think it's nice out," Aaron said.

They leaned up against Aaron's Mustang, and he lit up another Marlboro. It was beautiful out, warm but not hot or humid. The sun was heading down, but the sky was still bright.

"Dude, I thought you were going to get her car fixed," Dave said, nodding toward the Taurus.

Aaron rolled his head over to look at the car. "Yeah, well, I was going to take it in, but we got busy. We haven't been driving it. Arlene was complaining about the chemical smell at first anyway, and then it got a flat...."

"What'd you do with the money I gave you?"

"Paid some bills," Aaron said sheepishly. "Maybe waiting to fix it was better anyway, what do you think?"

"I think you need to fix it, the flat and the front end damage. You shouldn't be using your 'Stang as a daily driver. You need more money for that?"

"Nah, nah, I'm good."

They stood side by side for a while, just staring out at the neighboring trailers. The park wasn't loud, but it was filled with the sounds of people living their lives. Kids somewhere yelling in fun, the faint sound of the Tigers on the radio, and the occasional firecracker. The daylight had faded enough that the inside lights of the neighboring trailers revealed people moving around, and the blue flicker of TVs. Square golden islands in the gathering gloom.

"Sorry you had such a shitty time," Aaron said suddenly.

Dave looked at him in surprise, and saw he was serious. "No, dude, thanks for having me out, I had a good time. A real good time."

"Yeah, right."

Dave turned and looked at his friend. "No, Aaron, it was nice to be around a family for the holidays, even if it isn't my own. If I was at home, I'd just be sitting alone in an empty house, watching a movie or something."

"What about Gina? She got family or anything, you ever head over there and hang out with them?"

"I've never met her family. I don't know if she even sees them, she never talks to them. Or about them. And I think you know we don't have that kind of relationship."

"Well, I know how it started...."

"And that's pretty much how it's stayed. She likes me just because I'm the only normal guy she's ever dated. It makes her feel grounded, or normal, or something. All the other girls she works with are dating ex-cons or dealers or psychos, or just plain assholes."

"Yeah? So why are you still dating *her*?"

Dave shrugged and made a face. "Inertia. Habit."

"I'm guessing those big tits of hers might have something to do with it too," Aaron said with a smile, smoke curling up around his face.

Dave shrugged again and then gave a little smile. "She also brings girls from work home from time to time, too. For threesomes. I mention she's bi?"

The expression on Aaron's face made his whole evening.

PART III

MURDER CAPITAL

Detroit was the murder capitol for so many years not because we're more violent, we're just better damn shots.

Ted Nugent

CHAPTER THIRTEEN

They'd worked the guy twice before, and both times he didn't leave the house until after noon. In fact, there was never any sign of life at the place until late morning, so John had talked with the client about starting later and the adjuster had agreed.

Getting up early was part of the job, but Dave wasn't exactly a morning person. Getting on site at 9, instead of 6 a.m., was a welcome change, but then there was the traffic.

"Oh, come on!" he yelled at the row of cars in front of him, and checked his watch. Still on I-75 just past the 8 Mile curve, and he was supposed to be there in 20 minutes. Traffic was not cooperating. *Okay, time to test everybody else's reflexes with a little improvisational driving,* he thought with a grin. "Like a leaf on the wind," he said, and stomped on the gas.

He rolled into the neighborhood, if you could still call it that, right at 9 a.m. He saw one car backing out of a driveway, and a dog trotting down the sidewalk, but other than that nothing was moving. So much of the neighborhood was vacant, the abandoned houses having been torn down so long ago that there was no sign they'd ever been there.

The Cherokee crunched to a stop against the curb. He cracked the windows, grabbed his phone, and hopped into the back as quick as he could. It wasn't supposed to get that hot today, but it was going to be sunny, so he hoped this guy went somewhere. Otherwise it would be another day sweating. He called John on his cell phone.

"Monkey's in the box," he told his boss. "Tuna's in the can." Getting a full night's sleep always put him in a good mood. "You in the area yet?"

"Five minutes out. His car there?" John had spent even more time in traffic than his young employee, and was not happy about it.

"Yeah, I can just see the end of it. It's parked deeper in the driveway than usual, whatever that means."

"Okay. I'm glad he didn't skate out before he got here, I had to talk the adjuster into a late start to begin with, and if this guy wasn't here I'd probably have to eat today's billing. I'll call you when I land." John ended up being ten minutes late, but that was one of the perks of being the boss. He called Dave back. "All right, I'm here, I'll be in my usual spot in about ten seconds, you call him out when he moves."

John turned a corner and pulled the Expedition to a stop on Northfield in front of the second house in, right underneath a big oak tree. He could run the air if he needed to, but it was so much more pleasant to sit in the shade. He had the long eye anyway, and needed binoculars to see the two blocks down to the claimant's house. Speaking of which....

He pulled out the Bushnells from the back seat and put them up to his eyes. Nine in the morning and already he was getting heat mirage off the cracked concrete of the street. It wasn't that hot, but the sun was a lot hotter than the air and starting to bake everything. He cracked his windows an inch or so—enough for someone to get their fingers in, but that was it—and made sure all the doors were locked.

Dave's SUV was on East Cobb two blocks down and to the left, out of his view. John couldn't see the claimant's house either, for that matter, but knew roughly where it was, and where his driveway ran down to the street. They'd worked him before and knew his ride, a green Chrysler Concorde that desperately needed springs. He drove fast, and was a bitch to follow, which was how John'd gotten Nancy to approve two men on the case. Most adjusters hated to spend money, and had never done surveillance, so getting them to approve a second man on a surveillance was always an uphill battle.

As he was scanning the street he saw a dark car, an SUV or minivan, pull into view off a sidestreet two blocks up and head toward him on Northfield. After only a few seconds it pulled to the curb and parked. John kept his eyes on the vehicle, but never saw anyone get out of the driver's side, although it was pretty far away. Hmmm.

Cell phones had their uses, but were not great for rolling tails. John pulled out the Motorola handheld, turned it on, and hit the button. "You got your walkie on?"

"Yeah, I'm here," he heard Dave reply. "I can tell this is going to be a long day, I'm hot already."

Marsh thought that the day was going to be a bust after the target lost him in traffic. Detroit traffic wasn't as bad as either coast, or Chicago, which was part of the problem—the kid had room to move, and zigzagged in and out of the slow moving lanes of cars faster than Marsh could follow.

Before he knew it the target was out of sight. He'd given no indication he was aware of the tail, although given his part-time profession he was most likely a step above most people Marsh had followed, at least in awareness and driving skill. Better to lose him than risk exposure by doing something crazy, but he still hated to call the game so early in the day. He hadn't been given a deadline, but still....

The target had been heading into Detroit, so just for the hell of it Marsh decided to check out the locations he'd followed him to previously.

The first one, the long street with white houses in northeast Detroit, where he'd scared the crap out of that local with a screwdriver, was a bust. It took him a lot longer than he expected to make it to the other location, but damned if he didn't see the target's vehicle parked right in the same spot he'd taken the last time he'd come here. Marsh didn't stop and kept rolling on the cross-street, a block behind the Cherokee, which was facing away from him.

Marsh didn't know who the kid was watching, or even which house, and didn't much care. Whether it was for an insurance company or a divorce case it didn't much matter for what he had to do. He circled around the area and came in on a street which intersected the one on which the Cherokee sat.

Most of the houses were gone on the right side of the street, and as he coasted forward he saw the target's vehicle appear in a gap between two houses. He was pretty sure there used to be another house in there somewhere, maybe next to where the Cherokee was parked, but the only thing left was an empty lot with waist-high grass.

Carefully he pulled to the curb about eighty yards from the Cherokee. Only the front half of the vehicle was clearly visible above the unmowed grass of the vacant lot, and the driver's seat was unoccupied. The Cherokee's front windows were only lightly tinted, so he had no problem seeing the front seat was empty. The rear windows of the SUV had extra-dark tint, however, and he suspected the target was back there. There was no other likely place for him to be, not in this neighborhood.

Marsh scanned the houses in front and behind his van, and confirmed that they both appeared vacant—no windows, and minor smoke damage to the one in front, although in this city you never knew. There were a few houses on the driver's side across the street, but nothing was moving. If anyone was watching, the baseball cap and glasses helped change the shape of his head, plus the glare off the untinted front window would help make positive identification nearly impossible.

Marsh cracked the window on the right sliding door of the rental van, made sure the doors were locked, and climbed into the back, where the rifle was wrapped in a blanket.

Dave set down the camera, cracked his knuckles, and took a drink out of the bottle of Diet Coke he'd put in the freezer the night before. It still had good chunk of ice in it, and the cold soda burned pleasantly on the way down.

"You awake out there?" he said into the walkie talkie.

John was anything but asleep, he'd been on the phone for the last twenty minutes with his divorce lawyer. "Yeah, what?" he snapped into the radio.

"A neighbor just came over and yapped with him for a couple of minutes on the porch. I got video of it, but he wasn't doing anything other than standing there."

"He wearing his wrist braces?" John asked him. The claimant had stated in front of the work comp bureau's magistrate at the last benefits hearing that his bilateral carpal tunnel was horrifically painful, and he had to wear his wrist braces 24/7.

"Nope."

"Good. Nancy'll be pleased." Something caught his eye and he checked his side mirror. "I'll have to call you back, I've got the PD rolling up on me."

The squad car was half a block back and not moving fast, but after doing the job for over fifteen years John knew the chances were pretty good that they were coming to see him. DPD was too busy to just roll through a neighborhood. By the time they pulled up behind him he had the driver's door window down, and he had his driver license, PI license, and Concealed Pistol License all in his hands, which were in clear view on the steering wheel.

It was a two-man unit, and they got out and walked up either side of his vehicle. He noticed that they didn't hit their lights or siren, for which he was grateful.

"P.I., doing a surveillance," he said over his shoulder as they got close, before they had a chance to ask.

The lead cop was a thick black guy who looked like he had a dozen years on the job. He stopped just behind John's door and gave a little huff. "You call into dispatch?" he asked him.

John shook his head. "I figure they're a little too busy to be bothered," he told the officer. He checked his nametag—Ferguson. His partner stood next to the passenger door window and stared at John, his hand on his holstered Glock.

Officer Richard Ferguson made a face and took John's paperwork while giving him the eye. The vehicle occupant looked like an ex-cop, and wasn't nervous at all. A white guy, in this neighborhood, who looked like a cop? That, combined with all the licenses he'd just passed over told Ferguson he was exactly who he said he was. "You should still call in, Mr. Phault," he told him, relaxing somewhat. "P.I." he told his partner, Paul Gutierrez, over the roof of the car. Gutierrez nodded, but kept his eyes on John through the car window.

John didn't say anything, but they both knew that calling in to D.P.D. dispatch was a waste of everyone's time, as normally the cops were far too busy to roll out on a "suspicious vehicle" or "suspicious man in a vehicle" call, unless it was right next to a playground. Or the residence of a cop.....

"What kind of case you working?" Ferguson asked him.

"Simple insurance case," John told him.

"Which house you watching?"

John glanced down the street, then back at the officer. "Sorry, can't tell you. Several blocks down." The answer didn't surprise the cop, but it still didn't make him happy. "Am I parked in front of somebody's house?" John asked him.

"Narcotics," Ferguson told him. "You armed?"

"Wouldn't have handed you the CPL if I wasn't," John told him. His hands were still on the wheel at 10 and 2.

Ferguson nodded. "I'll be right back," he told the P.I., and headed back to the car with his paperwork. John watched the cop walk away. His partner, a thick guy who was maybe Hispanic, trailed after him, walking backward.

Undercover narcotics officers had eyes in the backs of their heads, but it was simple dumb luck that he'd parked near one's house. Although this was the third time he'd been out on this case, so either the officer wasn't that observant, or he'd never been home before.

John wasn't worried about the cops burning him for this surveillance—he was too far away from the claimant's house for him to see anything, unless he walked down to the sidewalk and looked down this way with a pair of his own binos.

Ferguson was back two minutes later, after having run his plate and his DL. "You come back here again, you need to call into dispatch," he told John. He handed him his paperwork, and John proceeded to put it away. "Tell them that you're calling in because of this, that you're parked near a narcotics officer's house. Maybe they'll actually make a note."

"Got it," John told him. "Also, I don't know where your guy's house is, but I've got a partner out here in a green Cherokee. He's down on Cobb, off to the left." He gave them his license plate. "He's tucked into the back right now."

Ferguson looked down the street, squinting. "What, is he right around the corner? Can't see shit when the city doesn't mow the grass."

"Yeah. Oh, and straight down the street, on the left side on the third block down, there's a black SUV or minivan. I think there's someone in it doing surveillance too."

"Oh?"

"Yeah. I saw it roll in just after we did, and never saw anybody get out. Maybe I missed them. I did a drive-by and ran the plate, wondering if it was the competition. If someone's in there they're tucked into the back as well." He handed Ferguson the piece of paper with the plate registration info on it.

Ferguson looked at the info. "Rochester Hills?" Talk about a whiter-than-white suburb.

"Yeah, they're not from the neighborhood. Like I said, I don't know if he's a P.I., or a fed, or one of your guys, but I'm pretty sure he's doing surveillance, and that there's somebody still in the vehicle. We could be watching the same guy, it's happened before with adjusters who forget who they've assigned to what, but since you've got an undercover living out here....."

"But he's not with you."

"Nope."

"Okay, we'll check it out. Thanks."

Marsh had a sniper's patience, and he'd done enough surveillance to know what was required, but that didn't mean he liked it. After about an hour he started to doubt himself, wondering if the target really was in the back of the Cherokee. Maybe he'd bailed out and was in some bushes nearby, closer to whatever house they were watching. Five minutes after that he caught a glimpse of brief movement behind the tint.

"Got you," he whispered to himself.

Eighty yards was practically point blank compared to some of the shots he'd made when he was in uniform or contracting, and so he spent most of his time just watching the car with his naked eye, waiting for the target to climb back into the front seat. The variable power scope on the rifle was set at 6X, which was more than enough to see what he needed to see to get the job done. He didn't have to worry so much about field of view on this one, and his target wouldn't be moving and he'd be shooting through the gap between two houses, so he kept the magnification on the 3-9X scope right in the middle.

He wasn't in the business of guessing, so instead of just a blind shot through the tinted window he'd have to wait for the target to climb back into the front sight. No telling how long that might take. He'd be hitting the side window glass at a slight angle, but the target would be inches away from the glass, so there wouldn't be much opportunity for the bullet, even if it was deflected slightly, to get far off course.

The .30-06, while it used to be a military cartridge, was possibly the most common hunting rifle round in the U.S. today, and powerful enough to kill anything on the continent. At eighty yards it would lose only a fraction of its velocity, and he wouldn't have to worry about drop or wind deflection at all. The Ballistic Tip round he had in the chamber was designed to expand in game animals and dump all of its kinetic energy into them, so they stopped quicker. One shot was all he'd have, but that's all he'd need.

Even without his eye to the glass, staring at one spot continuously was tough. He wiggled his head to keep his neck muscles loose — not a lot, even with the tint he didn't want to move around too much inside the van — and reached down without looking to the bottle of Gatorade. He just took a sip — this wasn't hot, not compared to Iraq or the 'Stan — but continuous hydration had been drilled into him like a religion.

As Marsh was putting down the bottle something caught his eye and he looked away from his target's car. There was a cop car down the street he was sitting on, maybe three hundred yards away from his van. He hadn't noticed it arrive, but as he watched he saw it pull away from the curb and head in his direction.

How long had the squad car been sitting there? Were they just rolling through the neighborhood on a random patrol, or had he missed something happening down the street? Maybe one of the residents had called about his car, or his targets. Wouldn't that be something? That would be a problem, though. If cops rousted his target, got him into the front seat, or even out of the SUV, there was no way he could take the shot.

Marsh watched as the white squad car rolled past the side street and his target and straight for him. Thirty feet away the unit angled right for the front of his van, nose on, and stopped when there was six feet between their bumpers. By the time the two cops were walking toward him Marsh was back in the front seat, the earplugs he'd kept halfway in his ears for when the time came tucked into a pocket.

He turned the key so he could roll down the window, then put his hands on the wheel. "Officers," he addressed them. "Doing a surveillance." Shit, he was blown, only thing to do now was get the hell out of there ASAP, dump the car, and assess his options. His heart was going a little faster, but outwardly he looked calm.

"You and everybody else on the block, apparently," the big black cop told him. "You got some ID?" The Hispanic cop walked around to the passenger side of the van and peered in at him, his hand on his Glock. The rifle was wrapped up in the blanket again and on the floor in back, although he hadn't had time to unload it.

"Yessir. It's in my wallet, may I?" He gestured at his hip, and when the cop nodded Marsh pulled out the prop wallet and dug through it for the driver's license. He handed it to the officer, then put his hands back on the wheel.

"Ohio?" The cop made a face. "You a P.I.?"

Marsh nodded. "Working a domestic. Parental kidnapping, waiting to see if a car shows up at a relative's address." He nodded down the street vaguely.

Ferguson studied the new guy. Late thirties or older, another white guy who looked like an ex-cop, and seemingly relaxed at being rolled up on. But there was just something about him...."You call in to dispatch?" he asked him.

"No. I guess I should have."

"Do you have a Michigan P.I. license?" Ferguson asked the van driver. He checked the ID – Robert Williams.

"No sir. I don't need one if I've followed the person from Ohio into Michigan. Exigent circumstances, I believe it's called."

Ferguson frowned. "I thought you were waiting to see if a car showed up." A work comp case in this neighborhood was par for the course, but a parental kidnapping was a little something different.

The guy blinked. "Yes. Today. But I've followed him to this house before from Ohio. Sylvania, actually, that's right outside Toledo."

"I know where it is," Ferguson said absently, thinking. Fuck it, this guy wasn't a local. He wasn't even a Michigan resident, and now his story is getting a little squirrelly. "Sir, please step out of the car," he told him, reaching for the door handle.

The man's face froze for just a fraction of a second, then he said, "Sure, not a problem."

Marsh could see the second officer in his peripheral vision, he was outside the front passenger door, and moving around the front of the vehicle as his partner opened the driver's door. Backing up his partner. Marsh slid off the seat, smiling and relaxed, as the big cop opened the door. In one smooth motion Marsh drew his Springfield from concealment and doubletapped the big cop in the face, and as he started to go down in slow motion spun to acquire his partner. The other cop was frozen in place, his brain still processing information that didn't compute. Marsh brought the Springfield up in a good two-handed hold, pressed it out, and as soon as his hands reached their proper index he started shooting, just knowing his sights would be in the right place. The first round hit the cop in the base of the throat, and while he pulled one just off to the right, two more bullets hit the cop in his big round face.

"Shit!" John jerked upright in his seat, spilling his pop. He'd only been peripherally paying attention to the cops down the street as they talked to whoever was in the van, and the sound of gunfire had startled him. Down the street, he could see what looked like someone lying in the middle of the street.

He grabbed his binoculars and threw them to his eyes. Both cops were down, and the guy had just gotten back into his car and started driving away.

"What the hell was that?" Dave's voice echoed from the walkie-talkie. "Is that shooting?"

"You've got cops down at your ten o'clock," John yelled into the Motorola, starting his SUV. In the distance he saw the van pulling away from the scene, heading toward him, and then it turned onto a sidestreet, maybe Cobb, heading away from Dave's car. Then it was gone. John threw the Expedition into Drive and roared away from the curb. "See what you can do for them. I'm chasing after the guy that did the shooting. You see a van go by you?"

"Yeah, it turned in front of me, heading away, then made a left at the first street. What the fuck is going on?"

John didn't have time to talk and threw the radio down. He hooked a right, tires squealing, and roared to the next intersection. Nosing out, he saw the van way down there to his left. Instead of turning and chasing it, he sped through the intersection to the next stop sign, then hooked a left. Praying no toddlers wandered into street, he got the Expedition up to eighty before hitting the brakes.

"Shit shit shit!" Warren Avenue was right in front of him, three lanes in each direction, and as John was three houses from the corner he saw the van pass in front of him. "There you are." He'd followed plenty of people before, but never anyone who'd just dumped two cops.

John grabbed his phone. 9-1-1 was answered on the third ring. "Nine-one-one, what's your emergency?" the female officer said in his ear.

He knew mobile 911 was operated by the Michigan State Police. "Connect me to Detroit emergency," he told her breathlessly as he turned onto Warren. The van was up there, in the middle lane, and John floored the Expedition for a few seconds until he realized the van was doing the speed limit. He tapped the brakes and stayed in the right lane, waiting on the line.

"Nine one one, what's your emergency," he heard the flat voice in his ear. She sounded so burned out it wasn't even a question.

"You have two officers down, shot," he told the dispatcher. "On Northfield Street, near Cobb. They were just shot. Um, fuck, what was...Ferguson, one of them was named Ferguson."

There was the very briefest of pauses, then she was back on the line, no longer uninterested in the conversation. "You say we have two police officers shot?"

"Yes ma'am, on Northfield near Cobb. East Cobb. I'm a P.I. and was in the area and saw it, and one of my employees is doing first aid on the officers right now."

"How bad are their injuries?" He could hear all sorts of frantic activity behind her.

"I don't know ma'am, I left the scene, but I heard multiple gunshots."

214

"You left the scene?" She couldn't decide whether to be shocked or angry.

"A white male did the shooting and left the scene in a dark minivan, Chrysler I think, and I'm currently behind him. I'm following him westbound on Warren Avenue. Just passed Epworth, and coming up on something else...Livernois."

"Do you have the license plate on his vehicle?"

"Yes." He gave it to her. "I can't tell if it's black or dark blue, but I ran the plate earlier today when I saw it roll up into the neighborhood, it registers to Rochester Hills. I haven't been close to him yet, so I don't think he's spotted me back here."

"Hold on the line, I'm going to get officers en route."

"Roger that."

John kept the phone to his ear, and a constant distance from the van. There were a few other cars on the road, but not as much as he would have liked to give him cover. Shit. Okay, where would this guy be going?

If I'd just shot two cops I'd get out of the area as fast as possible, without drawing attention to myself, he thought. *Where's the next freeway? Well, if he'd turned on Livernois he could jump on I-94 to the south or the Lodge to the north, but he was still heading west. What was up there?* John thought. Well, if the guy didn't turn off, the Southfield Freeway was three or four miles up.

The dispatcher was back on. "Sir, did you get a description of the suspect?"

"White guy, medium build, but I was too far away to see anything else."

"Are you still behind him?"

"Yes. I'm in a black Ford Expedition." He gave her his plate. "And I'm armed," he told her. Better they know ahead of time. "We're approaching a big field on the right, looks like a water plant past it. Seeing a sign up ahead...for Wyoming. Still heading west."

"Sir, stay on the line. I've got officers en route to your location as well as the Northfield location."

"My employee's name is Dave, a white kid. He's got first aid training. I'm pretty sure he's armed. I'd really appreciate it if your responding officers didn't shoot him. He'd probably appreciate it too."

"Yes sir. How fast are you travelling?"

John checked his speedometer. "Right about the posted. He's rolling in the left lane now, I'm in the right about six car lengths back."

"I'm going to keep you on the line as I coordinate the officers. Please call out your location, or if he makes a turn."

"Yes ma'am." He heard all sorts of cut-ins and outs on the line, and electronic beeps. He knew the call was being recorded, and was trying to sound as professional as possible, considering this was all going to end up in court one way or the other. What a clusterfuck.

"Did you see what kind of gun he had?"

"No. I was about two blocks away, and only looked over there with binoculars after I heard the shooting. Pistol, I think."

"How many rounds did he fire?"

"Four, five? Six? Both officers were down and if they were moving it wasn't a lot. Coming up on Schaefer now, still westbound, how far away are your units?" It seemed like they were taking forever, but he knew the adrenaline was skewing his perception. He'd only been behind the van for about three miles. Shit, wait a minute—this wasn't Detroit anymore, this was Dearborn. Fuck it, let their dispatch worry about that.

"We're working on it sir, I'm trying to get several there at once, and they're coming from different directions."

"Right." The more cop cars that showed up at the same time, the better chance they had of boxing the van in and preventing a car chase.

"Are you still travelling the speed limit?"

"Yes."

"Are you sure you're still behind the correct vehicle? You said you were pretty far back."

John gave the Ford a little extra gas and squinted. "Yeah, right van."

"Sir, just make sure you keep your distance, we don't need you getting shot too."

"No offense ma'am, but I've seen some combat and can take care of myself." Speaking of that, he had an AR-15 in a case in the back seat, in case of emergencies. He didn't want to have to pull the rifle out and chamber a round while driving, so hopefully this guy would just surrender without any drama. He had body armor back there too, but it was a little too late to put that on now.

"Are you still westbound on Warren?"

"Yes ma'am." *Motherfucker,* he yelled in his head, *were they driving here in reverse?* He knew that wasn't fair, he knew the DPD cops would be screaming to both locations as fast as possible, it just seemed to be taking forever.

"Units responding, be advised we have confirmed there are two officers down at the first location," the dispatcher said in his ear. "Multiple gunshot wounds."

"Coming up on Greenfield," John told her. "Uhhh, light's turning green for us."

He rolled up slowly to the intersection as the cars waiting at the light started pulling away. The van was to his left, two cars up, and had almost come to a stop at the light before it changed. John checked out the van as well as he could without being obvious about it. "It looks like there's only the driver in the van," John said into his phone. Then he saw the first cop car.

It was stopped on Greenfield at the light, southbound. In the right lane, first in line, waiting to turn. John flicked his gaze back and forth between the van and the cop car, but the van driver didn't do anything, and the cops just sat there. John rolled through the intersection, and a few seconds later saw the cop car in his rearview mirror as it turned onto Warren behind him. Lots of one-story businesses lining Warren here…pizza place, adult book shop, travel agency.

The van moved over into the right lane, four cars ahead of John's Expedition, but kept to the speed limit. The cop car moved out from behind John into the left lane, and slowly passed him. He glanced down at the cop in the front passenger seat, and saw the officer looking at him. The expression on his face was unreadable.

A hundred yards up, on the other side of Warren, past a CVS Pharmacy, John saw another cop car poke its nose out from a side street, and he instinctively took his foot off the gas. The cop car next to him accelerated and closed the distance to the van.

John heard no roaring engine, but he saw the van pulling away from the car behind it, and the police cruiser creeping up in the left lane. As the cruiser across Warren pulled out and headed in their direction, the first DPD car hit its lights, and gave a single *bloop* of its siren. "PULL OVER!" he heard one of the cops over their PA. It wasn't a shout, but it was close. Their adrenaline was up too.

Already pulling away, the van accelerated, and John could hear its engine, which was immediately drowned out by the big V-8s in the DPD Crown Victorias as they roared up and crowded its rear bumper, and both sirens went on full blast. There was no way the van would be able to outrun the cruisers, and the driver seemed to know it. After the first surge, the van's brake lights flared, suddenly, and one of the cruisers pulled up next to the van.

"PULL OVER!" the cop on the PA called out again. It was the passenger in the cruiser next to the van, John could see him on the handset, looking across half a lane at the van's driver, and then everything went crazy.

The air between the two cars went all sparkly and glittery, and something happened to the passenger side window on the cop car, which began to swerve. The sound of loud pops echoed around him, and John realized that the driver of the van had just fired on the first cop car, firing through his own window while driving.

The cruiser under fire took a dozen pistol rounds, and veered away from the van, into oncoming traffic. The first few cars were able to miss it, then a frantically swerving pickup couldn't help but tap the cruiser's rear bumper. The Crown Vic spun around and slammed into two parked cars sideways at forty miles an hour. There was a loud screeching crunch, and more glass went flying.

"Oh, shit!" John spat, and got back on his car's accelerator. "The driver just fired on one of the cop cars!" he yelled into the phone. "It crashed on Warren."

The van accelerated to the limit of its engine, and began weaving between the traffic on Warren. John kept pace, three car lengths back from the remaining squad car. He glanced into his rearview, and saw another cruiser flying up on him like he was standing still. He dropped the phone onto his passenger seat and put both hands on the wheel as the new cruiser rocketed by him. He was able to see two officers in the front, and as he watched them pass he saw two more DPD cars ahead on Warren Avenue, roaring toward them.

The cruiser swung wide, out into the center left turn lane, passed John's Expedition, passed the other cruiser still behind the van in the right lane, and then skipped across two lanes.

At seventy miles an hour the DPD unit slammed into the side of the van at a forty-five degree angle. With a crunch the van went up on two wheels and turned, sliding sideways, so that it was broadside to the cruiser embedded in its side. Somehow the van didn't flip over, maybe because it had been only travelling slightly slower than the cruiser before the impact, and the two now-bonded vehicles scraped to a stop, smoke and steam and flashing red and blue lights.

The window frame hit Marsh in the back of the head when the cruiser plowed into him, and his vision and hands went all tingly and sparkly for a second. The sensation disappeared almost immediately, and by the time his crippled van had come to a stop he was already trying to get his door open. It wouldn't budge, the impact must have buckled it.

He'd shot out his own window, and right out the empty frame he was looking at the two officers in the Crown Vic which had just broadsided him. Everything moving in slow motion, he brought his Springfield up and waited, as he couldn't get an angle on their heads inside the car, and shooting them in the vests was just a waste of ammo.

The passenger got out first, standing in the vee of the door and the car, his duty gun coming up as he started to yell at Marsh, everything happening in slow motion. At a distance of eight feet putting two rounds into the cop's face was easy, and by the time he was done the driver was sticking his face and gun out the crack between door and cruiser.

The cop fired several rounds at Marsh, which he assumed missed as he never felt them. He took an extra half second to aim, then fired three shots at his only target, the officer's forehead. The first round hit the door post, and the third he pulled above the officer's head, but the second 9mm bullet missed the officer's Glock by half an inch and hit him in the left eyebrow. The bullet continued on into his brain, and the cop dropped instantly.

The van was a bullet magnet, and Marsh knew it was time to find another ride. He could hear tires screaming, sirens wailing, and out the windshield saw three more cops cars hurtling at him, only seconds away. Time to go. Banged up from the vehicle impact but not actually injured, Marsh clambered out of his seat and tried the door on the passenger side. It worked. He jumped out, between his van and the cars parked on the street, and did a reload while moving slowly toward the rear of the van. He was right next to a used car lot, and if it hadn't been enclosed by a tall fence he would have run in there to use the cars for cover.

The other cop car had skidded to a stop thirty feet behind the van, and the officers were hunkered down behind their doors, using cover more than he could have preferred. Marsh fired twice at the legs of the cop behind the passenger door, then darted sideways behind a Jeep parked at the curb. Angry return fire spanged off the metal around him, and glass shattered, but he kept moving. He came quickly around the far side of the Jeep, and saw he had a great shot at the closer of the two cops, who was looking at where he'd been, not where he was. The cop on the passenger side instinctively straightened up to return fire, and between that and the new angle Marsh had him.

He brought the Springfield up and fired, but something went wrong. There was pain, and flashes, and spinning. He found himself on the ground, staring up at the blue sky. He tried moving, but couldn't. Why was he on the ground? He had to get out of there, had to....mouth working, he died staring at a wispy cloud drifting across the peaceful sky.

"Cover me!" John yelled. His vehicle was two car lengths behind the cruiser, and he stood up from where he was crouching behind the engine compartment and moved forward.

AR-15 at his shoulder, John advanced as fast as he could without bouncing the red dot off the downed gunman. The air was filled with sirens and the smell of burning brake pads, yells and screeches, someone screaming in pain, but he tried to tune it all out as he drew close to the killer. The cop who'd last been shot at was on the ground off to the left, yelling and kicking his legs.

A pistol was a few inches from the shooter's outstretched unmoving right hand, and John kicked it away. From the front, the man appeared unharmed, with only a tiny black smudge on his shirt visible where one of the two .223 rounds John fired hit him. Underneath him, however, there was a spreading pool of blood. His eyes were open and unseeing.

"Clear!" John yelled. Safing his rifle and holding it out away from his body, muzzle down, neither hand anywhere near the trigger, he was suddenly aware of a half dozen bodies flooding the empty space between the cars, everybody with a gun out.

"Who the fuck are you, a fed?" one of the uniformed cops asked him. At least half of them had seen him drop the shooter. Most of them were staring at the body on the ground, and everybody was still jacked up and looking for blood. The smell of burning plastic filled the air, people were moaning in pain, and glass crunched underfoot.

"We need EMS out here right NOW!" one of the cops was yelling into his radio. "We have officers down, multiple officers down."

"Stop staring at that fucker and secure the scene!" a Sergeant yelled at the massed officers, as even more squad cars came screaming up. He looked across the crowd of his officers at John, and their eyes met.

"You the P.I.?" he asked him.

"Yeah. If you let me put this away, I can help with first aid," John told him, motioning with the AR. "You got a lot of guys down. I've dealt with gunshot wounds before."

The Sergeant looked at him for a second, then grabbed one of the younger officers and pointed. "Lopez. Secure that rifle. Don't set it down, don't let it out of your sight." He then looked at the scene, left and right, then back at John. "What the fuck just happened?"

John could only shake his head.

Dave sat on the curb about fifty feet away and did his best to stop staring at the bodies. They weren't the first dead bodies he'd seen, but seeing dead bodies and futilely trying to do first aid on two men who'd been shot in the face was something completely different. He looked at his hands—he'd done his best to wipe the blood off, but it was still in the creases of his palms, in the corners of his fingernails.

Yet another DFD engine rolled up, the men jumping off in their blue shirts and thick pants held up by suspenders. "You okay?" one of the firefighters asked him, seeing the drying blood on his forearms.

"Yeah, not my blood," Dave told him. The man jogged toward the crime scene, where at least a dozen cops and firefighters were milling around at a distance from the bodies and the cruiser. His phone started ringing.

Dave looked at his hands, then made a face and dug his phone out of his pocket. He'd be able to wipe his phone off, but he didn't like the idea of rubbing the officers' blood into the pocket of his jeans. He saw it was his boss. "John? You okay?"

"Yeah, but I'm not going to make it back there. How about you? Are you okay?" John felt a little guilty, just tearing off to let Dave deal with the cops who'd been shot, but there'd been no other option. They'd just driven him to the precinct, where he knew he was in for a long wait.

"Me? Yeah, fine, why? You're the one who shot somebody." The officers who'd responded to this scene had told Dave what had happened to the shooter.

"It's not the first guy I've shot."

"Yeah, well, they're not the first guys I've seen shot," Dave told him.

John shook his head. He flashed back to the first time he'd ever met Dave, in his office. The kid looked great on paper, and in person he was very self-assured; not cocky, just confident. Then there was his personal history, which explained it all. *How is it I always run into guys like him? Or do they run into me?*

"Is there, uh, anything you want me to say to anybody here when they question me?" Dave asked him. "Or not say?"

"Answer any and every question they give you to the best of your ability. Tell them exactly what you know and saw and did."

"I don't know anything. I didn't see anything. And I couldn't do shit for these guys, they were dead before they hit the ground."

"Yeah. Me and you both, kid. I'll give you a call tomorrow. Forget about the surveillance, I think we both need a couple days off."

The detective opened the door and came in with a spiral notebook and a cup of coffee. "You want some—" he started to say, then saw John already had a cup.

"This is perhaps the worst coffee I've ever tasted," John told him, sipping from his cup. Even loaded with sugar and powdered creamer it was disgusting.

"Yeah. Welcome to my world." Bill Rochester set down his notebook and cup and then settled into the chair across the table from the P.I. Pretty much the entire precinct, hell, the whole department was in an uproar, but for the moment, in this room, there was just the two of them.

"You're sure you're ready to give a statement?" Rochester said to him, looking the man up and down. He seemed pretty composed for someone who, just a few hours before, had been in a car chase and then dumped a dude using his own assault rifle. That was the great thing about this job. No such thing as a routine day....

The P.I. frowned into his cup of coffee. "It's been a couple of hours. I presume you've run me. I've been involved in shootings before. Back in the day I worked for the DEA."

Rochester had run him through LEIN and CLEMIS, then Googled him just to be on the safe side. He'd found enough things to make him very interested in the guy. "Why'd you leave?"

John smiled ruefully. "Among other things, my wife—ex-wife—thought it was too dangerous, and I came into enough money to do something else."

Rochester gestured at the microphone on the table. "You ready to make an official statement? Okay if I start recording?"

John looked at the microphone, then up at the video camera in the corner up at the ceiling, then at the mirror taking up most of one wall. He knew there had to be people on the other side of it, watching him. "Shit, I figured you were recording already."

"Fair enough." Rochester hit the button, identified himself, the location, stated the day, date, and time, and the names of everyone present.

"Mr. Phault, are you aware that this statement is being recorded?"

"Yes."

"And do I have your permission to record it?"

"Yes."

"Are you currently taking any medication or drugs, prescription or otherwise, which might influence or affect in any way what you're about to tell us today?"

"No."

He didn't read him his Miranda rights, because he wasn't a suspect, and wasn't being charged with a crime. If that changed, well...."Well then, if you would, please tell us in your own words what happened today."

John sighed, then went through the incident step by step. John had taken—and given—enough police statements that he knew what details they were looking for. He'd also already told abbreviated versions of it to the uniformed cops on the scene, and the first detective, a female, so he had the details organized in his head. That female detective had only spoken to him briefly while he sat in the back of a squad car, handcuffed, on Warren Avenue. This detective didn't interrupt him at all but took furious notes.

"Have you ever seen the man you shot before?" Rochester asked him when he finished.

"Not that I know of."

"And the name, uh," Rochester checked his notes, "Robert Williams, is that familiar at all to you?"

John shook his head. "As far as I know, I've never seen the man before in my life, and his name is not familiar to me at all. Did you get anything when you ran his license?"

"We've got people working on that," the detective told him.

"He from Rochester Hills?"

Rochester remembered that the P.I. had run the plate of the van Williams had been in, and that it was registered out of Rochester Hills.

"No. He had an Ohio license. That mean anything to you?"

Ohio was less than an hour away, they saw cars with Ohio plates driving around all the time. Ontario too. The fact that the guy had an Ohio license didn't mean anything to John. "No," he said, shaking his head. "But I'll tell you something."

Rochester lifted his head up from his notebook. "Yeah?"

"It wouldn't surprise me if that guy was a combat vet. He knew what the hell he was doing, and I don't think he was rattled even with all the cops screaming up on him."

"What do you mean?"

John leaned forward. "He shot those two cops, killed both of them before they could even get a shot off, is what I heard from your people, and they're both wearing body armor. Then he takes off, but instead of panicking, he's driving the speed limit, doing whatever he can to not get noticed. Calm, after dumping two of your guys. When the cops do show up, and try to box him in, he takes out two carloads of your guys with a pistol. I think he might have had a chance of getting away if I hadn't been in the right spot at the right time." He sat back, and took another sip of his coffee. It was cold, and even more disgusting than before.

The detective sat and looked at him for a good thirty seconds, then glanced down at his scribbled notes. "Maybe you can help me with something," Rochester said.

"What?"

"You were there doing a surveillance on a worker's comp claimant. We talked to him—hell, the uniforms talked to everybody still living on the block, and none of them knew you or your employee were out there doing a surveillance. Ferguson and his partner rolled up on you just because you were sitting in front of another officer's house."

John nodded. "Right. A narcotics cop or something like that."

"And that's when you told them about the van down the street, that Williams was in. That you saw roll up a while after you did. They went to check it out, and that's when all hell broke loose."

"Right."

"So, based on your version of events, there was no way Mr. Williams could have expected being rolled up on by cops. If he'd only wanted to shoot a couple of cops, he could have driven to the precinct parking lot, or charged into the lobby here and done a suicide-by-cop. Hell, it's happened before."

"Yeah."

"So what the hell was he doing there?" the detective asked him.

"I don't—I don't know," John said, and suddenly realized where this was going. Where he should have realized it was going, where it had to go.

"Williams only showed up and parked on the street *after* you got there," the detective told him. "He parked in a spot where he could see *your* vehicle. The van he was driving turns out to be stolen, and he switched plates on it with another, identical van." They'd figured that much out already, and that marked Mr. Williams, if that was his real name, as having some sort of illicit intentions. "We also found a sniper rifle inside his van." He paused and took a sip of his coffee. God, that was horrible. "I think, Mr. Phault, that the person we should be talking about….is you."

CHAPTER FOURTEEN

Dave had just gotten out of the shower when his cell phone rang. He saw it was his PI boss. He actually hadn't talked to John in four days, since the day after the shooting. Dave had called him just to see if John was in jail. Even though it sounded like John had saved the lives of some cops by shooting that crazy dude, cops got weird about private citizens with guns. Local news couldn't seem to talk about anything but the shootings, but none of the channels had all the facts as he knew them right, so he didn't trust them to have anything right.

"John, what's up?"

"Hey, Davey. Sorry to spring this on you like this, but, uh...are you busy this evening?"

"I just got back from working for Absolute all day," Dave said. "Just got out of the shower. What's up?" He grabbed his watch off the counter, saw it was just before five-thirty.

"Well, I'm working a case..."

"You're back working?"

"Yeah. Gotta pay the bills. Anyway, followed somebody to a bar, but I can't get any video inside. Too dark...among other things. I talked to the adjuster, and she said that if I actually brought another investigator in, then there would be two people who could testify that they watched the claimant working here. Corroborating witnesses. Can you give me a few hours tonight? I don't know if you've got any plans….."

"All I was going to do was work out, maybe practice my draw for a while. Sure, I can come out. Where should I meet you?"

"Well, see, here's the thing," John said, then paused. "Claimant is a corrections officer, and I actually followed her to a strip club. She's in there working right now. Um, dancing. Stripping. I've never asked, so I don't know if you're religious or what…"

"You're wondering if I have any problems with *getting paid* to come down to a strip club and watch a stripper dance?" Dave said with a laugh. "I think I'll be okay with that. What club?"

"Goldfinger's. It's on Eight Mile near Schoenherr….what's so funny?" Dave was laughing his ass off.

"Nothing. You'll see. I'll meet you there."

Driving over, Dave got two texts from his boss. The first was LEAVE YOUR GUN IN THE CAR, THEY'RE WANDING EVERYBODY. The second was DON'T TAKE ANY PICS WITH YOUR PHONE, THEY'LL CONFISCATE IT. Dave smiled to himself.

Benny was working the door, collecting cover charges and checking IDs, and he smiled and nodded at Dave as he came in. Dave paused a second to let his eyes get used to the light, then headed in, AC/DC thumping in his ears. John was sitting at the bar, trying hard to look like he was happy to be there.

"Hi!" he nearly had to yell for Dave to hear him. His eyes moved left and right. "Glad you could make it." The topless bartender was heading their way and John saw her in the mirror. He wasn't sure whether or not it was polite to stare at her. Dave surprised him by addressing her by name.

"Hi Andrea. How you doing? Who's manager tonight?"

"Tony, you want me to send him over?" She had long black hair and a snake tattoo curling around her left upper arm.

"Yeah, could you? That'd be great."

She nodded and headed off. John looked up at him. "I take you've been in here before?"

Dave just smiled and held up a finger. A well-groomed middle-aged man in a two-thousand dollar suit approached them from the back. "David! Nice to see you again. What can I do for you?"

Dave pointed at John. "Tony, this is John, a good friend of mine. He just went through a messy divorce, and isn't quite sure he still likes women. I'm wondering if we can get that booth over there, maybe the better view will help him make his mind up?" Dave indicated one of the big padded leather booths in the center of the room between the two main stripper poles. Normally you had to slide somebody at least a hundred bucks to get one. Dave wouldn't have asked if it had been occupied.

Tony smiled. "Not a problem." He checked his watch. "You hungry? I can have Carlos whip something up."

Dave looked to John. "You eat dinner yet? I'm hungry."

"Uh, yeah, I could eat."

"Excellent," the manager said. "Barbeque beef tips? Carlos is an artist."

"Yeah, two," Dave told him. "But no alcohol for me, I'm carrying."

John's eyes jerked up at him, but the manager just said with a smile, "When are you not?" and strode off.

"You got stock in the club or something?" John asked him as they slid into the booth.

"I gave some shooting lessons to Tony and some of his guys after they got robbed earlier this year," Dave said. "So, who are we here for?"

Their table butted up to the main stage, and was about six feet from one of the brass stripper poles which stretched up twelve feet to the ceiling. There were two poles on the main stage, one near the far wall on a smaller stage, and one in the middle of the bar. Girls started on one side of the room and cycled through the poles, switching after every song. Usually by the time they were done with their fourth pole one of the guys in the audience had expressed enough interest to be talked into a lap dance, or even into paying for a trip to the VIP room.

John looked around. "She's not out now. You'll know her when you see her. Eight-pack abs. She can climb the pole like a monkey."

Dave envisioned most prison guards, male or female, as huge and fat, not stripper pole material. "What the hell's her injury supposed to be?"

John laughed. "Back. Got injured in a fight, supposedly."

One of the waitresses appeared at John's elbow. She had on a short pleated skirt that just covered her ass and a red bustier. "Something to drink, gentlemen? Oh, hey Davey, I didn't know you were here. Diet Coke for you?"

"You know it, Alisha."

"And for your friend?"

"Coke," John said. When Dave looked at him, he explained quietly, "Have to be able to say that our observations weren't impaired by alcohol."

Dave only paused a second, but in that time a whole flood of thoughts bounced around his head. "Fuck that. Alisha, do me a favor. Bring Tony back out here."

She looked confused. "Okay." Tony was back out a few minutes later.

"Dave, is there a problem?" Alisha hovered nervously behind her manager.

"No. I didn't want to mention it before, but fuck it. Tony, this is my buddy John. Shake his hand." Neither man knew exactly what Dave was doing, but they shook hands amicably. Dave went on. "You know that asshole who killed those three Detroit cops a few days ago, wounded like four more, that huge shootout and car chase shit all over the news?" Dave pointed at John. "This is the guy who killed *him*." John blinked and looked like he wanted to disappear into the booth cushion.

Tony didn't say anything for a second, and just stared at the muscular stranger sitting in front of him. Early forties, touch of gray at the temples, looked like he could handle himself. Looked like a cop. Worst day in the history of the department, one of the newspapers had called it. Word was a citizen had been the one who'd actually killed the maniac, a private investigator, but the cops were being very tightlipped with the details as the case was still "under investigation". The news media couldn't understand why whoever had done it wasn't begging to get his face all over the TV, but Tony did. He stuck his hand out again, and John instinctively took it. "I knew one of those officers," he said, actually fighting back tears. "Don't ever try to pay for anything in this club, ever." He turned to the waitress behind him. "Alisha, get this man whatever he wants."

"So much for low profile," John murmured as the waitress left with their drink order. But, he had to admit to himself, he did deserve to blow off a little steam. The divorce bullshit had been a giant pain in the ass, but it was almost over. Not as heartbreaking as the first time he'd gotten divorced, but it was still bad. And then there was the shooting. Not that it was the first time he'd ever killed a man, but it had been a while……..

John leaned back as a dancer climbed up onto the stage in front of them and began dancing to Lynyrd

Skynyrd. She started out in a bikini top and a micro skirt over high heels, but soon was down to nothing but a g-string. Michigan law stated that in any club which served alcohol the dancers had to keep on a g-string, or something that covered their pubic area. Across the river, in Windsor, the strip clubs were totally nude. Hell, escorts were legal, marijuana was legal, and the beer was stronger, but post-9/11 getting across the border was quite often a huge pain in the ass, with long delays. The waitress brought their drinks—John had decided on a rum and Coke—and he leaned back in the booth and sipped at it.

The stripper in front of them was a small-chested brunette with muscular legs and a shy smile that she kept flashing at him. The fact that she was half his age—or less—wasn't lost on him. He wasn't a prude, he'd been in he didn't know how many strip clubs over the last few decades, but he'd always felt strip clubs were a big waste of money. An expensive way to torture yourself.

"You know, they keep wanting to say that it was me he was after instead of just a whackjob thrill-killing cops," John told his young employee.

"Seriously? Why?"

"Just the way it happened. Guy didn't show up until after we did. Like he was following me."

"But he didn't shoot at you, he was only interested in killing cops. He had plenty of time to go after you, you followed him for four miles. Besides, who the hell would want you dead? I mean, besides your ex-wife?"

"Ha ha."

Three songs later the claimant appeared, and John nudged Dave's foot and nodded in her direction. "I think she's new, I haven't seen her before," Dave told him. He watched the sinewy young woman dance and strip and then climb the pole like a snake. "Damn. She's the first work comp claimant I've ever worked that I'd *want* to see naked."

John laughed hard at that, and took another sip of his drink. It was his second or third rum and Coke...he'd lost count already. He wasn't drunk, but he was feeling good. He watched the claimant work the pole for a while, then she got down onto the stage. "Okay," he said suddenly to Dave, pointing, "*that*. How the hell am I supposed to describe *that* in a report without upsetting the adjuster or crossing some professional boundary?"

Dave studied the claimant. "Um......*The claimant displayed the greatest flexibility of any dancer seen in the club, at one point lying on her back and spreading her legs until her knees touched the stage to either side of her body.*"

"Yeah!" John said. "That's great. Remember that, I don't think I can."

"She sure doesn't look like she's got any back problems," Dave smirked.

John tried to pay attention to the claimant as the song ended and she moved to the next stage, but the girl who got up after her was so hot he had a hard time not watching her as she danced. Blond, beautiful, toned body, and big tits. Probably fake, but who cared? "Wow, you see that one?" he said to Dave. "Who's that?"

"I'll introduce you after she's done her tour of the stages," Dave told his boss, smiling. He waved at Alisha and ordered more drinks for the two of them. Thank God he didn't have to pay for the tiny Diet Cokes, they would have cost him $8 apiece.

John was definitely feeling no pain by the time the blonde was done with all four stages, and it was a good thing, otherwise he might have felt shy as a teenager as she came over to his booth. "Gina, this is John, my boss," Dave said.

"Oh, hi!" she said, sticking out her hand. John shook her hand, but his brain was stuck in neutral as she hadn't put any of her clothes back on after her last dance and was clad only in a g-string and white high-heel shoes.

"Uh, hi," he said stupidly. He'd almost said *Pink nipples*, because that was what he was thinking.

"John, this is my girlfriend, Gina."

John blinked, and then turned and looked at Dave. "What? Girlfriend?"

"Yeah."

He looked at Dave's big smile, then turned back to the girl whose hand he was still holding. "Is he fucking with me?" She laughed hard at that, and it was glorious to watch.

"No, shit, he's not the first guy I've killed. Don't worry about me," John told him confidentially, leaning in close and trying not to slur his words. "It was a good shoot, I'm not going to get any TP...PC....PTSD or anything." He blinked and suddenly wondered what time it was. His watch was hard to see in the dim and flashing lights, but it looked to be close to eleven o'clock. Fuck it, he didn't have anywhere to go or anywhere to be until after noon tomorrow.

He probably shouldn't have been drinking so much, but a group of Detroit cops—regulars—had come into the club. The manager, after decades of experience dealing with liars and fakes, had asked them if John really was the guy who'd killed the cop killer. One of the officers had been on scene and seen John behind his rifle, so after a shitload of handshaking and backslapping they'd bought John half a dozen drinks. And he'd drunk them. All.

"You sure?" Dave asked him. "I mean, I got in that shooting a few years ago. Even though it was a good shooting, I had flashbacks and nightmares for a while. It's not like you've been in combat and killed a whole bunch of guys, right? Just shootings that happened when you were a fed?" John gave him a look. "What?"

"You ever hear of an, annnn.....NDA?" He had to say the letters very slowly and clearly to get them straight.

"A what?"

"Non-disclosure agreement." John blinked, then leaned back. "Never mind, I'm drunk. I should keep my mouth shut. 'Swhut nundishclosure means, right? Man, I'm drunk. You wouldn't believe me anyway." He looked pointedly at Dave. "But it's more like two dozen than two. I didn't get flashbacks after that shooting last week, I was getting flashbacks *during* it. Of the last firefight I was in. Which was a hell of a lot worse than popping a guy who didn't even know I was there. A cop killer. Shit, that was easy. Doesn't seem right to say it, but it's the truth."

Dave stared at him for a few seconds, then waved at the few strippers standing near the bar. Two of them came over, including the claimant. "I think he needs another trip to the VIP room," he told them with a smile.

"No, I..." John began to feebly protest, but by then the girls were pulling him out of the booth. "Make sure you pay very close attention!" Dave called out after him, pointing at the claimant and laughing. As the group headed across the club floor, Dave stared after his boss, a crooked smile on his face. What the hell? NDA? Two dozen? You always learned the most interesting things, being sober around drunk people. Maybe even some of what John'd said was true. He leaned back in the booth and watched Gina dancing around the pole on the bar. Great to look at, and a lot of fun, but he should have broken up with her long ago. What the hell was he doing?

Special Agent-in-Charge Mitchell Boehmer took a sip of coffee from his FBI mug and frowned. How the hell could hot coffee get lukewarm so fast? It just didn't seem physically possible. A few years ago his wife had bought him what amounted to a miniature hot plate designed specifically for keeping a coffee cup warm, but it had stopped working several weeks before and he'd been unable to find another one. It wasn't that important...except when he wanted his coffee hot and it wasn't, then it was very fucking important. His intercom beeped.

"Sir?"

"Yes?"

"I have Director Stephenson from the FBI Lab on Line 2 for you."

"Really?" Professionally he only ever saw Boone's name in memoranda several times a year, when the Lab issued new protocols for collecting certain types of evidence. He hadn't actually talked to Boone in....shit, had to be ten years.

He picked up the receiver and hit the button. "Boehmer."

"Mitch. You still sound the same."

They'd been a year apart at the Academy, but Boehmer had practically shared a cubicle with Stephenson for two years in the huge New York office. At the time they'd both been assigned to white collar crimes, but longed to be big fish in the FBI pond. Boehmer had to admit that Stephenson had risen a bit higher in the food chain than he had, but he didn't resent that. Stephenson was smarter than he was, but Boehmer was a shark, and had earned every promotion through a combination of skill, ruthlessness, and unwavering devotion to the Bureau.

Boehmer smiled. "I wish I looked the same. I'm a lot older than I used to be. What's the occasion for the call?"

"Um, we need to meet, actually. A matter of some urgency and importance."

Boehmer was a bit nonplussed. "Really? Is there a problem with one of our cases? Something to do with the evidence we've submitted?"

"Something like that. Something that we need to discuss in person."

"In person?" Boehmer's schedule was booked solid for close to two weeks. There was no way he could make time to fly to D.C. "Can you just email me the particulars? You know how busy it gets, and I really can't take any time away from the office to head out there. At least not for a couple of weeks." And Stephenson fucking knew that. His request was highly irregular, anyway. There was a proper procedure for these sorts of things. Hell, the FBI had a proper procedure for everything.

"I'll be downstairs in ten minutes," Stephenson told him. "Meet me in the parking garage. We can talk over lunch."

"You're in Detroit?" *What the hell?*

"Yes, I flew in this morning. I meant it when I said this was important. Parking garage, ten minutes." And he hung up.

Boehmer's head was spinning. He shook it and looked across the car at Stephenson, who had aged very well, and still had all of his hair. Bastard. "You're really hitting me over the head with a sledgehammer here. Exactly who did you reach out to to find this hotshot hired gun who managed to get himself killed by a stupid private investigator?"

"I didn't reach out, I reached up," Stephenson told him. And gave Boehmer a name.

"You can't reach out—up—and get another name?" Boehmer ran a hand through his thinning hair. What Stephenson was asking wasn't something in his usual skill set.

"I...." Stephenson stopped, and breathed hard through his nose. "I'd rather not. This is a problem we should be able to solve ourselves without further involving people who *really* don't want to know anything more about this. They just want to know that it's done. You can call him, if you want, just to make sure I'm not crazy or something, but you saw for yourself."

Anderson's file was sitting on the console between the two of them. In it Boone had copies of Anderson's fingerprints as well as full sets of the two men whose prints he matched, Beiers and Gutierrez. He'd even brought along a jeweler's loupe so his former white collar crime unit co-worker could see for himself that the world as they knew it had changed.

"Yeah," Boehmer said woodenly. "Ourselves." He was no fool. He knew what needed to be done for the good of the country, and it didn't really bother him morally, but.... He shook his head, then looked at the Director of the FBI Lab. "You work with a lot of trained killers in your position? And how are we supposed to pay for something like that, even if we knew somebody? Did this guy of yours who got killed get paid?"

He really didn't want to think about having to kill Anderson himself. Just walking up to him, and shooting him, or maybe pulling him in on one pretense or another, only to shoot him in some abandoned warehouse or something.....cold blooded premeditated murder took stones he didn't think he had. He'd bent the rules and a few laws to put people in jail before, but this was a completely different level of danger and illegality he was not comfortable with.

Stephenson shook his head. "I presume so, but that was handled above my head."

"Well, thanks a lot for dropping this in my fucking lap."

"I'm not going away, it's still both our problem." He looked at Boehmer. After New York Stephenson had been promoted to a supervisory position, and never worked in the field again. Not only had Boehmer worked cases longer, he was the SAC for Detroit—he had to be a little closer to the nitty gritty than Boone was. "You don't have any ideas?"

"Not right now, but I'll think of something. I guess I have to."

CHAPTER FIFTEEN

They were about an hour from their last stop of the day when Joe came over the in-cab radio. "Dispatch to all trucks, dispatch to all trucks, we just heard on the news that they expect a verdict in the Fellatia Washington case tomorrow morning."

"What did he say?" Aaron said from the captain's chair in back.

The radio clicked back on, and they could hear laughing in the background. "Felanie Washington. What'd I say? The Felanie Washington case." They heard more laughing, and someone muffled the mike for a few seconds. "No I didn't. Did I? Anyway, considering the Detroit Police Department has publicly admitted they have contingency plans for rioting if the officers are found innocent, I want everybody working tomorrow to pay attention. Don't let yourselves get caught in the middle of anything. You've got armored cars, use them. You don't like the look of something, you've got an angry crowd or whatever at a stop, just drive away. Screw the delivery, you can go back another day. Most of you have probably never seen a real riot. Trust me, you don't want to. Dispatch out."

Aaron came forward and pressed his face against the mesh. "Fuck, who am I with tomorrow? Am I with you? Are you working tomorrow?"

"Yeah, I'm your driver."

He sank back into his chair with a sigh of relief. "Thank God. Well, shit should be interesting, anyway. Should I bring my shotgun?"

"If the shit hits the fan, a rifle'd be a lot more useful."

Aaron always got there before Dave, and the next morning Dave was amused to see Arlene's pink Geo Tracker in the lot. Dave parked next to it and went inside.

"What's up with your ride?" Dave asked him when Aaron showed up pushing the day's deliveries on the metal cart.

"Just in case the city burns today, that's the one car we've got that I wouldn't mind so much if it got torched."

"Ah."

"You wearing your plates?" Aaron asked him, tapping his own chest. His knuckle made a hard thunk. Soft body armor did a great job of stopping pistol bullets, but rarely did shit when it came to rifles. Most Kevlar vests had pockets in front (and sometimes back) where the wearer could slip in hard armor plates—steel, titanium, and ceramic were the three most common types.

After they loaded up Dave headed out the long chute toward the armored overhead door, and they waited while it clanked up out of the way, sounding like a medieval portcullis. When it was clear he drove straight across the street to the parking lot and stopped next to their cars.

"You want to take bets?" Aaron said to him, as he opened the rear of the Geo.

"On what, the verdict? Or a riot?" Dave popped the rear of the Cherokee and pulled out his rifle case. He stowed it in the cab of the truck along with another nylon shoulder bag.

"Either." Aaron closed up the Geo and climbed into the rear of the truck carrying a black nylon rifle case with a number of pouches sewn on the outside.

"If the verdict was Not Guilty, and this was Chicago or Los Angeles, then yes, I think we'd have a riot," Dave said. "Detroit? I don't think so. I just don't think the people who live here will get that worked up about it. They had to bus in half those protesters at the courthouse." As Dave pulled the truck out of the lot they both looked out the windows and watched Reggie pulling a riot shotgun out of his Impala. The sight seemed a little surreal.

They'd just left their fifth stop of the morning when Aaron, from the back, asked, "Why don't white people riot?"

"What?"

"Nobody worries about white people rioting in this country. The entire city is on edge and thinking there's going to be blood in the streets if the cops get off. Because the blacks are going to riot."

"You getting philosophical today?" Dave asked him. "Those riots in London a few years ago. Those were all white people. Or a lot of them."

"Right. In England. So it's not a racial thing, if white people in other countries are rioting. But in this country, white people in this country don't trash whole neighborhoods and burn cops cars. Nobody anywhere has ever said 'I hope them white-trash burger eatin' beer drinkin' redneck motherfuckers don't smash in my windows and steal all the stuff out of my store.' It's not a skin color thing, it's a cultural thing."

Dave shrugged. "I think anybody'll riot, you give them a good enough reason."

Aaron snorted. "Like winning a Super Bowl?"

"Shit, if the Lions won the Super Bowl, I'd be looking around for the second coming of Christ, 'cause you know the end has gotta be near. Check the Bible, I'm pretty sure that's one of the signs of the Apocalypse. That and the Cubs winning the pennant."

They made two more stops, then Aaron checked his watch. "Eleven thirty," he observed. "They say when they thought the verdict would come down?"

"You know as much as I do."

"Did you bring your competition rifle?" he asked Dave.

"No. My competition rifle is a little long for inside the truck, plus it's got a muzzle brake on it. And I forgot earplugs, so if I fired that thing in here I'd be deaf." Muzzle brakes vented the expanding gases from a cartridge up and to the sides, to reduce felt recoil in competition guns, so the shooter could make quicker follow-up shots. Modern brake designs were very effective, but made the rifles much louder to fire, as much of the blast was directed almost back toward the person firing the weapon. "This rifle's a little shorter, and it's got a military flash hider on it. So if I have to fire it out the gun port I probably will only have partial permanent hearing loss. You bring that rifle I had Doug build up for you?"

"I've only got one rifle," Aaron told him. "How many do you have?"

"Just those two." Aaron didn't make any smartass comments about Dave being a spoiled rich suburban white kid, because he knew how Dave had come by his money. "If you need to grab mine, it's got a red dot scope on it, a small Aimpoint, and the dot's already turned on. Just put the dot on the target and pull the trigger."

"The dot's on? Won't you burn out the battery?"

Dave laughed. "Batteries last for five years on those things."

"Five years?" Aaron could hardly believe that. "Turned on?"

"Yeah, why do you think the military likes 'em so much?"

"What kind of ammo did you bring?"

"My competition stuff." Aaron gave him a look, and Dave explained. "The most popular kind of rifle ammo in 3-gun competition is the same damn stuff that was developed specifically for the Special Forces in Afghanistan. Black Hills....shit, what does the military call it? Mark 262 Mod something-or-other. Heavy, 77-grain stuff that will knock down targets way the hell out there. It will also do a good job of going through car doors, if it comes to that today."

"How many magazines did you bring? I've only got three twenty-round magazines, and two thirty-rounders."

"Shit, if I have to pull that thing out of the case I'd be surprised. Even if there are cars on fire everywhere, I'm just planning on driving out of any trouble," Dave told him. "Tires flat, engine smoking, wheels on fire, whatever. Chauffeur you straight home in this, I have to. Actually, we'll go to my place. City's on fire, time to head north. But, just in case, I brought a whole bag of loaded magazines, ten or twelve thirty-rounders. Between the two of us that's about five hundred rounds. Unless the zombie apocalypse happens while we're out here we'll be fine."

"That would be so cool." Aaron stared out the windows at the passing scenery. Some areas of Detroit already looked like sets out of a post-apocalyptic zombie movie, all they needed were the zombies shambling around.

"Yeah, for about five minutes. Then it would suck for the rest of your life."

Twenty minutes later they were at a Comerica bank on the west side of the city, almost in Livonia. Dave kept his head on a swivel as Aaron loaded the dolly at the side door with boxes of coin. The assistant manager of the bank walked into view, maybe coming back from lunch, and gave Dave a wave. Dave couldn't remember his name exactly, Lloyd or Roy or something like that. He waved back.

The manager walked around the front of the truck as Aaron was bent down facing away from him, and said with a smile, "Stick 'em up."

Aaron spun around, pistol already in his hand and coming up, even as Dave's mouth opened to yell "NO!", but he knew he was going to be too late. Aaron finished the turn as his Colt came up, pushing out toward the threat, and.....nothing. He paused. The manager's eyes were saucers, his hands open and in front of him in a defensive gesture.

"Oh, Jesus, I'm sorry, that was stupid, that was the stupidest thing to say," he said, his mouth flying a hundred miles an hour. "I don't know what I was thinking. Oh my God, as I was saying it...."

Aaron stuffed his pistol back into its holster. "The fuck, Roy? You know how close I almost came to shooting you. *Holy shit.*" Aaron looked a little freaked out himself. "'*Stick 'em up*'? Really?"

"I'm sorry, I'm sorry," the assistant manager kept saying. "Oh, man. Here, let me get the door for you. Christ, thanks for not shooting me..." his voice faded as the two of them went into the bank.

Dave's heart was pounding in his chest, and all he'd been was a witness. Aaron had reacted so quickly, Dave hadn't even had a chance to yell. Saying *Stick 'em up* to an armored car guy on the job, talk about stupid. Heart loud in his ears, he went back to idly scanning the parking lot and the few pedestrians, looking for anything out of place. Aaron was back out less than ten minutes later, and Dave hit the switch for the side door.

"Can you believe that shit?" Aaron said as he plopped back into the captain's chair. "What a dumbass. Fuck." He looked at his hands. They weren't steady.

"You okay?" As far as he knew, Aaron had never had to shoot anybody. He'd seen him point his pistol at a few people, justifiably, but that was it.

"My hands are shaking from the adrenaline or something. Hit me on the way out. Man. I heard him, and spun around, and all I was looking for was a weapon. Saw his hands. If he'd had anything in his hands, a cell phone or anything, I think I might have shot him. It wasn't until I saw his hands were empty that I looked up and saw his face, saw it was Roy. Fuck."

"I don't think he'll make that mistake again," Dave said. "I think you made him piss his pants. I know it scared the crap out of me."

"Yeah? Let's get out of here. I'm hungry."

Their third stop after lunch was a Kroger grocery store off Greenfield Road, and Aaron had to unload nearly two dozen boxes of coin out of the back door. The store manager insisted on only ordering coin once a month, so their shipment, when it came, was usually large.

"Might as well get this over with," Aaron said with a groan as he heaved himself out of the chair. "Keep an eye out."

"Yeah." The grocery store was one of their busiest stops, and there was always a large amount of foot traffic in and out. Like pretty much every grocery store in the city, the customers were limited to using grocery carts inside the store. Outside the exit doors at a ten-foot radius was a line of concrete-filled steel posts spaced about a foot apart; customers would push their carts up to the posts, then take their bags of groceries out and walk to their cars. This prevented the carts from being stolen or, just as likely, pushed by a senior citizen back to their home, never to be seen again.

There was no place to park where they weren't in the way, or weren't being passed on either side by shoppers going in and out of the store, so Dave's head was constantly moving. The Kroger was in an L-shaped strip mall, right in the corner between a beauty supply store and a dollar store. In the mall parking lot were easily fifty cars—too many to scan every one, and even if Dave did see someone sitting in their car, so what? Lots of people sat in their cars for a while after arriving, listening to the radio or talking on the phone or whatever.

He'd learned over the past few years to ignore the parked cars, as he couldn't do anything about them. The thing to worry about was anybody who got close to the truck on foot, or any vehicle that stopped nearby. However, there were always vehicles pulling up to the door, in front of or behind or sometimes right next to the damn truck. Because the shoppers couldn't push the carts out to their cars they had their spouse pull the car up to the front of the building to load. In short, the location was a nightmare when it came to spotting approaching threats.

Dave saw a guy walking along the front of the beauty supply store toward the Kroger. He looked messed up, drunk or stoned or something, not staggering but definitely not right. As he got about fifty feet away he paused, and watched Aaron for a few seconds. Aaron was still pulling boxes of coin out of the back of the truck.

The guy was stocky and in a dirty shirt and pants. He had a medium tan and looked Chinese, or Hispanic—it was weird how those two ethnicities sometimes looked similar. Nothing in his hands, no weapon, but he definitely was eyeballing Aaron. The man had moved into the *possible threat* category.

"Aaron," Dave said cautioningly through the mesh.

"Yeah, I see him," Aaron said quietly. He set a box of coin down and turned to stare at the guy. The guy just stopped where he was and stared back for a three count, then looked around, like he wasn't sure where he was.

"Jesus," Aaron grumbled, and grabbed the next box of coin. He set it on the dolly, then turned to look inside the truck at Dave, who was peering out at him through the steel mesh. "Well?"

"Coming this way slowly now that you're not looking," Dave said. There was a little tension in his voice now. *Possible threat* had now become *probable threat*.

Aaron turned and stared directly at the man, who was now thirty feet away and had moved off the sidewalk into the traffic lane, but still hadn't shown a weapon. He was in his mid- to late-twenties and wearing work boots below jeans and a button-down shirt that had seen better days. The man blinked back at Aaron, then started walking along the building straight toward the Kroger, like he'd changed his mind or realized he was walking in the wrong direction. He crossed directly behind the truck, then began angling away from it. Aaron shook his head, stared at the man for another second, then turned to grab the small bag of cash destined for the Kroger safe. As soon as Aaron turned back to the truck the man, who apparently was watching their reflection in the window glass, turned toward the truck and took two steps.

"Aaron!" Dave said quickly, and before the spacey-faced man had taken another step Aaron had spun around toward him, drawing his pistol but not pointing it. Holding his pistol down along his leg, Aaron stared at the man now twenty feet away. Dave heard the metallic click as Aaron popped the safety off on his Colt.

"What?" Aaron said flatly. And then he just stood there, not moving, not looking away. Aaron was prepared to stand there for the rest of the afternoon, waiting for the guy to make his move. He had all the time in the world.

After about three very long seconds, the man mumbled something, then walked unsteadily away, along the front of the Kroger, away from the truck. Aaron kept his pistol out until the man was a hundred feet away.

"That dude fucking comes back, you let me know," Aaron said. "I'll call you on the phone before I leave the manager's office. And keep your eyes open, maybe he's got a partner." The view of the parking lot from the manager's office, where the safe was, was almost nonexistent.

"Got it."

Once Aaron was inside the store Dave didn't spot a single suspicious thing, and ten minutes later they were driving away in the truck.

"All right, get ready, that's two," Aaron said.

"What?"

"Things always happen in threes. First Roy nearly got hisself popped, and then space cadet keeps trying to get behind me, the next thing's going to be *it*. How many more stops we got?"

"You tell me. You're the one with the run sheet."

Aaron looked over his list. "Four more. Shit, okay. And still no word on the verdict? Fucking Joe."

Aaron was inside their second-to-last stop, a furniture rental center, when Joe came over the company radio. "All trucks, dispatch. Be advised, the jury has come back on the Washington case, and it's a mistrial, a hung jury, they can't come to a decision. That's a mistrial on the Washington case. Don't know if that will make people riot or not, but that's the news. Hope to see you all back here at the end of your runs safe and sound. Dispatch out."

A few minutes later Aaron hopped into the back with a small cash bag. Dave told him the news. "So that's it, that's your third," he told Aaron.

"What do you mean? Ain't shit happened."

"Roy almost got shot, weirdo at Kroger just avoided getting filled with holes, and the city escaped riots. Three close shaves."

"I don't know....maybe. Keep an eye out anyway. I'm not going to feel safe until I pick Arlene up and we're back home. How long's it take for a retrial?"

"For those cops? Months, at least. Maybe years."

"You still going to be doing this shit then?"

Dave shrugged. "Probably not. Honestly, I'm surprised I haven't heard from the FBI by now to schedule a physical or a polygraph, they've had my application for almost two months. I know they're hiring, and my grades kick ass, but that's not what's going to get me in, it's the letters of recommendation from the two agents and police chief. FBI has so many applicants, you really have to know someone to get in these days, or at least that's what I'm hearing."

"Or be a lesbian transsexual accountant. Police chief and FBI agents? They write good letters?"

"Oh yeah. Killer."

"Then what's the hold up?"

"It's the government, dude. Bureaucracy. FBI's huge. Since when has the government ever done anything quickly?"

They made it back to base without any further incident, and Dave waited for his partner while he checked the cash they'd brought back into the vault. It didn't look like there was going to be any civil unrest due to the hung jury, but just in case they walked out together. They ran into Elmo on the way out.

"How was your day?" Dave asked the kid.

"Boring," Elmo said. He looked hot, and he'd already untucked his uniform shirt.

"Boring's good in this line of work, it means nobody's trying to rob you," Aaron pointed out.

"Hey, where's your Mustang?" Elmo asked Aaron when they got to the parking lot.

"Drove the girlfriend's car today."

"That's a sweet ride. I'd love to have that car. Put some spinners on it, it would look awesome."

Aaron turned to look at him, his mouth wide. "That sweet ride is a 1971 Ford Mustang Mach 1 fastback. All original interior. If you put spinning rims on it God would fucking smite you. The ghost of Steve McQueen would kill you, bring you back to life, and kill you again."

"I don't know," Dave volunteered while standing next to his Cherokee, not doing a good job of keeping the smile off his fact. "Spinners might look cool."

Elmo asked, "Steve who?"

John Phault opened the door, saw Bob looking over the front of the house. "This the new place? Not bad."

Smiling wide, John grabbed the man's hand, then swept him in in a tight hug. "How you doing? You look good. Tan. Come on in."

Bob smiled. "Yeah, well, not much for me to do in places that see a lot of snow." He followed John into the kitchen.

"If you're wearing a jacket in this weather, I'm guessing you're still spending a lot of time in hot places. You want something to drink? Beer, pop, water?"

"Water'd be good," Bob said, taking off his jacket. "What is it outside, eighty-five? Baghdad's about thirty degrees hotter than this right now, although the humidity's a lot lower."

John handed him a bottle of water and checked him out. He hadn't seen Bob in almost two years, although he talked to him several times a year. Still solid as a rock, he'd felt that in the hug, although the years—or the hot weather—had thinned him down some. Still the same damn Popeye forearms. "You look good." He eyed the Glock on Bob's hip. "I thought you just flew in this morning. Where'd the Glock come from?"

"Brought it with me."

"Oh." John was ignorant about international travel with a firearm, especially coming from countries most people tried to avoid. He was also a little fuzzy on whether Bob currently officially worked for the U.S. government, a

Defense Department contractor or sub-contractor, or a private company. It didn't matter, not really, and by not asking, Bob didn't need to not answer him.

He'd called Bob three days earlier, as he was the only person John knew who might be able to help him. He was actually surprised when Bob answered the phone. "Damn, I was expecting voicemail," he'd said, looking at his phone. "Where are you?"

The connection wasn't too bad. "Right now I'm in Turkey," Bob told him. "But I'll be home in two days, unless the Syrians invade. What's up?"

"I've got some business-related questions to ask you, but shit, I'd love to see you. It's been too long. You, uh....."

"What?"

"You don't have any problems getting into the country?"

"What? No, why would I? I never had any international problems."

"You weren't told to avoid the States for a while?"

"No, not technically, but shit, I didn't have a choice, they stationed me in Afghanistan for two years, then Thailand. Plus, you know....I had shit to work out on my own. I didn't want to come back, not for a while."

"You ever have any problems with law enforcement at Customs? People recognizing you?"

"No. All that was too long ago. Most people can't remember what they watched on TV last night."

"Hmm. Okay. Well, will you have time to get together when you're here?"

"Sure, not a problem. I should be getting in Tuesday morning, I'll call you when I land." And he had, right on schedule.

"You look good," Bob told him, sipping at the water. "Still working out."

John shrugged. "More muscle, more gray hair." He pulled a bottle of Diet Coke out of his refrigerator, and twisted off the cap. "I've got a name and a face, I'm wondering if you know the guy, or can run him by some people. I'm wondering if he's in your line of work."

"Which line of work is that?" Bob smiled at him.

"Shit." John laughed. "Private contracting, executive protection, I don't know. For all I know you're still in and doing super secret ninja stuff with Delta Force or CAG or Dev Group or The Unit or whatever the hell they're calling themselves now, seems like they change it every year. But it's a relatively small world, isn't it? Small number of guys at the Tier 1 level."

"Dev Group is SquEALs," Bob corrected him.

"Squeals? Nice. Okay, whatever, whoever. So?"

Bob shrugged. "Depends."

"On what?"

"On who you're working for, and what you're doing. Private contracting....yeah, that's a pretty small world. If you don't know somebody, you know somebody who knows them, heard of them, or worked with them. On the government side, though, the black work, the operations end on the spook side.... a lot of them originally come from the spec-ops community, but a lot of them are grown and trained in-house, and never interact with anybody else."

"I've got a picture, and a name," John said. He thumbed through his phone, and then handed it over to Bob. "Ralph Marsh is the name I have. He had fake ID in another name, Robert Williams, but was ID'd through his fingerprints. Marsh was 10th Mountain, Airborne, Ranger, two tours in Afghanistan, very early on. Don't know what he did afterward, which is where you come in."

Bob looked at the photo. "This guy looks very, very unhappy."

"Smart ass. That's a crime scene photo."

Bob shook his head. "Marsh?"

"Yeah. Ralph Marsh."

Bob shook his head again. "Name's not familiar, and I don't recognize him. Can you send me this photo? I'll check with a few people." He looked closer at the photo. "Who killed him, you?"

"Yeah. He gunned down a couple of cops who rolled up on him. Headshots with a pistol like it was easy. He could shoot. He was in a van, and I saw him pull up when I was on a surveillance. I actually pointed his vehicle out to the cops. Detroit thinks maybe he was there to take me out, because he had a rifle in the car, but I don't know him, and haven't done anything lately that would make somebody want to kill me."

"That you know of."

John shrugged. "That I know of," he admitted. "But I have pissed off a lot of people in the past, as you well know. Plus...." He sighed, and shook his head. "I'm the guy who sent the cops over to talk to him. I own a small part of what he did."

Bob glanced up from the phone at his friend, but didn't say anything. He knew all about survivor's guilt. He tried to expand the photo, but accidentally exited the photo gallery. He was about to hand the phone back to John when he saw the background photo. "Whoa. Who's this? You got a girlfriend?"

John took the phone and looked at the picture. "No, that was an EP gig I had about six months ago. It was taken by one of her people as we were leaving the club."

"One of whose people?"

John pointed the phone back at Bob. "Her. Gianna Michaels."

Bob shook his head. "Never heard of her. She's cute. She an actress or something? Nice rack." He figured she was probably an actress if she was paying for EP—Executive Protection, otherwise known as a bodyguard.

John smiled. "Or something. You sure you don't recognize her? How much time are you spending at home?"

Bob gave him an appraising look. "I moved out of my parents' house fifteen years ago. That's the last 'home' I had."

"What about the U.S.? How much time are you out of the country?"

"Out? More like how much in. In the last ten years, I've been in the U.S. maybe a total of a year. No shortage of work in the world today, and people who are willing to pay very well for it to get done."

CHAPTER SIXTEEN

Hartman waited until both her daughters were in the Macy's dressing room before he walked up. "Mrs. Wilson? I'm Pete Hartman, with the FBI."

She turned to look and saw a white man in a suit, and her brief confusion turned to anger in a heartbeat. "What the fuck are you doing here? Are you following me? This is harassment. I'm going to call our lawyer." Her voice kept going higher and higher.

And she'd seemed so level headed, Hartman thought to himself. He quickly cut her off. "This is me trying to keep your husband out of jail," he said, keeping his voice down. "This is me trying to work out an unofficial deal so that your daughters don't grow up visiting your husband in prison. My offer is no prison time, he and all of his guys walk, and nobody has to testify."

"We have a lawyer, you just can't—" she started.

"I'm not here, and we're not having this conversation," he told her. "If I talked to your lawyer, people would find out. We have your husband under surveillance. Tell him that if he and all of his buddies want to walk away from all of this, free, no jail time, he should meet me at the McDonald's at Fenkell and Telegraph tomorrow morning at 9."

"What?"

"Don't talk about this with him in your house, or even in your back yard, because we're listening. And tell him not to drive either one of your cars to the meet, we have GPS trackers on them. McDonald's at Fenkell and Telegraph, tomorrow morning, nine a.m.," he told her, then turned on his heel and walked away as quickly as he could without drawing attention to himself. He was as shaky and nervous as he'd been on his first raid, and was sweating so hard it was about to show through his shirt.

His wife had barely remembered the man's name, the guy claiming to be an FBI agent, but Wilson recognized it. He'd met him, briefly, during his arrest and processing. The man was a supervisor of some sort.

Contacting his wife like that, it was highly irregular, way over the line, and could get the fed in trouble, but the fed had to know it....so why had he done it? What bullshit was he talking about, walking away with no jail time? Wilson knew he should just pretend he hadn't heard a thing, that the man had never spoken to his wife, but.....he couldn't. He knew he and his guys were facing serious lockup. He wasn't quite sure what evidence the feds had, but he and his boys would need something on the good side of a miracle to stay out of prison.

He'd left the house before dawn, sneaking out the back door and hopping a few fences to cut over to Stahelin. He'd walked a good half mile to a bus stop, then waited impatiently for one to arrive. It had been years, decades maybe, since he'd ridden a bus in the city, and they hadn't gotten any nicer. He rode around for forty-five minutes, then got off and walked a zig-zagging mile through a neighborhood until he was sure nobody was following him. Then he cut three streets over to his cousin's house and borrowed her car.

"I'm glad you showed up," Hartman said, looking up from where he sat in the booth at the back of the McDonald's. There was a coffee sitting in front of him.

"No," Wilson said, shaking his head. "You want to talk, not here. Where you parked?"

"Out back. Toyota pickup." Hartman had driven his personal vehicle to the meeting.

"I'll meet you there," Wilson told him, then walked off.

Hartman was standing next to his truck when Wilson pulled up in an aging navy blue Lincoln Continental. Wilson rolled down his window, but didn't get out.

"You want me to get in?" Hartman asked.

Wilson shook his head. "Not yet. First, take off your jacket, tie, shoes, belt, and empty all of your pockets. Wallet, cell phone, pens, keys, everything, and put them into your ride."

"I'm not wearing a wire," Hartman said, but proceeded to partially disrobe anyway. "Gun too?" he asked Wilson.

"You're lucky I don't make you strip down to your underwear in this parking lot," Wilson told him. When Hartman was down to pants, socks, and shirt, he held up his car keys. "What about these?"

"No. Stick them under the bumper or something."

"Shit." With his luck, his truck would get stolen, with his FBI badge wallet and sidearm inside, but Hartman did as Wilson asked. "We good?"

"No, we not good, but you can get in the car now."

Hartman walked around the car in his socks and got into the passenger seat. "Okay," he started to say.

"No," Wilson said, shaking his head. "We're not doing this here. Just shut up until I tell you."

Hartman was getting a little pissed, but he figured that was good. If he was pissed, it kept him from that terrified feeling he usually got if he thought at all about what they were doing. He sat quietly as Wilson headed north up Telegraph, out of Detroit into Southfield, then got onto the I-696 freeway heading west. He stayed in the left lane, and just after passing over Inkster Road pulled onto the left shoulder, next to the concrete dividing wall. The shoulder was barely wide enough for their car, and the Lincoln rocked as the passing cars whipped by. I-696 there was four lanes across, with a 70-mph speed limit. Which meant everyone did 80.

Wilson turned and looked at the FBI agent. "Take off your pants, pull down your underwear, and pull up your shirt," he said flatly. "I don't know how small the feds are making bugs and wires these days, but I don't trust you one fucking bit, Mr. FBI Extra Special Agent Hartman."

Hartman stared at him icily for a few seconds, then did it. His mission was too important to let this asshole's petty games distract him from what needed to be done. It was a little awkward stripping in the seat, and he was trying not to flash anybody in a passing car, but finally he'd shown the cop everything he had. "Okay, satisfied? I'm not wearing a wire or any sort of recording device. I don't want a record of this conversation taking place any more than you do, trust me, but—empty *your* pockets, let me see your phone, all the same bullshit you just pulled on me."

Wilson gave him a dirty look, but complied. Hartman had to admit that the man had picked a good spot—it'd be impossible to do surveillance on the two of them, or record what was being said in the car. Four lanes of traffic whipping by them on the right, a four-foot tall concrete wall to their left, and not an entrance or an exit ramp to the freeway in either direction within a mile and a half. He idly wondered whose car they were in—it had definitely seen better days, and smelled dusty.

When Hartman was convinced that Wilson wasn't recording anything either, he sat back. "Okay, you remember who I am?"

"I saw you when I was getting processed," Wilson said.

"I am the Assistant Special Agent in Charge of the Detroit office of the FBI. The ASAC." He pronounced it *A-sack*. "I am the number two guy in the entire Detroit office. So I am the guy who makes things happen," he told the cop. "And let me tell you what I know. You are well and truly fucked. You're not buried yet, but you could be, very shortly."

Wilson just stared, and let the fed talk. "I'll tell you what we've got for evidence so far. First, the shell casing from the AK-47 that I believe Eddie Mitchell fired inside Coconuts, our lab guys have already matched it to the rifle we pulled out of his basement. Couldn't match the slug, that was too damaged, no fingerprint on the case, but we can put that rifle inside that club at the time of the robbery. Your partner Gabriel, he made the mistake of keeping his cell phone on him during three of the robberies. We went back and checked the GPS records, and they can place that phone within a couple hundred yards of those three clubs at the same approximate time of the robberies. Circumstantial, I admit, but it adds up.

"Motive is always something to look for, and with you I think it's pretty clear. You've got two daughters in private school, two new cars, and a wife who likes to shop. We ran the numbers, and it appears that you're spending several hundred dollars a month more that what you're actually pulling in from working."

"Lots o'folk livin' beyond their means."

"Sure. And we didn't find any cash hidden in your house, or in anybody's house for that matter. Haven't found any storage units filled with bills either. Everybody has been pretty smart about not spending their cash. Well, almost everybody."

"What do you mean?"

Hartman smiled. "I thought Mitchell would be the weak link in you four. He's twitchy, and he actually fought during the arrest. He hurt one of my guys, and Mitchell got pretty banged around. Had to take him down to St. John's and get him stitched up. Well, you know, they took a blood sample while he was down there, and that blood sample tested positive for both cocaine and marijuana."

Wilson stared at him, blinked, and then sighed. "Shit." He shook his head.

Hartman studied him for a second. "You didn't know?"

"He's been off for a while, not himself, but I just thought….well, not coke. I didn't think he'd be that stupid. He know better than that."

"Apparently not. And like I said, I thought he'd be the weak link of you four, especially since the case comes back to the rifle we found at his house, but he hasn't given us shit. Your buddy Gabriel, on the other hand…are you wondering why he didn't make bail? Why he's still in?"

Wilson shrugged. "I guess he didn't have the collateral. It was a lot of money."

"It was a lot of money. It's even more when you owe thirty-two thousand dollars to two casinos."

"What?"

"Yeah. For a quiet guy, he really likes to wager, Blackjack mostly, but apparently he's not very good at it. Or he's unlucky. I'm pretty sure he's got a marker at the Windsor Casino too, but that's Canada; they won't tell us shit. Motor City Casino, MGM Grand, they like your buddy Gabe. He's a high-roller. What do they call him? A whale. And he's been a little iffy during the interviews already. Showing cracks, maybe. So he's in debt, bad, and it's his phone that puts him near three of the robberies. He's the one who's going to flip on the rest of you, make a deal. Bet on it."

"Why are you telling me all this?" Wilson said to the man.

"I just wanted to make sure you knew where we stood. Right now what we've got is all circumstantial, but if we find any of that cash, or if one of your guys flips, you're done."

"You giving me all the goods, what put you on to us in the first place?" Wilson asked. He'd always been curious about that, ever since the FBI showed up at his door. There was always a chance they'd get caught, he knew that, but he always thought it would be during the robbery itself.

"When Mitchell fired that round into the ceiling? One of you guys, my money's on you, called him 'Roo'. And apparently the detective handling the case had heard that nickname before."

"Fuck," Wilson said, sagging in the seat. Of all the dumb luck. One word. And Ringo, one of the few detectives in the department who actually knew Mitchell's nickname, happened to be working the case. He knew Ringo just hadn't been wandering by that day he came by the house. Fucking Lady Luck was a cast-iron bitch. He looked at the FBI agent. "Okay, so what do you want? Why are we talking?"

"You could have a tape of the conversation we'd just had, and are about to have, and take it to my boss and you'd still end up with serious jail time for the robberies," Hartman told him. "We'd be in prison together. What I'm offering is a way to get all of you out of jail, charges dropped. Probably even back on the department."

"Now how the fuck you going to do that? And why?"

"The why is because you need to do something for us. But let's get to the how, first. The how is that I can make that shell casing disappear. Right now that case is the only thing that directly ties any of you to a robbery. There's no blood evidence, no fingerprints, all we've got is a fired case found at one scene that came out of a rifle we pulled out of Mitchell's basement. Without that case, the rifle is worthless.

The cell phone GPS records? They can only put him within a couple hundred yards of the robberies. The cell phone records are completely circumstantial, and not nearly enough if that's all we've got. If you get Gabe out of jail, bail him out and convince him everything is going to be fine, I can make that shell casing disappear. It's small, and I could toss it into my pocket easily, I'm in and out of the evidence vault all the time. As long as we don't find piles of that stolen cash laying around somewhere, there's no way we'll be able to prove shit unless one of you confesses. You guys have actually done a very good job covering your tracks. I can't imagine an AUSA even willing to press forward with what we'd have left. You might even be able to get that blood test on Mitchell quashed, because they didn't ask for his permission before taking it."

Wilson knew they'd never find his share of the cash, and was pretty sure the other guys had been smart with theirs as well. Hell, Gabe might not even have any left, the way this fed was talking, but without that shell case from Roo's AK....the man was right. They wouldn't have enough for a conviction. Not even close, not unless one of them rolled on the others.

"And why would you make that shell case disappear?" Wilson asked him. "What would I have to do?"

Hartman looked at the burly SWAT cop. "You'd have to kill someone."

Wilson blinked. "'Scuse me?"

"You heard me." Hartman made a face, then repeated, "We need you to kill someone."

"The fuck are you talking about? And who's 'we'?"

"'We' is the FBI, unofficially. I'm not here on my own, I'm not nuts, or a psycho, this is something that's come down from....well, all the way from the top, pretty much." As weird as it was for him to say it, it was pretty much true. *The things we do for the Bureau,* Hartman thought. Actually, he realized, it wasn't just for the Bureau, it was for every law enforcement agency in the country. If the kid didn't die...it would be bad for the whole country. Bad on an epic scale. Hartman gave a little smile. "You understand now why we had to meet in secret."

"Are you—what......who the fuck you want me to kill? What he do?" Wilson was stunned. Of course he'd had no idea why the FBI agent had wanted to meet with him in secret, and suspected that no good would come of it, but he'd had few options. His wife had put it very succinctly the night before when they'd been out walking around the block, talking under their breath.

"Don't go," she told him. "You don't know what that motherfucker wants. It can't be good."

"It can't be any worse," he told her. "I've been telling you not to worry, but that ain't cuz there's nothing to worry about."

Paul Wilson had shot three people in his twelve years on the job, two of whom had died, so killing a man was something that wasn't unknown to him. But just flat out murdering someone.... "Who is he? What'd he do?" he asked the FBI agent.

Hartman shook his head. "I can't tell you."

"Bullshit."

"I can't. You're better off not knowing, anyway. But I'm telling you the truth, killing him....it's actually the right thing to do. In....so many ways. He has to die."

Wilson sat there and thought for a long time. "Who is he?" he asked finally. "A drug dealer, a cop, the President?"

"He's nobody, really. He's a twenty-five year old kid. Lives in the area. Working as a private investigator right now."

"He such a nobody, why you need him dead?" Wilson growled. He huffed. "I suppose you need it to look like an accident or some spy bullshit like that too, am I right?" Candid Camera, that was the show, right? He kept expecting somebody to pop up with a camera, yelling "Gotcha!"

"No," Hartman said. "We don't care how it happens, we don't care what it looks like, he just needs to be dead. Although, making it look like a botched robbery or some other crime will be better for everyone. Less attention."

"Private investigator? You sure this kid wasn't snooping and saw you putting the wood to his wife, or your boss? Sure this isn't personal?"

Hartman laughed. "We had a female agent, a real piece of work, she had a bad break up with her boyfriend. He traveled overseas a lot, worked for a medium size company. She went to his boss. Told the boss hey, my boyfriend, your employee, he isn't who you think he is, he's actually a CIA NOC, an honest-to-goodness fucking spy."

"Yeah, so, she's nuts."

Hartman shook his head. "No, the dude actually *was* a CIA NOC. Hell hath no fury and all that shit. She blew his freaking cover to his boss.....lucky for her, the guy's boss already knew about his cover, and called our office. And you know what? She didn't get fired, she's still there. Still doing the job. The Bureau protects its own. So trust me, Channel 7 could get video of me banging a poodle in the Mayor's limo, and as long as I was wearing a condom all that would happen is I'd get assigned to desk duty in Kansas for six months. This....this is way beyond that. Way beyond."

Wilson sat silently and thought. The *why* of it bothered him. He knew he wouldn't be having this conversation with Hartman if they were just talking about some ordinary twenty-five year old kid working as a P.I. The FBI wanted him dead for a reason. Not knowing that reason, when you were the person they were asking to do it, really bothered him. Hell, maybe it wasn't even the FBI that wanted him dead, maybe they were the ones just delivering the instructions. Maybe the word was coming from above them, or from some other agency. Maybe Hartman's story about the CIA was a hint. Could this dude they wanted him to kill be a spy? Or maybe a terrorist? Shit. What the hell had he gotten himself into?

"Why you don't do it yourselves?"

Hartman shrugged. "In case something goes wrong. If you fuck it up, it's on you, not us."

"Yeah. Even if I agreed to do this, what guarantee would I have that you'd make that shell casing disappear?"

"I can't give you one. But why wouldn't I? It'd be so easy. It's just one case, in a plastic evidence bag. We misplace stuff all the time, and something that small….nobody would even miss it until they went to look for it. Stealing that case will be a lot easier and simpler than not doing it, with me then wondering how you're going to react, what you're going to say to who about what we've talked about today. Not that you'd have any evidence we ever talked, but you could make my life uncomfortable for a while."

Wilson shook his head. "Fuck. This….fuck…this kid got a name, an address?" He still hadn't decided he'd do it, or at least that's what he kept telling himself.

"I've got everything you need on a flash drive back at my truck," Hartman told him. "If my truck's still there."

Wilson sat in his car in the McDonald's parking lot for ten minutes, long after the FBI agent had driven off, staring at the flash drive in his palm. Finally, shaking his head, he stuck the flash drive in his pocket, then reached underneath the dash of the big car. The digital recorder was right where he'd left it.

CHAPTER SEVENTEEN

The more time he spent on the road, the more convinced Dave was that the majority of people who had driver's licenses....shouldn't. Either they didn't have the mental capacity to process traffic patterns, the reflexes to avoid trouble, or the innate intelligence to know texting in rush hour traffic was bad.

The driving style of most Michigan drivers seemed to resemble children on a playground. Fierce surges in speed, abrupt changes of direction, and a complete randomness in decision-making that couldn't be anticipated or defended against. No sense of impending collision. When he was first driving Dave didn't really understand road rage. After three years of trying to follow people in thick traffic, he understood it all too well. He pulled into a parking lot and called his boss.

"Yeah, what's up?" There was no background noise on John's end of the phone, and Dave assumed he was at home or the office.

"He took off about eleven thirty, got gas at the corner, then ran the red light at Greenfield. I couldn't because I was blocked by cars. He was almost out of sight by the time I cleared the light and the idiots blocking the road, and when I got to Southfield I had no idea if he kept going west on 7 Mile or jumped on the freeway. I picked Southfield northbound and tried that, then circled back and searched the lots around Northland Mall. Nothing. You want me to head back to his house, see if he shows up?"

John thought for a bit. "What time did you start, six? Go ahead and break it off, we're about up against the budget on this one. He look like he was going anywhere in particular?"

Dave shook his head in the car. "Dressed in a t-shirt and jeans, wasn't carrying anything."

"Yeah, forget it, you're done for the day. Head on home and work out, maybe do something with Gina. Uh, I mean..." He hadn't meant it the way it sounded, but Dave just laughed. John couldn't believe Dave was dating a stripper and hadn't told anyone. Shit, if he was dating a stripper, especially one who looked like her, he'd be telling *everyone*. And showing pictures. "When are you working for me again?"

"You've got Brad and me doing that two-man surveillance on Leticia Matson Thursday."

"That's right, the Indy Car racer." She owned a little Honda and drove like she was trying to qualify for the World Rally Cup. They'd tried working her twice with just one guy, and she'd lost the investigator both times. John didn't even think she was aware she was being followed, she was just crazy. Maybe they'd have better luck with two cars on her. "Okay, talk to you then."

Dave was back home and pulling into the garage before 1 p.m. Short days were nice, as long as they didn't happen too often. Even though he didn't have many bills, thanks to the inheritance, he still had some, and getting home early cut into the bottom line when you were getting paid by the hour.

The house had nearly been paid off when his parents had been killed; in fact, the Mustang had taken a larger chunk out of his bank account than paying off the house had. However, even though he didn't have a house or car payment, he had property taxes, utilities, grocery bills, insurance payments — the regular expenses everyone had living their life — and he didn't want to have to dip into the remainder of his inheritance to pay for those. So he always tried to work forty hours a week, if not more. Sometimes the claimants didn't cooperate.

Once he got on with the FBI, he knew he'd be making a lot more money, but he wasn't there yet. They were taking forever to process his application. Until he got on the government dole himself, he had to watch the money coming in and going out, and earning interest on the leftover inheritance was a smart move. He had a chunk of the money invested in CDs, and some more in municipal bonds, because by the time he was old enough to retire he knew Social Security will have collapsed under its own Ponzi Scheme weight. He was no genius, but he could do basic math — too many retirees living too long, and too many young people already on government aid, balanced against an ever-shrinking workforce, equaled disaster. It couldn't continue.

The house echoed with the sound of the interior garage door banging against the side of the refrigerator, as it had his whole life. His parents had bought the house two years before he was born, and he'd grown up in it. Unlike those kids whose parents moved every few years, it was the only home he'd ever known. He'd thought about selling it when his parents died, but there were no bad memories for him at the house. Maybe if they'd died there he might feel differently, but they'd died twenty miles away, while he was away at school. Coming home after the funeral, the house hadn't filled him with sadness, it had just seemed....empty. Quiet. If it had continued to bother him he believed he would have been able to sell the house, but he'd grown used to living alone in a house big enough for a teeming family.

The keys to the Jeep clanked as he tossed them onto the kitchen counter. He cracked the refrigerator out of habit, but as he stared at the nearly bare interior he realized he wasn't hungry or thirsty. Hmm. He looked around, and saw the latest book he was reading on the table in the breakfast nook. It was a hugely long thriller by Neal Stephenson about computer gamers and Russian mobsters, but he was having a hard time getting into it.

The clock above the sink ticked loudly with every advance of the second hand. The refrigerator hummed and vibrated slightly in his hand, which was still on the handle. Shit. He had all sorts of time to do whatever he wanted, he just didn't feel like doing anything. Didn't feel like working out, or practicing his draw, really didn't feel like mowing the lawn. He was glad Gina was working, because he didn't feel like company, either.

He headed upstairs with the vague idea of changing his clothes. The house was a hair over 2400 square feet, which was far bigger than he needed. Honestly, it was larger than his parents had needed, but they'd bought the house when they had plans to start a family.

Dave had actually had a brother, an older brother who'd died of meningitis when Dave was only a few months old. He of course had no memories of Robby, and his parents never talked about him. Once he got old enough he knew not to ask. Occasionally he wondered how that had changed them as people, and as parents. Losing a child, especially a two-year-old, to some random disease, had to have been devastating for them. He wondered how his life was different because of the death of his brother. Dave hadn't been an only child, and yet he had. Were his parents easier on him because he was all they had, or all they had left? He'd asked them once why he didn't have any other brothers and sisters, and his mother had just replied, "I guess because God wants it that way." Which, he supposed, meant they'd tried, but it had never happened. And so the house had always seemed a bit big and empty.

In addition to the master bedroom, there were three bedrooms on the second floor. The master bedroom had its own bathroom, and walk-in closet, but the other bedrooms shared a bathroom off the stairway. His engineer father had turned one of the bedrooms into his home office, and his mother had claimed another as her sewing room. Dave had boxed their stuff up and put in the basement, but that was it. He knew, someday, he'd have to do something with it, but he hadn't gotten there yet, even though it had been years.

The master bedroom was huge, with windows on three sides. While he'd left the furniture in the rest of the house alone, he just couldn't sleep in his parents' bed. He'd replaced it with an expensive king-sized mattress and new wrought iron bed frame. The house was so quiet that he could hear the birds chirping outside even with the windows closed. Sunlight was slanting in through the back window, and dust particles sparkled in the golden light.

He walked to the dresser beside the bed, a chest-high dark brown walnut piece probably older than he was. With a sigh he pried his shoes off and kicked them under the dresser. As he did that, his eye was caught by a photo. The frame was dusty, and he realized he probably hadn't cleaned it off since the house had become his. Hell, he hadn't looked at it in years, even though it was right there. The photo was of his parents standing side by side in the sun — in the back yard, actually — his mother's hand on top of Dave's head. How old was he there, four, five? His parents looked so much younger in the photo than he remembered them. Happy, even though their dream of a big family hadn't worked out.

Dave sat down on the bed, photo in his hands, and burst into tears.

CHAPTER EIGHTEEN

John had a rule—and it was a good rule—that you didn't shit where you ate. Doing surveillance on someone anywhere near your own house was a very bad idea. If they spotted you, spotted your vehicle, and you lived four cities over, that was one thing, but if you lived two blocks over, that could cause some serious problems. Which was why he hadn't even considered giving Dave the domestic surveillance right around the corner from his house, in the same subdivision, even though it was supposed to be a cake walk. The wife was heading out of town Friday morning, and she wanted her husband followed from work on Friday. She thought he had a girlfriend, and figured her long-arranged trip out of town would be a perfect opportunity for him to misbehave, if that's what he was actually up to.

The wife had given John a description of her husband's vehicle, including the plate, the address where he worked, the names and addresses of the guys who were his closest friends, everything he might need to know and then some. If her husband went straight home after work, she wanted John to sit on him until eleven o'clock, then he could break off, because her husband never stayed up past eleven.

"And Saturday?" John had asked her.

"Oh no, if he does anything, it will be on Friday night," she told him.

"But you're not coming back until Sunday afternoon, right?"

"Yes?"

"It just seems to me he could just as easily do something on Saturday as Friday. Maybe more likely, as he doesn't have to work."

"Do you give a discount for working on the weekend?" she asked him.

"Uh, no, sorry."

"Then just Friday."

So that was how John had found himself doing a surveillance roughly three hundred yards, as the crow flew, from Dave's house on a Friday night. To add insult to injury, Dave went jogging by about eight o'clock, and gave a little wave as he passed John's SUV. Fucker.

Before Dave was back from his run, John left him a voicemail on his cell phone. "Yeah, ha ha, enjoy your run. Listen, I don't think this guy's going anywhere tonight, and we're wasting the client's money. I really think he's more likely to do something tomorrow. Even though she's too cheap to pay for it, I want to sit on this guy tomorrow for a few hours, but I've got something to do tomorrow morning. Can you sit on him until about nine? Maybe start at seven? Give me a call, let me know."

Dave listened to the message when he got back, and called John. "He still there?"

"I can see the TV. He's not going anywhere."

"Girlfriend could stop by."

"Yeah. Can you sit on this for a couple hours tomorrow? I know it's a little close to home."

The only plans Dave had for Saturday were to head over to the range and get some practice time in with the rifle. Considering the range didn't open until nine a.m. anyway.... "Yeah, sure, not a problem."

"All right. I'll email you his info. Right now he's parked in the attached garage, the only car in there, and there's nothing else in his driveway or parked anywhere near the house. You show up and there's anything parked nearby, get the plate. Make sure to call into the Troy P.D., otherwise they'll roll on you. And I'll be back at nine."

"You know, this isn't….." Wilson began, turned in the driver's seat of his Charger.

"Even if you're just gonna take a look at him we should be there," Parker said from the front passenger seat. "I don't trust the feds for shit." He looked to Gabe in the back for agreement.

"This whole thing is fucked," Gabe said. He was looking decidedly depressed.

"We're fucked," Wilson said. "Even if this is a clear way out, not knowing why they want this kid done really bothers me. We don't know what we're getting into." In his heart he still hadn't decided whether or not he could go through with it. If everything Hartman had told him was true, then it was a way out, but that was a real big fucking *if*.

He hadn't told any of his crew about the digital recording he had of his meeting with Hartman. That was his insurance. The only person he'd said anything to was his wife. And with her he'd only hinted that he had something that might help. He could always offer the recording to the FBI, in hopes the trade of a dirty agent would make them go easier on him, allow him to plea to a much lesser charge, but what about Gabe, Eddie, and Parker? No way the FBI would go easy on all of them. "Where is Eddie? Wasn't he going to be here?"

Wilson looked around the parking deck of the MGM Casino. He'd pulled the FBI's GPS tracker off his car—because he could, fuck 'em—and he'd told everybody else to meet him there, but to make sure they slipped their tails and didn't take their own rides. If the FBI still had them all under surveillance—and that was a good bet—they wouldn't be expecting them to be out this early on a Saturday. Only Parker had seen any hint of a tail car when he'd left his house, and he'd lost them pretty quickly — FBI didn't know how to follow shit unless they had eight cars, a helicopter, and a GPS tracker in the wheel well. The parking deck was remarkably full of cars, and Wilson idly wondered if they belonged to people who'd arrived early to gamble, or had just never gone home.

"I talked to him last night," Parker told him. "I gave him what info you had, and he was going to try and run the kid, see if he had a record."

"With who?"

"I don't know, but you know Roo, he knows a lot of people. I told him nothing official, nothing that could be traced back to him. But I didn't hear back, and he knew you wanted to meet this morning."

"We might as well do a drive-by," Gabe said from the back seat. "Got nothing else to do. What am I going to do, go home and sit around listening to the FBI listening to my ass?"

The flash drive Hartman had given Wilson had been full of information on the kid they wanted gone. In fact, there was almost too much info on it. It worried him. Where'd they get all the info? From who? Kid's work history, medical history, vehicles, photo, everything. Satellite photo of his house, so at least Wilson didn't have to worry about that. Punching an address into his home computer....at this point he assumed everything he did online was being monitored by the feds. There it was, that twinge in his gut again. Was it an ulcer? Wouldn't surprise him, all the stress he'd been under. Worst fucking month of his life.

He was carrying his Glock. He'd be damned if he'd roll around unarmed in this city, he'd put too many assholes behind bars. The department had pulled his badge, and his issue Glock, but he had his own spare Glock .40 and a

Concealed Pistol License. The FBI hadn't found it when they'd searched his house, and he wasn't about to turn it over. Until he got convicted of a felony, he was still legal.

"Fuck it, let's at least check out the house. Maybe he's got a 'I Want To Kill the President' sign on his front lawn, swastikas in the windows. Nobody's got their phones, right? I don't want the feds tracking us."

"I've got a dump phone," Parker said. "Never been used. Eddie has the number. Maybe he'll call while we're out."

"I ain't holding my breath on that coke-head," Gabe grumbled.

Parker turned around to look at him as Wilson backed out of the parking space and headed toward the exit.

"Roo's got his issues, but he's fucking solid," Parker said angrily. "I'm not worried about him turning rat. He's the only one of us fucking fought when they knocked on the door."

"What are you trying to say?" Gabe said. "I haven't said shit."

In fact, through a concerted effort organized by Parker, enough money and collateral had been raised or donated by fellow DPD officers to get Gabe out on bail. They'd been worried that sitting in jail was wearing down his resistance, and wanted to get him away from the FBI agents who kept trying to get him to talk.

"Chill, both of you," Wilson told them. "Let's just get an eye on this kid's house, and see what's up."

"Shit's early, he's still going to be in bed," Gabe said from the back, ducking his head so he could see the house through the windshield.

The house was unremarkable. Two stories, aluminum siding, attached two car garage. It looked a hell of a lot like every other house on the street. The garage was closed, and they couldn't see any lights on inside, although it was almost fully light out. There were curtains or drapes across the big front window, and what looked like blinds covering the upstairs windows. They sat and watched the house silently. There was no movement in the neighborhood, although the street echoed with the early morning calls of birds. There'd been a sign entering the neighborhood— Stoneridge. He assumed that was the name of the neighborhood, or subdivision.

"I'm glad it's early. This neighborhood's a little pale for us."

Wilson grunted in assent, but then said, "My car fits in fine." His black Charger R/T was less than two years old, and didn't have a scratch on it yet.

"How long you want to sit here? You want to bang on the neighbors' doors, ask if they know if little Johnny's been up to no good?"

Wilson sighed. He didn't have an answer for that. He'd hoped that seeing the kid's house might help him, but it was just a house. And they couldn't sit there all day. Any minute now some coffee-sipping busybody was sure to peer out her curtains and see a car full of negroes parked on the street, call 911, and then they were fucked if they ever did decide to kill the kid. First thing the detectives would do is check all the reports and dispatch calls in the neighborhood, to see if there'd been anything suspicious noted prior to the murder. Three grown black men loitering in a car down the block from his house would definitely qualify as suspicious.

"All right," Wilson said, staring the car. The engine turned over with a deep rumble. Gotta love the hemi. "That didn't do shit for us."

"Hold up, garage door's going up," Gabe said.

"Early," Parker said. "Date heading home early, you think? Walk of shame?"

As the garage door opened all the way, they saw brake lights flare in the dim garage, then white reverse lights. They couldn't quite ID the car until it was halfway out of the garage.

Parker whistled. "Nice ride. That his car?" The Mustang looked new or close to it, and had obviously been treated to a few aftermarket parts. A black GT, it sported oversize tires and wheels, and the low growl of its exhaust could be heard all the way down the block, over the sound of their own car.

"They both are. His house too." Wilson could see the other vehicle in the garage was a Cherokee.

"How old is he? Twenty-five? He's got some money. Maybe he's into drugs. What you gonna do?"

"Shit," Wilson said. The Mustang waited for the garage door to close, and he could see the driver, a white male who looked like the photo he'd seen of the kid, was alone in the car. The Mustang then headed away from them on the street. On an impulse, Wilson put the Charger into gear and headed after him. Just then Parker's pre-paid cell rang.

"Yeah? Roo, whatchoo doing, where are you? No, we were sitting at his house, but he just got into his ride, the Mustang. Top's doing a loose tail through the hood right now. You find anything?"

Wilson looked at his partner. Parker shook his head. Shit. "Where is he?" he asked Parker.

"On I-75. Heading this way."

"No," Wilson said firmly. "We don't need any more exposure out here. Tell him to stay there, after we break off here we'll hook up with him and have a sit down."

"You catch that?" Parker said into the phone. "No, shit, Roo—" he pulled the phone away from his head and looked at it.

"What?"

Parker shook his head. "I don't think he ever went to sleep last night, he wasn't even listening to me. Mouth going a mile a minute." He looked out the windshield. Wilson turned a corner in the subdivision and saw the Mustang up ahead. "Where the fuck are we—watch out, he's pulling over. Shit, did he see us?"

Wilson quickly pulled the Charger to the curb about a hundred feet behind the Mustang. There were two parked cars between their vehicles. "I don't think so, that was the first time we were behind him in view for more than a second. He didn't have a chance to make us."

They couldn't really see into the Mustang, there were too many layers of car glass between them, so they had no clue what the kid was doing. The three of them were silent as they stared at what they could see of his car. Wilson kept expecting him to get out and walk to a house, but there was nothing.

"The fuck he doing?" Gabe asked after close to five minutes.

"I don't know what the fuck he's doing," Wilson said in exasperation." Maybe he's doing a surveillance, he works as a P.I."

"Around the corner from his house? In that car?"

"Am I Melvin the Mind-Reader? I don't fucking know. Maybe he picking up a friend."

After another three minutes, Wilson was getting antsy, and wanted to leave, but he was afraid that pulling away from the curb would actually draw more attention to their car. And they'd have to drive past the kid, unless they did a U-turn. Both options sucked when it came to not being noticed, although there wasn't any movement on the street. Parker's drop phone rang again.

"Yo. No, he drove like two blocks from his house and stopped. No. I don't know. Um..." Parker looked out the window for a street sign. "Larkins, why? Wait, what? No, Roo, I don't think that's a good idea."

"What's he want?" Wilson asked.

"What's he doing?" Gabe asked.

"He's, uh...." Parker said, hesitating, and then Wilson caught movement in his rearview. He looked up and saw Eddie's burgundy Monte Carlo turn the corner behind them.

"The fuck? Gimmee that phone. Roo?" Now he was seriously pissed.

"The fuck we doing here Top?" Eddie said into his ear. Wilson watched as the Monte coasted to a stop a car length behind them. He could see Eddie behind the wheel.

"Eddie, I said to fucking back off and wait for us. This ain't Detroit. We don't exactly blend."

"He just pull to the curb there? Why?"

"I don't know. He just drove off from his house, and he's sitting here. I don't know if he's waiting for somebody or not. He didn't see us."

He heard Eddie huff in his ear. "No, not that, I mean, this is the dude we have to pop, right? Why don't we just do it here?"

"Roo, we're right in the—"

"No, seriously, if killing this asshole keeps us out of jail, why don't we just fucking do it? You're clean, I'm clean, nobody's on us, nobody's even fucking awake. Let's just fucking do it. I'm gonna do it."

"Eddie—" Wilson began, but the phone was dead. In the rearview, he saw Eddie open his door and step out. He just pushed the door gently to, then walked around the front of his vehicle to the curb.

"The fuck is he thinking?" Wilson said, turning his head. Parker and Gabe both looked over and saw Eddie walking past them on the sidewalk. His eyes were red, and he looked terrible, like he hadn't slept in days.

"Is he back on the rock? The fuck's he doing?" Parker said.

Wilson was frozen in indecision and borderline terror. Meanwhile, Eddie walked down the sidewalk like he didn't have a care in the world. He passed the first parked car, then the second. As he approached the Mustang, he suddenly veered off the sidewalk onto the grass strip between the sidewalk and curb, and they saw a pistol appear in Eddie's hand.

Dave had noticed the black Charger in his rearview right as he'd pulled to the curb. He wouldn't have paid it any attention if it had driven by him, but he saw it park three cars back. After so many years of surveillance he tended to notice everything, and even though there wasn't anything particularly suspicious about a vehicle parking on the street in this neighborhood, his antenna were always up when he was working. He'd been followed himself a few times by angry claimants, and always checked his six when he was working.

Staring at what he could see of the car in his side mirror, Dave kept the 'Stang running and shifted it into neutral. He gave a little tug on the e-brake to keep the car from rolling. The house he was supposed to be watching was six up on the left. Garage door closed, no vehicle in the drive, no cars parked any closer to it than his. So much for the wife's suspicions.

His eyes flicked back to his side mirror. Still nothing. Nobody had gotten out of the Charger. He wondered if it was a Troy cop. He couldn't remember what color their cruisers were, but almost every department in Michigan was rolling Chargers for cruisers now. Nobody'd had a chance to call the cops on him for looking suspicious, but maybe they'd been driving through the neighborhood....

Keeping an eye on his mirror, he grabbed his phone and called in to the P.D.'s non-emergency line.

"Troy dispatch."

"Good morning. I'm a P.I. doing a surveillance in your city today, thought I'd call in and let you know where I'm at, in case you get any calls about me sitting in my car, looking suspicious."

"All right. Where you going to be?" Dave gave the female dispatcher his location, color and type of vehicle, license plate, and contact phone number. "Okay. Are you armed?" she asked.

"Yes ma'am."

"How long are you going to be out there?"

"Only until nine or so, but then I've got someone relieving me."

"Make sure he calls in." There was a pause. "Do you—don't you live right in that subdivision?" Dave realized she must have run his plate while he was talking to her.

"Yeah. Long story."

"What kind of surveillance?"

Dave didn't have to tell her, and he wouldn't tell her which house he was watching, but it didn't hurt to be as nice as possible. "Domestic."

"Good luck."

Dave disconnected the call and dropped the phone into his passenger seat. Still nothing from the Charger. Maybe somebody had gotten out of the passenger side, and he'd missed it. He thought about shutting off the Mustang, especially with the price of gas, and his hand strayed toward the keys. Then he saw another car pull onto the street and park behind the Charger.

Must have been waiting for a friend, he thought, but he still kept staring into his side mirror. Fifteen seconds later he saw the door of the new car open and a guy get out and walk between the cars to the curb.

Golfers, he thought. In this neighborhood, at seven on a Saturday morning? He'd bet money on it. Michigan had the highest number of golf courses per capita in the country, or had until recently, which was odd considering it was too cold to golf six months out of the year. It was a few seconds later that he caught movement in his passenger door mirror. The guy hadn't walked to a house, he was heading down the sidewalk. Toward Dave. Dave watched him walk closer, simply because there wasn't anything else to watch. The street was dead, nothing happening.

The guy was in his thirties, nothing unusual about his appearance. Black, but there were a number of black families living in the neighborhood. But as the man grew closer, even though he wasn't looking at the Mustang, Dave began to get a weird feeling. He didn't fidget in the seat, and kept facing more or less forward, but he pushed in the clutch with his left foot. Then, very gently, he deactivated the emergency brake. The big engine continued to rumble, but the car, two wheels against the curb, didn't move.

"Where are you going, dude?" Dave muttered, watching the guy. The man was so close now that he wasn't visible in the rearview at all. He was small in the side mirror, OBJECTS ARE CLOSER THAN THEY APPEAR, but suddenly Dave noticed that he'd stepped off the sidewalk and was on the grass, right at his rear bumper. He whipped his head to look over his shoulder just as the man raised his hand, and Dave saw the pistol.

In slow motion Dave slammed the car into first, left foot coming off the clutch even as his right foot stomped down on the gas. His side window exploded as the engine roared, the car filling with razor-edged glitter, back end sliding out as the crazy horsepower was unleashed on the rubber. More explosions, gunfire, back window shattering, guy now in the middle of the street, rapidly growing smaller, bucking gun in a two handed grip.

"The fuck is he doing? Eddie!" Wilson yelled, watching Eddie stand in the middle of the street and fire half a dozen rounds at the Mustang roaring away. Eddie then turned and sprinted back down the middle of the street toward them.

"Jesus, fuck, let's get out of here," Gabe said.

Eddie ran past them and piled into the Monte, and a second later was roaring past, tires squealing. He wasn't driving like he was trying to get away, he was taking off like—

"Is he fucking chasing him?" Parker said, staring.

Roo had been like a kid brother, lovable but always on the edge of getting in trouble. Wilson had been keeping him out of trouble for years, and the reflexes took over. He started the car and took off after Eddie.

Dave wasn't thinking, he'd reverted back to primordial caveman terror mode, blindly running from the monsters, and almost wrecked his car at the end of the long street. At the last minute he slammed on the brakes and just barely made the turn, then floored it again. The houses whipped by on either side, then he had to slam on the brakes again and downshift to take the corner hard right onto Square Lake Road.

There was hardly any traffic at that time of the morning, and it was a good thing, because he hit the corner wide and sloppy, all the way across both lanes and nearly into the grass on the far side. Thank God there was no oncoming traffic. He got back into his lane and floored it, feeling the G forces push him into the seat.

Panting, his brain finally started working, and he began to back off the accelerator as he saw how fast he was flying down the nearly empty street. Then he saw the Monte Carlo slewing around the corner behind him, tires squealing. Dave couldn't take his eyes off his rearview as he stomped on the gas. Two seconds later the black Charger came around the corner onto Square Lake in a power slide, both cars hurtling after him. It was like a horror movie. What the fuck was going on?

There was a car in front of him but no oncoming and Dave swerved around it like it was standing still. The intersection with Dequindre was up ahead, and there were cars stacked up before it. Cars in front of him in his lane stopped at the red light, cars on the other side of the intersection. He couldn't see to the right because of a liquor store, but there was a vacant lot to the left, and past it he could see there was no southbound traffic. Dave downshifted and hit the horn hard as he angled across the incoming lanes and took the turn left at fifty miles an hour, tires squealing. Dequindre northbound had almost no cars on the road, and he stomped the gas. The Mustang's engine roared, and the wind coming in the blown out window buffeted him. He checked the mirror, and saw the Monte, with the Charger only a second behind it, take the corner just as fast as he had.

"Why are you chasing me?" he screamed.

Half a mile up Dequindre expanded to two lanes in each direction across from Beaumont Hospital. He was going crazy fast. Knuckles white on the steering wheel, he checked his speed. A hundred miles an hour, over double the speed limit. A check of the mirror showed the other two cars still behind him, a few hundred yards back. Were they gaining on him? A hundred miles an hour and they were gaining on him? What the fuck? Who were these guys? He pushed the accelerator down.

Intersection with South Boulevard up ahead. Yellow light, one car just coming to a stop in the right lane, Dave flew through the signal just as the light turned red. Everything a blur. Bridge under M-59 up ahead, no traffic in sight. Checked the rearview as he went under the freeway, big green sign flashing over him—the cars chasing him had had to stomp on their brakes to avoid hitting the cars on South Boulevard, but they were still coming. Who the fuck were these guys? Had he been shot? It didn't feel like he'd been hit, but he had so much adrenaline pumping through his body he felt like he could rip the steering wheel off the column. He didn't dare take his hands of the wheel no matter what, it felt like they were vibrating. Driving way too fast to take his eyes off the road even for a second to check for blood.

Shit, he realized, he should have jumped on the freeway. No way they could keep up with him on a straightaway, not with his horsepower. Too late for that now.

Jim Bonniker put his change in his pocket and then balanced the plastic-wrapped Danish on his coffee cup lid so he could have a hand free to open the door. As he stepped into the sunlight he looked down past the Danish to his gut and sighed. Married twelve years to the same wonderful woman, but he'd put on five pounds for every year of marriage. And not five pounds of muscle. Shit. It wasn't working too many hours, it was the kids. Three kids, all of them involved in something different, gymnastics, Boy Scouts, swimming... who had time to work out? At least the vest made it look as if some of that weight was muscle.

A totally random thought popped into his mind as he walked across the gas station's lot to his cruiser — Danish pastry was capitalized, as was Dumpster. Who would have thought that Dumpster was capitalized, but apparently it was a trademarked name. You learned the weirdest stuff helping your kids with homework. And yet deputy wasn't. Somehow it didn't seem fair. Another random thought — thank God their uniforms were brown. All the coffee he'd spilled on himself over the years......

He put the coffee cup — with the Danish capital D still perched precariously atop it — on the roof next to the light bar and grabbed for the keys hanging off his duty belt. He'd left the car running to power the radio and computer, but had locked the door. Over the roof of the cruiser he could see the BMW dealership next door, all the shiny new cars waiting to be bought. Wouldn't that be nice? Maybe one day, when he wasn't paying private school tuition for three.....A sudden roar made him snap his head around, and he saw a black Mustang burst out from underneath the M-59 overpass. It went flying past...holy shit, how fast was he going? Eighty? A hundred? The engine sounded massive.

Bonniker ripped open his door and jumped into the Crown Victoria. Before he could even get his door closed two more cars whipped past going almost as fast as the first. Were they chasing the first car? Racing? On a Saturday morning? He threw the car into gear and let the acceleration slam his door shut, and never noticed the coffee and Danish flying off the roof.

"Radio, I've got three vehicles northbound on Dequindre from M-59 at triple digit speeds!" he yelled into his handset breathlessly, forgetting to even identify himself. Even with his cruiser floored, the cars up ahead were still pulling away from him. What the hell were they doing? Somebody was going to end up dead.

Dave almost lost it at Auburn Road, zig-zagging through the cars stopped at the light with his horn going, sliding through the intersection almost sideways, but he straightened it out. He downshifted and stomped the pedal again. Once he was sure he had the car under control he checked the rearview. Shit. They were still back there, although he'd gained some ground on them, maybe a quarter of a mile. If he kept driving this fast, he was going to die in a spectacular fireball. How long were they going to chase him? For that matter, where the fuck was he going? He was driving this route because he'd driven it a hundred times, because it was familiar, but there weren't any cops or police departments ahead. He knew what was, though.

Two cars behind him, he didn't know how many people, but if they caught up to him they were both bigger and heavier vehicles, they'd be able to force him off the road easy. He was done being terrified, that had worn off; now he was angry. Pissed. The whole thing was out of control. Better to regain control of as much of the situation as he could, and he was a better shooter than he was a driver, anyway. Fuck it.

Trusting to fate, he flew through the intersection with Hamlin blindly, a row of spruces blocking his view of the westbound lanes. Behind the spruces was a trailer park—yep, done surveillance there, a tiny corner of his mind said. Past the combination gas station and 7-11 he pounded the brakes. A narrow blacktop road ran off to the right and he nailed the turn onto Forest, downshifted and hammered the gas for just a few seconds, then hit the brakes and turned off onto the dirt road to the left. A cloud of dust obscured his view of the two cars behind him as they roared up on Dequindre.

High grass-covered berms, the highest berms in the state, came down close to either side of the road. He knew the range would be empty this early in the morning, and if he parked across the road his pursuers wouldn't be able to get by him. Past the berm on the right was a small pistol bay, and—

Dave slammed on the brakes instinctively as he saw the half dozen vehicles parked on the grass ahead. What the fuck—he suddenly realized they must be having a club member work bee. Not good. Not good at all. At the last moment he twisted the wheel to the side and yanked the e-brake, and the Mustang spun sideways on the dirt road. The following dust cloud engulfed the car as Dave bailed out of his door and ran to the trunk. Did he have time? As he ran to the back of his car he looked up but he couldn't see anything past the swirling road dust. *Focus, focus!*

He opened the trunk and for a second didn't see it, but the black rifle case had been thrown off to the corner. The roar of approaching engines was loud in his ears as he found the zipper on the case and ripped it down the side.

Don't look up, don't look. Smooth is fast. He as much ripped the case off the rifle as pulled the rifle out of it, then scrabbled at the flap of one of the exterior magazine pockets.

His hands were clumsy as he finally extricated a loaded magazine and looked up from the open trunk. The Monte Carlo was almost on top of him, skidding to a stop through the dissipating dust cloud. Dave moved sideways, behind the Mustang, shoving the thirty-round magazine into the oversized mag well of his rifle, and for some reason he looked over his shoulder behind him. Three or four guys he recognized, fellow shooters, were standing outside the nearest bay and staring curiously in his direction, one of them with a circular saw in his hand.

"Line's going hot!" Dave screamed at them reflexively, chambering a round. After years of hearing the range warning, it just flowed naturally from his lips. The black guy who'd shot at him on surveillance jumped out of the Monte Carlo gun in hand.

"Just fucking die!" Eddie yelled wild-eyed, running at Dave. He fired and Dave flinched as he felt the bullet whip past his head. He fired again as Dave got his rifle up to his shoulder in practiced movement, thumb down, safety off, finger on the trigger, big glowing red rectangle of the Trijicon scope's reticle centered on the man's chest. Dave pulled the trigger but it had no effect, the man kept running at him, shooting wildly. Shit, had he missed? There was no way he'd missed. Trigger, press, trigger, press.

Dave fired and kept firing until the man went down, a hurt look on his face. Brass cases glittered in the air, the sound of the rifle huge in the quiet morning, but it seemed distant, as if his ears weren't working right. The Charger came sliding sideways to a stop, passenger door six feet from the rear door of the Monte. The cloud of dust enveloped Dave, and he couldn't see the Charger for a second. Realizing he was just standing there, wide open, he dropped to one knee behind the hood of his car. As the dust blew by him he saw the passenger door of the Charger hanging open. Someone popped his head around the back of the Monte and fired at him, and Dave heard the thuds as the bullets hit the Mustang.

He felt oddly calm, and didn't flinch at all. Everything seemed to be happening to someone else, almost as if he was watching a movie in slow motion. Fuck these guys, whoever they were. He'd been shot at before and walked away, and that was before he'd ever fired a round in competition, before he knew anything about anything. The back end of the Charger wasn't more than twenty-five yards away....he'd shot plenty tougher matches than this, and he had his favorite rifle in his hands.

Dave put the glowing red triangle on the man firing at him and began pulling the trigger as fast as possible. His competition rifle had almost no recoil, and he could see the bullet impacts in the scope—dark holes appeared in the Monte Carlo's bumper and the plastic tail light shattered as the high-velocity rounds ripped right through. The man, plastic shards of tail light in his hair, fell to the ground underneath the car, yelling, and then the driver's window of the Mustang blew out beside Dave's head.

He ducked behind his car instinctively, but not before he saw someone running behind the Monte Carlo, maybe trying to flank him. Dave dove sideways, planting his shoulder into the dirt, and in rollover prone stuck his rifle underneath his car. He was looking for feet to shoot but saw nothing. Where was he?

A pistol fired, and he could hear the bullets hitting his car. A tire blew, his car sunk a few inches, more glass shards flew over him, but he couldn't tell where the shooter was. The man kept firing, hitting the car, the ground, what was left of the windows, emptying the pistol, trying to keep Dave's head down. Dave saw the man he'd just dropped, crawling in the dirt. The bits of red plastic from the tail light looked like confetti in his hair as the man reached for and grabbed a pistol lying in the dirt. Shit. Dave fired at him with half his rifle barrel underneath the Mustang, and the concussion in the enclosed space raised such a dust cloud he pulled back from the car, spitting.

"Parker!" someone yelled. Their voice was very faint.

Dave didn't know who Parker was, didn't care. He backed off from the Mustang and rolled around the rear bumper, rifle up, dialed in. Get some. He caught a glimpse of movement at the rear bumper of the Monte Carlo and fired twice, past the open driver's door. A man popped up behind the Monte Carlo and fired quickly at him over it, then ducked back down. Dave hammered the car with rounds, trying to hit the man through the thin layers of steel.

"Gabe, get out of there!" Dave heard a man yell. Someone stood up behind the Charger — fuck, how many guys were there? — and fired four times at him. Dave flinched but apparently not as much as they'd expected or hoped. The man between the Monte Carlo and the Charger decided to make a run for the open door of the Monte Carlo, and Dave saw him. Left forearm braced against the rear bumper of the Mustang, rifle in the pocket of his shoulder, Dave pulled the trigger as fast as he could, shooting into and through the door of the Monte. He could see his hits, the tiny holes in the door panel just below the window, the man running to meet them. The bullets zipped right through the car door, as he knew they would. The running man staggered, tried to raise his gun, then fell, half-in and half-out of the Monte Carlo. Dave could see his legs and pelvis underneath the door, and shot him four more times for good measure. *Because FUCK YOU, that's why!* a small part of his brain screamed.

Wilson saw Gabe go down. Saw the kid shoot his unmoving body. It was fucked, they were all fucked. Eddie, Parker, Gabe....it made him want to cry. What the fuck had happened to them? What had gone wrong? Part of him wanted to charge the kid with the rifle, just end it all — and where the fuck did he get that? Who drove around with a loaded rifle in their car? What the fuck was wrong with these gun nuts?

Instead he threw the Charger into reverse and floored it, looking over his shoulder through the rear windshield. He hadn't killed anybody, hadn't trashed his car, there was a chance no one would even know he was—and then he saw the Oakland County Sheriff's Department cruiser skid to a stop on the asphalt road behind him.

Jim Bonniker slid his unit to a rocking stop on the blacktop at the end of the dirt road. Even over the sound of the siren he'd heard the shooting, but hadn't been sure exactly what was happening as, well, it was a shooting range. But as he looked down the narrow road he saw two cars at angles, and bodies in the dirt. There was a black Charger racing down the road toward him in reverse. Bonniker expected it would stop as soon as the driver saw his cruiser, as it wouldn't be able to get by, but instead he heard the deeper growl as the Charger accelerated.

"Fuck!" the deputy yelled, and grabbed onto the steering wheel with both hands as the Charger slammed into the front corner of his cruiser. Bonniker bounced off the exploding airbag and fell half across the passenger seat, not having worn a seatbelt since he'd put on the uniform. He discovered the Charger had shoved his unit halfway across the pavement, and tasted blood.

With a grunt he grabbed the handle then kicked his door open. He was drawing his Sig as the driver's door of the Charger opened, and a big black guy climbed out. The cruiser's flashing red and blue lights bounced off his expressionless face. Somewhere in the distance he heard yelling, but as his vision tunneled everything else faded away. "Freeze! Get on the ground!" Bonniker yelled. It was then he saw the pistol in the man's hand. "Put the gun down!" he screamed even louder, his voice cracking. Instead, the man raised the pistol and pointed it at Bonniker.

In fifteen years on the job, Jim Bonniker had found occasion to point his duty weapon at a few people, but never anyone visibly armed, and he'd never had to pull the trigger. Never even came close. With a sense of disbelief he felt himself pulling the trigger on his pistol, saw it buck in recoil. He viewed himself from above in a near out-of-body experience firing over and over, firing at the man who kept trying to point a gun at him, firing at the man who just calmly stood there and took it, firing until the big man slowly fell to the ground.

Bonniker climbed out of his cruiser and approached the body, face down on the ground. The deputy's gun was in front of him, and it was quivering. He kicked the Glock away from the man's lifeless hand, then looked up the dirt road at the pile of cars, at the bodies, at the whole scene. It was then that his brain caught up to his ears, and he remembered what he'd heard someone shouting from the pile of cars up ahead.

"You wanted a gunfight?" an unseen male had yelled in the distance as Bonniker was confronted by the driver of the Charger. "I'll give you a gunfight. I'LL GIVE YOU A FUCKING GUNFIGHT!"

"What the fuck is going on here?" Bonniker yelled at the distant pile of cars, at the man he'd just killed, at the world.

PART IV

UNGOVERNED

A government is a body of people usually, notably, ungoverned.

Captain Malcolm Reynolds

CHAPTER NINETEEN

Two more Oakland County cruisers were the first to arrive. By that time Bonniker had approached the scene down the road, put Dave in cuffs, secured his rifle and pistol, and verified that the three guys on the ground were well and truly dead. He ordered the gawkers at the range to back away, and had Dave sit on the side of the road behind his cruiser, as his car wasn't going anywhere. Not only wasn't it drivable, it was part of the crime scene now.

"I have multiple fatalities at my location," he told the dispatcher. "I need command staff out here, ASAP, Fire, and as many units as you can spare to secure the scene and the witnesses."

"Ten-four," she told him.

With everything that had happened Bonniker had forgotten he'd never called out anything but speeders and the dispatcher assumed that the deaths were due to an accident caused by the pursuit. In the modern age of smartphones there was no such thing as a day off, but the Sheriff was actually out of town on vacation with his family. The Undersheriff, however, answered his cell phone on the third ring, sounding sleepy. He told the dispatcher he'd be out to the scene as soon as he got dressed.

"You walk into the middle of a gunfight, Jim?" one of the responding deputies asked Bonniker, staring at the bodies littering the road and the shot-up cars. Gunfight at a shooting range. "Holy shit. You okay?" Bonniker was looking a bit shaky. Except for car wrecks, none of the deputies had seen that many dead bodies in one place—at least in the States.

"I shot this guy, but all that other shit happened right before I got here. I don't know...get those people over there," he pointed at the club members standing on the far side of Dave's Mustang, "get 'em separated. I don't know if any of them saw anything. Keep them away from the cars."

"You're good?"

Bonniker felt anything but good, but near as he could tell he hadn't been shot. His face hurt from the airbag, and he'd probably have a stiff neck, but thank God, he hadn't been shot. "I'm good, don't worry about me." As the air pulsed with the sound of approaching sirens, he walked over and looked at the kid sitting on the ground in cuffs. He wanted to ask him what the fuck had just happened, but knew before he did that he probably ought to read the kid his Miranda rights, and he just didn't have the energy for that. "Don't move," he finally told him.

The kid, looking exhausted, just nodded. After a few seconds he said, "This started in Troy, you might want to call them."

Bonniker turned back to look at him. "What?"

"I'm a P.I. and was doing a surveillance in Troy, and one of those guys started shooting at me, and chased me to here."

"Why? Who are they?"

The kid looked up at him, complete confusion on his face. "I wish I knew."

Mrs. Maddie Bridger's arthritis was so bad that she couldn't sleep more than two or three hours at a stretch, and some nights just didn't have it in her to climb the stairs to her bedroom on the second floor. Friday night she'd had one too many Tom Collins' during her monthly bridge club party, and after her guests left had fallen asleep on her recliner while watching the news.

She awoke at four, the alcohol having helped her sleep five hours straight, but when she got out of the chair she felt halfway crippled. No one to blame but herself, she knew that, and had Jack still been alive he would have laughed at her hobbling up the stairs to take a long hot shower. At least she wasn't hungover. For some reason, on those rare occasions when she did celebrate a little too much — at the birth of her last grandbaby, for instance — she never got a hangover. Her knees and knuckles and elbows might be putting up a mighty racket, but her head, while a bit stuffy, didn't hurt at all.

After seventy-two years she knew her own body, and what aches and pains the hot water didn't erase she knew activity would. After putting on her old housedress she spent a good forty-five minutes getting her kitchen clean. Virginia Walker had helped her put away the leftovers the night before, but the counters still needed to be wiped off, the dirty dishes rinsed off and put in the dishwasher, the folding chairs put away, and then there was the vacuuming. Holy Moses, it looked like a crumb bomb had gone off in her front room. Did none of her old buzzard friends know how to use a napkin? Vacuuming worked her hands and elbows hard, but for some reason they hurt less when she was done. They always did.

She was staring out her front window sipping a nice big steaming mug of coffee — decaf, her intestines couldn't handle caffeine any more — when the hot rod parked on the street in front of Betty Green's house across the street. She kept waiting for the driver to get out and walk to a house, but he didn't.

"Nine one one, what's your emergency?" she heard in her ear after dialing.

"Yes, this is Maddie Bridger at 5725 Larkins. I've got a very suspicious person out here."

The woman dispatcher didn't seem to share her worry, and instead said flatly, "A suspicious person? What are they doing?"

"He's sitting in his car in front of my house. He's been just sitting in his car for ten minutes. I saw him pull up. I'm a widow and I can't have just any suspicious characters lurking around the neighborhood."

"What kind of a car is it?"

"I don't know. It's a race car of some kind, black."

"Can you see the license plate?"

"No, it's sideways."

"And he's just sitting in the car? I—wait, hold on a second. No, ma'am, you don't have anything to worry about, we know exactly what he's—"

"Oh my God!" Maddie screamed, dropping the phone, and the dispatcher heard loud noises in the background. A loud roar, and multiple *pops*.

"Ma'am! Ma'am! Are you all right? What's going on?"

There was rustling, then the phone was picked up. "He just shot him! They're chasing him!" She sounded nearly hysterical.

"What? Who shot? Who's chasing who?"

"A black man just shot the man in the car, he just shot at him right in front of me! I saw the whole thing. Oh my Lord! He drove off, but they kept shooting, and I think they're chasing him."

"Hold on ma'am, I'm sending units to your location." The dispatcher had heard gunshots over the phone before, and to the experienced ear they didn't sound anything like fireworks or slamming doors or car backfires, not that anybody had cars that backfired anymore. Gunshots were very distinctive. There was a pause, and Maddie Bridger heard some electronic beeps in her ear. Her heart was racing in her chest, and it felt like she was going to faint. The dispatcher got back on the line, exuding professional calm. "Tell me exactly what you saw."

Two Troy cruisers responded to the scene. The tire tracks on the street were immediately visible, as was a single 9mm cartridge case, but it took them a little longer to notice the shards of glass by the curb and the other empty cases. Officer Paul Taylor was just talking to Mrs. Bridger when their dispatcher came over the air. "Units responding, be advised that Oakland County has just reported an officer-involved shooting, it sounds like the vehicles from your scene were involved. Location is Dequindre north of Hamlin."

The two officers looked at each other, and Taylor got on the radio. "Dispatch, show me responding to that location. The other unit will remain on scene here. Have an evidence tech roll out here, we've got some shell casings, skidmarks, and glass. We'll also need a detective. And whoever the highest ranking officer on call today, you better call them. This looks like it's going to be big."

"Ten-four."

"What are you guys doing here?" a harried deputy asked the four of them, standing about fifty yards back from Dave's Mustang. They couldn't leave — the dirt road blocked by Dave's Mustang was the only way off the range.

"Club members. Here doing some maintenance."

"Work hours," another one told him.

"Did you see what happened?"

"Hell yeah."

"Some of it."

"Okay," he told them. "Someone is going to need to take your statement. Go stand over there, don't go anywhere."

Frank walked over to the picnic table as the deputy instructed, pulling out his cell phone as he did.

"Hello?"

"Dude, wake the fuck up. You're never going to believe what just happened. Oh my God. Jesus."

"What?"

"Gunfighter just got into a fucking gunfight, right here at the club!"

"What?

"Dave just got into a gunfight, right here."

"Dave Anderson shot somebody?"

"Shot somebody? Dude. *Duuude.* No, he got into a fucking Hollywood gunfight with two fucking carloads of fucking bad guys right fucking in front of Bay Seven and killed them all. With his fucking TTI AR. I mean....Jesus. I saw the whole thing and I can't fucking believe it. He had four guys shooting at him and he just fucking stood there and filled the air with fucking brass like a fucking action movie. It was the most awesome thing in the history of....awesome. Fuck."

"What? Who were they?"

"I don't know. Buncha black dudes, chased him down here and started shooting. There's about a thousand fucking cops screaming here, can you hear all the sirens?"

"Carjacking?"

"I don't fucking know."

"Is he hurt?"

"No, but you should see his Mustang. Shit's messed up."

By the time Troy PD Officer Taylor arrived at the second crime scene it was a sea of swirling red and blue lights and he couldn't park anywhere close. Dequindre was completely blocked off in both directions by units, and he could see two ambulances and a fire truck. He parked on the shoulder of Dequindre and walked the hundred yards down Forest, the narrow asphalt road. There he ran into the first crime scene, a tape line strung on poles at distance around an Oakland County cruiser with its nose crushed.

"Who's ranking officer on scene?" he asked the crowd of officers.

"Sergeant Leven," one of the deputies told him. The man squinted at his uniform. "What's Troy want with this?"

"Sounds like it started in our city. What kind of cars do you have involved?" He could see the black Charger by the damaged cruiser, but a berm blocked his view down the dirt road. He could also see a body in the road by the Charger.

"That Charger there, a black Mustang, and a burgundy Monte."

"Yep, same vehicles."

"We've got four dead here. What the hell happened?"

Taylor shook his head. "I think there was a P.I. on a surveillance, and somebody started shooting, then chased him here."

"What, a jealous husband kind of thing? Somebody catch somebody cheating?"

"I don't know."

"The kid, is that the P.I.?" someone asked him. They pointed at a young man sitting in the back of one of the squad cars in handcuffs.

"I don't know."

"Well shit, I guess you know as much as we do then, which is nothing. You should probably talk to the Sergeant."

Undersheriff Raymond Marx arrived ten minutes later. He'd forgotten to grab his prep radio, and no one had called him on his cell since he'd talked to dispatch, so he didn't have any further details of the incident. He wasn't surprised at the amount of activity at the scene, if in fact there were multiple fatalities, but what the hell was Troy doing here? The dark blue uniform stuck out among the brown sea of deputies.

"All right, somebody give me a rundown, what have we got?" He looked around at the faces — shit, there had to be twenty deputies and EMTs wandering around — looking for a detective. He didn't see one. "Any dicks on scene yet?"

"No," Leven, one of his sergeants told him. "But I think we've pretty much figured out what happened, although why is another question."

"Let's hear it."

"A young man, David Anderson, called in to Troy dispatch, saying he was a P.I. and doing a surveillance in a neighborhood. Not five minutes later a neighbor calls in to their dispatch as well, thinking Anderson looked suspicious. While she's on the phone with Troy, somebody walks up to his car and shoots him, or at least shoots at him."

"Shoots him? I thought this was a high speed chase."

"What?"

"The call I got said this was a high speed chase, with multiple fatalities. There was a shooting?" Well damn, there went his Saturday. "What the hell happened?"

"Anderson drove off at a high rate of speed, followed by two vehicles. Headed up Dequindre. Blew by Jim Bonniker who was parked at the Mobil at M-59, and ended up here." He saw the Undersheriff looking at the Charger and Bonniker's unit, then looking around for the other vehicles.

"The other vehicles are around the side of the hill, closer to the range. You can go up on the hill no problem, just stay off the road. Not sure if the techs are treating the whole road as a crime scene, or if they're considering this two separate ones here, but we're figuring everything between the cars off limits until we're told otherwise. Anyway, triple digit speeds, Bonniker estimates. That Charger and a Monte Carlo chased Anderson here. He stopped in the middle of the road, and according to the witnesses the men in the other cars started shooting at him. There were four men between the two cars. Anderson grabbed a rifle out of the trunk of his car and fired back, killing three of the men. The fourth drove away in the Charger, and rammed Bonniker's unit. When he got out of the Charger he pointed a pistol at Bonniker, and Bonniker shot him."

"Holy hell." Marx thought for a second. "Did Bonniker identify himself as a police officer?"

Leven bit back what he wanted to say to a commanding officer asking a very stupid question and instead observed, "I don't know, but he's in uniform, and his unit's pretty damn well marked." He turned his head and pointedly looked at the damaged cruiser.

"Okay, I'm probably going to assign two detectives to this. I think Linklater and Cashman are on call this weekend. Leven, get dispatch to call them to the scene. Is this kid, Anderson, talking?"

"Oh, I forgot. The witnesses know Anderson, he's a club member. At least one of them thought that he worked as a security guard of private investigator or something, so that's some sort of confirmation."

"Anybody talk to Anderson yet?"

"No, and he hasn't been read his Miranda rights yet, either. Bonniker cuffed him, and I stuffed him in the back of my unit. He told Bonniker that this started in Troy, and he had no idea who the other guys were, but that's it."

Marx pointed at the Troy officer standing in the group. "What do you have at your scene?"

Taylor shrugged. "Tire marks where he accelerated away, maybe some window glass. Plus half a dozen nine millimeter cases. The witness insists Anderson was just sitting in his car when a black male walked up behind his car and shot at him. Shot at him while he was driving away, too, then ran back to his car and gave chase. We've got an evidence tech who just arrived at our scene, and a detective's been assigned, but that's about as far as we've gotten."

"Black male? Is Anderson black?"

"No," Taylor told the Undersheriff. "White kid, lives about a quarter mile from where the shooting took place. Somebody ran him, and he's got no record, he's clean — nothing criminal, not even anything on his driving record. He's got a CPL. I guess he even had a pistol on him, but he didn't use it."

"Oh, shit," one of the assembled deputies said loudly. It got the attention of everybody. The young deputy was staring at his smartphone.

"What?" Marx asked him.

"Sir, I was the first unit on scene — after Bonniker. I checked the bodies for vitals, just to make sure, but I didn't check them for ID or anything else after I verified they were dead. I didn't want to disturb the bodies. But I did run the plates on the Charger and the Monte. The Charger is registered to a Paul Wilson, and the Monte Carlo to Eddie Mitchell, both out of Detroit. Their names sounded slightly familiar, so I just Googled them." The deputy turned his phone around, and showed the screen to the Undersheriff. It was a several-week-old Detroit Free Press Headline, "Detroit SWAT Officers Arrested for Strip Club Robberies". The deputy pulled the phone back, and announced, "'The four officers arrested were Randy Parker, Eddie Mitchell, Paul Wilson, and Gabriel Kilpatrick.'"

Marx just stared at him for a second. His peripheral vision got gray, almost as if he was about to pass out. He liked being Undersheriff because he got a title, more money in the paycheck, and never had to do anything more difficult than shake a few hands and pose for some pictures. He never had to make any of the tough decisions, and almost never had to get involved in the political in-fighting that took place at the highest levels of county government. That job fell to the Sheriff. Except…the Sheriff was out of town.

He shook his head and said, "Find an EMT, tell him to check the bodies for ID. Tell him to do it right now."

The officer ran off. He was back less than two minutes later. "It's them," he said, panting. It sounded like he could hardly believe it.

"Oh shit," someone murmured. They'd all heard of the case of course, it had been huge news for quite some time. Crooked cops, then the officers dying in the huge shootout they had a few weeks back....the Detroit Police Department was having a really bad summer. As for which one was worse, well, police work was a dangerous business. Occasionally, cops got shot. But having a whole armed robbery crew be active members of a major metropolitan SWAT team? That was a first. Detroit already had such a bad reputation, and *that* had to happen. Maybe it was better that it had happened in Detroit. Bad cops made all cops look bad, but Detroit was in such sad shape anyway, had such a bad public image, maybe the public would just ignore one more outrage from the Motor City.

Marx stood there thinking. This was going to be a jurisdictional nightmare. "You need to call your Chief," he told the Troy officer. "Started in Troy, ended in Oakland County, involving DPD officers, arrested by the FBI? He and I are going to need to talk." Sheriff Brooks had said not to call him when he was on vacation unless "Jesus reappears or the dead start walking the earth", but Marx figured this was big enough to count. There was a good chance Brooks would cut his vacation short, especially with this case involving the FBI. Brooks knew just how much his Undersheriff hated the feds.

"Uhhh...." One of the other Oakland County deputies began, then asked, "Any of you guys looked at a map recently? We're on the east side of Dequindre. This is Macomb County. Shelby Township."

Marx looked around, then shook his head. His man was right. "Shit. Anybody call them yet?" He heard a sound, and lifted his head. There it was, the first news helicopter.

As he was en route John called his young employee twice to find out what he'd found at the house, or if there was any activity, but got no answer. The second time, he left a voicemail. "Don't know if you're busy following him, or filming, but give me a call as soon as you get this." While there was always a chance that Dave had overslept, he figured the chances were much greater that Dave was busy in some way working the case. When John turned onto the street at five minutes to nine, he felt a cold rush up his spine. Six Troy cop cars, including an SUV belonging to an evidence tech, crime scene tape everywhere, two news vans, plus at least twenty residents standing on their front lawns watching the activity. When he saw no sign of Dave's Mustang, he breathed a little easier, but he was still concerned.

John parked as close as he could to the yellow tape blocking off the street and got the attention of an officer. "What's going on?" He hadn't had the radio on at all during the drive over, so if there'd been announcement of a big incident he'd missed it. He stared at the two cameramen from the local TV stations filming the cops, who seemed to be searching the street for something. One plainclothes guy, so it looked like there was already a detective on scene.

"We're in the middle of investigating a crime scene, sir. If you live on the block you're going to have to park there and walk to your house, the street's going to be roped off for a while."

"What happened?"

He could see the officer was tired of answering questions. "I'm not really at liberty to say, sir."

"I'm a private investigator. I had an employee doing a surveillance on this street early this morning. He's not answering his phone, and I don't see his car. Can you give me *any* idea what happened?"

The officer looked at him, for the first time seeing him as something other than an annoyance. "What kind of car does he drive?"

"A green Cherokee," John said. He saw the cop relax a bit. "He also has a black Mustang," he added. The cop immediately pointed a finger at him.

"Stay right there," he told John, and turned away. He got on his radio, but John couldn't hear what he said.

"Is he okay?" John asked. Jesus, what the hell had happened? Had Dave been carjacked?

Marx opened the rear door of the squad car and looked down at Dave. "Mr. Anderson, I'm Raymond Marx, the Undersheriff with Oakland County."

Anderson looked tired, and maybe a little bored. What he didn't look like was someone who'd just killed three people. He didn't look like someone who thought he was going to be going to jail for murder. He looked almost....defiant. "Undersheriff?" he said. "Sorry, I don't think I've heard the term before. So you're the number two guy?"

"Yes." Marx was treading very lightly here. Whether or not Anderson was guilty of a crime was yet to be proven, but he had just killed several people, so questioning him without reading him his Miranda rights was a very bad idea. But..... "I just wanted to let you know that I've talked to your boss, John Phault. He confirmed that you were doing surveillance for him, on a domestic case. He's talking to a Troy detective. I've let him know that you're okay, but at the moment in our custody."

"Thank you."

Marx pursed his lips. "I'm...I'm wondering if there's anything you can tell us that would help in our investigation. We're at a bit of a loss to explain what happened. Or rather why."

Dave's mouth curled into a half smile as he stared at the seatback in front of him. "I've got a CJ degree, done an internship with Warren P.D., and I've been working as a P.I. for three years," he told Marx. "So I know that the only thing I should be saying to you is that I want to speak to a lawyer." He turned his head to look directly at the Undersheriff. "But the truth is I have no fucking clue who those guys were or why they were chasing and shooting at me. I've been sitting here this whole time, trying to remember if any of them looked familiar from a case, but...." He just shook his head, then took a deep breath. "I was in fear for my life," he said very clearly and slowly. It was obvious he'd decided to make a statement. "They shot at me first. Both here and there." He pursed his lips. "And now I don't think I want to say anything else until I talk to a lawyer. But then I'll be happy to make a statement."

If he was waiting for Marx to get mad, that wasn't going to happen. Marx just nodded. "Fair enough. But you're uninjured? You're not hurt?"

"My ears are ringing, but that's about it. I think I might have some glass inside my shirt." Dave was actually surprised at how calm he felt, but as soon as he had made the decision to stand and fight....the fear had left him. For whatever reason. He remembered the last time, in Warren, and expected that he'd get the shakes soon enough, and nightmares and trembling flashbacks for weeks or months, but right then all he felt was tired. Adrenaline dumps really wore you out. But still....he'd just been in a car chase and gunfight with four guys. Shouldn't he be just a little freaked out? The fact that he wasn't was weirding him out a little bit. Who was calm after a shootout?

The Undersheriff pulled out his phone and looked at it. "You don't have to answer of course, I heard you when you asked for a lawyer, but I'm wondering, do any of these names sound familiar to you? Randy Parker, Eddie Mitchell, Paul Wilson, Gabriel Kilpatrick?"

"No." Dave looked out the window toward where the bodies were, not that he could see them. "Is that them?" He shook his head. "I don't think so. I don't think I've heard the names. But….I've done a lot of surveillances, I'd have to go back and check my records to make sure."

"Okay. Sit tight. I'll have a paramedic look you over, and we'll get you back to the station in a little bit."

When Marx walked back to his car, Sergeant Leven asked him, "So when's the FBI going to show up and start throwing their weight around?"

Marx shrugged. "I made the call. We'll see. Brian, I've got a question for you."

"Yes sir?"

"We've got a, what, twenty-five year old kid sitting in that car over there? What question pops into your head first?"

"Why'd four Detroit cops just try to kill him?"

"Mmmm. You know what question pops into my head? How many people do you know who could get into a gunfight with four highly-trained SWAT cops, kill three of them, scare the fourth off, walk away without a scratch, and sit there looking bored?"

Leven scratched his head, and looked back at the squad car, where the top of Anderson' head was visible. "What, you think he's not who he says he is? That he's….undercover FBI or something?"

"It sure seems like something else is going on here, that's all. Bonniker's a lot more shook up than that kid. I'll be curious to see how hard the FBI will fight to take over the investigation."

Hartman wiped dampness off his forehead and put the phone back against his ear. The phone felt hot, but maybe it was just him. He was sweating freely beneath his clean white shirt and tie. "I'm heading to the scene right now."

"What exactly happened?" Boehmer asked him.

"I don't have much, just a few details over the phone and what I've been hearing on the news. They're all dead, Wilson and his whole crew. Apparently there was some sort of gunfight involving an Oakland County deputy."

"Jesus Christ. And the kid?"

"It sounds like he was there. I believe he's still alive, but I'll be able to give you more details when I get there."

Hartman listened to profanity for a while, then Boehmer said, "What's our exposure on this? What's worse case scenario?"

Worst case scenario is we all go to prison for life is what he thought, but what Hartman said was, "Zero. We're covered. There's no way to tie us to this….in that way. The only thing we have to do if at all possible is make sure nobody prints this kid but us. We need to make it clear that we believe it was obvious self-defense. Put all the focus somewhere other than on him. As to motive, well, maybe we can work on that. Maybe we can come up with something." He'd made sure there was nothing tying the FBI to this attempt on the kid's life, if that's what it was — and he had to assume. The flash drive he'd given Wilson had been generic, and the information on it had been sanitized. There was no way to tell which computer it had come from, or that the info had come from FBI files.

"We need to corral this. Lock down the investigation." Boehmer was thinking out loud. They both were. "I don't know if we'll be able — well, shit. We can't fight too hard, even though my first instinct is to threaten to stomp on their necks with the full weight, power, and authority of the United States government. If we can't find an excuse to take over the investigation, we need to do our best to direct it. Head up the task force, if there is one. We have to make them look at something other than the kid. We need to give them a motive that doesn't involve him. Case of mistaken identity, something. You got any ideas?"

Hartman sighed. "Not yet. We're going to get questions, like why weren't they under surveillance? And if they were, how they slipped away. Well, I checked into that, I checked the records from the SSG surveillance guys. It looks like Wilson pulled the GPS off his car, and so did Mitchell. No matter how they got away from us, we can say that these were highly trained SWAT officers, and they didn't become stupid when they decided to start breaking the law. They've done surveillance, and knew what to look for. We'll spin it so that we don't look too bad. I think the judge who gave them bail will look worse than us. In fact, maybe we can put the onus on her with a comment or two."

"And you're sure there's no way to tie this to us."

Hartman thought back on his meeting with Wilson. He'd spoken to his wife in a public place, very briefly, and it hadn't been pre-arranged, he'd surprised her. He'd only met Wilson the one time, and they'd checked each other over thoroughly for recording devices. The only thing he'd given the man was the flash drive, and if that ever turned up, it wouldn't be a problem for them. If it was found, maybe make it look like someone had hired them to take out the kid for other reasons? No, they couldn't do anything to put any more attention on Anderson. Shit.

"Hartman?"

"Sorry, sir, just thinking. No, there is no way to tie this to us."

"John George."

"Ringo? It's Bill Rochester, from the Northwestern Precinct. We've met, but I'm not sure if you remember me."

"Sure, Bill, I know you. What's up?"

"Sorry for calling you on a Saturday afternoon. Got your cell from command. Have you, uh, been watching the news today?"

Ringo sighed. "I thought that might be what you were calling about. Yeah, I got a call a few hours ago, and I've been on the phone since then with Oakland County, Troy, and the FBI, not that they're saying shit." In fact, he was standing in front of his big screen, which currently was showing an overhead view of the crime scene from the Channel 7 news 'copter. The first time he'd seen the shot he'd immediately picked out Paul Wilson's Charger. "What's your interest?"

"You hear the name of the guy they were reportedly chasing?"

"Yeah, somebody Anderson." The name hadn't meant anything to him. He wasn't actually sure how reliable that identification was, as no police agency would officially release it this early. He supposed a reporter somewhere had been owed a favor. The TV switched to a ground-level view of the scene. All he could see was cop cars with flashing lights and ambulances, officers milling about, and yellow crime scene tape.

"David Anderson. Working as a private investigator."

"Okay."

"I'm working the Warren Avenue case. The one where the guy two weeks ago killed three officers. Shot two, then when we chased him down he shot four more. Three dead, and two more that I don't think are ever going to come back to the job." It was the single worst police loss in city history. Ringo had attended the triple-funeral, but he didn't know which detectives had actually been assigned to the case.

"You still working the case? It's not closed? I thought he was killed."

"I'm still working the case because the shooter had fake ID. We know it was fake because when his prints finally came back, they came back to a name completely different than the Ohio driver's license or the credit cards in his wallet. Shooter was Ralph Marsh, Army veteran. Did several combat tours, then got out, and as far as I can tell he just disappeared, at least until he showed up two weeks ago with fake ID and shot our boys."

"That's.....weird. That's some weird shit right there, Bill."

"It gets weirder. Don't know if you heard, but we didn't kill him. A P.I. on a surveillance witnessed the initial shooting, and followed Marsh. When Marsh started ramming cars and shooting again, it was the P.I. who put him down. With a rifle."

"Anderson? Anderson killed him?"

"No. His boss. His same boss that gave him the surveillance he was working today, John Phault. But Anderson was there. On my case. Hundred feet away. It was a two-man surveillance. I interviewed the kid myself. He said he didn't see anything, but he was close enough to hear it, and he tried to do first aid on Ferguson and Gutierrez. You a big fan of coincidence?"

Ringo didn't say anything for a good long time. "What the hell?" he finally wondered aloud. "We need to talk."

CHAPTER TWENTY

Dave rubbed at his left eyebrow, trying to massage away the headache deep in his skull as the deputy walked away. His cell phone was back in his possession for the first time in......he looked around, tried to find a window. Shit, maybe it was tomorrow already. He checked the clock on his phone. No, still the same day, just late. Seemed like the shooting had happened days ago.

He saw he'd received twenty-four calls since the last time he'd seen his phone, and had sixteen voicemails. Aaron had called more than anyone else. He'd also gotten calls from Gina, two of the guys he shot with at matches, and a number of numbers he didn't recognize. He couldn't bear the thought of listening to all those voicemails, and instead just called Aaron. As he listened to it ring he idly wondered if the cops had browsed through his phone, looking for something incriminating. The only thing on his phone he knew they'd want to look at were the pictures. He'd taken quite a few of Gina wearing almost nothing and less, and she'd taken a few of herself as well, for his enjoyment. Some of the ones she'd taken could best be described as "action photos".

"Dude, what the fuck? Was that you they were talking about on the news?" Aaron said as soon as he answered. That was the problem with having a common name like David Anderson. There'd actually been another Dave Anderson in his graduating class in high school, as well as a Dan Anderson.

"Yeah," Dave said tiredly.

"Are you okay? You didn't get shot, did you?"

"I'm fine. Just tired. Been talking to cops all day. They're trying to figure out if they should arrest me, charge me with murder." Currently the consensus seemed to be, *Maybe not right now, but……*

"For what? What the fuck happened? You actually gun down three fucking cops at the range? Every channel is saying something a little bit different—"

"Aaron. Aaron!" Dave interrupted his friend. "I'm too burnt to talk. Just wanted to call and let you know I was still alive. I don't know what they're saying on the news."

"Why would they charge you with murder? Wasn't it self-defense? Reporters were talking to an old bag in Troy, she said some dude just walked up and started blasting at you, then chased you out of there."

"Pretty much what happened. But cops never believe anybody." He was also pretty sure part of the problem was they weren't used to dealing with good guys with guns. Only bad guys—or cops—shot people in their world. And he'd shot—wait for it—three cops. When he'd found that out he'd almost cried. He'd killed three cops? He'd stayed all wrapped up in that news for a few minutes, before he moved on to the logical question—why the hell had they tried to kill him? Because that sure was hell was what they'd seemed to be doing. And so far he'd come up with nothing on that. Which really had him worried. "Can you do me a favor? Can you call Joe at Absolute? You have his cell phone or something? I don't think I'm going to make it in to work on Monday."

Aaron laughed. "Dude, I don't think you *should* come in to work on Monday."

"What? Why?"

"Coming to work in Detroit?" Aaron laughed again. "You didn't kill people, you killed *four Detroit cops*. Black guys. And somebody dug up the fact that you got into that gunfight a few years ago, those bank robbers you told me about. The fact they were all black? News channels can't decide if you're a racist serial killer or just a racist murderer, but they're willing to talk about both them possibilities for hours."

"Shit, really? Shit. But dammit, I only killed three guys, the deputy killed the fourth. And I didn't give a fuck that they were black, only that they were trying to kill me." He thought back, trying to remember if the fact that any of them was black even registered on him at the time. Mostly he was just trying to shoot them before they shot him. And had everyone forgotten these cops were the same ones arrested by the FBI? What that had to do with him he had no idea, but at least he hadn't gunned down true-blue heroes, the guys after him apparently were bad guys with badges. But again, *why?*

Aaron laughed again, mirthlessly. "It's the news, dude. They're not interested in the actual truth. Ain't nobody got time for that."

Dave saw his attorney and John, his boss, come out of the big meeting with half a dozen detectives from at least three jurisdictions, plus a guy he was pretty sure was an FBI agent. "Gotta go. Will call you when I can. Don't forget to call Joe." He disconnected and put the phone away. Maybe if they didn't see he had it back they wouldn't take it away again. Apart from the few words he'd spoken to the Oakland County Undersheriff, he hadn't actually talked to the cops at all. He hadn't even said all that much to his attorney. How many different ways could you say, "I was just minding my own business when….."?

Dave didn't really have an attorney, but John did, and that's who he'd called. The two of them stopped in front of him. "Time to go home," John told him.

"I'm not being arrested?" Dave croaked. He felt like lying down on the hard bench, but was pretty sure if he did that he'd fall right asleep.

"For what?" the attorney said. "The most clear-cut case of self-defense anybody in there has ever seen? We've got witnesses at both ends of the car chase saying they attacked and started shooting at you first, without provocation, and one of them tried killing an Oakland County deputy to boot."

John smiled thinly. "Cops just don't like it when citizens kill people," he told Dave, then said everything the young man had been thinking. "They think that's their job. Plus, all the guys you killed are cops. That's got a few of them more than a bit twisted up. Having a hard time seeing past that."

"Crooked cops out on bail," the attorney felt obliged to point out. "They seem to grudgingly admit that it looks like self-defense, the thing that's bugging them is *why*. Why did four Detroit cops out on bail head up here and apparently try to kill you." He looked over his shoulder, and lowered his voice. "You sure you don't...." His eyebrows went up.

Dave shook his head. "Not a fucking clue. Seriously. Wish I did."

The attorney in his sharp, dark blue suit looked down at him for a few seconds, then shrugged his shoulders. "Whatever. I guess we'll find out. The 'what happened' seems pretty clear, but they really wanted to keep you locked up until they could figure out the why. That's what we've been arguing about for the past four hours. But you're a fine upstanding citizen without so much as a speeding ticket, and even though they were cops they were dirty cops out on bail. And the FBI seemed to take my side."

"Which was weird," John said.

The attorney nodded. "You're right about that. It was downright bizarre, but I'm not going to look a gift horse in the mouth. Just imagine what they've got going on over at the McNamara Building right now, agents scrambling trying to figure out if they screwed up. What they missed in their investigation that would make those officers do…whatever the hell they were trying to do."

"You're going to get your face all over the news no matter how this plays," John said to his lawyer with a smile.

The lawyer smiled back. "You're damn right I am. And after being your lawyer for all these years I've got Massad Ayoob on speed dial. I just hope we don't need him for this one." Dave recognized the name—in addition to being a well-known gun writer, Ayoob was the preeminent expert court witness on firearms and shootings. Heck, he'd practically invented the job.

The lawyer checked his watch. "They—meaning the FBI, Sheriff's Department, Troy Police Department, and representatives of every other agency involved in this thing—have requested that you not speak to the media. And for God's sake, don't ever talk to them without me present. We don't have anything scheduled, but assume that within a day or two they're going to want you to come in again, answer some more questions. I'll be there for that. Part of the agreement to not arrest you was that you'd cooperate, stay close. Not go on any surprise trips to countries without extradition." The attorney smiled at his own joke.

"Well, if I'm not under arrest, they can go fuck themselves, I'm going to go wherever the hell I want," Dave said with sudden vehemence. "This is America, and I didn't do anything wrong. I was minding my own fucking business." Not that he had any plans to go anywhere, but he was tired of being their punching bag. All he'd been trying to do was earn a few extra bucks on a surveillance. All he'd done was defend himself. "They've got my cell phone number."

John held out his hands in a calming manner. He understood Dave's attitude completely. "Just......call me if you think you're not going to be immediately reachable."

"Fuck. Whatever," Dave said defeatedly.

The attorney looked at John. "I'll keep in touch." He shook both their hands, then headed out of the station.

"How much does that asshole cost an hour?" Dave mumbled.

"Don't you worry about that, I'll pay for him. You were working for me when it happened. Hell, with as much as his face is going to be on TV after this you should charge him." He smiled and looked over, then saw how Dave was nearly asleep sitting up, and checked his watch. "Jesus, it's almost midnight. Come on, I'll drive you home."

"No, I'm good," Dave said, blinking bleary eyes.

"Yeah, you're so good you forgot you don't have a car to drive home. The Mustang's evidence, remember? It's got about twenty bullet holes in it. You'll be lucky to get it back next year. C'mon, don't make me carry you."

John dropped him off at his house just after 12:30 a.m. Dave was half-expecting news trucks to be parked in front of the house, but either none of the cops had given up his address (unlikely) or they'd gone home once it got late. Someone said the satellite trucks left the police station not long after the reporters did their live remotes for the 11 o'clock news, but Dave never saw them.

"You okay?" John asked him as they sat in his SUV idling in the driveway. "You in shock or anything?" He liked the kid, and knew what he was going through.

Dave looked at him with bleary eyes. "No. I don't think so. Maybe I should be in shock, but I'm just numb. Anybody in that big meeting, FBI or whoever, even give a hint about whey they thought those guys were after me?"

John shook his head. "I heard twenty different theories, about half of which painted you as the bad guy, but they don't have any evidence of anything. They're turning those guys' lives upside down right now, even more than after their arrest, trying to figure out what the hell they were doing in Troy. But nobody knows anything more than you." He looked at Dave, saw he was about to fall asleep.

"Get what sleep you can," John told him. "Give me a call tomorrow. You may not want to talk to anybody, but you're going to have to."

"Like who?"

"Like your insurance company, for one thing. To let them know about the car they insure. Their adjuster probably won't be given access to it for a couple of weeks, but they still need to know." John leaned forward. "Just so you know, since your car wasn't in an 'accident' per se, there's a good chance they're not going to cover the damages to it. Or at least try to deny the claim. Find a copy of your policy and look it over, and if I need to, I'll have my lawyer talk to the adjuster. This thing is so high profile, we can give them huge negative publicity with just one word to the press."

This was not what Dave wanted to hear. He just wanted everything to go away, to be left alone; the thought of fighting with his insurance company over the damage to the Mustang drained whatever energy he had left.

"Okay," he said dully.

He trudged up the driveway to the front door. John waited in the driveway until he got in, and Dave used the glow from his headlights to get the key in the lock. He hadn't left any lights on, and the house was completely dark. Once he got the door open he gave a wave over his shoulder and headed in. He turned on the porch light, then the light in the foyer, and then trudged into the dark kitchen. Hungry; he needed to eat something before he went to bed, all he'd had to eat all day was a pre-made sandwich one of the deputies had brought him, probably bought at a gas station.

Blinking in the light of the fluorescents, Dave was reaching for the refrigerator door when someone said, in a very tired voice, "Please don't shoot me."

Dave spun, his hand already on his hip, touching his empty holster, but of course he wasn't wearing a gun. The cops had taken it for evidence, as they had his rifle and his car. Peering below the cupboards, he saw someone sitting at his kitchen table. A skinny guy, sitting awkwardly in the chair. His hands were out in front of him, flat on the table. He wore a t-shirt and a dark windbreaker and looked like he hadn't slept in a couple of days.

Moving with his hand still on his hip, trying to give the impression there was a gun in the holster, Dave moved to the side so he could get a better view of the trespasser. "Who the fuck are you?" He assumed the guy was some hungry young reporter who'd broken into his house, trying to get a scoop.

"Michael Mitchell," the man said, sounding as tired as Dave felt. "FBI.....shit. Sort of. You can call me Mickey."

"What's the 'sort of FBI'?" Dave demanded.

"I was with the FBI before they killed me," he said with an odd sad smile. "Now I'm just with me. And, I guess, since they're trying to kill you too, I'm with you."

The pain as Boehmer shot him made Mickey clench up, his mouth going wide in shock. Then, without even thinking about it, forgetting the pain, he lunged for the man who'd ended his life as he knew it, and fought for the gun. It was dark in the back of the car, and he couldn't see anything. Then Boehmer fired again, and again. Mickey went weak, and Boehmer shoved him backward, against the door.

Mickey reached behind himself, trying desperately to find a way out, and somehow, unexpectedly, got the door open. He was falling backward out the opening door as Boehmer's gun flashed again, and he felt a burning pain in his neck. Then he hit the moving pavement hard, rolled once, and lay there, his ears ringing.

Face down on the gritty surface, he heard the car accelerating away, but the sound seemed distant. His ears were pulsing from the gunfire inside the back of the Lincoln. His neck was on fire, and searing pain shot through his body with every ragged breath. His body was curled into a ball, eyes clenched shut from the pain. Did death hurt this much? Seemed pretty unfair.

Gradually the night sounds of the city returned. The constant hum of traffic, isolated tweets of birds, the occasional distant shout. Then voices that weren't so distant, and the hum of a different kind of tire.

"Shit, man, I told you I heard a gunshot. Somebody just smoked a dude. Lookit that."

"Is that a dead guy? Why'd they leave him in the middle of the street? Probably just a dummy."

Mickey wheezed and rolled half onto his back, and the two boys yelped in surprise. He was able to crack his eyes and saw them sitting on their bicycles about fifteen feet away. "Not dead yet," he said with a groan. There was enough light to see the boys were maybe eight or ten, their arms and legs nearly as skinny as the frames on their bikes.

"You get shot? What are you doing in the street?"

"D'you get jacked, man?" the other boy asked. "Somebody take your ride?"

"Somebody took my life," Mickey said. Grunting with the effort, he slid a hand up to his neck and gasped with the pain. There was a big chunk taken out of his neck muscle, and his hand felt wet. He couldn't tell if it was still bleeding, but thought it probably was. He knew he should put pressure on the wound, but didn't have the strength. That was probably a bad sign.

"You gonna die?" one of the kids asked him. They both still sat on their bike seats and stared at him like he was an interesting exhibit at the zoo. Kids.

Mickey looked at the kids, then at the darkness beyond them. "Isn't it past your bedtimes?" he said wearily.

"Ain't got no bedtime in summer vacation." The boy paused. "So, you gonna die or what? You want us to call the po-lice?"

"Shit, Manny, look at all that blood." The other boy had rolled a few feet closer to Mickey and looked over his handlebars. He could see a large puddle of blood under the man's head.

"No, don't call the police."

"Why not? You white."

"Police are the ones who shot me," he told them. He hadn't moved his forehead off the street, and still was curled up into a tight, pain-wracked ball.

"Shit, really? Why? Who you be?" But they didn't get a response. He'd passed out.

Jorge Eligio was leaning one hip against the grille of his pickup, relaxing. He had an ice-cold Budweiser in his hand, the Red Sox were on, and he didn't have to work tomorrow, so all was right with the world. Didn't even matter that the Sox were down by three in the eighth inning. Lots more games in the season.

Most Saturdays he worked, and today had been no different. He was still wearing his paint-splattered coveralls. He'd take a shower before bed, and tomorrow was church and family dinner, but now was his time. Time at the end of a long week to unwind. He'd had to replace the radiator hose on the Ford, but that had only taken ten minutes, and had only been his excuse to go outside. Not that his wife didn't know he was out here by himself, relaxing. Graciela knew a man needed some time alone. And maybe, later on, she'd be in the mood for some company herself.......

Manny rolled up with his friend on their bikes, out of breath. "Papa, papa, we found a dead guy!"

"What?"

"He not dead. He's only maybe half dead," D'Shaunte said.

"What are you talking about?" Jorge asked his son. Sometimes he just didn't understand children at all. The only thing he could remember about his childhood was working every day after school for his father.

"Dead guy—almost dead guy," Manny corrected himself, "in the middle of the street. Got shot. I thought he got jacked, but he said the cops shot him."

Jorge looked down his nose at the boys. "Are you telling me another story?" Even if you took away the video games they made up stories all day long, played cowboys versus aliens.

"No!" Manny insisted.

"He's a cop too," D'Shaunte added.

"What?"

"He white, in a suit, wearing body armor." D'Shaunte beamed proudly. He'd been the one brave enough to first approach the man and poke him, feel the hard vest under his shirt.

"What? You touch his gun?" Jorge stood tall and looked down at them.

Manny knew how his father was when it came to keeping them away from guns. "No, no, we didn't see no gun." Not that D-Shaun hadn't been looking for it, but when he touched the man's body armor he'd groaned, they'd gotten scared, and pedaled for home as fast as they could.

"Go get your cousin Emilio," Jorge told his son.

The next memory Mickey had was of pain as he was lifted into the bed of a pickup truck. There were silhouettes of men around him, but he couldn't see their faces. He could smell cigarettes and beer and spicy food. "Please, no ambulance," he gasped. It felt like he was getting stabbed by flaming knives, it hurt him just to breathe.

"Your wallet says FBI," one of the men said to him.

"Don't call them," he pleaded with his rescuers, if that's who they were.

"Why. The ID fake?"

"No, they're the ones who shot me." It sounded ridiculous even to him, and he knew it was true.

"Why?"

"I know the wrong secret."

"Shit." He was lying in the back of the pickup, he could feel the steel under his shoulder, the vehicle shift as the men moved around him. "Then what the fuck we supposed to do with you, mister?"

Mickey groaned and cracked an eye. "Give me til morning. If I'm still alive, I'll leave. If I'm not…..then bring my body back here. You can have whatever money I've got, it isn't much." Mickey slid back into unconsciousness with the colorful sound of what he guessed was Spanish profanity ringing in his ears.

Mickey wasn't sure what was real and what were his dreams, but he remembered opening his eyes and seeing a hulking Hispanic teenager staring at him from a chair. There was bright light coming in a window, but exactly where he was he couldn't remember. He had no recollection of falling asleep again, but found himself waking up to the sound of steps. Lots of footsteps, on creaky wooden stairs.

Mickey cracked his eyes. The teenager, who looked like a fifteen-year-old linebacker with a peachfuzz moustache, was still sitting in the chair, just putting away a cell phone. There was a window above and just to the left of the kid, and golden sunlight was streaming into the room. Dust particles danced in the light. Looking around the room, Mickey saw he was in a young girl's bedroom. The walls were white, and there was a lot of pink in the room—wood trim, stuffed animals, assorted items on a small dresser sitting nearby.

The steps arrived outside the door, which opened to admit a couple that looked Mexican. She was small woman and the man, while he wasn't huge, had the same thickness as the teen in the chair. The man was in a suit, the woman a very pretty flowered dress. "Emilio," the man said, and jerked his head toward the open door. The teen got up with a scowl at Mickey, and as he passed him the man muttered "Gracias."

"We are not Maria and Jesus," the man told Mickey, giving the name the Spanish pronunciation, "so this is not Heaven. You did not die." It appeared he wasn't sure if he was happy about that. The woman gave him a dirty look and moved closer to the bed.

Mickey could tell he wasn't dead, because he was in too much pain. His entire neck was stiff and sore, and the left side of it burned like it was on fire. He reached up and found there was a fat bandage there. His chest hurt as well, and he could feel it every time he took a breath.

"You have a hole in your neck, you need a doctor," the woman told him. "I think you have broken ribs, too. There were bullets in your vest when we took it off. Some of them fell out, but we saved them."

"That's okay," Mickey said. For just having slept through the night, he didn't feel rested. He felt like he'd just had his ass kicked by a gang armed with baseball bats. With great difficulty he pulled the sheet and comforter down off his chest. Hell, it *looked* like he'd had his ass kicked by guys with baseball bats, his chest was covered with angry red swollen circles the size of quarters. What hurt the most were the two down by his floating ribs.

"Drink some water, take some pills," the woman said, gesturing. Mickey looked and saw that on the bedside table was a glass of water and a half-full prescription medicine bottle. With some difficulty he reached over and saw it was a six-month old prescription for amoxicillin for Graciela Eligio. Take three a day until gone. There was also a big bottle of ibuprofen. "I never finished the pills, and they should help. But you should see a doctor, your neck looks very bad."

Mickey got a pill out of the bottle, stuck it in his mouth, and washed it down with water. He did the same with four ibuprofen. "Thank you," he said in a tired voice. He'd told the man that if he was alive he would leave in the morning, and he'd meant it. "I will go." He tried, he really did, but it hurt too much to even sit up, much less get out of bed and walk down stairs.

Panting and sweating, Mickey said, "I don't think I can. Not on my own. Can you help me downstairs? Maybe drive and drop me off somewhere where I can sit for a while? Get my strength back?" He had no idea where he should go, but he didn't need to put them in any more danger by his presence.

The woman turned to the man, whom Mickey presumed was her husband, and they had a long and very intense conversation in Spanish. The man was on the receiving end most of the time. Mickey caught the name "Jesus" several times. Finally the man, frowning, turned back to Mickey. The woman looked at Mickey, nodded, then headed downstairs. "You are lucky today is Sunday, and the priest talked about compassion until my ears bled," the man said. "My wife wants to be a good Samaritan, and use you to get into Heaven. You may stay two days. If you can't walk then....I drag you."

Jorge thought about the body armor he'd peeled off the unconscious stranger's body, currently stored on the top shelf of the closet, along with the misshapen bullets that had fallen out of it. "Are we in any danger? From the men who shot you?" He'd examined the FBI identification as well. It looked authentic enough, although he had no idea what a real one might look like.

"Not if no one knows I am here. Although...did you find a cell phone in my clothes? You should take the battery out and throw it away, just in case. Somewhere away from here."

Mickey changed the bandage on his neck twice a day, and Graciela Eligio was right—it did look ugly. It looked like someone had stuck a finger in the muscle on the left side of his neck and ripped it out sideways. Even with the antibiotics he was taking it seemed to be a little inflamed, but he didn't dare go to the hospital. They were required by law to report gunshot wounds, and this didn't look like anything but that. He couldn't really turn his neck more than two inches in either direction without the wound pulling, and he was careful not to tear it open. He was taking 800 milligrams of ibuprofen every four hours, but it still was only taking the tiniest edge off the pain. Kevlar saved lives, but it didn't keep getting shot from hurting.

They never left him alone in the house, and never with just Graciela home. Either Jorge or his surly nephew Emilio made sure to let him know they were around, even if they were just outside in the driveway tinkering on the car. Mickey got the impression they were calling in sick those days, for which he felt both grateful and ashamed.

By the second day the bruises from where the bullets had hit his soft body armor had doubled in diameter and turned a nice shade of dark purple. He was pretty sure he had two fractured ribs just from the amount of pain he caused himself by moving around the room. While everything still hurt—a lot—he was able to get up and walk around. Admittedly, he moved like someone three times his age, with bad arthritis, but he could move under his own power. Then it was time to go.

"My clothes will be baggy on you, but are the right length," Jorge told him, handing Mickey an old t-shirt, button-down shirt, and fraying blue jeans. When he had the jeans and t-shirt on, Jorge said, "Oh, wait." He strode to the closet and opened it, then pulled out Mickey's vest.

Mickey examined the vest. It had definitely been damaged by the bullet impacts, there were deep divots in the woven polymer material. Charcoal-hued circles. Mickey wasn't positive, but he was pretty sure that unless he was shot again in the exact same place, the vest should still stop more bullets. With a few grunts he got it on over his head and secured it with the elastic Velcro straps. The button-down shirt was blue, and he let it hang, as tucking in the shirt was beyond him in his current state. He was the same height but barely more than half the width of Jorge, and the shirt was more than baggy, but as long as it didn't have bullet holes or bloodstains he didn't care. His FBI ID went into his pocket.

He didn't have much money, but he still tried to give it to Jorge. "For the food," he told the man. Three meals a day, that's what they brought up to him. He ate it all, every time, even though it hurt him to both chew and swallow.

Jorge wouldn't take it. "I think you'll need it more than we do," Jorge told him. Mickey had been studiously avoiding thinking about anything beyond the moment for days, as when he did the world seemed a crushing weight on his head. The thought of where he'd go when he left the safety of their little girl's bedroom—he hadn't seen her, they wouldn't let the children up to even peek at him, but he learned her name was Esmeralda—Izzy—was just one of a number of questions he didn't have answers to.

He had enough amoxicillin pills left for another two days, enough ibuprofen in the bottle for maybe a week. Not a full dose of antibiotics, but it would have to do. "Take this too," Jorge said, handing him a paint-splattered hooded sweatshirt. "It's too hot to wear now, but you might need it."

"Thank you," he said sincerely.

By mutual consent he'd waited to leave until after dark. Less for prying eyes to see. Going down the creaky wooden staircase hurt like hell, and took him over a minute. At the bottom a rail-thin boy and a doe-eyed girl stared at him.

"Mister, you look like a zombie," the boy told him. His mother, standing nearby, shushed him, but Mickey smiled. He hadn't shaved in two days, but that was deliberate. He figured looking like himself was a pretty bad idea. Between the dark stubble and the whiter than usual skin (from the blood loss) he didn't look like the man who'd climbed into the Lincoln belonging to the Director of the FBI Lab. And he wasn't.

"Thank you for letting me sleep in your bedroom," he told the little girl, who quickly ran and hid behind her mother's legs.

Graciela lifted a plastic bag off the kitchen counter and handed it to him. "Vaya con Dios." Mickey looked inside and saw it was filled with food.

"I sure hope so." He looked at the food again. "This is very generous. I hope to repay you someday."

Graciela shook her head. "We did what we did because we are good people, and I think you are good people too. You repay someone else with a kindness."

And just like that, Mickey realized where he needed to go, and what he needed to do.

"I'm sorry—believe me, after seeing what happened today—yesterday—I'm really sorry I wasn't able to get here sooner," Mickey told Dave. "But those six days in the hospital in Philadelphia because my neck got infected really set me back."

The treating physician had notified the police, but Mickey had hidden his FBI employee ID, wallet, and vest in an alley three blocks away from the hospital before walking into the emergency room with a swollen purple neck and 104° fever, giving a fake name.

When the exhausted and overworked cop had shown up Mickey flat-out refused to answer any questions, saying he couldn't remember anything. The cop didn't believe him, of course, but he couldn't arrest Mickey for getting shot. The wound was old, that much was obvious. He checked with his department to see if there were any recent reports of shootings, and when he could find no connection between Mickey's wound and any recent police activity, he just cursed at Mickey for being stupid, completed his report, and left. They kept him in the hospital much longer than he thought they would, because the infection was so close to his spine and brain, and was initially resistant to the first antibiotics they tried. The only thing that really surprised Mickey was finding his wallet and vest undisturbed behind the dumpster after almost a week.

"I was actually surprised how willing truckers were to give me a lift," Mickey observed. "I guess they like the company. As long as you're polite and don't seem crazy, hitch-hiking from truck stop to truck stop is pretty easy. It's just not as quick as you think. Sometimes you have to wait a whole day for another ride in the direction you want to go."

He'd remembered the name of the street Dave lived on, and the city, but he couldn't quite remember the address. A few internet searches using a borrowed cell phone hadn't helped at all; apparently Anderson didn't have a home phone number, so he couldn't call ahead. Not that Mickey was sure he would have — what were the chances Anderson would believe his crazy story in person, much less over the phone? But Anderson's profile picture on Facebook was him standing in front of a black Mustang in the driveway of a house Mickey assumed was his home, and after arriving in the area he'd pretty much figured out which house that was. He also saw all the police activity two streets over, and quickly learned what had happened from neighbors standing on their lawns. Mickey'd then bounced around between three local fast food restaurants until dark. The house was still dark when he returned. He'd walked around back and tried a few windows, and was surprised to find the one over the kitchen sink unlocked.

"Shut up about your fucking hitch-hiking," Dave told him. He was sitting across his kitchen table from him, Mickey's FBI ID in his hands. "I don't care about your goddamn hitch-hiking. I had two car-loads of SWAT cops just try to kill me this morning. Yesterday morning. And you're telling me that they were trying to kill *me*. Not some random person, not some stranger, *me*. Because my fingerprints match two other people. Because *you* matched my fingerprints to two other people."

Mickey had borrowed a little cash from some good Christian folk along the way, so he'd been able to eat at least once a day, but he'd dropped close to twenty pounds and had been skinny to start with. Between that and the stress of having life as he knew it end, he looked and felt horrible. Dave pointing out that it was his forensic skills—and naiveté—which had put both of them in this position didn't make him feel any better. "Yes," he said simply. Mickey was pretty sure he was still in shock, or psychological denial, or something, because everything seemed so surreal. This couldn't be his life now, could it? He had a great job at the FBI Lab. This whole thing seemed like it had to be a dream, or a movie, or something. He kept waiting to wake up.

Dave felt as tired as this FBI asshole looked, and was having a hard time focusing his eyes, but he put down the ID and pulled out his cell phone. "What's this other guy's name? The one in Jersey that my finger matches?" As he said it he glanced at his fingertips. He found he'd been doing that a lot ever since the news. They looked....normal. Not something worth killing him over.

"Beiers, Jerome Beiers." He spelled it. "I think he was in Newark? Somewhere in that area."

Dave's thumbs were moving over the phone. "How old was he?"

"Maybe ten years older than you? I can't really remember." Mickey wondered exactly what the kid was doing, then remembered that this 'kid' was the same age as him, and had been working as a private investigator for several years. He was probably pretty damn good at tracking down information.

Dave's thumbs stopped, and he peered at his phone in silence for about thirty seconds. His eyes moved back and forth. "Shit," he finally said.

"What?"

"'Jerome Beiers, age 38, of Newark, died as a result of complications from his injuries yesterday,'" he read. "This was....shit, almost a couple of weeks ago." He read the newspaper story further. "Looks like he was stabbed in an attack, and his attacker cut off his finger. Doesn't say which one. The finger was not recovered. "Police have no motive in the attack, and no suspects. Anyone with any information....blah blah blah. Fuck."

He threw the phone down and rubbed his eyes. He was so tired he was weaving in the chair. Now he knew the why of the gunfight yesterday, but he sure as hell didn't feel any better about it. He now knew that it wasn't just a one-time random occurrence. If what the FBI evidence tech said was true—and he didn't have any reason to doubt him, everything he'd said made sense—the Detroit cops coming after him wasn't going to be the last excitement he'd have in the near future.

Shit, he thought, *could that thing a few weeks ago, when I was on surveillance, be tied in with this? The crazy cop killer? Had the guy been coming after me and been interrupted?* "I've got to go to sleep, think about this tomorrow."

Dave looked at the FBI—former FBI employee, and saw how exhausted he looked as well. "You can take the couch. Anybody comes through the door, jump on them and start yelling. I'm going to bed."

CHAPTER TWENTY-ONE

Mickey opened his eyes, not quite sure where he was. He heard someone moving around nearby, but didn't recognize the room he was in. Well decorated, somebody's living room.....with a groan he sat up on the couch, remembering where he was. Anderson's house. That's probably who he heard, walking up and down stairs.

He checked his watch. Nearly ten a.m. Jeez, he'd slept nearly nine hours. He hadn't slept that much since before....this all happened. He'd never been able to relax enough to catch more than two or three hours in a row, even when he was in the hospital. There he kept waiting to hear the heavy tread of the police, or worse yet, the FBI. He'd refrained from Googling himself since Boehmer had left him for dead; he wasn't sure exactly how much activity on the internet the government monitored, but he knew they did it. No reason to make them suspect he wasn't, in fact, dead.

Stiff-legged, he levered himself off the couch and went in search of a bathroom. He found one off the kitchen, used the toilet, and stared at himself in the mirror. He looked horrible, like a scarecrow. There were dark hollows under his eyes, and his neck....his neck would never look the same. Seventeen stitches, that's how many it had taken to close up the wound, after the doctor had cleaned out the pus and scolded him for leaving it untreated for so long. The left side of his neck was a lumpy tangled mass of pink flesh. Plus, his chest still hurt, his broken ribs had not healed all the way. He hadn't mentioned anything about broken ribs to the medical staff at the hospital, and if they'd noticed the yellowing bruises across his torso they'd never asked about them. It didn't hurt him to breathe anymore, but if he leaned too far this way or that pain shot up his side.

Anderson was coming out of the garage when Mickey emerged from the bathroom. He looked like he was busy doing something, harried and grumpy. "Can I grab something to eat?"

Dave stopped and looked at him. "Yeah, sure. Food's in the fridge, and some in the cupboard. Get whatever you want."

Eating a bagel and drinking some Diet Coke, Mickey watched Anderson make two more trips to the garage. "What are you doing?" he asked the young man. Actually, Anderson wasn't that young, he reminded himself, he was the same age as Mickey. But Mickey felt old. Older than he was. Running for your life tends to age you.

"Packing."

Mickey blinked. "Packing for what?"

Dave stopped and shook his head. "I'm not staying here. I need to get the hell out of here." He rested his hand idly on the Glock in his holster. His spare gun, the one Taran had used at the match, as the other had been taken into evidence even though he'd never fired a shot out of it. But the cops couldn't take his word for that.

Mickey was confused. "What do you mean? Where are you going?"

"I've got a house—a cabin, more like—in Arizona. I'm going to head out there." He'd already called Joe at Absolute earlier that morning, told him he was going to take a little time off.

"Davey, you take as much time as you need," Joe told him. Actually, he'd been glad Davey wanted to take some time off. While the local TV stations only had his high school graduation photo to post during their stories, Dave was still recognizable, and driving around Detroit after killing a handful of black Detroit cops—whether they were dirty or not—could cause serious problems. Armored car personnel were already targets.

"But—" Mickey started to say, but stopped himself. He looked around the kitchen. He'd just gotten there, and now Anderson wanted to leave again? But, he supposed, it made sense. Anderson wasn't safe, not until they could go public with this.

"But what?" Dave said angrily. Mickey found himself getting angry in return.

"You know, you're not the only person they're trying to kill here." He jabbed a finger at his ugly neck. "I got shot, almost died. In fact, they—my boss—shot me so many times he thought he killed me. My ribs are still messed up."

Anderson's mouth opened like he couldn't believe what he was hearing and stepped close, like he was going to hit him. "Do you actually want sympathy from me? Is that where you're fucking going? This is all your fault! If you'd just kept your damn mouth shut I'd probably be in the FBI Academy right now. You'd still have a fucking job, and your neck wouldn't look like a pussy with third-degree burns."

Mickey opened his mouth, closed it, then said, "Is that really what it looks like?"

Dave took a couple of breaths and calmed down. "It looks bad, yeah."

"No, I mean, does it really look like a vagina?"

Dave frowned and cocked his head. "Yeah, it does. A sideways one."

"Shit". He'd been afraid of that. Mickey looked at Dave. "What are you planning to do when you get to Arizona?"

"I'm not planning on anything. I just want to get out of here. Those cops didn't come after me on their own, somebody put them up to it. Probably dirty FBI, the same ones who shot you. And they're still out there."

They both looked around. For the first time Mickey noticed how big the house was, how empty it seemed. "We should stick together," he said. He didn't know if Anderson had been planning on leaving him there, but he wasn't about to let him get away after travelling across half the country to find him.

Dave stared at him for a long while. "Can you shoot at all, if it comes to that?" he finally asked. Opposite the Glock 35 on his hip were two spare magazines on the left side of his belt. He'd already put his spare rifle and competition shotgun into the Jeep.

Mickey blinked. It wasn't a question he'd been expecting. "My uncle took me shooting once. He was an FBI agent."

"Did you have to do any shooting or qualifying for the FBI Lab?" Mickey shook his head. "Shit."

"What?"

Dave told him, "You don't get good at something by only doing it once in your life, and shooting, especially with a handgun, is a perishable skill." He eyed Mickey's rumpled clothes. "How soon can you be ready to leave?"

"Um….can I take a shower first? And maybe borrow some clothes?"

While the FBI Lab geek was in the shower, Dave called John Phault. "Hey," he said, sounding tired.

"Hey," John replied. "Have you turned on the news yet?"

"No."

"Good, don't."

"Why, is it that bad?"

"Let's just say you were there, so you know what happened, but everyone else on TV just keeps guessing, and talking about everything. They're fascinated by the fact that these guys were out on bail when this happened, and they're giving the FBI a giant public screwing about it. The usual suspects also keep pointing out that it was a couple of white guys—you and the deputy—who killed a bunch of black guys. And somebody dug up the fact that this isn't the first time you've killed black guys."

"Jesus. I don't care what color they were. I didn't even notice, I was too busy shooting back. Both times."

"Yeah, I know. Hey, did you call your insurance company yet?"

"No, not yet. It's Sunday, anyway. I was calling you to let you know I was going to take a few days."

"Dude...." He heard his boss laugh. "You take as much time as you need, shit. Hey, um, if you, you know, need to talk to anyone about it, I know someone who's really good."

"You mean a shrink?"

"Yeah. Well, a therapist."

Dave made a face that his boss couldn't see. "No thanks."

"No shame in it," John told him. "PTSD's a real thing, I've had it. I know a lot of people who have, professional badasses."

Dave knew it was a real thing. Hell, he'd hardly slept the night before with all that had happened, and all that he'd learned. When he did sleep, he kept reliving the gunfight, except his rifle malfunctioned, or the bullets had no effect. PTSD....the gift that kept on giving. "Talking about it's not going to help me." *Bombing the FBI lab, that might help me. Maybe going back in time a month or two.*

He heard John sigh. "Okay, but if you do feel the need to talk, you can talk to me, too, you don't have to talk to a shrink."

"Thanks," Dave said grudgingly.

"You call me in a day or two, okay?"

Dave agreed and hung up the phone before he did something stupid like tell John about his little fingerprint problem. John couldn't help him, and telling him would only put him in danger. He quickly finished packing the Cherokee, then waited while Mickey got dressed.

"How long of a drive is it to Arizona?" Mickey asked him, tugging on a borrowed t-shirt. He only had a vague sense of the geography east of the Appalachians.

"With two of us, we can drive straight through. You can drive, can't you?" As un-American as it was, especially from the view of someone who lived so close to the Motor City, he knew a lot of D.C. and New York City residents couldn't drive because they always depended on public transportation.

"Sure, I can drive."

"Good. Straight through, depending on traffic and construction, should only be twenty-eight, thirty hours. Plus stops for gas and bathroom."

"Thirty hours? Really?" Holy shit, that was forever.

"What? Oh, you're an east coast kid, aren't you? You forget just how big this country is?"

Mickey asked him, "Why don't we just fly?"

Dave just stared back. "Dude, seriously? You live your whole life in a box? First off, I want to have a car when I'm there. I'm not going on vacation in Cancun. Second, third, last, and most important," and he pointed at the gun on his hip, "this is staying on me til I die. Which probably is going to be a lot sooner than I'd like."

"Christ, can you turn on the music, the radio, something?" Mickey exploded after nearly six hours of complete silence.

"What? Oh, sorry," Dave said. "Thinking. And I spend so much time in the car doing surveillance, I'm sort of burned out on the radio. You want some music?"

"That would be good, thanks." Six hours felt like twelve, and they were still only in Illinois.

Dave kept the Cherokee in good shape since he depended on it when following people. He'd just gotten an oil change a few weeks before, and the tires were only six months old. The interior wasn't in good shape, but that's what happened when you lived inside your car three days a week. He grabbed his iPod off the center console, turned it on, and flicked on the radio on the dash.

"Oh my God, what is this?" Mickey said about thirty seconds later.

Dave glanced down at the iPod, touched it so the display would light up. "Truck Stop Tuna. A lot of people say they sound like early Pink Floyd."

"The only people who would say that are those who have never heard Pink Floyd. It's like Down's Syndrome set to music. I need to change this or I'm going to lose my mind." He grabbed the iPod without waiting for permission.

Dave shot him a dark look, then glanced back at the road. "What the hell do you like? Lady Gaga?"

"Actually I do like a lot of her stuff, but I prefer classical music in the car."

Dave rolled his eyes. "This is going to be a long fucking trip."

Mickey thumbed through the iPod, trying to find something he liked. "Sooooo," he said slowly. He still didn't have a read on Anderson. "What exactly happened yesterday with those cops? I talked to some of the neighbors, but....did they just come at you?"

Dave really didn't want to talk about it. He was pissed off at this fingerprint tech, this was the guy who'd ruined his life. And yet...he knew that wasn't quite fair. The guy couldn't have known what would happen. No one could, and to be honest, he'd suffered more loss than Dave had — no job, no life, and a bullet wound in the neck that just looked nasty. Hell, it looked pornographic. Hands gripping the steering wheel tight he frowned, then told Mickey, "I was sitting in my neighborhood on a surveillance when they came up in two cars behind me. One of them walked up and just tried to shoot me."

The road in front of him faded out as he flashed back to the scene; the glass filling the cabin like glittering dust, the back end of the 'Stang threatening to break free as he floored it, the taste of fear in his mouth.

"Yeah, that's what the people I talked to said. And then they chased you down and what, ran you off the road?"

Dave shook his head. "I couldn't outrun them. They were better drivers than I was." He shrugged. "So I said 'Fuck it' and made a stand."

"You stopped on purpose?" Mickey said, eyes wide. He tried to picture it and couldn't. It made no sense to him. He stared out at the passing scenery for a few seconds. "But weren't there four of them?"

Dave shrugged. "I didn't know how many there were. I knew there were at least two, because there were two cars."

"Did you set them up in an ambush or something?" Mickey was trying to figure out how Anderson was still alive. Four veteran SWAT cops versus one scared young private investigator. The math didn't add up in his head.

Dave was having a hard time talking about it but he figured Mitchell had a right to know. "No. I just stopped and they came at me."

"Were you in the military or something?" He didn't remember that from Anderson's application packet, but he was still trying to make sense of what he was hearing.

"No."

Mickey stared at him. "How are you not dead?" he asked frankly.

Dave had replayed the incident a thousand times in his head and knew the answer to that....but explaining it to the FBI lab guy might be difficult. "I was in a gunfight a few years ago," Dave told him. "I was still in college, doing an internship, a ride-along, with a local police department. And we ran into a carload of bank robbers. I mean," he shook his head, a grim little smile on his face, "we actually ran into them. Or they ran into us. And they started shooting the shit out of our car, and the officer in the car with me, he got hit in the head and was out of it. So it was up to me." He frowned. "And I fucked up so bad both of us almost died. I missed a guy not much farther away than the end of this car with a shotgun. A shotgun! We should have died, but the assholes shooting at me were even worse shots than I was." Images from that firefight flashed through his mind.

"I was scared, but not that scared. I was more scared afterward than I was during, just like the Detroit cops the other day. So I should have shot better than I did." He shrugged. "Considering that I was going into law enforcement, and even wanted to get into the FBI back then, I thought actually becoming a better shot might be a pretty good idea if I didn't want to die stupid. So I started shooting competitively. What you'd call 'combat style' shooting. And I practiced, and practiced, and practiced, and practiced, with the idea being that if I ever found myself in the same kind of situation I'd have practiced shooting so much that I *couldn't* miss. That the muscle memory would kick in no matter how freaked out I was."

Mickey heard what he was saying, but it still didn't make sense. "But that's target shooting, right? They were SWAT cops."

He tried to put it in terms the guy from the FBI lab might understand. "I have a criminal justice degree, and know a lot more than the average CSI viewer about fingerprints. But compared to you I'm probably a moron. Think of it in those terms. Those cops, they are probably great at kicking in doors and putting handcuffs on assholes, but even though they're SWAT I bet they only go shooting once a week, if that. There is so much more to the job than shooting people, which, if they're doing their job right, they will rarely if ever have to do. Hell, what they do every day on the job is drive, and you see what happened there, I couldn't outrun them even though I had a faster car. A much faster car." He silently mourned his brutalized Mustang for a second. "But when it comes to shooting, I practice every day. *Every* day. Hell, I had the rifle in the car because I was going to practice at the range later."

He looked at Mitchell and saw the tech still wasn't quite following him. "Okay, what about golf. You know anything about golf? If shooting was golf, I'm good enough to get onto the PGA. I'd never beat Tiger Woods, but..." he thought back to the state match and Taran Butler, "I've competed alongside him. And didn't embarrass myself. Those SWAT guys weren't professional golfers, professional shooters, they were just guys who worked with and usually go up against people who aren't any better than them. Cold honest truth is I was just better than they were. A lot better, and by the time it happened I wasn't scared any more. I was just pissed. Being not scared makes a huge difference, trust me, you're in front of the curve. I was pissed, I had cover, and I had my rifle. I'm really good with that rifle, and if I died I knew it wouldn't be for lack of shooting back. Shit, the farthest shot was maybe twenty yards, which is nothing for a rifle. Looking back on it, once I got my rifle in my hands it was all over. They were already dead, they just didn't know it."

Mickey stared at him. "But how are you? I mean....you killed three guys. Yeah, they were trying to kill you, but....you know....." Mickey'd been shot, but that was entirely different from killing someone, much less three people.

Dave stared out at the passing road for a while. "You mean do I have PTSD or whatever? Sure. Maybe I'm in shock, I don't know. I sure don't feel normal, but then again my whole life's been turned upside down. You want me to break down because I've got nightmares and the shakes and I'm freaking out and barely holding it together? I keep reliving the gunfight over and over, seeing it every time I close my eyes for more than two seconds. Want me to sit down and have a good cry?" He gave a little laugh. "I'd love to, if it would solve any of my problems."

Boehmer's phone beeped, and he saw it was the receptionist calling. "Yes?"

"Agent Boehmer, I have an Agent Colman from the CIA here to see you." She knew better than to call him *Mr.* Boehmer, that pissed him off to no end.

Boehmer frowned, and looked at the appointment book on the desk. He didn't have anything penciled in, and he probably would have remembered an appointment with someone from the CIA. "Did he have an appointment?"

There was a pause and he heard muffled conversation. "No."

"Then what is this about?" Boehmer didn't have time for more inter-agency political bullshit. That's all he did all day, seemed like.

"He said he talked to Agent Hartman on the phone yesterday?" The receptionist didn't sound like she knew exactly what the man wanted either, but Boehmer's blood ran cold. The only conversations he'd had with Pete Hartman yesterday had been about the Detroit cops who had been killed. Hell, those were the only conversations he'd had with anyone yesterday. The damn news reporters, what were they thinking? The FBI had argued for no bail, it was the damn liberal woman judge that had not only set bail for the four Detroit cops, but set it so low they could afford to get out.

"Send him in. Uh...." he had to think for a second. "Nancy? Is he armed? Make sure whoever is out front runs him through the metal detector. If he's not FBI I don't want him carrying a gun in our offices. He can leave his gun in one of the lock boxes if he's armed."

"Yes sir."

Boehmer didn't know what he expected, but it wasn't the unassuming man who poked his head in the door of his office. "Got a few minutes?" Boehmer pointed at one of the chairs in front of his desk, and frowned when the man closed his office door before taking a seat. Colman was maybe forty years old, medium build, brown hair, clean shaven, wearing a well-made but off-the-rack suit. He smiled as he sat down.

"What can I help you with...is it Agent Colman? Can I see your creds please?"

Colman dug into his jacket pocket and handed over his credentials. As Boehmer was looking at them, Colman pulled a small black box out of another pocket, activated a switch on it, and set it on the desk.

"What's that?"

"We call it a jam box," Colman told him. "It will disrupt any listening devices in the room."

"There aren't any bugs in my office," Boehmer told him indignantly.

"Special Agent Boehmer, I don't believe you're that ignorant," Colman told him, not trying to be insulting. "If there's an active phone line in the room, a land line, we can listen through it. If there's a cell phone with any power in the battery, we can turn the microphone on remotely and listen. The same goes for computer microphones, webcams....this has been public knowledge for years. I suppose the disconnect is that nobody thinks the government will ever listen to *them*. Did you think we wouldn't do it to you because you're the FBI? Please."

Boehmer stared at the man, then looked down at his CIA identification. Over his eighteen years with the Bureau he had had occasion to work with the CIA on a handful of cases, and what he was holding in his hand looked like an authentic ID, but......"Are you with the CIA? Or the NSA? Is this an authentic ID?" Boehmer waved it at the man.

"It is a completely authentic CIA ID, made by them in Virginia where they produce all of their credentials." Colman smiled. "They're very useful. Everyone ought to have one. But I think you're avoiding the subject."

"I am? What subject?"

"Your unsuccessful attempts to have David Anderson killed."

Mike Boehmer froze, then set the CIA credentials down on his desk. He stared at the blank leather on the exterior for a few seconds, then looked up at Colman. "I'm sorry, could you repeat that?"

"I could, but you heard me quite well the first time I said it. I am here to tell you to cease and desist."

A thousand thoughts raced through Boehmer's head. The one that his mind kept circling back to was—*Am I going to prison?* He had a hard time getting past that one. It had been large on his mind from the first minute he'd learned about David Anderson's unique predicament. He'd been eating Tums like they were candy, snapping at his wife and son, just waiting—expecting—it to all go sideways. And now it had. An entire career in the toilet because of one shit-ass kid with copycat fingerprints.

"I'm surprised they only sent one of you," the FBI Special Agent in Charge said finally. "I would have thought everybody wanted to get in on the arrest."

Colman blinked, and sat further back in the chair. "I don't think you've been paying attention to me, Mr. Boehmer. I am here to tell you to stop, to not do anything else where David Anderson is concerned. Or at least anything else illegal, I know you have to investigate the shooting of your suspects, but I trust you can keep a lid on that. I am not here to arrest you."

"You're.....then what's going on?"

"What's going on is that the adults are going to handle this now," Colman told him. "Your incompetence has gotten I don't know how many cops killed. Leave this problem to the professionals. This is what we do, and we're very good at it." He stood up and dusted off his pants. With studied indifference he picked the black box off the desk and tucked it away in his pocket. Colman then leaned over the desk, picked up the CIA credentials and slid them inside his jacket. Boehmer just watched.

"What are you going to do?" Boehmer asked him.

Colman raised his eyebrows and pointed at the pocket where he'd put away the "jam box", then lifted that same finger to his lips. "Shhhh," he said, with a twinkle in his eye, then opened the door and walked out.

CHAPTER TWENTY-TWO

Mickey knew they had to be getting close when Dave pulled onto the shoulder of the road about an hour northwest of Phoenix. The road was two lanes of blacktop in each direction, and had been gradually climbing in elevation ever since they'd passed Phoenix.

"What's wrong?" Mickey asked him. Dave didn't answer, he just waited for the next car to pass, got out of the vehicle, and retrieved a red tennis racket case from the back of the Cherokee. He set it on the console between the two front seats.

Mickey wasn't feeling nearly as sharp as he could've been, but still it didn't seem the right time or place for a bit of exercise. "Feeling sporty?" he asked Dave.

Dave just gave him a dirty look as he climbed back in. "Yeah," he said. He then proceeded to take the two broken-down halves of an AR-15 out of the racquet case and assemble them. He finished by slapping a loaded magazine into place and chambering a round. "That's why I have a 'modern sporting rifle'. Stick this between your legs, muzzle down," he told Mickey.

Mickey did as instructed, but even so he asked, "Why?"

"Because a rifle's better than two pistols," Dave said, putting the car into gear and accelerating off the shoulder.

Even though Mickey had next to no firearms training, Dave had given him his small Kahr that he wore while jogging and an inside-the-waistband holster. If something happened, it was probably better if the fingerprint tech was armed — although Dave reminded himself to try to stay behind him if at all possible. The one mistake most new shooters made was accidentally pointing their guns at things they didn't want to shoot.

They continued to go up and down hills. Mickey was pretty sure they were gradually climbing, but sometimes it was hard to tell. He glanced over at Anderson. He'd known thirty hours in a car wasn't going to be pleasant, because it was, well, thirty hours in a car, but Anderson hadn't done anything to make the trip enjoyable. Between Anderson sitting in sulking silence for hours at a time to being outright hostile, Mickey wasn't at all happy about deciding to come along. Not that he could really blame Anderson for having mood swings. Then there were the music choices. Radio stations in the Midwest just plain sucked, and Anderson had 500 songs on his iPod, 475 of which didn't qualify as music. Who the hell named their band *Explosions For Charity*?

Mickey thought they'd talk during the trip; talk about their plans, talk about what they'd do when they got to Arizona, hell, maybe just talk to talk, seeing as they were stuck in this together and close to the same age, but after their initial conversation Anderson had pulled inside himself. It had almost been worse than being in the car by himself, because then at least the guy in the other seat wasn't making you feel guilty for ruining his life. Not that Anderson had really mentioned that again, but he didn't need to; Mickey had long ago internalized that guilt. Apparently a Catholic upbringing was good for something.

Dave pulled off the main road onto a narrow blacktop road and followed that for a while. His original plan had been to drive straight through, one driving while the other slept, but after about eighteen hours in the car they'd found they were both so sleepy they had to stop. Dave found a mom-and-pop no-tell motel south of Tulsa and they'd slept there for six hours. After a quick breakfast at Denny's they'd moved on, stopping only when the gas tank needed to be refilled.

From the narrow blacktop he turned off onto a gravel road and followed that for several miles, going up and down hills, each one of which was taller than anything in Michigan. The land here was rolling hills, thinly dotted with pine trees, mesquite bushes, and saguaro cacti. There were houses, usually low and earth-toned, every quarter to half mile. Not too far to the east was Skull Valley, which as a kid he thought was the coolest name he'd heard of or seen on a map, ever. The closest town of any size was Prescott. It was maybe thirty miles away to the east as the crow flew, but there was no quick way to get there. As a kid 'stuck' at the family cabin on vacation, wanting to go see a movie or the mall, the isolation sucked, but as an adult he'd come to enjoy it. For this visit, the isolation was preferred.

Dave loved the high desert, but realized he'd need to head to the store to get some supplies, especially lip balm. He could feel the dry air sucking the moisture out of his lips as he drove. The sun was getting low in the sky to his left as he spotted the end of his driveway. A narrow dirt track running off the dirt road, it was almost impossible to find in the dark if you didn't know where to look. He turned onto the driveway and stopped.

The driveway was visible for about a hundred and fifty yards, making a gentle S before cutting through a low ridge and diving out of sight to the right. He looked around. There were no other houses visible here, and he knew from years of wandering around the land as a kid that the closest house belonged to Richard Henderson—"Old Mr. Henderson"—about half a mile further on. Henderson had died about a year before, and the tiny house there had passed to his son, Paul. Dave had no idea if Paul had sold the house, or if he ever visited.

Dave grabbed the rifle from between Mickey's legs and climbed out of the Cherokee. He looked around, but there were no other vehicles visible, and no sound but for the wind and the faint cry of some sort of bird.

"Oh my God," Mickey groaned as he climbed out of the car. He stretched. Strange and ominous clicks and pops emanated from random areas of his body. Two days in a car had not done him any good. He did a few squats to loosen up his legs. It felt like he'd landed on an alien planet, where the gravity was all wrong.

"Yeah, that last stretch was a bit long," Dave agreed.

"You mean the stretch that started when we left Detroit?" Mickey grumbled. He worked the kinks out of his arms, then looked around. A lot more trees and green than there had been around Phoenix, and it wasn't nearly as hot. Maybe eighty? It was hard to tell when the air was so dry. Dry air didn't retain any of the heat from the sun, and he expected the temperature to plummet as soon as the sun finished setting.

"You should try doing surveillance some time," Dave said. The only real difference between a long car trip and surveillance was that the car was moving.

"Are we parking here?" Mickey asked him, looking around. "Where's the house? What's with the rifle?"

'Time to see if anybody's here waiting for us," Dave said. He bent down inside the car and pulled a second magazine for the rifle from the tennis racquet case, stuck it in his back pocket. "You have your pistol? Good. Don't point it at or anywhere near me. Don't slam the door, move when I move, and shut up."

Muzzle at low ready, buttstock planted in his shoulder, Dave strode up the gravel driveway. His crunchy footsteps seemed loud to him, maybe because they were the only sound. His eyes constantly scanned left and right, then to the wide-notched V the driveway cut into the small brown ridge. The sun was angling across the front of the ridge, leaving the notch itself dark in comparison.

The ridge was a gentle lip that rose maybe half a dozen feet above the surrounding land. Once through, the driveway angled down into a hidden depression. As he reached the top of the slope, Mickey behind him, Dave paused. He could see half the small house his grandfather had built, and most of the oval depression in which it sat. Other than the house, there was nothing to see—no visitors, no cars, nothing. He'd been studying the driveway on the way up, and there was no sign anyone had driven or walked on it since the last time he had been there. Listening for a minute betrayed no noises, nothing out of the ordinary, so he continued on.

Down a gradual slope, the rest of the small house revealed itself to him, nestled at the west end of the oval depression. If it had been round the shallow formation would have looked like a crater from some extraterrestrial impact, but meteors didn't make oval craters. The ridge was just higher than the top of the roof of the single-story house, and the bottom two-thirds of the house was already in shadow from the setting sun.

Soundlessly Dave gestured for Mickey to go around the right side of the house, while he went around to the left in the narrower gap between the house and the slope. There was nothing to see, and Dave cupped his hand and peered through the rear bedroom window. Nothing. He gestured for Mickey to follow him and walked around to the front.

The front door was still locked and showed no signs of tampering. Dave unlocked it and quickly checked the small house, which took about six seconds, seeing as there were only three rooms; the big main room which held a living area next to the open kitchen, a small bedroom in back, and a tiny bathroom in the corner.

"All right, go get the car and drive it down here," he told Mickey, and handed him the keys. "I'm going to walk the perimeter."

Mickey gave him a funny look, but headed out for the car. Dave walked back up the driveway and turned left. He followed the base of the small uneven ridge around the bowl, checking for any human footprints or vehicle tracks. On the north side of the oval bowl the ridge was cut by a deep gulley. On the rare occasions when the area saw rain, that was where it washed out of the bowl. It was completely dry now, hard-packed sand and white gravel.

Dave completed his circuit around the ridge just as the light was getting low enough that spotting any tracks would have been problematic. He found the car parked on the flat expanse of sandy dirt in front of the house. Mickey didn't have any luggage, other than the clothes on his back, and he didn't feel comfortable making himself at home in the cabin, so he was waiting outside, leaning against the fender of the SUV.

"Nice flagpole," he said to Dave. "That you?" His foot touched the square of concrete at the base of the pole where he saw both an R.A. and D.A. scratched in.

Dave looked down. "Me and my dad. Put it in when I was....six? Something like that." At the thought of his father a wave of sorrow hit Dave hard, and he shoved it back down out of sight. He'd had a lot of practice at that, and it was almost a reflex.

"How do you keep the pole upright when the concrete's still wet?" Mickey asked him. The flagpole had to be twelve or fifteen feet tall.

"Guidelines, three rope guidelines attached to tent pegs." Dave looked up the length of the pole. He'd last painted it white what, five years ago? Years of wind and sand had worn the paint nearly off the aluminum. "But it's buried in two feet of dirt under the concrete."

"You going to put a flag up?"

Dave shook his head. "Not right now. No spotlight, it's not illuminated." He saw the FBI fingerprint geek didn't know what he was talking about, and shook his head. "Nobody knows flag etiquette anymore. If you're going to fly an American flag at night, it is supposed to be illuminated. Otherwise, you take it down." That was just one of the many things Dave had learned from his father as they'd put up the flagpole and repaired minor things around the small house.

"Oh."

"There might be a few things to eat in there right now, but we'll need to go out in the morning for supplies," Dave told him. He grabbed his dufflebag out of the back of the Cherokee and headed into the house. He'd have to flip on the circuit breaker for power, light the pilot lights….making a list in his head. He needed to keep his mind busy, think of little things, think of *other* things. Thinking about why he'd driven out there, why he'd *had* to drive out to Arizona, twisted him all up.

The parking lot was asphalt and very well-maintained. It looked like it serviced a very fancy strip mall, and Mickey could see signage for the Scottsdale Gun Shoppe. The shadows of the small decorative trees were shortening in the morning sun. "Why are we here, exactly? You've brought an arsenal…."

Dave got out of the Cherokee and stared at Mickey over the roof. "Seriously? Okay, first, never mind the fact that the FBI—the F-fucking-B-I—just tried to kill us both, exactly what constitutes an arsenal in your world? More than one gun? Between the two of us we've got two pistols, a rifle, and a shotgun, which, when you consider what we're up against, ain't shit."

"And a zillion bullets and magazines," Mickey said defensively.

Dave just sighed and shook his head. "You've spent too much time on the East Coast," he told Mickey, and then shrugged off the button-down shirt he'd been using to cover his Glock.

Mickey looked around the parking lot in a panic. "What are you doing?"

Dave smiled. "This is Arizona, dude. You don't need a permit for concealed carry, and open carry is legal too. Hell, it's legal in a lot of states, Michigan too, but nobody who lives there knows it. In Arizona, things are different. Welcome to America. You ever even been in a gun store?"

Mickey thought about that. "No."

"Well, I've never voted Democrat, so I guess we're even. Come on, let's bust your cherry."

"Wow. Are all gun stores this nice?" The interior of the Scottsdale Gun Shoppe was all almond and cherry wood and chrome trim. All the shelving was new, and the place was huge, much bigger than it looked from the outside. There were only a handful of customers in the store, as it had just opened for the day. Mickey was dazzled by all the military-style weaponry on the walls. Were they machine guns? He just didn't know enough to even ask. He'd called Dave's rifle an "assault rifle" early that morning, and been treated to a ten minute harangue on the historical origin of that term, and how no semi-auto rifle sold commercially in America fit that technical definition.

"Semi-auto...that's a machine gun, right?" Mickey had asked.

Dave looked at him in horror. "No! Oh my God, are you serious? How can you know nothing about guns and work in the FBI lab? Shit, you're a forensics guy, don't you deal with guns all the time? No, semi-auto means you get one bullet every time you pull the trigger. Fuck."

Dave looked around the gun store. "No. This one's actually pretty well-known around the country, it's bigger and nicer than just about anything you're going to find anywhere else. They've got a public indoor range, and a private range only for members that has an honest-to-God retinal scanner. Looks just like the ones you see in the movies. Well, shit, where you work, you probably know what one of those looks like."

"Yeah." Mickey lowered his voice. "But seriously, why are we here? Don't we have enough ammo?"

"You can never have too much ammo, but that's not why we're here."

Mickey followed Dave up to the counter. One of the clerks in their red polo shirts and pressed khakis walked over. "Can I help you gentlemen?"

"Yeah, I'm wondering what you have in night vision," Dave said to him, looking around. "And do you carry Turnerite? I've got a lot of family coming into town for a big birthday celebration, and they all love to shoot."

"How the hell is a binary explosive legal?" Mickey asked once they were back in the car.

Dave shrugged. "I'm not sure. You've got to mix it, plus you can only set it off by shooting it. Bullet has to be travelling at least two thousand feet per second, so you've got to shoot it with a rifle."

Mickey violently shook his head. "That shouldn't matter. C4 and other traditional explosives, you can't set them off without some sort of electrical current or blasting cap, how is this different?"

"I don't know, but the ATF says it's legal." Dave had first seen Turnerite at a big charity match the year before. After it, the teenagers with cancer to whom the proceeds were going to be helping got to shoot at various objects—oil drums, refrigerators, even junker cars—packed with the explosive. Upon seeing the huge explosion, and feeling it in his chest, Dave had had the same reaction—how the hell was it legal for commercial sale? But it was, and it wasn't much less powerful than good old-fashioned dynamite. "I guess because it's sold un-mixed, and it's a low order explosive as opposed to a high explosive, like black powder. Most of the gun laws in this country were made by people who don't know anything about guns, and don't make any sense, why should laws about explosives be any different?"

"Where'd you get all the cash?" The Turnerite had been hundreds of dollars because Dave had bought it in bulk for his "birthday party", but the night vision scope Dave had purchased had cost ten times as much. And Dave had paid cash. Mickey had known better than to ask any questions while they were inside the store.

"Rainy day fund." Otherwise known as his inheritance slash retirement fund. Not much need for that now. "Let's go get some groceries, I'm starving."

"Okay, what do you have for me?" Smith asked. He sat down in the chair across from Colman.

"I've got a high priority target for you. Currently don't have a location on him, but when we do we're going to want you to move on him. Quickly. So you need to assemble a team."

"How many guys? And do I need any specialists? Language skills?" John Smith was a compact man, with veins bulging in his biceps and grey starting to appear at his temples. He was deeply tanned, but could never be mistaken for anything other than pure Caucasian. Everybody who'd ever worked with him assumed that "John Smith" was an intentionally unimaginative pseudonym, but he'd actually had it placed on him by his Lutheran parents – John James Smith. If anyone lacked imagination, it was his parents.

Colman thought about the question. While most cops did not have a combat mindset, Anderson had gone up against four experienced SWAT officers and walked away without a scratch. SWAT cops weren't the same thing as true operators of course, but that was still pretty impressive. And this problem, which he'd inherited, needed to be taken care of promptly and properly. "Six man team. Language and looks aren't important, as this is going to be a home game. I'll get you some sterile domestic commercial hardware."

He pushed a flash drive across his desk with the eraser end of a pencil. "Here's everything we know about him so far. Was living in Michigan, but he seems to have rabbited within the last few days. He's not a pro, though, so I know we'll track him down pretty damn quickly. I'd like you to have a team picked out in twenty-four hours. Keep them on a two-hour standby until I tell you otherwise."

"He driving a car with OnStar or anything like that that you can track?" Smith picked up the flash drive and stuck it in his pocket.

"No. Cell phone's dropped off the grid, and he hasn't logged on to email or Facebook in days. We've actually got the FBI doing field interviews of all his friends and co-workers, and I'm reading their reports as they upload them. We're all over everybody's phones, if he calls anybody we'll know about it."

"The FBI? Do they know they're working for you?"

Colman just smiled. "No, but they can be so very helpful at times."

"What's their interest in this?"

"It's in the file. Let's just say that you're not the first team to get this assignment, but you're the first pros. The amateurs have made quite a mess of things, and it's our job to tidy them up."

"Great." Smith got up to leave. "Any special instructions when we find him?"

"If you can destroy his fingerprints, when the time comes, that would be wonderful. If not...." He shrugged.

CHAPTER TWENTY-THREE

Cashman had a pounding headache, and neither the six aspirin he'd swallowed, nor the coffee he was washing and keeping them down with was making a dent in the dull pain behind his right eye. Probably shouldn't have stayed up so late watching the Tigers go into extra innings, or had that extra beer (okay, maybe two), but hell, he'd gotten five hours of sleep. Maybe he was just getting old. Or maybe it was just this case.

He hit Backspace again as what he'd meant to write in the report ended up gobbledygook—shit, if he had a stroke maybe he could go home early—and then just cursed. Too many questions and not enough answers, and what he was doing was just make-work, status updates. There hadn't been anything new in the case since the autopsies yesterday. Now those had been....interesting.

Bodies that had been dead so long they'd started to bloat and rot were bad. Dead kids were the worst. Four dirty cops who'd died in a shootout with a civilian and a fellow deputy, now that was interesting as hell.

The Oakland County Coroner's office had scheduled all of them for the same day, Monday, two days after the shooting, and the Medical Examiner, Dr. Eichstadt, did them all himself. That had been a long day for the doc, and just as long for everyone else in attendance. Cashman had been there for all four, although Linklater, his partner, had come and gone. The detective from Troy had stayed for the duration, as had three grim-faced detectives from Detroit. Cashman, for one, didn't know how to act around them. He'd nodded to them, but what the hell do you say? It's not like their guys had died in the line of duty. They were dirty cops who'd died trying to gun down a P.I—and a deputy. An FBI agent was there too, being uncharacteristically friendly.

The bodies themselves weren't that bad. Cashman had seen a suicide by train, and more than one suicide where the person in question had stuck a rifle or shotgun in their mouth and given the room a new paint job. He'd seen a minivan full of kids after it had rolled down an embankment. An autopsy on a three-week-old rotting corpse so foul the stench wouldn't come out of his shirt and he'd had to throw it away. Compared to those, these bodies were nothing. Just a quartet of adult black males who were in pretty good shape, or had been. Most of the bullet holes— at least the entry wounds—weren't even that easy to see, because the kid had been using a .223. A .223 caliber bullet was small in diameter, but very fast, so the entry wounds were tiny and sometimes almost invisible from more than a few feet away in the cops' graying skin. Where they'd exited, though, there were often large chunks of flesh missing.

Anderson had shot the hell out of three of the officers. There was no other way to accurately describe it.

Eichstadt found at least nineteen separate and unique entrance wounds in the three men Anderson had killed. Two of the men also sported what Cashman thought of as shrapnel wounds, bits and pieces of car metal and plastic in their skin from the bullets hitting them after they'd gone through car doors or bumpers.

Considering they'd found twenty-four empty rifle cases at the scene, those SWAT cops—who'd all been armed with pistols, pistols that had been matched to ejected cases found at the scene, so they were shooting too—had been seriously outgunned. Shit, Cashman had to admit, they'd been *outmanned*. Jim Bonniker had fired eight rounds from his department-issued SIG P226 from a distance of eight yards, and only hit Paul Wilson four times—and one of those was a superficial arm wound. If the kid had been shooting like that, there was a good chance he wouldn't have survived, not against 4-to-1 odds. Cashman wasn't putting it all on his fancy scoped rifle with its hair trigger, like some of the guys working the case. He knew he couldn't shoot a rifle that well, even one with that thousand-dollar scope, and Anderson had done it with four people shooting back.

Since the autopsy, all their efforts had turned up was a big fat pile of nothing. He growled as his phone range for what had to be the fifteenth time that morning, but politely said "Cashman."

"Yeah, I'm told you're the lead detective on the...well, I don't know what you guys are calling it, the 'SWAT team shootout' that happened over the weekend?"

"Yes sir, can I help you?"

"Detective Billy Dixon with West Bloomfield Township. I'm working a case that may involve one of your people, and I'm hoping we could share a little information."

Cashman checked the caller ID on his desk phone, but nothing had come through. That was a good sign that this was a detective calling from his blocked office phone, but before he started talking about his case with someone who called out of the blue...."West Bloomfield Township? You in your office right now?"

"Yeah, you want to give me a call back?" Dixon knew the score.

"Yeah, Dixon? Give me a minute." Cashman disconnected the call and used his computer to Google the phone number of the PD—it actually was quicker than digging out his county-issued directory of all the police departments in the state, in part because he didn't know where *that* was. Google, he could find.

He dialed the main number first, then asked for Dixon by name. "Dixon."

"Cashman. Okay, what do you have?"

"News reports are that the Detroit officers were shot by a David Anderson. I'm wondering if he's the same David Anderson who's a person of interest in a case I've got." He gave Cashman the date of birth.

"Hold on." Cashman pulled up his report, and looked up Anderson's info. "Yep, same DOB. What are you looking at him for?"

"A hit and run. I actually have nothing to tie him to the crime, but the guy who was killed in the hit and run, just about a year before that killed Anderson's parents in a drunk driving accident. Third offense."

"And he wasn't in jail? The drunk driver? How the hell did that happen?"

"Because he is—was—Paolo Bufonte."

"The name's….familiar."

"Big Paulie. Son of Pietro Bufonte. Think *Sopranos*, *Godfather*…."

"Oh, yeah. Yeah, I remember that, I heard about the accident on the news. I think I assumed it was some sort of mob hit on him. I mean, what are the chances, with *him* getting hit, that it was really an accident, you know? Wasn't he out walking his dog or something?"

"Yeah. Which he did pretty regularly. What we didn't release to the press was that it looked like that whoever hit him then backed up and ran over him again."

"Soooo, probably not an accident, then."

"Nope. Not a scratch on the dog. And like I said, about five months prior to that Paulie skated out of any jail time. The judge threw out the case due to irregularities in the arrest. That happened with the guy who killed my parents because he was a serial drunk driver, I know how I'd feel."

"Anderson ever make any threats?"

"Nope."

Cashman thought. "Didn't this happen like a few years ago?"

"Yeah, just about three."

"And you're still working it?"

"Do you know how many unsolved murders we have in this town? None. Well, one, this one. And the fact that I haven't been able to close it has been bugging me for years."

"You get a description of a vehicle, or...."

"Yeah, sort of. Two neighbors remember seeing a car on the street, maybe parked, right around the time of the accident. Nobody saw the accident, though, or anybody in the car. You know what our neighborhoods are like. Big houses, set way back from the road, usually walls or hedges along the street. The vehicle description I have is a green or black or blue Crown Victoria or Impala or Taurus. A dark colored full size sedan, basically. No plate info."

"And he was walking his dog in the street?"

"We don't have sidewalks. Sidewalks are for the poor neighborhoods."

Cashman smiled. A cheap house in West Bloomfield went for about half a million bucks. "And Anderson didn't own a dark-colored full size sedan?"

"I checked him, his family members, any friends I could track down, co-workers. Put out an alert to any body shops in the area if they got in any vehicles with front end damage. Checked with all the rental car companies. The family put out a reward. Nothing panned out."

"Alibi?"

"Home alone for the evening. Watching a movie. Says he went out jogging, and I found a neighbor who thinks they remember seeing him jog past."

"Any other suspects?"

"No. And I've got nothing to tie him to this, but after all this time, his motive's the only thing I've got. I like him for it, but liking him isn't enough."

"Honestly, though, he can't be your only suspect. I mean, somebody kills the son of a mobster—"

"Only son," Dixon interjected.

"Yeah, that just makes it worse. Kills the only son of the top mob guy in Detroit. I mean, aren't there a lot of suspects? In theory?"

"In theory. But as for solid names and faces, all I've got is him."

"How much you question him?"

"Just enough to get his alibi. He wasn't having any of it. 'Why the hell would I talk to you? You're trying to prove I killed someone,' I believe is what he said."

"Yep. He's not dumb, I've talked to him a little on this one. Not that he's really talking to us either, he's lawyered up. So what you're telling me is that you've still got nothing, and you're calling me because you're grasping at straws."

"Basically. I've been sitting on this one for months with nothing new. You got anything weird going on with yours that maybe might help me with mine? I mean, just what the hell happened out there?"

Cashman sighed. "Near as we can tell, exactly what we're telling the press. Kid was doing a surveillance, just a suspicious wife thing, sitting in a neighborhood, watching the husband while she's out of town, and those four Detroit officers roll up on him in two cars and try to take him out. Just start shooting. He peels out, they chase him to his local shooting range, and they get into a gunfight."

"Why?"

"The fuck if we know. He says he has no clue, and I….shit, I think I believe him. We have not been able to turn up any ties between him and the cops. Hell, the FBI is all over this one, actually being helpful for once, not officious pricks, but they haven't found anything either. Right now the most popular theory is it has something to do with a PI case he worked, but we don't actually have any, what's the word....oh, yeah, *evidence*. We're just guessing."

"There's got to be a reason. They just didn't pick this kid at random."

"Maybe they thought he was somebody else. Eddie Mitchell, the cop who first started shooting at the kid? His blood tested positive for cocaine and marijuana."

"And so he just went nuts? Started shooting at a....at a kid who was a good enough shot to take out a whole SWAT team? What's up with that?"

"The more I look into this, the weirder it gets, but right now it still looks like this kid was sitting there minding his own business, and they just picked the wrong fucking dude. He had a Glock on him, and a rifle in the car because he was going to go shooting later. Practice. He shoots competitively, and is supposed to be really damn good. He shot the state championship not too long ago, came in third or something, and is friends with a professional shooter who actually trains actors for movies. *Avatar*, I think. What are the chances, right? Reminds me a little of the whole Marcus Luttrell dog thing."

"The what?"

"Marcus Luttrell, he's that SEAL won the Medal of Honor I think, wrote *Lone Survivor*, which they made into that movie with Marky Mark Wahlberg. He was sitting at home one night and a couple of assholes shot his dog. Dog that helped him with his rehab from getting blown up in Afghanistan. He chased them across like three counties at a hundred miles-an-hour plus, with two guns in the car, on the phone with 9-1-1. That 9-1-1 call is posted on YouTube, and trust me, Luttrell doesn't sound panicked, and he doesn't sound scared, even doing triple digit speeds. He just sounds *pissed*. I'm guessing the only reason those guys are still alive is because the cops got to them before he could.

Hell, it's like that guy with the bad luck to try carjacking Audie Murphy back in the day."

"What? Who?"

Cashman smiled and waved his hand as he talked. He loved this story. "Audie Murphy. Little scrawny guy, maybe five-six, buck thirty soaking wet. So small the Marines turned him down when he tried to enlist. Ended up being the most decorated soldier of World War II. Killed three hundred Germans from the top of a burning tank. Three *hundred*, and that was just one gunfight. Well, sometime in the fifties, I think in Texas or Oklahoma, some big dude with a Colt .45 tried to carjack some little guy, steal his car." He laughed. "Foot taller than him, outweighed him by maybe fifty pounds, and he's got a gun, sticks it in the little guy's face. When the deputy showed up this big guy looked like he'd been mauled by a pack of Rottweilers. When he found out that the smaller gentleman was Audie Murphy, the deputy turned to the bad guy and told him he was just plain lucky he wasn't dead."

Cashman shook his head. "Last few days, I've gotten calls from half a dozen Warren cops, vouching for this kid. I guess he was doing a ride along with the Warren P.D. about five years ago, and he and the training officer ran into—I mean literally *ran into*—a car load of bank robbery suspects. From what everybody is telling me, Anderson killed several of them in a shootout that left a bunch of cops in the hospital. I checked into it. It's true, but it appears Anderson did everything he could to keep his name out of the press."

"What? When was this?"

"Five years ago. It puts it before his parents getting killed, sounds like. He got sued civilly by family members of the deceased, but the suits didn't go anywhere." Cashman shook his head again. "So, gunfight with a bunch of bank robbers, gunfight with SWAT cops, and he walks away without a scratch both times. Some bad guys get lucky, but some just pick the Wrong. Fucking. Guy."

Dixon was silent for a while. "You believe in coincidence?"

"No, but detectives from Troy, Oakland County, Shelby Township, Detroit, and the FBI have been looking into this one for four days, and right now you know everything the task force does. We're also looking into that original shooting of his, to see if any of the guys he killed are somehow related to the Detroit officers he shot, but so far that avenue of inquiry, as they say, is going nowhere."

"I don't suppose Anderson was driving a dark-colored full size sedan, was he?"

"Sorry, black Mustang."

"Hmm. He didn't own that at the time of the hit and run. Well, shit. Okay, you've got my name, I guess if you turn up any cars buried in Anderson's backyard or he happens to mention running over someone, can you give me a call?"

Cashman laughed. "Yeah."

Dixon hung up his phone and looked around the office. He was the only one around, but there are some things you didn't do inside a police station. "I'm heading out to Starbucks," he told Joyce Rubin, who was manning the front desk.

"You want to grab me something?" she asked.

"Sure, what do you want?" Not even a Kevlar vest could hide the fact that she had a big rack, and Dixon was a sucker for a big rack. He was also quite the ladies' man, but Rubin liked having sex with women as much or more than he did, so she was a lost cause.

Armed with her order Dixon headed out to his department-issued detective's sedan, a new black Charger. It was a three minute drive to Starbucks, but when he got there he sat in his car and pulled out his cell phone.

"Oops, shit," he said, and put that one away, and pulled out the other phone, the prepaid one he'd bought with cash.

"Yeah."

"I'm calling you back about that purchase your client wanted to make," Dixon said.

"Okay."

"It definitely was the same model that he saw, but I haven't been able to learn anything about whether or not it had anything to do with that purchase he wanted to make."

"My client is definitely interested in buying *something*." The emphasis was impossible to miss.

"I'm well aware of that. But we don't want him wasting his money now, do we? Having to buy the same item twice?"

"You're going to keep looking into it?"

"Yes. And if I find anything, I will—" Dixon found he was talking into a dead phone. "Fuck," he muttered, and realized his armpits were swampy with sweat.

At the other end of the call, Miller closed the cell phone and slid it back into the pocket of his suit coat. He turned to his boss. "The West Bloomfield detective says that the Anderson kid involved in that shootout with the SWAT cops is the same one he likes for Paulie, but he still can't prove anything."

Pietro Bufonte, his black hair faded mostly to gray, face deeply lined with wrinkles, frowned and sipped at his Espresso. He looked around his back yard. The lawn was as flat and closely trimmed as a putting green, and the arborvitaes had been trimmed by professionals into geometric shapes. He didn't see any of it, didn't hear the birds tweeting at each other. "I'm beginning to think he never will."

Miller clasped his hands in front of his body and waited. "Just say the word."

After a long pause, Bufonte shook his head. "Enough boys are dead. I'm not going to do anything until I know. And even if I found out today, I'd have to wait. There are too many eyes looking at him right now." He took another sip of his espresso and stared out at his huge empty yard.

Ten minutes after hanging up the phone with the West Bloomfield detective, Cashman's partner came walking up with a shit-eating grin on his face.

"Guess what I've got?" Linklater said.

"Crabs," Cashman replied. His headache hadn't gone anywhere. His partner ignored him.

"Two things you're not going to believe. One, we've finally found something that ties Anderson to the SWAT guys."

"Really? What?"

"One of the strip clubs they hit was Goldfinger's. Turns out Anderson's girlfriend works there. Not only that, after they got hit, as a favor or something to her, Anderson took out a couple of the bouncers and the manager and gave them some shooting lessons."

Cashman thought. "So....what? You saying the Detroit guys were so pissed at him that, if they ever decided to take up a life of crime again, he made their job more difficult if they hit that same club?"

Linklater shrugged. "Doesn't make sense to me, but shit, at least we actually turned up a connection."

"You said two things, two things I wouldn't believe. What's the second?"

"You know who gave us the info? The FBI."

"The FBI shared information? Holy shit, miracles really do happen. I better go out and buy a lottery ticket." He paused. "You been getting a weird vibe from the FBI? Normally they seem to love playing the jack-booted thugs, but in that big meeting right after the incident their agent in charge was almost acting like Anderson's second attorney. Marx didn't know what to make of it. You hear his conspiracy theory yet, that Anderson's FBI, undercover?"

373

"No, but...." Linklater thought for a few seconds. "That sure would explain a few things. Like how he didn't get shot."

"I don't buy it, but who knows. Anyway, the FBI's why the kid's not still locked up while we try to figure this out."

"This is really the first time I've ever dealt with them on anything."

"Hmm. Hey, wait a minute, did you say Anderson was dating a stripper? Seriously? This fucking guy, Jesus."

PART V

TROUBLE

You never have trouble if you are prepared for it.

Theodore Roosevelt

CHAPTER TWENTY-FOUR

Ringo sat on the hood of his abused Impala and sipped coffee. It was standard McDonald's coffee, with a little cream and sugar, and tasted just fine. He wasn't one of those who'd drunk the Starbuck's Kool-Aid (so to speak), and been brainwashed into spending $4 for a cup of coffee. Actually, he'd tried Starbuck's a few times, and thought their stuff tasted too damn burnt. $4 for a burnt cup of coffee? No thank you.

The sun was bright, and he squinted behind his sunglasses. He checked his watch—9:28 a.m. Still no human movement on either Northfield or East Cobb, and nothing to hear other than a lot of small birds and the distant sound of traffic. It was peaceful, actually. The sun was off to his right and slightly behind him, and for the moment he was in the shadow of a decaying abandoned house. The air was still cool, but he could feel the humidity on his skin; as soon as the sun got to work it would turn into one of those muggy miserable days that made every Michigander appreciate winter.

"It's like breathing soup," Detective Sergeant Bill Rochester said, standing off the passenger side of the sedan. He was looking around, and had his own cup of McDonald's coffee.

"Not yet, but that's why I wanted the meet to be early," Ringo agreed.

Rochester, a dark complected black man, shook his head. He had a big round belly that looked hard as a basketball. "The wife's family is from Tennessee, and she keeps talking about moving down there when I retire." He spit onto the cracked asphalt, then looked at Ringo. "You know how hot it gets in Tennessee this time of year? And it's just as humid as here."

"You might like the heat in a few years," Ringo said, suppressing a smile.

"I want to move someplace hot, I'll move to Arizona or Texas, someplace dry. I don't want to live in soup. Every year we go down there in July for the family reunion, you know? My wife's aunt always gets everybody matching t-shirts in these bright colors, you know? Red, yellow, fire engine green, makes everybody look like Skittles, and they say Rochester Family Reunion on the back. But she never washes them before she hands them out, and I've got allergies. So I can put the t-shirt on my bare skin and break out in a rash, or put it on over another shirt, and wear two shirts when it's so hot it's like I'm sitting in boiling water. Only reason I haven't snapped and shot somebody down there is they're all family. And the bar-b-que."

Ringo looked at him, the smile now playing around the corners of his mouth. "You know, it's the cold that you're not supposed to be able to take." He nodded at Rochester. "With your tan, you strike me as coming from someplace....warm."

Rochester looked down at his nearly black skin. "Tan. Shit," he said with a laugh. "You ever been to Africa? I've been to Africa. Did it when I was in college, with a bunch of my fraternity brothers. Getting in touch with our roots, you know? Place is goddamn miserable. Anybody that complains about anything in this country should go there for a few days, see how good we have it."

"Where'd you go?"

"Kenya and Nairobi. Talk about an education, wow. Didn't realize at the time how dangerous it was. We thought that since we were black, and everybody over there was black, that things would be cool, you know? Everybody would be our friend. Shit. Ignorance of youth."

"So that's where you're from?"

"Me. No, I'm from the East Side, born and raised. My family might have originally come from Africa, but that was long before I was born. It's not home to me. Not after having gone there, and seen it myself. I'm from the D. This is my home." He saluted the city with his coffee cup and took another sip.

They heard the sound of an approaching car and Ringo looked over his shoulder. Bonneville, about ten years old. Had to be a cop, seemed like the only people who'd ever bought those sedans were old white people and suburban police departments.

The black Pontiac pulled up behind their car and a middle-aged white guy wearing khakis and a black polo climbed out with a Starbucks cup in his hand. He had a gun on his right hip and a badge on his belt. Ringo smiled, and got off his car. "Are you Cashman or Reed?" he asked.

"Cashman, Oakland County," he said. Ringo introduced himself and Rochester, and they all shook hands. Cashman looked up and down Northfield street, then up East Cobb, eyeing the vacant overgrown lots and sagging houses. "City stop mowing the grass on all the vacant land?" he asked.

"Not all of it," Ringo said, finding the suburban detective made him feel a little defensive of his city. Cashman nodded, and sipped at his coffee. "We're waiting for one more," Ringo told him.

Cashman just nodded, sipping at his coffee and eyeing what he thought of as the ruins of a once-great city rotting around him. Damn shame.

Two minutes later a new white Charger came speeding up from Warren Avenue and pulled up beside the three men standing at the corner. The driver rolled down the passenger window. "Reed, Troy," he said. "Where should I park this?"

Ringo pointed in front of his unmarked unit, where there was enough space for a car between his bumper and the corner at East Cobb. "Right here's fine," he said, and they all moved out of the way.

The Troy detective got out of his unit and there was another round of introductions. Reed was tall and skinny, with dark hair. Ringo noticed the man from Troy didn't have a cup of coffee or any other beverage in his hands. Apparently he didn't get the memo.

"Hey, somebody forgot to invite the FBI," Cashman said with a smile, and that got a laugh.

"Okay, who called this?" Reed said. He pointed to Ringo. "You're George, right? Detroit? So what's up? Why are we here?"

"I'm just the messenger," Ringo said. He pointed at Bill Rochester.

Rochester stepped away from the unmarked cruiser and wiggled his fingers for the other detectives to follow him. He walked out into the intersection with East Cobb. No danger of getting hit by any traffic, they hadn't seen a car moving since they'd arrived. "On June fifth," Rochester told the assembled detectives, "you might have heard we had the worst day ever for the department. We had two officers roll up on a guy in a van. He shot them, killed them both, then took off. Our units eventually ran him off the road, but he ended up killing another officer, and putting four more in the hospital."

Rochester pointed behind Cashman's Bonneville. "He was parked over there. He actually got called out by a private investigator doing a surveillance. John Phault. He was sitting two blocks down over there," he pointed in the opposite direction down Northfield, "on the other side of the street. Phault was doing a work comp surveillance, and our two-man car rolled up on him because he was across the street from an undercover narcotics officer's house. Phault saw the van pull up down here, and told the officers about it. They rolled down here, and the guy, Ralph Marsh, just shot them down in cold blood and took off."

"Phault ended up killing Marsh, right?" Cashman said. He remembered from the news that a PI had been the one who'd killed the man.

"Right."

"And we're here why?" Reed said. The Troy detective was impatient.

"Phault wasn't working alone," Ringo said. "He had an employee with him that day. David Anderson. Anderson stayed on the scene and tried to do first aid on the officers while Phault went after the shooter." The Detroit detectives now had the full attention of the suburban ones.

"Anderson was at the scene?" Reed said. He rubbed his ear. He and Cashman began twisting their heads, looking this way and that. What, exactly, they were looking for neither would have been able to say.

"Yeah," Rochester said. "For a while I was thinking that the shooter wasn't just a random nutjob that snapped, that he was here for Phault, because he didn't show up on scene until Phault was already here. I really liked Phault for the motive on this one, but couldn't get anywhere with that. Then I heard Anderson's name mentioned in connection to the shooting last week, and……"

"And he called me," Ringo said. "And I came out here. Looked around." He looked around at the faces standing there. "I want to try something." He looked at Reed. "You have your cell phone on you?"

"Yeah, why?"

Ringo pointed up East Cobb. "According to the report, Anderson was parked in his Cherokee on East Cobb, facing west, approximately one hundred feet from the intersection with Northfield. Walk down that way, to where he was parked. I'm going to go to where the shooter's van was parked when the cops rolled up on him."

The Troy detective frowned. He didn't like anybody telling him what to do, and he didn't see the point in this exercise, but he grabbed his cell phone out of his pants pocket and began walking up the street, counting his paces. Paces were thirty inches or something, which meant about forty paces for a hundred feet. Math. Now they had him doing math.

Ringo went back to his unmarked unit and pulled the case file out of the back seat. Followed by Rochester and Cashman, he walked past the parked cars as he flipped through the crime scene photos. He stopped when he got to one which showed the dead officers' bodies in relation to the two ragged houses and an upthrust square of sidewalk concrete just visible in one corner of the photo.

Studying the photo very carefully, trying not to look at the bodies or the pools of blood, he took two steps to the right, then one forward. He was almost in front of one crumbling house, maybe fifty feet from the intersection with East Cobb. It shared a driveway with the house to the left, a tall narrow Addams Family-looking thing made of dark brown brick. The driveway looked like it had once been made of concrete, but now more closely resembled a gravel two track with two-foot tall weeds sprouting from....everywhere. If it had once led to a garage, now it seemed to lead to nowhere, vanishing into the overgrown backyard which sloped gently upward. Past the tall grass between the houses he could see nothing but blue sky. He had a tall rectangular window of blue over green fifteen feet wide to look through. He dialed Reed's cell phone.

"Reed."

"You a hundred feet from the corner?"

Reed looked around. Facing back the way he had come, there was nothing but waist-high grass to his right, a small house with dirty white siding behind him to his left. "Just about."

"Walk away from the corner slowly."

"Okay. And should I be looking for something?" Reed looked around, but there was nothing to see but grass, weeds, and random litter blown against the curb. He walked, and walked. "Okay, I've gone about forty feet."

Ringo frowned. Bill Rochester was to his left, and Cashman was behind his right elbow, wondering exactly what was happening and staring in the direction he was looking. "Okay, that didn't work. Try walking the other direction, toward the corner. Let me know when you get to your starting point last time."

Reed huffed into his phone and pulled it away from his head as he strode quickly back to the approximate spot he'd stopped at before. What the hell was he doing? Were the Detroit cops fucking with the white boy from the suburbs? Playing a practical joke on him? "Okay, back at my original spot, walking toward the corner now," he said into the phone. He'd only taken four steps when the Detroit cop yelled in his ear.

"Stop!"

Reed stopped. "Okay, why did I stop?"

"How far are you from the corner?" Ringo asked him.

Reed eyed the distance, then looked back at the spot where he'd paced to. "Maybe eighty-five, ninety feet."

"And how far from the right curb?"

Reed looked down. "Maybe five feet."

"About where you'd be in a parked car. Look to your left."

The house with peeling white siding was behind him, and directly to his left was a dense clump of bushes and young trees, growing wild. Between the tangle of foliage and the brown-bricked house at the corner of East Cobb and

Northfield was a vacant lot covered in long grass and mysterious lumps that, perhaps a decade ago, might have been piles of trash but had long since been overgrown. This is where aspiring archeologists should go on digs, he thought absently. Detroit. The airfare would be a hell of a lot cheaper, too.

As he stared at the tall green grass waving in the gentle breeze, he realized the empty lot fell away from him, and past it were the dark back sides of two houses on Northfield. Reed saw movement, and squinted. Between the two houses he saw the Detroit detective waving at him. Behind him were the other two cops. What was that on a diagonal, a hundred yards away? Less?

"Where are you standing?" Reed asked.

"Right about where the back of the shooter's mini van was," Ringo told him. He squatted a little, trying to guess how tall someone sitting in the back of a minivan would be. He could still see the Troy detective, standing on East Cobb, from the waist up.

The two cops stared at each other across the open land for a long while. Reed looked around him, but there was nothing to be seen in the street. Finally, Ringo pulled the phone slightly away from his mouth and said, "Did Bill or I remember to mention that the shooter had a scoped rifle in the back of his van? And fake ID so good we didn't know it was fake until we ran his prints."

The Troy detective stood there and stared across the lot and between the houses at the other cops. "Son of a bitch."

Back together in front of Ringo's unmarked cruiser, the four detectives clustered in a tight group. "What do we know about the shooter. Marsh?" Cashman asked.

Bill Rochester shook his head. "Not a whole hell of a lot. Army veteran, that's how we matched his prints, but he left active service six years ago. Since then, nothing. No criminal record."

"Combat vet? Who was he with?"

"I'm still—*still*—waiting on official copies of his records, but what I was told over the phone was that he was 10th Mountain Division, Airborne qualified, Ranger tab, eight years in, and that he did two combat tours in Afghanistan. Bronze star, two purple hearts. So yeah, combat vet."

"And he had a sniper rifle in his van, and was parked right where he could see Anderson?" Reed said, trying to wrap his head around it. The Troy detective was used to cases that were a little simpler; husband kills wife, teenager steals car, that kind of thing. This thing had him using muscles he hadn't exercised in a while. "What about the rifle, what do we know about it?"

"Winchester Model 70 in thirty-ought-six, bought new in 1979 by Raymond Meadows of Evansville, Indiana. Near as I can tell after making a few calls, talking to the widow Meadows in a nursing home, Raymond owned that rifle until he died, and it was bought in an estate sale about two years ago. By who, nobody knows."

"And the pistol?"

"A Springfield......" Rochester had to check the file. "Springfield Armory XDM, whatever the hell that is. Nine millimeter. Stolen from a gun store in Oklahoma about two years ago, along with a shitload of other guns. ATF said this was the first one that's even turned up. Nobody ever arrested for the burglary."

"Well hell." Reed rubbed his neck. "You say you looked into Phault. I've been looking into Anderson after that fiasco last week. We both have." He gestured at Cashman. They'd had a dozen phone conversations, and met on-scene in both Troy and Shelby Township several times. "If he's dirty, I haven't been able to find it. Two jobs, no criminal record, and he's got a CPL. The only thing I found was an eight-year-old speeding ticket. So if this asshole Marsh was here to kill somebody, why Anderson?"

Cashman stood there, thinking, and slowly started shaking his head. The conversation with the West Bloomfield detective kept replaying in his head. "Shit," he said. "Shit shit shit." He looked at the assembled detectives. "I think I know who might want to kill the kid," he admitted. "The name Pietro Bufonte ring a bell?" And he recounted the details of the phone call he'd had with Billy Dixon.

"Fuck, I'm getting a headache," Ringo said, pressing his palms against his temples. "So you're saying that Bufonte hired this guy to kill Anderson because he suspects him of killing his kid?"

Cashman shrugged. "Anybody else got anything resembling a motive?"

"The FBI learned that Anderson gave firearms training to the employees of one of the strip clubs Wilson's crew hit," Reed volunteered.

"That's not a motive, that's just a connection. And a damn thin one at that," Rochester observed.

Cashman informed them, "None of the Detroit officers had any sort of a connection to Absolute Armored that we could find, and while he won't let us look at his files, Phault insists that he's not aware of any cases he's worked either on those officers or anybody with the same last name, like family members."

"But do you think Bufonte'd risk a murder rap, taking out someone he wasn't even sure did it? You said the detective didn't have anything other than his gut, right?" Reed had started to write in a small notebook.

"Right. He liked Anderson for the hit-and-run, but had absolutely nothing in the way of proof. And I got the impression he'd been looking hard."

"Have any of you guys ever worked any cases on connected guys?" Ringo asked the group. "I haven't, so I don't know. Is Bufonte old enough or sick enough that he'd be willing to say 'Fuck it' and take the kid out anyway? On a 'maybe'?"

"Big Paulie was his only son," Rochester told him. "And he's not getting any younger."

"Fuck." Ringo shook his head again. "We're going to have to call the FBI again."

Ringo and Bill Rochester had ridden over together from the nearest precinct house in Ringo's unmarked, and he dropped Rochester back in the lot just before noon. "Call me after you talk to the feds," Ringo said to him through his open window. They were both very surprised the feds hadn't taken over everything already. Maybe this not-so-thin connection to the grandfather of Detroit's organized crime community, who they had been chasing for thirty years, would be the final straw the FBI needed to claim eminent domain over every competing investigation.

Rochester stopped and looked at him, eyes shining and teeth visible in a big grin. "Do you not just love this job some days?" he said.

"I like putting bad guys away," Ringo said. "I don't know exactly what this is."

"This, Ringo, is a sho 'nuff mys-ter-ee," Rochester said. "And I'll take this every day of the week over dead kids, you know?"

Ringo nodded and gave a wave as he pulled away. He'd just exited the parking lot when his cell phone rang. He didn't recognize the number, but it was local. "John George."

"Detective George, this is Diana Wilson. Paul's wife."

Ringo didn't have anything to say for a couple of seconds, his brain vapor locked. "Um, uh, Diana, I—"

"We need to meet," she told him. "Paul left me something to give you."

Ringo met her in the parking lot of a Murray's Discount Auto Parts, against his better judgment. When she pulled up and got out of the car he said, "Diana, I...." He was about to say that he didn't know what to say, but how stupid was that? "I'm sorry," he ended up telling her lamely.

She nodded. She was thinner than he remembered, and her eyes looked hollow, but she had some strength in her. She'd always had steel in her backbone. "This is for you," she told him, and held her hand out. What she laid in his palm was a small audio recorder.

"What's this? I mean," he corrected himself, because he knew what it *was*, "what's on it?"

She looked haunted. "Let's sit in your car."

Diana Wilson held it together for about five minutes, listening to her husband's voice on the recording, then started weeping silently, tears running down her cheeks. Ringo didn't say anything to her, he was too engrossed in what he was hearing.

"Oh my fucking God," Ringo said when he heard the FBI agent proposition Paul Wilson, offering to make evidence disappear if he murdered David Anderson. "Oh my God." Hartman—he knew who that was, he'd met him. Several times. Shit, Hartman was the Bureau liaison on the Anderson shooting!

He sat there when the recording was over, unable to even think clearly. Finally he asked, "And he told you to give this to me? What, in case he died?"

Diana Wilson smiled ruefully and wiped at her cheeks. "No. I found it in his desk, in a box marked R.I.P. After I listened to it, I knew I should bring it to you."

"Why? I mean.....shit....did Paul tell you? I was the one who figured out that it was him and his crew hitting the clubs. I was....I was the one called the FBI." *R.I.P.?* He didn't know whether to laugh or cry at Wilson's morbid sense of humor.

She nodded. "He told me. And I told him to pay you off with some of the cash he took. To forget what you learned, or make evidence disappear, or something. He laughed, said you wouldn't even take a half-price meal. He told me some stories of when you were in uniform together. Called you a 'motherfuckin' Boy Scout.'" She paused. "I know you called the FBI. I want to hate you, and maybe I do, but you called them because you thought it was the right thing to do, not because you knew this was going to happen. Which means you're the only cop I know that I can trust to do the right thing with this. I know I don't want it. Don't want it anywhere near my daughters." She climbed out of the car. "It doesn't matter where you got it, you can say you got it in the mail." She bent down and peered through the open door at him. "You do the right thing, Ringo. See if my baby girls can get some justice out of this. Because they sure as shit cain't get their daddy back." And she slammed the door.

Ringo sat in his car and stared at the biggest piece of evidence he'd ever had. Biggest piece of evidence he was likely to have in any case, ever. It felt hot in his hand, heavy. When cops were dirty, you called in the FBI. Who did you call when the FBI was dirty? For the first time in a long time he had absolutely no idea what to do.

CHAPTER TWENTY-FIVE

In Michigan, Dave usually ran four times week. During the winter he ran on a treadmill, but in the summer he did his usual path around the neighborhood. Four miles, and he'd been running four miles four times a week long enough that he didn't even start sweating until he'd gone a mile and a half. Four flat miles was easy, unless he had a chest cold or was running on only a handful of hours of sleep.

In Arizona, he wasn't running on the road because he didn't want the people he was trying to avoid driving up on him when he was only armed with a small pistol. So he ran cross country, up and down the hills on trails that had been there for years. He didn't know if they had originally been game trails or something else, but he was able to stay off the roads and still get a three mile run in. Three miles up and down hills, however, on dirt that often wasn't packed hard, at five thousand feet of elevation, was kicking his ass. Hard.

Wheezing and gasping, he stumbled into a walk as he reached his driveway halfway between the house and the road. Four times he'd run the route, every morning, and four times it felt like someone had ripped his lungs out of his chest with burning tongs. He supposed — eventually — he'd get used to the elevation, but how long would that take? Probably more time than he had.

The sun was barely up, and it was only about sixty degrees, but he wasn't cold. He wasn't cold, but he wasn't sweating — or at least that's what he would have thought, if he'd never exercised in the desert before. Jogging in an arid environment was nothing like jogging in Michigan. In Michigan, and pretty much everywhere else that it wasn't near desert, you knew when you were sweating. In the desert, it often evaporated so quickly you weren't aware just how hard you were working.

Every day they'd been there he'd been waking up long before dawn. The combination of surveillance hours plus two days travel west meant he would have been out jogging at three a.m. local time if he wasn't afraid of twisting his ankle on the uneven ground. Plus, of course, he wasn't sleeping well. He was surprised he was sleeping at all, actually.

If the elevation wasn't kicking his ass so hard he probably would have been able to appreciate how pretty the surroundings were. The ground itself was shades of brown, and it was far too dry for more than occasional clumps of nearly dry grass, but the slopes were dotted with all sorts of green bushes and scrub trees. He'd learned the names of most of them when he was younger, but remembering which was which now was tough — acacia, hackberry, mesquite and ironwood were trees and bushes. Buckwheat and primrose were low to the ground. As for cacti, he'd always been fascinated with them and remembered which was which. Around the property they mostly had prickly pear and cholla cacti, with a few saguaros.

Dave walked back and forth on the driveway for a while until he was cooled down, then headed into the house. A check of his watch showed him that it was just eight o'clock. "It's me," he called out when he opened the door, just in case.

Mickey was in the small open kitchen, making coffee and still looking half asleep. While Dave was running with the Kahr, he left his Glock sitting on the kitchen counter, but Mickey didn't seem to be a big fan of guns. "I'm going to jump in the shower," Dave told him.

Dave took off the Kahr and took a quick shower, then got dressed in jeans and a long-sleeved button-down shirt. That was another thing he'd learned in the desert; clothes that were a little warmer, but covered your skin from the intense sun, were a good thing. Exiting the tiny bathroom, Dave grabbed a cup of coffee, unloaded his Glock, and proceeded to practice his draw. He'd been doing it every morning and night since they'd arrived at the house.

Mickey stood with one hip against the kitchen counter, sipping his coffee and watching Dave as he practiced his draw and reloads and shooting on the move, over and over and over and over…..gun clicking and snicking, timer beeping…..it was maddening. How could he do that? He must have drawn his gun a thousand times since they'd arrived, not to mention putting a new magazine in it, shooting while moving left or right.

Shit, Mickey thought, *I guess that's how you get good at something, you do it ten thousand times.* Dave was amazingly fast, Mickey had never seen anything like it. His go-to "dryfire drill", as Mickey had learned they were called, involved two 8x10 pictures hung on one wall across the room, "Because I don't have any proper targets," as Dave told him. At the beep of his timer Dave would draw his Glock, "fire" twice at one picture, twice at the other, reload with a spare (empty) magazine off his belt, then shoot each picture twice again. He was consistently able to do it in 4 seconds or less. Impressive as hell, but Mickey was bored numb just watching and listening to the routine. He didn't know how Dave could do it, it was like imitating a sewing machine. Dave had calluses on his right hand in weird places (the inside of his middle finger, the web of his hand) just from practicing his draw.

After watching him, he understood how Anderson had not just won a gunfight against SWAT cops, but expected to win. He didn't understand that kind of bravery, or physical confidence, or whatever you wanted to call it, but he recognized it. Mickey was confident in his abilities when it came to technical expertise, but knew that was an entirely different animal than what cops needed to charge into dangerous situations.

"We need to talk," Mickey said to him, when it looked like he was done for the morning. Mickey was on his second cup of coffee, and checked his watch. Only half an hour this time. Dave looked flushed, and he was massaging his right shoulder with his left hand.

"About what?"

"About what?" Mickey waved a hand around. "About this. About what we're doing. We've been here for three days, three and a half, doing nothing. We need to have some sort of plan, we can't hide out here forever, you know. The problem is not going to go away. I've been thinking about this a lot — as I'm sure you have — and I think our best bet is a press conference. Contact as many media outlets as possible to announce what's going on. But — they just can't take our word for it on your fingerprints, they're going to have to print you, probably by one of their on-call experts. Because we're going to need a station or three that has those kind of resources, plus wanting to make as much noise as possible as fast as possible, we're going to need to head to a major city. Major news outlets. I don't know if Phoenix is big enough. Dallas, maybe? What's the closest really big city to here?"

"A press conference?" Dave said, looking at him. His expression was hard to read. "That's how you think we're going to solve this problem?"

"Sure. Why, do you have a better idea?"

Crossing his arms, Dave said, "Jerome Beiers only had one offending fingerprint tying him to this whole mess.

They snipped that off, and that's all they needed to do. Instead, they took his finger and fucking killed him. Your boss, the head of the damn FBI Crime Lab, shot you, what, six times? And they've made two attempts on my life, near as I can figure, the second because the first one got so fucked up. That sound like people who are going to give a shit about a little tiny press conference we give?"

"What alternative do we have? Unless you're willing to cut off your fingers—and heck, *I* can't do that, they tried to kill me because of what I know. But what else can we do? We have to do something that makes them realize killing us will no longer solve their problem. If everyone knows about your fingerprints killing us will just bring them under more suspicion."

"Don't you know how this government works? The way all governments seem to work these days? They will paint us as nuts, as kooks. If we trot out a fingerprint expert, they'll trot out ten that say the exact opposite. Then find kiddie porn on our computers to completely discredit us." He pulled out his cell phone from somewhere. Mickey hadn't seen Dave use a cell phone since they'd left on the trip. He fiddled with it as they talked.

"But I worked for the FBI Lab!"

"When they killed you, nobody ever found your body. I'm guessing that has them a little concerned, and on the off-chance that you do show up again, I bet that you'll find out you embezzled some money, forged some checks, faked evidence in some cases you worked, downloaded donkey porn on your office computer, something. Something that will completely ruin your credibility, and put you in handcuffs, under their control. And you'll commit suicide in your jail cell. Me too. Or one of us will get murdered by our cell mates. It doesn't have to be pretty, or clean, they just need us out of the picture." He set the cell phone in a kitchen drawer and closed it. Mickey could hear the phone beeping inside as it turned on.

"If you think they're going to do that, they don't need to kill us then, they just need to destroy our credibility."

"Destroying our credibility doesn't destroy my fingerprints. Even if they have experts from around the world saying my prints don't match anything, someone else can always print me and see for themselves. They could have just framed you for something, and instead they drove you out to the hood and shot the shit out of you."

Mickey was starting to get irritated. "Okay, so you don't like my idea, what's yours? How are we going to get out of this?"

Dave stared at him. "We're not," he said, in a tone that indicated he couldn't believe Mickey hadn't realized that already.

That shut Mickey up for a few seconds. "What do you mean, we're not?"

"We have the whole fucking weight of the U.S. government coming down on us," Dave told him. "Didn't you ever hear the phrase, 'You can't fight city hall'? These guys are a lot bigger than city hall. They have a lot more resources."

"I don't think the whole government knows about us."

Dave made a face. "No, just the parts of it that are in the business of killing people."

Mickey shook his head. Anderson wasn't making any sense. "So you're just going to, what? Give up? Why don't you just turn yourself over to the FBI then? Why did we come out here?"

"If I was going to give up I wouldn't have brought all my guns," Dave told him. "I wouldn't be practicing my draw, and planting Turnerite around the property."

Dave drawing his gun over and over again had been annoying, but it was the Turnerite that had unnerved Mickey. Anderson had mixed the binary explosive, poured it into buckets with lids, then wrapped each one in layer after layer of drywall screws and duct tape, then two layers of white plastic bags to keep moisture and bugs out. He'd planted them around the property, just sitting out in the open. Even close up it wasn't obvious what they were. "I thought you just said that you can't fight city hall."

Dave smiled grimly. "Well, you can fight it. You just can't win."

"What the hell are you even saying? That you came out here to die?"

"Why do you think I was such a dickhead in the car on the way out here? You think I'm happy about this? It's not easy to come to grips with your impending death. I'm fucking depressed as hell, dude. Jogging and working out and practicing my draw and painting the flagpole and putting the flag up and taking it down are what I'm doing to keep me from thinking about things."

Mickey shook his head rapidly. "Wait wait wait, what are you talking about? That you *did* come out here to die?"

"I came out here to fight. I can't sing, I can't dance, and I can't paint, but I can shoot. I can fucking shoot, *that* I can do. I've got no illusions about winning. Of living through it. Shit, for all I know they're going to fly a drone out of White Sands and put a missile through the window. Training accident, that missile wasn't supposed to have a live warhead. Oops, sorry, GPS error. We're nothing but a crater, no fingerprints to worry about. The local sheriff's department might get a hot tip about domestic terrorists from the feds and roll up here in armored personnel carriers and burn the place down with us inside. The people who are out to get us can do that, they can do all of those. They've just got to pick one. I'm just hoping to take a few of them with me before I go."

Mickey didn't accept that, he'd never been a defeatist. "Come on. You're young. You're the same age as me, and I know I'm too young to die. Don't you have anything to live for? Girlfriend, family, parents?"

"Well, I've got a girlfriend, sort of," Dave admitted.

"What's a 'sort of' girlfriend?"

Mickey saw him smile ruefully. "It's a long story. And you said you'd read my file, you know my parents are dead. Shit, for the last ten years, all I've wanted to be was an FBI agent. And now it's the FBI that wants to kill me. Talk about irony."

"I don't accept that. I didn't come out here to give up. I don't understand how you can feel that way. You've got fingerprints that match two other people. We can go to the press. We can raise so much of a ruckus that the government won't dare to do anything."

"Two dead people, my prints match two *dead* people, and they're still trying to kill me. And who are we? You're a rookie FBI fingerprint examiner, not even an agent, who walked away from his job, so you have no credibility. And I'm a cop killer. A racist cop killer. No matter what, both of us will end up dead, sooner or later. Accident, homicide, whatever. I don't like it, goddammit, but I'm looking at the facts. I'm not giving up, I'm going out on my own terms."

Dave collapsed into a chair, looked around the small house, which was barely more than a cabin. "I've always loved coming out here. As a kid, the desert's cool. After my parents died, I came out here for a couple weeks. To think. It's quiet."

Mickey slumped against the refrigerator. "I'm sorry about your parents," he said.

Dave glanced up at him, then looked down at the floor between his feet. "I.....really, I've felt lost since they died. Just going through the motions. Like the FBI thing, it wasn't nearly as important to me after they were gone. But....what else was I going to do?" He sighed. "Criminal justice degree, looking toward that career in law enforcement...and the guy who kills them is able to walk away, just walk away. Because of the law." He frowned and shook his head angrily. He stared out of the window for a minute.

"I like coming out here because it reminds me of them. Especially my dad. He would always find all sorts of make-work projects for us to do, so we could spend time together. Just us guys. His dad, my grandpa, built this house, and he worked on it as a kid. I remember, my mom would smile as we geared up. Dad would usually have me carry all the tools. I felt like such a grownup, swinging the hammer, helping to pour concrete. And you never know what you're going to find outside. We found scorpions, saw a few rattlers, lizards. Scary, but cool. And he pulled more than a few cactus thorns out of my hands and butt."

Mickey saw a potential opening for Dave to see reason. "Your parents. You think they'd want you to give up? Want you to just wait for the end?"

"You trying to guilt me with my dead parents? Dude, you have no idea...." He shook his head as if to clear it. "No, what I *want* doesn't matter. Shit, what I want is for this to be over, one way or the other. Why do you think I put the battery back in my phone and turned it on?"

"I don't know, why?"

"To make it easier for them to find out exactly where we are. And if that phone rings, don't answer it. Just leave it in there."

Mickey huffed, stared at the drawer where the phone was, and stomped out of the house. He stood on the small concrete porch, staring at nothing. The sun was off to his left, warming that side of his face, and he turned to it and closed his eyes. It felt comforting, the heat. Eventually he turned his head and opened his eyes, scanning the cloudless pale blue sky. Would he even be able to see a drone? Would he even hear the missile before it hit? He had no idea at what elevation they flew, or how big the ones the government used domestically might be. Scanning for drones in the sky....it felt paranoid, but then again he still had pain in his ribs from where the Director of the FBI Lab, his boss, had shot him six times. This couldn't be the end of his life, could it?

"Come *on*," he sobbed, long pent-up emotion suddenly overcoming him. It was ridiculous There had to be a way out of this, for both of them, him and his semi-suicidal partner. He went back inside.

"Okay, Death Wish," he said to Dave. "I don't know anything about guns, but they can't be harder to work than a microscope. Show me how to use that rifle you brought, and the shotgun. You've brought enough ammo with us, maybe we can do some shooting out back." If he played along, maybe Dave wouldn't be so confrontational with him, and they'd be able to talk. Seriously talk, about life, death, and their future together. Mickey was very persuasive. He figured it wouldn't take him more than a few days to convince Dave that going to the press was the best solution to their problem.

"That's the spirit," Dave said.

Smith walked into his office, but didn't bother sitting down. He knew it wouldn't be a long visit. Colman handed him a file. He opened it to see visible light spectrum satellite imagery.

"Found your target. He's in the middle of nowhere Arizona."

Smith was looking at what looked like a small, nearly square residence, with an SUV parked in front. "What's there?"

"Small house. He owns it, and we knew about it, but Arizona's a long way from Michigan. His phone went active there four hours ago, and a satellite pass two hours ago puts his vehicle there as well." Colman pointed at the photos in the file. "We've tried listening in on his phone, but so far no audio. He's barely got a signal out there."

"Middle of nowhere?"

"Pretty much. You'll be flying into Vegas. Farther away than Phoenix, but it's a bigger airport, much easier to not get noticed. Plus, more equipment in the area at our disposal. I'm arranging a vehicle there, all the gear you'll need inside. You should be able to get eyes on before dawn."

"You want us to move that quick? I'd like to work up a plan with my team."

"Work it up on the flight down. I want this done tomorrow if at all possible."

"We're not flying commercial?"

"No. Like I said, I want this done ASAP."

Smith nodded. "Copy that.

CHAPTER TWENTY-SIX

Ringo sat at his kitchen table, eight in the morning, a cup of coffee in front of him, and stared at nothing. He looked up. "What?" He belatedly realized that his wife had been talking.

His wife frowned at him and repeated, "I said, whatever the hell has you in a funk, you need to get over it. You've been dragging around since yesterday. You have a mistress die in a car accident or something?"

"What? Jeez, Mary." He shook his head. Sometimes she just came out of left field with the things she said. Mistress? Like he needed more feminine headaches in his life on top of a menopausal wife and bitchy teenage daughter. He looked around the kitchen. It was filled with knick-knacks, candles, baskets, rosy-cheeked figurines...it was hideous. How had he never noticed that before? This was no way for a man to live. Idly he wondered why the hell gay male couples ever broke up—shit, there was no woman involved, so everything had to run pretty smoothly, right? Lot less drama?

"Well, whatever it is, you need to get over it, or get on with it. Is it work?"

"Yeah, sort of. Shit." He'd been running on autopilot for a day and a half, completely shell-shocked by the recording that Diana Wilson had dumped on him. He hadn't known what to do, but knew he had to do *something*. Even if that recorder hadn't turned up, the discovery that David Anderson was probably the target in the Northfield murders, and that Pietro Bufonte was a potential suspect, had flipped a lot of switches. Bill Rochester had called the FBI, and they'd seemed very interested in the possibility that Detroit organized crime was involved. Yeahhhhhhh, no shit.

Ringo assumed that Bufonte had bought Hartman and maybe a few other local FBI agents, and they were now trying to control the investigation. It seemed like Ringo'd made and received a hundred calls over the past two days, monitoring the progress of all the other detectives he'd met at that crime scene, but not doing much himself. Two things he learned—1. Nobody knew anything more than they had two days ago, and 2. Nobody had been able to track down Anderson. He wasn't answering his cell phone, and three different detectives had made at least four trips to Anderson's residence without finding anyone at home. His front door was stuffed with business cards. Both Bill Rochester and Cashman from Oakland County had expressed serious concern. Shit.

With what he knew, Ringo was more than just seriously concerned. He wondered if maybe Anderson was already dead in a ditch somewhere. They wouldn't need to make the body disappear; you kill three cops, even if they're dirty, you automatically make a lot of enemies. Anderson showing up dead wouldn't surprise anyone.

Time to not just make phone calls but get off his ass. Actually do some detective work. He stood up, and handed the coffee cup to Mary. "Here, drink up," he said, and started looking for his shoes and gun.

"What am I going to do with this? I don't drink coffee."

"Maybe you should start," he called back to her. "Give you the pep you need to do some cleaning."

Some quick phone calls from the car confirmed that Anderson hadn't worked since the day of the shooting. He didn't blame him for that, but he still felt a small wiggle of doubt. Dammit, he never should have sat there and done almost nothing on the case for two days, not when he knew the FBI had tried to kill the kid. That was unforgivable. Nobody knew he had the recording, and until they did he was free to work the case any way he wanted. He left a message on Anderson's voicemail, then checked the file and called John Phault.

"Mr. Phault? Detective John George with the Detroit Police Department." They'd met at the Oakland County Sheriff's Department substation in Rochester Hills right after the shooting, as the many and varied jurisdictions tried to figure out who was in charge, and whether or not Anderson was going to jail.

It only took John half a second to place the voice. It belonged to the tired looking guy he remembered from the long meeting that ran until midnight. "Yes, detective?"

"Have you talked to Mr. Anderson recently? I'm trying to get hold of him and getting voicemail."

"No, I haven't. Actually, I haven't been able to get in touch with him for several days, which has me a little worried."

"Has he worked for you since the, ah, incident?"

"No, I told him to take some time off. I talked to him the day after, that morning, but since then haven't been able to get him on the phone. Went to his house the day before yesterday, but he wasn't there. Have you talked to his partner Aaron?"

"Aaron. Um, from the armored car company?"

"Yeah, they're friends. If he's talking to anybody, it's him."

"Do you have a phone number for him?"

"No, sorry, but Absolute can probably give you a cell phone number. Have you been by Dave's house?"

"Not personally, why?"

John frowned. "Just wondering. I'm worried about him."

Ringo grunted. If Phault only knew.

There was no answer at Anderson's house, and none of his neighbors reported seeing him for a couple of days at least.

"Shit," Ringo muttered. He walked around the outside of Anderson's house, peered into all the windows, but there was no sign of anything amiss inside. "Shit." He walked around to the last side of the house, and looked through the window into the garage. No car. "Where are you, boy?" he mumbled.

He remembered that Arlene had a 7 p.m. appointment with her son's school guidance counselor, and that she wanted him to go with her, so Aaron started putting together tomorrow's lunch for the both of them not long after getting home from work. He was using the provolone and the pepper jack cheese slices in alternating layers with the capicola, mortadella, and hot sopressata, making sure not to drop any cigarette ashes into the sandwich as he worked. He was just reaching for the Worcestershire sauce when someone knocked loudly on the door.

Aaron pulled open the door and looked out the screen at the man on the step. Short, dressed in a well-fitting off-the-rack suit, Aaron made him for a cop right away.

"Yeah?" he said, Marlboro bobbing in the corner of his mouth.

Detective Billy Dixon blinked at the man standing in the door. The 70s porn star moustache and too long jet black hair were to be expected in a trailer park, but the uniform shirt and holstered gun—and it was big damn gun—put him a little off his game. He knew both Anderson and his partner worked for an armored car company, but why was this guy wearing his uniform and gun at home, in his house? "Aaron Abruzzo?" he asked. "I'm Detective Dixon, wondering if I could ask you a few questions about David Anderson?" He flashed the badge on his belt, and his own gun.

Aaron frowned some more. "You got any ID?" He made no move to open the screen door.

Dixon dug out his ID and opened it so Abruzzo could read it through the screen. "Is Mr. Anderson back working at Absolute?" Dixon started out by asking. He hadn't planned on asking it first, but he was curious.

"What's West Bloomfield's interest in this?" Aaron asked him. He'd looked everything up on a map, knew the shitstorm had started in Troy and ended in Shelby Township, dragging an Oakland County dep in on the fun, but West Bloomfield was way the hell on the other side of Woodward. "You here because of the shooting?"

"I'm here on a related matter," Dixon told him. "Do you mind if I step inside to ask a few questions?"

He was starting to reach for the handle of the screen door when Aaron said, "Yep, I do. I was in the middle of something. Something more important than talking to you."

That brought Dixon up short. "Is there a problem?" he asked the armored car employee. Maybe he didn't like Anderson.

"No problem, I'm just not talking to cops. It might have something to do with the fact that Dave just dumped three of them, and I don't know which ones of you might be pissed at him and looking to return the favor." *It also might have to do with the fact that you're from West Bloomfield*, he said to himself.

That made some kind of sense, but Dixon wasn't about to get shut down by mullet-wearing trailer trash. "I can assure you I'm here on official police business, and interfering with or obstructing my investigation is not something you want to do."

"I don't remember," Aaron told him.

"I—what? You don't remember what?"

"The answer to any question you're going to ask me. Ever since my ma dropped me on my head as a baby, I can't remember shit. It also did horrible things to my manners, so you'll have to excuse me when I tell you to fuck right off." And he closed the door firmly on the detective.

"Asshole," Aaron muttered as he went back to his sandwich construction. Although that reminded him, he should call Dave. He hadn't talked to him in a few days. Not that he hadn't tried, but Dave wasn't answering his phone.

"Motherfucker," Dixon swore as he stared at the closed door, then walked back to his department sedan. Beside the driver's door he looked back at the ratty trailer. There was just the concrete parking pad in front, and two vehicles, an old classic Mustang and a tiny pink SUV. No dark-colored sedan, and nothing parked on the street nearby. Abruzzo had been working with the suspect for at least three years, near as he could figure out, and he didn't have any vehicles other than the Mustang registered to him, but Dixon'd hoped bracing him might turn something up. He hadn't turned up shit.

For a smart, apparently personable kid Anderson didn't seem to have very many friends to talk to, and Dixon felt like he was banging his head against the wall. He'd read something in the notes of one of the detectives working the shooting that Anderson had a girlfriend, but he'd yet to find out where she lived. Maybe he could work on that. Guys always said shit to women they shouldn't.

With a grunt he climbed into the Chevy and pulled away from the trailer. Getting turned around trying to find his way out of the maze of a trailer park didn't put him in a better mood.

Aaron had the big sandwich sliced up and in the refrigerator, and was changing out of his uniform, when Arlene showed up. "Hey, you back there?" she called out.

"I thought the thing wasn't until seven," he yelled from his bedroom.

"It's not, I wanted to stop by and see your ma."

Aaron popped out of the open bedroom door wearing boxers and a tank top that had once been white but was now faded to a dishwater gray. "She's not here, she's at Julie's for the rest of the week." Aaron's sister lived about forty-five minutes away, and had taken some time off of work to spend with their mother, seeing as they didn't think she had a whole lot of time left. Peanut was with her as well, she didn't travel anywhere without Peanut, even though she was officially Aaron's dog.

"Oh, crap, I forgot about that. Well, anyway, you should check out the car."

"Yeah? Hold on." Aaron tugged on a pair of black jeans and a polo shirt, then took care of priorities and kissed his girlfriend. When that was done he swung the front door the rest of the way open and looked out at the Taurus parked on the street behind the other vehicles.

"What, he couldn't find a green bumper?" He pushed out through the screen door and headed toward the Taurus in bare feet.

"Nope, but he said you could spray paint that easy, and hardly anybody'd be able to tell," Arlene said, holding open the screen door.

Aaron checked out the repair job, walking all around the front of the car and then getting down on hands and knees to peer under it. "Looks okay," he said. "Although I'm pissed about the black bumper. How much did he charge?"

"Only a hundred and fifty bucks, plus you have to make him spaghetti. Black was all he had at the junkyard. But he sprayed the hell out of the inside with Febreeze or something. Almost smells like a new car inside, now, instead of a pool."

"You and your bionic nose, I never could smell a thing. Well, I wish it looked like a new car, but for a hundred and fifty bucks plus spaghetti I can't complain." Aaron looked at the front end of the car. It didn't look new, but with the hood, grille, and front bumper replaced it just looked tired, not tired and beat up. Remembering the detective, he looked up and down the street, but there was nobody in sight. The asphalt was hot against the soles of his feet. Arlene headed toward the trailer, and he pulled out his phone. He got Dave's voicemail again.

"Dude, you're really starting to piss me off. And get me worried, too. Give me a call back, let me know what's going on. I hope to shit they didn't decide to arrest you after all." He made a mental note to watch the evening news, see if there was anything new on the shootout or Dave.

"What are you doing?" Arlene called to him. "Get in here. We've got an hour to kill, and I'm not going to drive all the way over here for nuthin'." Through the screen door he could see her pulling down the zipper of her Brinks coin room coveralls, then she stepped out of view.

Smiling, he forgot about the detective and headed back to the trailer.

Billy Dixon didn't get to where he was in life by giving up easily, but he was damned if he knew what to do next. He found himself driving all the way across Metro Detroit to stare at the crime scene on the range driveway in Shelby Township. There wasn't anything to see, just a dirt road leading off a narrow asphalt one. The cars were still in evidence, actually being stored by the Michigan State Police as they were the only ones who had an evidence garage big enough to handle four cars from one incident. Dixon had seen the crime scene photos, and imagined the evidence techs had been having orgasms at the sheer number of bullet holes in the cars.

Seeing as he was in the area, he drove to Troy and checked out the first crime scene. The only evidence still remaining of what had occurred there were the skid marks of Anderson's Mustang as he accelerated away from Edward Mitchell. Dixon tried to imagine what that must have been like—just sitting there, minding your own business, in your own damn neighborhood, and some dude walks up and blows the shit out of your car. Whatever else he may or may not have done, Anderson had big clanking balls. Dixon stood in the street next to his car for a while, thinking. *Own damn neighborhood.....*hmm. He'd been to Anderson's house before, years ago, right after his parents had been killed. Talked to him—for as long as he was willing to do that, which wasn't long—and did a neighborhood canvass, trying to verify his alibi that he was home alone.

Dixon got back into his sedan and drove down the block, seeing if he could find his way through the neighborhood to Anderson's house without pulling it up on GPS. He had a good head for numbers, and remembered Anderson's street address.....all he had to do was find the street.

After a few lefts and rights he found Willard, but had no recollection of where the house was on the street. As he coasted along at walking speed he suddenly saw he was in front of Anderson's house, and there was a girl getting out of a car parked in Anderson's driveway.

"Excuse me," Dixon called out, then threw the sedan into Park and climbed out. He badged the young woman as he walked up the driveway. She didn't seem surprised to have a cop walking up on her, but after what Anderson had been through the neighborhood had probably seen more than its share of police officers in the past week.

"If you're looking for Davey, I don't think he's home," she told Dixon. "You here about the shooting?"

"Are you his girlfriend?" Dixon asked. "I think I remember something in the interview files about him having a girlfriend."

She nodded. "Gina." Between the slope of the driveway and her high heels she had three inches on him, and he tried not to stare at her tits.

"How's he handling all this?" Dixon asked her.

She made a face and shrugged. "He doesn't really talk about stuff like that, you know? Not really a share-your-feelings kind of guy."

"Still, he shot three guys. Three cops—dirty cops. Dirty SWAT cops. Had to freak him out a bit. He talking to any of his friends?"

"He doesn't really have that many friends. Aaron, at the armored car place, that's about it. A few guys he shoots with."

"He seeing a counselor or therapist or anything for post-traumatic stress?"

She snorted. "A shrink? Please."

Dixon nodded. "So, how long have you and Dave been seeing each other?"

"Three, four years, something like that."

"Is it serious?"

Gina tilted her head. "I don't know."

Dixon smiled. "Four years and he hasn't proposed yet? He got cold feet?" If Anderson had been dating this smoking hot sex popsicle for four years and hadn't proposed, then either he was a closet fag or she was a cast-iron bitch.

"Nah, it's just.....neither one of us has ever gotten too serious. I don't know....he wants to get into the FBI, and with my line of work...."

"What do you do?"

"I'm a stripper," she told him.

Dixon blinked. After a second he said, "Most girls that do what you do say that they're 'dancers'."

She laughed. "Oh, I dance, but what I get paid for is to take my clothes off. I just don't lie about it, to myself or anybody else. And I make a shitload of money doing it." She put a hand on her hip, and Dixon glanced down at her jeans. How the hell did women even put on jeans that tight?

"Where do you dance—er, I mean, strip?"

"Goldfinger's, on Eight Mile."

"Did you meet Dave there?"

"Yeah. No….." She thought for a while. "No, I guess I met him before that, when I was at another club."

"Which one?"

"Gatsby's."

Dixon licked his lips. "Really? I think I've been there on a case. Three or four years ago? Who was the manager?"

"Wow, that was a long time ago. Uh…" he could see her thinking. "Paulie. Paulie…something Italian. Big guy. Total asshole."

"Hmm. And you met Dave there? He was watching you dance?"

"No, I got a flat tire leaving work one night. It was almost three o'clock in the morning and he was driving by and saw me. I didn't have a spare, but he waited with me until the tow truck showed up."

"What was he doing out so late?"

"Coming back from a surveillance, I think. I saw he had a gun, but it didn't scare me. I thought he was a cop, a rookie, at first. He looks like a cop."

"That's nice. What kind of car?"

"What?"

"Your car. With the flat. What kind of car were you driving at the time?"

"A new VW Bug."

"Hmm." Dixon glanced at the house. "So he's not home?" The house was dark.

Gina glanced over her shoulder. "No, I don't think so. He called me a couple of days ago, said he had to get out of town for a few days, and asked me to get his mail until the post office Stop came through."

"Where'd he go?"

She shook her head. "I don't know."

"Did he say when he'd be back?"

"Nope."

"He really doesn't tell you a lot, does he?" He checked out her car, but it was a tiny little two-door coupe. "Well, I've got his cell phone number, I'll try calling him again, leave him another message. Nice meeting you."

As he walked back to his car, he was thinking, *Gatsby's, Big Paulie, a convenient flat tire….*holy shit. He'd been looking for some kind of connection, and boom! There it was. *Anderson just happened to date a girl who worked for Big Paulie, meet her what sounded like only a couple of months after Paulie's case was thrown out? Coincidence my ass. Had the kid been doing surveillance on the club?*

The meeting with the school guidance counselor hadn't gone that well. Aaron knew it wouldn't. Arlene's son was a foul-mouthed little snot, and the only reason Aaron hadn't broken his nose for him was because he was thirteen, and Arlene's son. Billy had called the cops on his mother when he was nine and she'd taken his Xbox away, then started cursing at the cops when they wouldn't grab it back from her. Complete asshole, just like his father, wherever that loser was.

Aaron wouldn't be surprised if Arlene kicked Billy out of the house when he was old enough, if the kid didn't leave on his own first. Hell, he was hardly home to begin with, and Arlene had no idea where he was going. His grades were horrible, and Aaron was pretty sure he smoked, but where he was getting the money for the cigarettes was anybody's guess.

It was almost nine o'clock when there was a knock on his front door. "Seriously?" he bitched. It better not be that short asshole cop from West Bloomfield.

"Who's that?" Arlene called from the back of the trailer.

"I don't fucking know," he yelled back as he headed to the door. "All right, who are you with?" he asked the obvious cop standing on the steps.

Ringo held up his badge. "Detroit. Detective John George. I'm actually trying to locate Dave Anderson, but I'm not having much luck. When was the last time you saw or spoke to him?" Ringo could have called, but he'd wanted to drive by Abruzzo's residence in case Anderson was hiding out there.

"I think the day after the shooting. How'd you track me down?"

"Anderson's boss at the PI company, John Phault. So you haven't talked to him for several days? Do you know where he might be? I went to his house, but no one answered, and there wasn't a vehicle in the garage." A woman appeared behind Abruzzo and Ringo nodded at her. "Ma'am."

"He hasn't been answering my calls for a couple of days. Actually, I haven't talked to him since the day of the shooting. Late that night." Aaron looked at the detective. "What do you want with him?"

"I've got to talk to him about the case."

"Detroit detective....you must be pretty pissed that he killed a bunch of Detroit cops." Aaron cocked his head.

"Shot the hell out of your guys," Arlene added helpfully.

"No, that's....not something I'm concerned with. Investigating. Actually, I'm the one who figured out who it was hitting the clubs."

"I thought the FBI did that."

"Armed robbery isn't federal unless it's a bank. We passed it on to the FBI. We can't investigate ourselves, not on something that big." He got back on topic. "You sure you don't know where he is? Do you have another phone number for him? I've tried his cell several times."

"He's only got the one phone." Aaron crossed his arms. "You've talked to John, been to his house....."

"Called Absolute," Ringo offered.

"You talk to his girlfriend yet?"

Ringo shook his head. "No, I wasn't aware that he had a girlfriend. Could he be staying with her?"

Aaron blew out air and shrugged. "I don't know, maybe."

"You have a phone number, or an address?"

"No, I...." he thought for a second. "Hmm, maybe, hold on." He tracked down his cell phone inside the trailer and scrolled through incoming calls as he walked back toward the door. He waved Ringo inside the trailer. After a while Aaron said, "Umm, maybe this is it." He tapped the screen with his thumb, then put the phone up to his ear.

"Hello?"

"Yeah, is this Gina?"

"Yes?"

"Hi Gina, this is Dave's partner Aaron, at the armored car company. I'm trying to track down Dave, but he's not answering his phone. Have you seen him?"

"No, not for a few days. Seems like everybody's looking for him, I met a cop at his house earlier tonight looking for him."

"Shit. You have any idea where he might be?"

"No. He just said he was going out of town, asked me to get his mail for a few days."

Aaron quickly said, "Hold on, what? He said he was going out of town? For how long?"

"He didn't say, but the way he said it I'm guessing a while."

"When was this?"

Gina thought. "I don't know, three or four days ago. I think it was the day after the shooting. I'm not sure."

"No shit? You seen him when he left? Just wondering if he took the Cherokee, since it's gone."

"No, he left without me seeing him. He called me on the phone."

"Okay, thanks. You hear from him, you tell him to call me." He looked at the Detroit detective and chewed on the inside of his cheek. "I know where he is," he admitted to the man. "He's fine, he just escaped that circus you call a city."

"Where?"

Aaron shook his head. "No, sorry, I'm not going to tell you. If he went out there, it's because he wanted his privacy. Get away from this mess."

"I don't think you understand. I really need to talk to him."

"Yeah, I bet. Listen, if I hear from him, I'll have him call you. You got a card?"

"No, sir, I'm deadly serious, I need to know where he is, right now." Ringo paused, and took a deep breath. "He's in danger. Somebody's trying to kill him"

Aaron barked a laugh out. "Well no fucking shit somebody's trying to kill him, there's a bunch of dead bodies in the Oakland county morgue that could tell you that. Probably a bunch more Detroit cops would like to make him just as dead as their buddies."

"No, I mean somebody is *still* trying to kill him. And not us," he felt obliged to add. Ringo looked from Aaron to Arlene. "I was told you're his friend. That you're almost his only friend."

"Well, I don't know about that, but we're close. He was over here for the Fourth, had spaghetti with me and my mom and Arlene."

"I know why the shooting happened," Ringo told him. "And it's going to happen again, I think, unless I can talk to him. The two of us, we need to figure this out."

"What do you mean, you mean that wasn't some random bullshit? They were trying to kill *him*? Why?"

Ringo shook his head. "It's a long story, and I don't have all the facts. But I know who, and I know it's not over. He's still in danger. And don't ask for any more details, you don't want to know." He looked into the middle distance. "Hell, I don't want to know, it's tearing me up, but I've got to do something. I can't not." Ringo stared into the face of the man who might be Anderson's only friend. "You know anything about his parents' death?"

"Yeah," Aaron said slowly, frowning.

"I think this whole thing is tied to that. And if I'm right....it's probably going to get worse."

"You going to give me any more details than these fucking vague warnings?"

"No. I've already told you too much. So can you help me? Help Dave?"

Aaron stared at him for several long seconds. "Shit." He turned to Arlene and kissed her. "Babe, you want to turn on the computer? We've got to buy some airplane tickets."

"No, no, no," Ringo said quickly. "I can't have you going with me."

"Well then, I'm going without you," Aaron told him. "Because I'm not giving you the address."

"I don't think you understand," Ringo tried. "This is something very dangerous. When I find him, I'm going to have to put him into protective custody...."

"Dude, really? Dangerous? I ride around Detroit in an armored car five days a week. I'm dancing in the lion's cage wearing steak pajamas every day for $15.89 an hour. When's the last time you even had to pull your gun? For me it was last Tuesday. So shut up about that shit. Besides, I don't actually know the address, I just know how to get there."

Which wasn't really true, but fuck this asshole, he wasn't going without Aaron. "Anyway, how do I know that you're not part of the reason people are trying to kill him? DPD doesn't exactly have clean hands in this."

"You're going to have to trust me."

"Yeah? Back at ya, dude." He stared at the cop. "So, we flying together? Or am I going alone?"

"Shit," Ringo said finally. "So where are we going?"

"Phoenix. To start. I can take care of my own ticket, but you're going to have to cover the rental car. And on the plane, you're going to tell me everything you know. No bullshit."

CHAPTER TWENTY-SEVEN

"You mean I've got to pay for my carry-on as well as my goddamn checked bag?" Aaron said, outraged. "'American Spirit' Airlines my ass."

"You want to fly cross-country on only a few hours notice, in the middle of the night, your choices are sort of limited," Ringo told him tiredly. Abruzzo was already wearing him down, and they'd only been together a few hours. But he didn't see how he had much of a choice.

He was pretty sure Anderson was still in danger, and finding him and telling him that, sooner rather than later, was a priority. Ringo wasn't exactly sure what kind of witness protection he could offer Anderson, but he had to do something.

Doing research, he'd learned that normally it was the Office of Professional Responsibility who investigated the FBI....but the OPR was still a department *inside* the FBI. Their own version of Internal Affairs. And the feds were well known for circling the wagons whenever they were challenged. His faith that the FBI would properly investigate itself, especially with something this huge, was slim to none.

Internet research showed him that, on various cases when the OPR was called in, it usually discovered the FBI— big shocker—hadn't done anything wrong. Nothing to see here, folks, move along. Apparently if the incident was big or important enough the Department of Justice might get called in, but he didn't have any confidence in that arrangement either. It was more than a little incestuous.

But who the hell did that leave? Who he could hand over the recording to? The press? Honestly, he didn't want to go that route. He wanted the people responsible for this investigated and punished, and he'd never trusted the press. They rarely did anything right, and true news organizations—as opposed to those who had devolved into editorializing shills and gossip mongers—were almost extinct.

"What are you checking luggage for anyway?" he asked Aaron. "We're only going to be gone a day or two."

"I'm checking my guns," Aaron said. "The plane would be safer if they let me carry on board, but they don't feel the same way. Shit, the FAA barely lets the pilots carry guns anymore, it's like Nine-Eleven never happened. Assholes." He looked at Ringo, then Ringo's hands, then the area around him. "Aren't you checking a bag? Where's your gun? I didn't think they let locals carry on board, just federal agents."

"I left it in the trunk of my car." It had been a reflex—he never flew on department business, the only time he flew was on family vacations, which had been fewer and less frequent as the years had gone by. No need to bring a gun to the beach, or Disney World.

"Are you shitting me? We find him, what the fuck are you going to protect him with, your shitty ties?" He checked his watch. "We've got time. Go back out to your car and get your gun. I've got room in my case."

"I don't even think I'm legal to carry in Arizona," Ringo said, pissed, not happy about being told what to do by anyone, much less someone with a Harry Reems moustache. He glanced down at his tie. It looked fine, there wasn't anything wrong with it. What the hell did Abruzzo know about ties anyway?

"Everybody's fucking legal to carry in Arizona," Aaron told him. "It's like drinking beer in Europe. Go get your goddamn gun."

Smith stepped away from the small table and opened the mini-refrigerator. "Anybody want anything?"

"What do we have?"

Smith looked. "Gatorade, Monster, water. We're going to the high desert, so I'd stay away from anything with caffeine, it's a diuretic."

"Thanks, ma," Bailey said sarcastically.

"If he's there, it's going to be a quick in and out," Marcus remarked.

"That's what your mom said," Kyle couldn't help but say. That got a laugh all around.

"It's like playing grabass with a bunch of PFCs," Smith said, fighting back a smile. "Anybody want something or what?" He ended up returning to the table with two Gatorades and a water.

"If he's not there, we're going to sit on it until he shows," Smith reminded them. "So pack all your empty pouches with water bottles." He glanced around the interior of the Gulfstream G4. As private jets went, it was spacious, and renting one of the things out cost something ridiculous, like a thousand dollars an hour. Flatscreen TVs, leather reclining chairs with cupholders, real wood, carpet, fresh flowers in vases.....too bad every job wasn't like this. Six big guys clustered around the G4's small table, though, and it got a little claustrophobic. He wondered which shell company owned the jet.

Marcus, who'd spent a lot of time in the mountains of Afghanistan, said "I'd feel a lot better if we had Camelbaks."

"Shit, I'd feel a lot better if we could have brought our own gear, or at least had a chance to sight in our shit," Randy said.

"Yeah, but everyone knows SEALs are whiners," Haney said to him.

"Did anybody bring any of their kit?" Smith asked the team.

"Heard we were jumping a flight, assumed it was commercial," Marcus said. "I didn't bring anything other than a carry-on full of clothes. Just stuff that would make it through an x-ray." Everyone else indicated they'd done the same. Smith looked around. They were, for the most part, dressed in button-down shirts over cargo pants and boots, typical private contractor attire.

"Well, we've all worked compressed timeline jobs before, and sometimes you have to make do," Smith told them. "I've been assured that everything we need is going to be in the vehicle waiting at the airport for us."

"And if it's not?"

"Then I call it. Can't do the job if you don't have the tools. But I have no reason to doubt there will be a problem this time."

"Anybody else worked a domestic job before?" Kyle asked. He looked at Bailey. "Shit, all you've ever done is ops for the Company. So what's the deal?"

"What do you mean?"

"All domestic ops this rushed?"

Bailey, who had sandy brown hair and looked ten years younger than his age, shook his head. "No, and they're usually a lot more....covert. Make it look like an accident, or at least leave no evidence of foul play. Just disappear the body. Here, this one, the fact they don't seem to care.....might be important."

"Can we get back to the fucking file?" Haney said. He was one of the two former SOF-D operators on the team, the other being Smith. He was the second oldest on the team, and showing gray, although Smith had a few years—and gray hairs—on him. Unlike Smith, who rarely brought up his elite roots, Haney relied heavily on the cachet of being former "Delta Force". It hadn't earned him a lot of friends in the business, but then he wasn't looking for friends.

"Fuck you, Delta," Kyle said, but Haney chose to ignore it. That might have been because Kyle was the youngest, strongest, and biggest member of the team. He fought amateur heavyweight MMA matches in his free time, with a fighting weight of 265.

The satellite photos were spread around the top of the small, round-edged rectangle of a table, and the flash drive containing the rest of the information was plugged into the side of an open laptop sitting open. "The only way to approach on the road is from the southwest, but it's open as hell," Randy said. "If we're going to come in that way, we might as well drive all the way up to his front door and hit the horn."

"I don't know. See this around here," Kyle said, his finger tracing a feature on the photo, "I think this is a low ridge around the house. It's set at one end of a shallow oval." They studied the shadows in the photo closely.

"Yeah, but how shallow?" Marcus asked what they were all thinking. "If the house is in a hole, and he's inside, he won't see anybody approaching. Hell, he might not even hear a car until it's right there."

"And if that depression is only two feet deep, and he happens to be looking out an attic window, he'll see our vehicle half a mile out," Smith said. "All our asses are on the line, but I'm on the line for your asses. No unnecessary risks. I think parking here," he pointed to a narrow gravel road running north/south a mile east of the subject's property, "and walking cross country is the best bet. I don't know if we're getting NODs, but the moon is almost full, and the weather forecast for the area says no clouds. We should be able to work our way in from the road and get into position without a problem." He checked his watch. "We're what, ninety minutes from wheels down? Then we've got a four hour drive, probably less at this hour of the night. Nothing gets screwed, we should be in position by oh-two-hundred local, maybe oh-three-hundred at the latest."

"And then what? Pop him as soon as he sticks his head out? I'm not against that," Marcus assured them, "but we're going to be bringing weapons we've never fired, that were zeroed by other people. Shit, hopefully they've been zeroed. What are we picking up? M4s? AKs?"

"I was told sterile domestic commercial stuff, so I'm guessing they'll be ARs or M4 variants. Semi auto. We'll find out when we get there."

"Optics? Handguns?"

Smith shrugged. "I don't know."

"Shit."

"What the hell are you guys getting your panties all tied up in knots for?" Haney asked them. "This is a fucking kid, barely out of college, never been in the military, never even been a cop. I can't figure out what the fuck they're doing sending six of us out on this douchebag. Between us we've got what, like twenty combat tours? I mean, is there something we should know?"

Smith looked at him. "You've served with guys younger than him."

"Yeah? Well, this isn't that. It's not like he's got combat experience."

Smith paused. "He does now."

Haney snorted. "Getting into a shootout with a bunch of fat, crooked cops doesn't count as combat."

"What kind of weapons is he likely to have?" Bailey interrupted them.

Kyle pulled the laptop over to him and scrolled through the information. "According to the ATF, he's registered a number of handguns over the years, one shotgun......and two AR-15s. No way to tell what he might have sold. Or bought used, in private sales."

"One of the rifles is now in the police evidence room," Smith reminded them. "Along with one of his handguns, if I remember correctly. But he could still be armed. We should assume he will be. No way to know how hot he might be. Don't know if he's hiding out there or just getting away from it all. But let's assume he's got his head on a swivel, looking for bad news."

"Top, you have any more detail on why they want us to hit this guy?" Kyle asked Smith. That got him stares from everybody.

"How long you been doing this shit, you don't know better than to ask that?" Haney said.

"How much more detail you want, we've practically got everything but his favorite color," Marcus said, pointing at the open file on the laptop.

Kyle held up a hand. "I know, I'm just wondering, because this thing is so rushed, if we need to worry about him or his house. I'd prefer not to end this op glowing in the dark."

Smith nodded and smiled. "Roger that. Honestly, you know everything I do. But we weren't told to secure any intelligence or materiel on this one, so all they're worried about is him. He's the mission. I don't think you have to worry about any dirty bombs or uranium surprises."

"What about you?" Kyle asked Bailey, since he had a lot more intelligence contacts and time with the Company. "You got any special insights into this one?'

Bailey shook his head. "I don't know anything more than you guys," he said. Even though it was true, nobody else on the plane believed him. Working for the spooks just wasn't the same as doing contracting work. You could never really trust them to tell you the truth. The only thing you could ever trust was the weapon in your hand, and the guy next to you....and with these jobs, not even him.

Smith looked back at the overhead photos. "So, how do you want to handle this? Marcus, you don't like the sniper angle, because of the uncertainty with our gear. And I don't disagree. You got any suggestions?"

"Yeah," the former Army Ranger said brightly. He smiled. "I was thinking I could walk up and knock on his front door."

The G4 landed two minutes ahead of schedule and taxied to a small hangar at one end of the airport. They were met by a sleepy-looking guy in a polo shirt and khakis.

"Who gets the keys?" he asked, holding them up. Smith took them, and the man pointed, then headed off in the opposite direction.

"Seriously? Well, I guess we won't be doing any offroading," Marcus said, eyeballing their transport.

The team walked over to the Chrysler mini-van and Smith opened the rear hatch. There were several gear bags inside. "All right, gloves? Everybody got their gloves? I'd prefer not to leave a print on anything, in case we have to ditch it." Everyone on the team pulled out well-worn tactical gloves in varying colors from their bags and put them on. There was no one else around, but still they were careful as they looked through the provided equipment.

"M4s with Aimpoints, short-range headset radio mikes, looks like some handguns as well. Glocks."

"Armor?" Bailey asked.

Smith said, "I see plate carriers with mag pouches mounted on them. Looks like we've got at least a couple loaded mags for each rifle, ball ammo. All right, everybody pile in. Bailey, you finish inventorying what we have, we need to get on the road. Check to see if all the Aimpoints work, count the mags and make sure they're loaded all the way, you know the drill."

As Smith closed the rear door of the van, Haney asked him, "We got cans on anything?" He was hoping at least some of the weapons had sound suppressors, so when the shooting started the target's neighbors didn't call the local authorities.

"Nope. We're going loud on this one. So hopefully we'll only need one shot."

Kyle shook his head. "It's Arizona. Unless it sounds like a war, nobody is going to call anybody. They'll just figure it's someone out plinking."

Dave opened his eyes, completely alert. Nothing like nightmares to clear the cobwebs from your head. He checked his watch in the darkness, and the glowing hands told him it was just after one-thirty in the morning. Damn, that was early. His body still hadn't adjusted to Arizona time, three hours difference, and he'd been getting up early for so long for surveillance that he'd yet to sleep past 3 a.m. local. No chance of his going back to sleep tonight; he was a little sweaty from the nightmare, yet another version of the gunfight with the dirty Detroit cops where things turned out worse for him than they had in real life.

He sat up on the couch with a grunt and looked toward the bedroom, which was a narrow space set behind the house's small kitchen. The door was closed, and he assumed Mickey was still asleep. There was no light on under the door. For being just as much of a target as Dave, the young FBI agent didn't seem to be having the same nightmares. Then again, he still thought there was a way they could get out of all this alive. Press conference; yeah, right.

Dave lifted his pants off the floor, stood up, and pulled them on. He'd left his belt threaded through his belt loops, his holster and double mag pouch still on the belt. After securing his belt he grabbed his Glock off the coffee table and slid it into the holster, then pulled his shoes on and laced them up. Walking gently across the length of the house—the wood floor creaked something awful—he grabbed a windbreaker.

The air outside was crisp and cool in a way that seemed unique to the desert. Maybe it was the dry air, he didn't know. He could smell a few things....definitely a hint of sage, and maybe mesquite. Sure didn't smell like southeastern Michigan. The Cherokee was bright in the light of the nearly full moon, and he looked into the night sky.

"Wow," he breathed. There really was no comparison between the Detroit sky and what he was seeing above his head in the middle of the Arizona high desert. He might have been on another planet, there were just so many more stars visible. The Milky Way was there in all its fuzzy mysteriousness. One thing he never understood, if the Earth was in the Milky Way, why did it look like it was *over there*? There was Orion's belt, and the Big Dipper, follow that to the North Star....he turned around, searching for and finding most of the constellations that his father had taught him all those years ago. The moon was so sharp-edged it looked cut out and pasted above his head. Like he could reach out and touch it.

As crisp as the air was, it really wasn't that cold. He walked across the dry crunching earth toward the east side of the valley, as he'd always thought of it since he was a kid. It had seemed a lot larger when he was younger, now it was just a little bowl in the middle of rolling dry hills. He was looking for something.....would it still be there? No reason why it wouldn't. Reaching the far incline, he searched around for a bit, finally finding what he was looking for. He hadn't seen it at first, because a few desert weeds had grown up around it, and in part because the ground looked different in moonlight.

Not sure whether it was the start of an abandoned project of his father's, maybe the floor of a never-realized tool shed, or the final resting place of an unneeded bit of road construction, the ragged slice of concrete jutted out from the inside of the ridge. He wasn't sure how far into the ground the concrete went, but a good four feet of it stuck out from the ridge, sloping down and in, with a slight overhang at the bottom. It was at least six, probably more like eight inches thick. A serious slab. He'd have to break it up if he ever wanted to move it. Not much use thinking about that now.

Dave picked up a few rocks and threw them at the overhang, and stamped his feet, but no snakes or other creatures announced their annoyance with him. Satisfied, he climbed up and sat down on the slab. The afternoon and evening sun baked the concrete for hours, and even this deep into the night he could still feel the residual heat under him as he leaned back.

Staring up at the infinite universe couldn't make him forget his troubles, but they slid further back in his mind as he gazed up at the tiny winking pinpoints of light. Checking once again for any bugs or creatures, Dave lay back on the slab, his head on the dirt slope above the piece of concrete. He crossed his arms over his chest and marveled at all there was to see, and tried not to think of anything else.

CHAPTER TWENTY-EIGHT

"Okay," Bailey called from the rear of the van. "I've got an inventory."

"What do we have?" Smith said from the passenger seat. Marcus was driving. The van came with turn-by-turn directional GPS, which was very helpful at night, in unfamiliar territory.

"Six semi-auto ARs with sixteen-inch barrels. Various makes and models, all topped with Aimpoint M2 red dot scopes, and with single point slings."

"Are they new?"

"The rifles? I think they've been test fired, maybe — hopefully zeroed in — but yeah, I think they're new. It's sort of hard to tell back here, I'm working off a flashlight. I've got fifteen fully-loaded 30-round magazines for the rifles, which doesn't split equally."

"Two mags for some, three for others," Smith said.

"Two magazines?" Marcus complained.

"Between all of us that's almost five hundred rounds, for one civilian target," Haney said. "I think we'll be fine."

"Ball ammo, federal headstamp," Bailey announced. "Probably military contract. We also have two Glock 19s, loaded with ball ammo as well, two fully-loaded magazines per pistol."

"Sure there's only two Glocks?" Kyle asked.

"Positive. So that's sixty rounds of nine-millimeter. We've got six commercial Motorola walkie-talkies with plug-in push-to-talk headsets. They advertise them as having the range of a mile, but I've used them before, that's pushing it. In the open, they'll reach half a mile for sure, and in a downtown they'll reach a quarter mile no problem. Shouldn't be an issue for us. All the batteries are fully charged. Oh, and I checked the Aimpoints as well, all the dots turn on." He moved his flashlight around. "Six plate carriers with rifle magazine pouches. Look brand new, never been worn."

"They have plates?" Randy asked him.

Bailey nodded, unseen in the dark of the van. "Front and back. Feels like steel."

"What about body armor?"

"No, just the plates. Ummm, I've got a bunch of zip-cuffs here, if we'll need those…"

"NODs? Please tell me you have NODs in there somewhere."

"Nope," Bailey told them. "No night vision, no suppressors. I do have a smaller bag filled with bottles of Gatorade and Power Bars. Oh, and there's a first aid kit with a pressure dressing and a tourniquet. And that's it," he finished.

"All right. That's not bad," Smith observed. "Geared up nice. Anybody bring anything else that might be of help?"

"I've got a handheld GPS," Haney announced.

"I've got a compass as well," Kyle told the group. "Shouldn't have any problems walking a mile in a straight line, not with this moon." He looked out the window.

"Now we've just got to get there. How long?"

Marcus glanced back at the van. "GPS is saying it's another three hours to the drop-off point."

Smith nodded. "Say a slow, careful walk the mile to the house, add another thirty minutes.....we should have eyes on by oh-three-hundred. Perfect."

Until Dave opened his eyes, he hadn't realized he'd fallen asleep. He was surprised, actually, that he'd dropped off, laying there. He supposed he hadn't been getting enough sleep since driving to Arizona, what with the time change and the nightmares. Still on his back, arms crossed, he hadn't moved at all in his sleep.

The night sky was a black velvet blanket above him, a thousand pinpricks of light showing through it. Still dark, no hint of dawn. It didn't feel like he'd been asleep for more than half an hour, he wasn't stiff from lying on the ground, and the concrete was still emitting faint warmth. He wondered what had caused him to wake up, maybe an animal nearby had made a sound. No nightmares, for once, for which he was grateful.

There was a faint crunching above him, and the nearly silent hiss of sand running down the slope. He turned his head to see if there was an animal moving down the slope toward him—didn't want to surprise a snake, especially if it was a rattler—but couldn't see anything. The slope reached maybe four feet above his head, and glowed nearly white in the moonlight. Dave was just about to get up and investigate when he heard, seemingly right over his head, a man quietly say, "Alpha's in position, eyes on. No movement, no lights, vehicle is present." Dave froze, his heart suddenly racing.

Aaron couldn't sleep sitting up for shit, so he was dragging when the flight landed at Phoenix Sky Harbor airport. The detective had arranged to rent a car before they'd left Aaron's trailer, which was a good thing seeing as their flight landed at 4:22 a.m, but they still wouldn't be able to pick it up until the counter opened at 7 a.m.

"My ass is kicked," he told Ringo as they walked up the jetbridge to the concourse. "You get any sleep on the flight?" They hadn't been able to get seats together, for which Ringo had been very thankful.

"About an hour." Ringo actually felt pretty good. Maybe it was the thrill of the hunt, of putting his nose to the ground, but he always felt like a younger man when he was out and doing something case-related. He reflexively checked his pocket — the recorder was still there.

He hadn't made a copy of the digital recording of Hartman, and he wasn't quite sure why. He told himself that it was because he wasn't sure how to do it without leaving traces on whatever computer he used, but the fact of the matter was....the recording scared the shit out of him. If there was only one copy, and something happened to it......not that he would willingly destroy it or let it be destroyed, but accidents happened. He shook his head, and pushed that ugly thought away. "I'll drive," he told Aaron as they walked. "Get some time under the wheels, then maybe we can get some breakfast. You can nap." *Please God*, he thought.

"We didn't sit together on the plane, you still have to tell me what the fucking hurry is about all this. How you know that more people are gunning for Dave." Aaron pointed at the baggage carousel. His locked case full of guns and ammo was already sitting there. "I can load and strap on my shit while you drive and talk."

"Don't get in a hurry, we've still got a couple hours, right?" And Ringo wasn't looking forward to it, either, or the two hour drive to Anderson's place. He was getting to the age where extended sitting hurt both his ass and his back. "Can you give me the address now?" He gestured at the closed rental car desk. "I'm not going to leave without you."

Aaron hoisted his hard-sided padlocked Pelican case off the baggage carousel and looked at the detective. "Sure, as soon as you tell me why we're out here. What has you so worried?"

Ringo huffed. "Shit." He looked around the deserted terminal, and pointed to some out-of-the-way chairs against the far wall. "Let's go sit over there. You're going to want to be able to hear this."

For what he estimated was an hour, Dave hadn't twitched, hadn't scratched, hadn't dared to do anything other than breathe as quietly as possible through his open mouth. He'd never sweated so much doing so little.

Whoever it was above him, they were still there. Every five or ten minutes Dave would hear the man shift his weight, or breathe heavily. It sounded like the man was only a foot above his head, but Dave knew with the thin desert air the man could be much further away than that—however, if he had "eyes on" the house and vehicle, he had to be just over the top of the ridge.

Twice Dave had lifted his head slowly and looked around the valley in front of him, moving only his eyes, but he hadn't seen anything or anyone. If whoever above him was "Alpha", calling into someone on the radio, it stood to reason there was somebody else out there, somewhere.

Dave didn't know who, how many, or where, but he assumed they were close. Actually, the "who" of it didn't matter so much. He knew *somebody* would be coming for him, eventually. FBI, or whoever the FBI would hire to do the job. The only surprise was in how quickly they'd arrived. Well, he had to be honest with himself, there was a small part of his brain that kept hoping Mickey had been lying to him, or delusional, that there really wasn't a conspiracy to remove him from the gene pool because of his matching fingerprints. So having a guy show up to do just that wasn't completely unexpected, he just hadn't been 100% sure it would happen, even though he'd told Mickey otherwise. Dave wasn't happy being right. Depressed didn't even begin to cover it.

There was a faint sound above him, and it took him a while to place it—the man up there was drinking something. So he'd brought refreshments....great. His—or maybe their—plan was to sit there and wait him out. They'd assume he was in the house. *Shit, they might have thermal scopes,* he realized. They might be able to *see* that he was in the house, or see who they thought was him. Dave was stuck where he was, in the open laying on the slope with just a few weeds for cover. He couldn't move, couldn't even make a sound, and was nowhere near the house, his rifle, his shotgun, or the night vision scope he'd just bought. Plus, Mickey was in the house sleeping away, without a clue. Fuck. At least he had a gun with him out here. A Glock wasn't a rifle, but it was sure as hell better than nothing.

He lifted his head again, slowly, and looked around the depression in which his house sat. If he was planning to hit the house, the guy above him was in a good position. He was side-on to the house, and as soon as Dave stepped out the front door he'd be in perfect profile and not looking anywhere near where the shots would come from. The distance was maybe seventy-five yards, not a problem at all for someone with a rifle, and he could cover nearly the entire valley except the far side of the house, the narrow slot between it and the far ridge. But....if there was more than one guy, where would the other person be?

Neck starting to quiver from the strain of holding his head up, he moved his eyes left and right. Someone on the ridge directly to the south, facing the front of the house, would have a good view, but might get spotted out the front window. He didn't think there'd be anybody on the opposite ridge; two people directly facing each other with guns was never a good idea.

The washed out V-notch gulley behind the house at an angle, that would be a good spot to put someone as well. Someone in that notch would be out of sight from the rear window of the house, and yet only twenty yards away from the back corner—there was no way to get closer without being spotted. He squinted, looked a little to the left and right, but if there was anyone there he couldn't see them.

Dave gently lowered his quivering head and rested. If there was more than one guy, and they'd had a chance to recon the property, he knew they could be anywhere. He actually might be in full view of them right now, and the only reason they hadn't spotted him was because he hadn't moved and drawn attention to himself. Actually, thinking of that....

Very carefully, very slowly, moving in increments, Dave uncrossed his arms. The windbreaker had a nylon shell over a thin fleece layer, and made a faint hiss as it rubbed against itself. Was color was his windbreaker? He couldn't remember. How the hell could he not remember the color of the fucking jacket he was wearing? It was a solid color, and he was pretty sure it was dark, but his brain just couldn't pull up the image.

He moved his arms in slow motion, hands going down and in until they met near his waist. Then he placed his right hand over the glowing luminescent face of his watch, and took a deep, slow breath. No yelling, no gunfire, no pain as bullets tore through his flesh. So far, so good.

"Are you shitting me!" Aaron nearly yelled.

"Keep your voice down," Ringo growled at him through his teeth. He knew this had been a bad idea.

"The fucking FBI? Do we know for sure this guy actually is FBI, and not just saying he is?"

Ringo nodded reluctantly. "Yeah, I've met him. He's FBI."

"Working for the mob."

"Maybe, I don't know."

Aaron shook his head violently. "You know of any other reason somebody would want to kill him?"

"No, do you? Do you know anything about that accident? The hit and run of Paulo Bufonte."

Aaron calmed down and looked at the detective. "Yeah. Dave mentioned it. I can't say he was upset about it."

"I can imagine. So you were working together at the time?"

"Yeah."

"Did he own a dark-colored sedan at any time?"

Aaron shook his head firmly. "No. He never owned a dark sedan."

"Do you know if he had access to one?"

"Seriously, dude? Is that why we're out here? You still trying to pin that fucking hit and run on him? All this shit happened years ago. Look, apparently it doesn't fucking matter whether or not he did it, Big Paulie's dad thinks Dave killed his kid and hired the FBI to take him out."

"We can't say that for sure."

"Hired, bribed, blackmailed, whatever, I don't care. Shit, how long have you known this? Dave's been out of contact for almost a whole week. How do we know he's even still alive?"

"How would the FBI know about this place we're going to?" Ringo asked him.

"Well shit," Aaron said, "Dave fucking applied for a job with them guys. You need Top Secret clearance and all that. He showed me the application, it was a mile goddamn long. Have to put down every one of your relatives, if they have any criminal records, all that. I bet he had to tell them that he owned this house out here. Don't you think so?"

Ringo sat and thought for a few seconds. Abruzzo was probably right.

"Fuck, how long till the counter opens?" Aaron checked his watch. "And then it's at least an hour and a half drive. Shit." He looked at the detective. "Isn't there anything we can do?"

Ringo wasn't convinced that they needed to be in such a hurry.....but he had sat on the file for over a day, doing next to nothing, even after he knew the FBI was trying to have the kid killed. If Anderson ended up dead.....hell, he didn't want that guilt. "I can call the local PD. Ask them to do a drive-by of the house this morning before we get there, a welfare check, make sure there's not a problem. But to do that, you'd actually have to give me the address."

With only a brief pause, Aaron did just that. "And it's Tohono County, that's who has jurisdiction," he told Ringo. "Call their Sheriff's Department."

"You sure?"

"Yep." Ringo pulled out his smartphone and went about tracking down a phone number. The airport had wi-fi, and it didn't take him very long.

"Yes, could I speak to your shift commander, please? My name is John George, I'm a Detective with the Detroit Police Department. What? Detroit, *Michigan*. Yes." He looked at Aaron and rolled his eyes.

The sky above him was beginning to lighten, but it was not yet dawn. For being in the open, he was in a pretty good spot. The sun would rise behind him, and lying on the slope he'd stay in shadow for hours, probably until close to ten in the morning. Not that he'd be lying there that long. Something would have to happen before that, he was sure.

While there were a few weeds to either side of him, about a foot tall, he was pretty much in a completely exposed position. The guy on the other side of the slope behind him wouldn't be able to see Dave until he came down over the ridge, and Dave would hear him as soon as he started to move. If there was anybody else out there... His only camouflage was silence and stillness — that and being where nobody would think to look.

Dave's mouth was dry, and he had to piss. How unfair was that? Either he should be thirsty, or have to pee, but not both at the same time. Hell, now that the sun was about to come up, he was starting to get chilled, lying on concrete that had finally cooled.

Carefully and ever so slowly (his neck muscles were going to be sore as hell if he lived through this) he lifted his head to survey the small valley in front of him. No movement, as usual, and nothing to see, although his eyes were drawn to the gulley behind the house. He was increasingly convinced there had to be somebody there, in that narrow notch, if there was anybody else in the area. He hadn't seen any movement down there, but he had a feeling.

Laying his head back down, Dave silently cursed. Should he move before it got fully light out? He'd surprise the hell out of the guy behind him. But other than knowing there was a man on the ridge behind him, he didn't know anything — who he was, if he was armed, if he was alone, if he wasn't alone, where the other guys were. Assuming he was going to die a violent death at a young age didn't make Dave happy about it or eager to make it happen. Just because he'd survived two gunfights didn't mean he was looking forward to a third. He decided to wait. If he had to move, had to do something, he hoped that surprise would be on his side.

Aaron cracked the window enough to let some of the cool dry air into the stuffy rental car. "Aah," he sighed. "This is what I like. More desert, less people, and fewer 'I'm With Stupid' bumper stickers."

It took Ringo a second to figure out what he meant. "You're a real piece of work," he said. "Die-hard Republican, hunh?"

Aaron shook his head. "No, I'm a Libertarian. Democrats don't want anybody to have guns or religion, but the Republicans don't want anybody to have sex or drugs. Everybody is always trying to control everybody else. I just want to be left the fuck alone." He was happy to be armed again, loaded Colt back on his hip. "You want to let me drive so you can load your gun, you let me know."

The last thing in the world Ringo was going to do was let this guy drive a rental car he'd put on his own personal credit card, but he just said, "I don't think we're going to have any problems on the drive up there, thanks." Besides, Abruzzo was ready for war, he had a huge shiny pistol on his hip and two spare magazines on his belt. Even if he couldn't shoot worth a damn, just pulling the thing out would probably scare off anybody giving them trouble. "No answer on his phone?" Aaron had just tried calling Dave again.

"Nope, but I think it's turned on. I got a lot of rings before it went to voicemail."

Mickey yawned, and stretched. The bedroom had thin curtains across its one window, but they did very little to block the light. He was sleeping later and later, adjusting to the time change, and saw that it was full daylight outside, although the light had the quality of early morning.

He climbed off the old narrow bed with a grunt and pulled on the sweatpants Dave had loaned him. That's what they should do today, go clothes shopping. Mickey hardly had anything to wear, only had the clothes he'd been wearing when he'd broken into Dave's house and the few he'd borrowed since them. Plus boots and that pack of underwear from Wal-Mart.

His ribs still gave him twinges of pain if he moved a certain way, but overall they seemed to be healing nicely. His neck still bothered him, though. Not the way it felt — the way it looked. Maybe he could get some cosmetic surgery on it one day, reduce the scarring.

He pulled on a borrowed "Bravo Company" t-shirt — whatever the hell that was — and opened the bedroom door. He shuffled into the bathroom, used the toilet, then flushed and came out. The couch was bare, and a quick glance around the one-room house showed him it was empty. Dave was probably jogging again.

Heading into the kitchen, which was an alcove barely big enough to turn around in, Mickey ground some beans and filled the coffee maker with water. Hip against the counter, he listened to the coffee brew as he slowly woke up. Another quiet morning.

If Arizona actually got enough rain for farming there probably would have been fields of crops all around them, but there was nothing surrounding the little cabin but rolling dry hills dotted with shrubs and trees. No neighbors within shouting distance. He'd heard some dirtbikes the day before — or had it been two days, he couldn't remember — but other than that the only sound were the cheeps and tweets of small birds and weird clickety-clacking sounds that probably came from insects. He kept forgetting to ask Dave what the hell was making those bizarre alien sounds.

Between the morning cereal and the coffee they were running out of milk. He put in a little less than he would have liked, a spoonful of sugar, and then drank it staring out the front window at the Cherokee sitting on what passed for a front lawn in Arizona — dirt and gravel. No movement on the driveway, which headed up to the right, cutting through the ridge and then ending at the pale blue sky. In Arizona, putting your vacation cabin at the bottom of a bowl was no big deal. No way you could have a house set up like this in any area of the country that got any rain, though, the foundation would end up underwater. The house would wash away. And the nearly flat roof would get crushed under the weight of Michigan snow.

The desert was interesting, that was for sure, but he couldn't really say he liked it. Too foreign, too alien. He was an east coast kid. Indiana was about as far west as he'd ever gotten before this adventure.

Adventure. Shit. He shook his head. That's the thing they never told you in the movies or books. Adventures were only great when they were over, or happening to other people. When you were in the middle of them, you were miserable. Adventures were uncomfortable.

Finished with his coffee, Mickey glanced over at the table by the front door and saw the flag still sitting there. *Might as well*, he thought. He could only spend so many hours a day reading, and there wasn't a working TV in the whole tiny house. He set the cup of coffee down on top of the bookcase, slid his feet into the boots without lacing them up, grabbed the properly folded flag, and opened the door. He almost jumped back and shrieked like a little girl at the man on the porch, whose hand was raised to knock.

"Jesus Christ, you scared the shit out of me," Mickey said with a nervous laugh. He'd startled the man as well. After blinking quickly, the guy, who was pretty big and dressed for the desert, smiled. There was a mini-van with Arizona plates parked next to the Cherokee, Mickey hadn't even heard him drive up. The wood floor of the cabin squeaked like hell.

"Yeah, sorry about that." He peered at Mickey. "Is, uh, Dave around?"

"Somewhere," Mickey told him. "I think he's probably out jogging. You a neighbor?"

"Yeah," the man said. He looked at the flag in Mickey's hands. Mickey followed his gaze.

"Let me put this up," Mickey told him. "You want to come inside and wait? I don't think he'll be too long." He unwound the rope from the tie down at the base of the newly repainted flag pole, attached it properly to the flag, and then raised the colors. It flicked and twitched in the fitful morning breeze. The wind was always stronger later in the day, it seemed.

"Yeah, if it's not a problem. Sorry to stop by so early."

"Don't worry about it," Mickey told him. He headed back inside, hearing the man follow him. Mickey turned to say something to him, and as he saw that the man had left the front door of the cabin open, the man struck him full in the face with his elbow, and Mickey went down hard, his head sounding like a coconut as it hit the wood floor.

The sun had been up for quite some time, and Dave was getting increasingly nervous. He was still in the shadow of the ridge, but for how much longer? He knew that once the sun got high enough, hit the right angle, the shadow would recede up the slope practically in the blink of an eye. Whether he wanted to or not, he was going to have to do something. He was going to have to move. But in which direction?

Running forward and down the slope would get him away from whoever was hiding back there, but he'd be exposed the whole way. Even if he didn't trip and fall, he'd be an easy target for anyone with a gun for ten seconds or more. Running the other way, up the slope? Towards someone he could only assume had a gun? That didn't sound any better, although it would probably surprise the fuck out of "Alpha", whoever he was. Dave would be popping up right in front of him, like a jackrabbit.

He still hadn't made up his mind what he should do when he heard the man hidden behind him quietly say, "Copy that, still no movement here." It was the first thing he'd said since he'd arrived hours before. Copy what? What did he copy? And who was he talking to? It was less than a minute later when Dave heard the faint sound of a vehicle. A few seconds after that, a mini-van appeared in the driveway.

It coasted down and came to a stop next to the Cherokee, and a guy in tan pants and a button-down shirt got out. Dave didn't recognize him, but he didn't see any weapon, and the guy sure didn't seem to be trying to be sneaky. Dave had a perfect view as the man walked up to the house and started to knock, then almost jumped back. There was the faint sound of talking. He was too far away to hear exactly what was being said. Mickey walked into view carrying the flag. Up the pole went the flag, and then the guy followed Mickey into the house.

Who the fuck did you call, Mickey? Dave wondered. *What the hell?* And then he saw the sliding door of the mini-van open and a second man climb out. He looked around carefully, but not too long in Dave's direction as that was staring almost directly into the sun. The man then removed a heavy-looking gear bag from the rear of the van and carried it into the house. Dave heard the front door of his house shut. Seventy-five yards was a good distance, but with the sun shining directly on the man it had been easy for Dave to see the man was built like a heavyweight boxer and wearing a pistol on his hip. Probably a Glock.

Dave's head was spinning. He wasn't exactly sure what was going on in the house, who those guys were, if Mickey had called them, if they were somehow connected to Alpha on the ridge behind him, but he knew he didn't have much time, and the situation had just gotten a lot more complicated.

The skinny guy, whoever the fuck he was, went down hard with the elbow strike, and Marcus put a knee on him and pulled out the Glock from under his shirt. He swept left and right, but there was nothing to see. There was a tiny bathroom to the right rear, and he could see most of it from where he was. Empty. The only areas of the cabin he couldn't see were behind the small kitchen counter, and the back room. He suspected it was a bedroom, and the door was open. He kept his Glock 19 trained on the open doorway as Kyle came in behind him. Kyle set the bag down with a thump, pulled out his Glock, and advanced without a word. He cleared the counter, then the back room.

"Clear," he said, coming back to Marcus. "What the fuck are you doing? Why didn't you drop him?'

""Cause it's not him. Couldn't you hear?"

"No."

"He's the only one here, and it's not him. Check his face against the picture."

Kyle squatted down. "No, I can see that. So where the fuck is the target? Hey." He pointed, then stood up and walked over to the wall. There was an AR-15 leaning there, and it wasn't one of theirs. Kyle unloaded it and stuck it on a shelf.

Marcus flipped the mystery man onto his stomach. Knee on the man's back, he dug zip-cuffs out of the bag and secured the man's wrists, then went to work on his ankles. He grabbed a radio out of the bag. "Alpha, Bravo, are you fucking napping out there? I've got a guy in here, not the one we're looking for, who says our guy is probably out jogging. Car's still here, but nobody else is. How'd you geniuses miss him leaving on foot?"

"Bravo is negative on any movement since arrival."

"Alpha is a negative on that as well. Are you sure of what you've got?"

Kyle came in from the back room, held up a small pistol with one hand and handed him something else. Marcus looked at it and shook his head. What the hell? "Roger that, I've got federal ID on this one. Bunch of hardware lying around in here." They were using unscrambled commercial radios, so even if their range was short he didn't want to say 'FBI'.

"This is Bravo One," Smith said quietly into his mike, crouched in the notch behind the cabin. "Federal ID?"

"Affirmative. With a capital F," Marcus informed them.

"Bravo One, everybody hold in place," Smith told them, until he could figure out exactly what the hell was going on. Anderson wasn't there, but an FBI agent was? Was this some kind of setup, a sting or ambush? "Cover six," he murmured into the mike, and glanced over at Bailey. Bailey nodded and spun on his knee, now facing away from the small valley.

"This guy wasn't expecting company," Marcus said over the radio. He also couldn't take a hit. One to the face and he was down for the count. Kyle wrapped duct tape around his mouth and tossed him into the back room, out of the way, while they figured out what the fuck to do. They pulled their rifles out of the bag. Marcus set up on the front door, and Kyle moved to where he could see out the front window.

"He wasn't *acting* like he was expecting company," Smith corrected him distractedly.

Mickey never lost consciousness, but it felt as if he had been disconnected from his body. After the hit—which for some reason didn't hurt—he found himself on the floor, unable to move, eyelids at half mast. Like a passenger riding in the plane that was his body, he felt the man flip him onto his chest, zip-tie his wrists and then ankles, then wrap a piece of duct tape around his mouth. It wasn't until he was heaved into the back bedroom like a sack of potatoes and landed on the wood floor that he came fully to.

Squinting against the blinding pain in his head and ribs—so much for the healing—Mickey fought the panic rising in him. *Reason, logic, reason, logic, think, think!* he told himself.

The back bedroom was dim, but he didn't need bright lights to know that he was lying on his left side, facing away from the door, his wrists were zip-cuffed behind his body, and his ankles were secured as well. The duct tape around his mouth was more of an annoyance than anything else, but it helped him fight the panic—panicking required panting, and panting worked a lot better when you could open your mouth.

Moving his throbbing head, he looked over his shoulder to see the door was still open. He could hear the two guys in the main room, talking quietly and moving around. They'd left him alone, and alive, but he didn't know for how long. Dave might come back at any minute, and then it would be over for both of them.

Shit. His heart fell. *Dave had been right all along.* He gritted his teeth. *Don't think about that. Focus. Focus. You get out of this and there's still a way to bring the media in on it. There had to be.*

The one thing he had going for him was that he was skinny. He hadn't been this skinny since junior high. Trying not to make any noise, Mickey pushed his arms down and hunched his torso as he lay on the dusty floor. You don't realize how dusty hardwood floors get until your face is pressed into one.

With a lot of pain but only a little noise, he was able to get his cuffed wrists under his ass, and then he began the arduous—because he never stretched and wasn't nearly as flexible as he should have been—process of pulling his legs out from between his arms. Doing it without making any noise was the hardest part. Lying half on a hard wood floor and half on his own elbow, his re-abused ribs were complaining loudly. Finally, his hands were clear of his feet, and he pulled them up his body and studied the zip cuffs.

White plastic, about half an inch wide, they were cinched tight enough to hurt. He'd heard from other lab employees talking shop that sharp blows at the right angle would break the plastic ratchet/lock inside zip-cuffs. Plastic hard enough to resist the chewing teeth of protestors tended to be brittle, and zip-cuffs were vulnerable to brute force attacks on their weakest point. However, smashing his wrists hard against his bony hips one or three times to break the cuff ratchet would be sure to bring one of the bad guys into the bedroom, and he had no doubt that, at that point, they'd just kill him.

If only he had a lighter or some other heat source, then he'd be able to burn through them pretty quickly. No lighter, nothing in the pockets of his sweatpants. A quick check showed him that he'd even lost one of his boots — the big guy had knocked him right out of it. Shit, the one boot he was wearing wasn't even laced up, he'd just slipped it on, and —

Son of a bitch! Mickey reached down and, as quickly as he could, began unthreading the lace from the boot his still had on. It was a round, black nylon lace, military style.

Getting it all the way out of the eyelets in the boot seemed to take forever, and the sound of the black lace flopping around seemed huge to him in the small room. Thank God the entire floor of the cabin was creaky, the guys out in the main room sounded like thundering elephants just shifting their weight. He wished they'd talk some more, cover the sound of what he was doing.

After what felt like an hour he finally had the lace all the way out of the boot. He tied one end of it to the top eyelet in the boot, and with great difficulty (because his hands couldn't bend inward enough) made a loop around one of the plastic ties around his wrist.

Mickey looked around, looking for something to tie the other end to, but there wasn't anything. Shit. Gritting his teeth, he reached up and grabbed the edge of the duct tape around his face. Pulling it down hurt like hell, it felt like he was ripping his skin off, especially the skin of his lips.

Finally his mouth was more or less exposed, and he fed the end of the shoelace into his mouth and bit down on it. Hoping this would work, he then slowly began running his hands up and down the length of shoelace, from his face to his boot. It didn't make much noise, but then again it wasn't doing anything either.

In the dim light he squinted, and realized there was too much slack in the shoelace. He pushed his foot down, felt the tension in his teeth, and began sliding his hands back and forth again.

The faster he went, the more noise it would make, but he had to move at a speed fast enough for it to work. This was no different than making a wood and string bow for starting fires. Wrapped once around the plastic cuff, as he moved his hands up and down the tight shoelace would generate heat. If he did it right, the friction might even—should—generate enough heat to melt through the cuff.

The shoelace made a buzzing hum as he worked his hands up and down. Was he wasting his time? Would this even work? He'd managed to work his sweatpants down off his ass and around his knees as he lay on his side and wiggled like an earthworm.

The theory was sound, but maybe the shoelace would break from the heat, or deteriorate under the strain. Could he even move fast enough to generate heat? Yes—there it was! He was starting to feel some heat on his wrist, starting to—ow, that hurt, it was burning his skin, don't stop, keep going, the pain was causing his eyes to tear up—and suddenly the shoelace burned through the plastic cuff with a small popping sound. He pulled his hands apart.

Yeah! Science, bitch! he exulted. Now he just had to do the same thing with the cuff around his ankles. Then what? Maybe try to jump out the back window? He'd seen them take Dave's Kahr.

If only there was—he stopped thinking, and instead just looked underneath the tall, old bed. There, leaning against the wall, in the dark corner, was Dave's shotgun. He could see the buttstock sitting on the floor. Holy shit, they hadn't seen it?

Mickey looked down his body. Even if he could walk, going around the end of the bed he would cross right in front of the open doorway. Without a second thought he began crawling under the bed toward the black stock of the shotgun. Getting the gun was more important than undoing the cuff around his ankles.

Both Kyle and Marcus heard the sound from the back bedroom. They looked toward the open doorway, then at each other. "I'll check it out," Marcus said. He was closest, anyway, and Kyle could cover the front door from where he was, staring out the big front window. It was only about four steps from the front of the cabin to the bedroom door. Rifle at low ready, Marcus looked in to the left, where he'd thrown the unconscious FBI agent, and saw....just his feet. Sticking out from underneath the bed, sweatpants bunched up around his shins, ankles still cuffed. What the hell? He stomped around the foot of the bed, rifle up. What the hell was this guy doing?

Mickey crawled underneath the high narrow bed, the floor creaking under him, expecting any second to hear shouts, to feel his feet being seized and pulled back. Still under the bed, he reached a hand out as he continued to hunch forward, and his fingertips brushed the shotgun. As his head cleared the bedframe the shotgun twisted where it leaned against the wall, and fell. On his head. With a clank.

Mother − ! With a growl, Mickey pulled himself forward on his elbows as he heard footsteps approaching. He grabbed the shotgun and rolled onto his back, his head in the narrow gap between the bed and the wall. What was it

Dave had told him? That it was ready to go, fully loaded, nine rounds of buckshot, he just had to turn off the safety. Which was....where?

One of the men appeared at the end of the bed, looking down at him over his rifle, just as Mickey remembered where the shotgun's safety was located.

Dave was sweating again. The sun wasn't on him, not yet, but he knew the time was fast approaching for him to do something. The two men had been in the house for maybe ten minutes, and for all he knew they were torturing Mickey — or the young FBI Lab employee was already dead. Well, they probably weren't torturing him, Dave was sure he'd be able to hear that, the walls of the house were pretty darn thin.

He didn't want to move, didn't want to get up, but he knew he'd have to, sooner or later. Either that, or he'd get shot where he lay. He had a gun; even though it was only a pistol, it was better than nothing, and he damn sure didn't want to die for lack of shooting back. It was just.....he knew this was it. However it started, he figured it would end up with him dead.

Just like at a match, he pictured what he'd do in his head. Getting up from his prone position on the slope would be a bit awkward. So would drawing his Glock from beneath the windbreaker, especially if he was trying to sit up or stand at the same time. So how best to do it?

After working through several solutions in his head, he guessed that sitting up sharply while shoving his hands down to either side of him, when combined with the slope, would get him to his feet the quickest. Alpha was the biggest threat to him, he was closest, so Dave envisioned himself turning, sweeping the jacket away, drawing, and then advancing up the slope. Have to make sure not to look up too high, or he'd be staring at the rising sun and be blinded.

One or two steps and he'd be at the top of the slope, and then....whatever happened, happened. Front sight, press. Repeat as necessary.

Just thinking about it had his heart hammering in his chest. If this was a match, he'd try to calm his nerves, take a couple of breaths, stand in the shooting box, and wait for the Start signal. Except he was afraid to take more than shallow breaths in case Alpha heard him, and these targets would be shooting back. Shit.

Dave jerked as the unmistakable BOOM! of a shotgun came from inside the house, rattling the windows in their thin frames, with an answering volley of rifle fire.

The man fired, the muzzle of his rifle flashing in the dim bedroom, just as Mickey shoved the long shotgun toward him and pulled the trigger. The buttstock was nowhere near his shoulder as the gun BOOMED. Mickey felt pain; pain in his chest where he was pretty sure he'd been shot, and pain in his face where the shotgun's buttstock had come back and punched him.

The man with the rifle stepped back, but Mickey couldn't tell if he'd hit him. Maybe he'd just been surprised. Mickey pulled the stock against his shoulder as he pulled the trigger again, and again. The shotgun wasn't just loud, it felt like he was setting bombs off inside the room. He knew he'd hit the man, because as he fell down Mickey saw his face had changed shape, and color.

Struggling to sit up behind the bed, Mickey flinched as the man in the front room began firing blindly through the wall at him. The bedroom filled with flying bits of wood and bullets, the hot pieces of metal zipping easily through the entire house to hit the ridge out back. Yelling incoherently, Mickey fired the shotgun through the open doorway, then brought it across the bed and fired it twice through the thin wall between him and the rest of the cabin.

Then he dove back down to the floor as the wall before him began disintegrating under concentrated rifle fire.

The sound of the shotgun inside the house seemed to stop Dave's heart, and his mind went blank. Then he moved.

Up and forward off the slope, hands pushing him to his feet. Spin left, right hand going down and sweeping the windbreaker back, away from the holstered Glock, even as he looked up the slope.

Hand on gun, gun coming out, left hand moving to gun, eyes moving up to see—shit, he was higher up the slope than he thought, he was right fucking THERE, staring over the top of the ridge, right into the face of a prone guy, Alpha, with a rifle who was so surprised it should have been funny. He was so close Dave could have spit on him. Dave pushed his Glock out in a two-handed grip, red fiber optic insert in the front sight glowing nuclear red from the sun hitting it straight on, and fired three times into the man's face from a distance of maybe six feet. He pulled the last shot, rushing it, as he pivoted left. Shit, there wasn't one guy lying there, there were two, and the second guy was rolling onto his right shoulder, bringing his rifle up to bear. He fired at Dave, the sound massive at that distance.

Dave fired at him as he charged up the hill, kept firing, moving targets were harder to hit, then he tripped and fell and rolled down the opposite slope, landing against a body with a thump. His thigh was burning, and Dave knew that he'd been hit, but the pain seemed distant. Gun up, a quick check of the two men told him they were dead. Both men had taken multiple rounds in the face. They'd been so close, holy shit. They'd been right on top of him, all night. Alpha had powder burns on his face.

Somehow alive between two dead men, Dave lay his head back down on the dirt and gasped for air.

Smith nearly jumped at the sound of shotgun and rifle fire almost directly in front of him. Almost instantly the back wall of the cabin began splintering as someone with a rifle began pounding it from inside, the rounds impacting the slope to his right.

Almost at that same moment he caught a glimpse of movement off to his left, and heard a quick volley of shots. He spun his head to see someone disappearing over the ridge, right about where Alpha was positioned. What the fuck? Who was that, where had he come from? It was like he'd appeared out of nowhere, blinked into existence.

"Contact, contact, I see one on foot at Alpha's position," he said into his mike. "Alpha, what's your status, over?" He turned his head and saw Bailey was looking at him with a 'What the fuck?' expression on his face. Smith jabbed a hand at and past Bailey, telling him simply, "Alpha."

Bailey nodded, and took off around the outside of the ridge, heading toward Alpha's position.

Kyle fired left, right, high, low, peppering the wall and cabinets and kitchen appliances between his position and the back bedroom. He wasn't sure where the FBI agent was inside the room, how he'd gotten loose, or how the fuck he'd snagged a shotgun, but he could sure as hell ruin his whole day.

He paused his trigger finger, ears ringing. "Charlie One is down," he said into his mike. He fired the last few rounds from his magazine through the wall, then did a quick reload. He could see Marcus' body through the open doorway. What the fuck had happened in there? "Subject is in the back bedroom. I've got him pinned down, don't know if he's still alive." After those first few shotgun blasts, one of which had definitely come through the wall in his direction, he hadn't heard anything.

"Hold in place," Smith told him over the radio.

"Roger that," Kyle said. The fresh magazine in his rifle was his last, but he had the Glock 19 and two fifteen-round magazines. More than enough to complete the mission. He glanced over his shoulder out the front window, making sure there were no surprises heading in his direction,, then moved closer to the kitchen, tucking himself in the corner. It was a better spot, one where he could cover the doorway without immediately being a target, and not likely to be hit if the FBI agent started shooting through the wall again.

Rifle up, covering the doorway, Kyle waited. And realized that he could smell smoke.

Dave sat up between the two dead men, holstering his pistol, and glanced at his leg. Blood soaking his pantleg over his thigh, but he didn't see any chunks missing. He didn't even see an entry wound, .223s were so tiny. Pain just a dull throb.

He quickly glanced left and right, then took hold of one of the dead men's ARs. That was a shotgun versus rifle fight he was hearing in the house, no way he'd join that gunfight with only a pistol. At least that meant Mickey was still alive—hopefully. He tugged on the rifle and nearly fell on top of the man when the rifle tugged back. What the hell? Then he saw that it was wrapped around the man's body on a sling. Were these guys wearing body armor? Dave was trying to figure out how to free the rifle from the dead man when the bullet came so close to his head he felt something—air, heat, the soundwave of the supersonic projectile—as it whipped past his ear.

Dave dove sideways to the ground even before he consciously realized what had happened, before his brain catalogued the sound he'd heard as "gunshot". Now continuous rifle fire, bullets flying all around him. Dave twisted onto his back, trying to get as flat as possible. He yanked massively at the rifle again even as he looked around to find out where the shooting was coming from.

The man's body flopped from his efforts, but the rifle remained attached, and past the dead man's head, around the outside corner of the ridge, Dave saw a man advancing toward him, shooting as he came. The bullets were hitting all around Dave, throwing up dirt and sand, and he could feel them thudding into the dead body next to him. Jesus, where did *he* come from? How many of these guys were there? The man was visible from the waist up, maybe twenty-five yards away, pinning down Dave as he advanced with suppressive fire, until he could get a better angle on him.

With an angry growl, Dave drew his Glock and rolled onto his left side, pushing his pistol out in a two-handed hold above the head of the dead body next to him. A bullet hit right in front of him, showering him with dirt, as he settled his sights on the man starting to run toward him. Dave fired, kept firing as the man fired, pulled the trigger until the slide locked back on the Glock.

The man was down, Dave could see the top half of his body in the dirt, not moving. Dave had panicked, barely seeing the sights, just shooting in the general direction of the threat. He couldn't even remember where he'd been aiming, had no idea how many times he might have actually hit the guy.

Taking a couple of ragged breaths, Dave waited to see if any new pain hit him, if he'd been hit again. His right arm felt weird, and he looked down. He couldn't see anything on the windbreaker—no, shit, there was a hole in the sleeve. He rolled over on his back between the first two men he'd killed and tentatively touched his upper arm—and bit back a scream. Fuck, yes, he'd been hit. He could still move his arm, even flex his muscle a little bit, so the bone hadn't been hit, but it hurt so bad.... Gritting his teeth, he pulled a fresh magazine from his belt and reloaded his Glock. Right hand was still working, but dexterity had taken a hit. At least he wasn't shaking. Yet.

He didn't want to get up, but he couldn't stay there. With a deep breath, he lunged forward, to his feet, and then slowly advanced toward the man he'd just downed, gun up and now shaking just a little bit. His leg was starting to burn and he couldn't walk normally, but he could shuffle step around the outside of the ridge. It didn't help his stride any that he was on a slope partially made of sand.

A quick glance to his left showed him the top of the ridge, and beyond that, the roof of the house. No more gunfire from inside the house, he didn't know if that was good or bad. But he saw smoke. That was definitely not good. Ignoring the house was tough, but he pushed forward toward the man face down on the ground in front of him, sights of the Glock bobbing over his inert form, right arm both burning and tingling.

Mickey dragged himself to a seated position behind the bed. He knew he was more exposed to incoming fire, sitting up, but he was starting to get weak. There was a lot of warm wetness on his chest and back. He'd been hit in the high chest, but the bullet had missed his lungs, he didn't seem to have any problem breathing. That was a good thing, right?

Shotgun laid across the top of the mattress, Mickey pulled the butt into his shoulder and kept it trained on the open doorway. How many rounds did he have left? At least a few, he knew that. His left hand was pressed against his chest. The pressure seemed to make the pain less. Mickey didn't want to pass out from blood loss, and then get killed when he was unconscious. There was still at least one guy out there, he knew that. What was he waiting for? And what was burning? He realized he'd been smelling it for a while, but now he could see the smoke up near the ceiling.

Smith turned his attention back to the valley as Bailey moved off behind him. He inched forward far enough to see the entire rear of the cabin as the shooting inside stopped. The bedroom window had been shattered by at least one bullet, but he couldn't see any movement. "Charlie One is down," Kyle said over the radio. "Subject is in the back bedroom. I've got him pinned down, don't know if he's still alive."

"Hold in place," Smith told him. How the fuck had the FBI agent gotten hold of a gun? Didn't matter now.

"Roger that."

Smith was going to sit there, cover the rear of the cabin, and the window, when there was a ferocious volley of fire off to his left. Bailey, presumably, and whoever Smith had seen go over the ridge. It was over in seconds. "Bravo Two, what's your status?" Smith called. No response. "Bravo Two, status?" Still nothing. "Shit."

After hesitating for maybe fifteen seconds, Smith moved into the bowl, angling left, heading toward Alpha's last location. He'd moved about twenty steps when he realized that Bailey wouldn't have had enough time to work all the way around the ridge to Alpha's location before he'd heard the shooting. Shit. He pivoted left, rifle up, and slowly began climbing the ridge.

Dave reached the body and crouched down with a lot of difficulty. His leg was stiffening up. The man was face down, and had no visible wounds. Muzzle of his Glock against the back of the man's head, he checked him for a pulse. Nothing. And his rifle was trapped beneath him, Dave would have to flip him over before he could even start to figure out how to detach the sling, and he didn't think his aching arm was up for that. Shit. He would feel better with a rifle in his hands, but was getting nervous standing still. How many other guys were out there, wandering around the property? Was this the last one? Two gunfights so far, two fucking bulletholes in his body. And what the hell was going on in the house? Shit.

Dave stood up, his injured leg starting to shake, and caught movement out of the corner of his eye. He spun left, Glock coming up, and saw a man coming up the slope behind him.

Both eyes open, the bright red dot of the Aimpoint superimposing itself over everything he saw, Smith inched up the slope. As he crested the ridge, he swung right. No movement, but he could see a pile of bodies in the distance—movement off to his left, he whipped around, there was someone standing up, turning toward him. Smith was pulling the trigger as the dot moved onto the man's face, and in that briefest fraction of a second he recognized the target, Anderson. Then the rifle bucked in his hand, and nothing.

Mickey was finding it hard to breathe. The smoke was a foot thick near the ceiling, but he didn't think that was it. His body was cold, and no matter what he couldn't seem to take in enough air. It was getting darker in the room, and he was getting weaker. The shotgun was still pointed at the open doorway, and.....and what? What had he been thinking of? His brain seemed to be working in slow motion. He wasn't sleepy, not really, but his mind wasn't working right. He couldn't focus. Was that because of the smoke?

He reached down with his left hand to prop himself higher and put his hand in a puddle. Where had that come from? He lifted his hand and his palm looked dark in the dim bedroom. He knew that wasn't good, but he couldn't quite remember why. He'd heard a lot of shooting from outside. Was that Dave? He hoped it was Dave. But who was he shooting?

The long black barrel of the shotgun began wiggling and moving, reflecting odd colors. Confused, Mickey looked up, and saw pretty orange flames licking the ceiling. And yet the room seemed to be getting darker. Interesting.

Dave came to, found he was staring up at the sky. His face was searing agony, pain throbbing like a bass drum in his skull. How long had he been out? He had no idea, didn't even know if it was the same day. Lying there seemed like such a good idea, but he knew he had to move, had to get up. Preparing to roll onto his side, he clenched his teeth, and his head exploded in white stars. Someone had stabbed a burning knife into the side of his head. He screamed weakly. He'd been shot in the face, there was something wrong with his jaw.

Panting harshly, he forced himself over onto his left side, letting his forehead rest on the cool dirt. He could feel sticky blood on his neck, and in his new position he felt it running up his head, dripping off his ear. If blood was running, it meant his heart was still beating. Good news. Sort of.

"Not dead yet," he whispered, lips barely moving.

Right arm wasn't working quite right. He pushed himself into a sitting position with his left hand. Where was he? What was going on? Body facedown in the dirt near him, that was the guy whose vitals he'd been checking when the other asshole showed up with a rifle. Fuck—*he'd* been fast, fast as Dave.

Dave blinked and looked down at his hands. No gun. Where was his Glock? He looked around, saw it in the dirt nearby. Half buried. Picked it up with his left hand, shook it to get the sand out of the cracks. Right arm wasn't working well anymore, going to have to hold the gun left-handed. Shooting weak-handed, they called it in competition. *Strong hand and weak-hand shooting, should have practiced that more*, he thought absently. What did the FBI call it? Something different. Oh, yeah, 'primary and support hand' shooting, because 'FBI agents don't have weak hands.' Who'd told him that, Al Safie? Well, with his right arm hurting like hell and tingling as if it was asleep, it wouldn't be supporting shit. Although he doubted his application with the FBI was going anywhere. He laughed, then sobbed.

Struggling to his feet, Glock held out in front of him, Dave limped up the ridge and looked over. There he was, halfway down the slope, on his back.

Breath ragged, Dave stumbled down a few steps and then fell to his knees beside the man. His closest eye was open, staring at the sky. Dave's bullet had hit him in his other eye, and there was a big exit wound in the back of his skull. Gray hair…he was old. That was weird. What was an old guy doing out here? Leaning over the body, Dave saw blood begin dripping from the end of his nose. How much was he bleeding? He felt a little light-headed, how many times had he been shot? He couldn't remember.

Dave sat back against the slope, exhausted. After a while he sighed, looked at the body, looked past it, raised his eyes all the way to the house. Oh yeah, it was on fire, he'd forgotten. The smoke was everywhere, coming out of every window and from under the eaves, and flames two feet tall were shooting out of the center of the roof.

Kyle stayed in place for as long as he could, until the flames were rolling halfway across the ceiling, but then it just became too hot. He had to retreat to the alcove by the front door. Still no movement, no sound from the back bedroom, which was filled with smoke. Hell, the whole place was filled with smoke. He was coughing, finding it hard to breathe, to see.

Finally, Kyle opened the front door and backed out of the cabin, keeping the back doorway covered with his rifle. There was no way the guy back there could still be conscious, there was too much smoke, and even on the concrete porch the heat was so bad it felt like his face was cracking. The flames had broken through the roof and were sending tongues and black smoke upward. His eyes followed the twisting pillar up into the sky. Shit, the neighbors were sure to see that. Fire department was probably already on the way. House roaring and crackling like a bonfire on the beach.

"This is Charlie Two, sitrep, over," he said into his mike. He coughed, and had to back away from the house, past the flag pole. He got no response. "Alpha, Bravo teams? Anybody out there?" He looked away from the house, left and right, but there was nobody close to him, nothing moving. Then a faint crunch, different from the rush and pop of the cabin flames, made him turn around. A police cruiser was pulling to an abrupt stop at the top of the driveway.

Dave heard more shooting, looked up, and past the edge of the house saw a big man with a rifle firing upward, at a cop car whose nose was just visible at the top of the driveway. When did the cops show up?

Tiredly, Dave looked back down at the dead man before him. His rifle was lying across his waist, connected to his body by a sling. Single point sling. Well hell, he knew how to take those off.....buckle, buckle, who's got the buckle? Shit, there it was. Set his Glock on the dead man's chest. He reached forward and with a simple squeeze of the black plastic buckle the rifle popped free. Sat on the slope.

Picking the rifle up with his left hand, Dave put his feet in front of him and rested his left arm on his knee.

Why am I so tired? he thought. *It's still early in the morning.*

Buttstock back against his right shoulder, he reached his right hand up to the pistol grip. This was easier than holding the Glock in a two-handed hold, the rifle was wedged between his left hand and right shoulder. All he had to do with his right hand was work the trigger. It was very comfortable, sitting in the sand, sun on his neck.

The big man was still down there, standing next to the Cherokee, once more looking back at the front of the house after firing half a dozen shots at the cop car. What was he, seventy-five, eighty yards away? And just standing there, looking around a little bit. *I can't sing, and I can't dance, but I can shoot......*

Dave lowered his head and peered through the familiar Aimpoint. The coated lenses in the tube tinted the world slightly, but that helped the glowing red dot stand out. No magnification, but he didn't need it. Wow, the dude was big, and his tactical vest made him look even bulkier. Were these guys wearing armor? Probably.

Dave settled the dot on the top of the man's ear, took a breath, held it, began squeezing the trigger. And squeezing. *Jesus, was this a shitty trigger, like dragging an anchor through gravel. Had he forgotten to take the safety off? The trigger on his competition rifle* — the strange rifle barked in his hand, jumped a little, and when it settled back down he saw through the Aimpoint the big man was down on his knees and one hand, the other holding his neck, scrambling behind the Cherokee.

Shit, he'd missed. Dave heard return fire, bullets hitting the dirt around him, but he was too tired to be scared, or even flinch. He fired over and under and around the Cherokee, blowing out windows and tires, making the man keep his head down. This sort of reminded him of something....what? Oh, yeah, the last gunfight, when he'd been the one ducking and diving around his Mustang. Having a flashback of a gunfight in the middle of a gunfight....who had told him they'd done that? John, his boss John. At the time, Dave thought it had sounded weird. Crazy.

More return fire, and a bullet thudded into the ground between his feet. Dave hammered the hood of the Cherokee, flying brass rifle cases glinting in the early morning sun, and the big man dove to the side, then crabwalked backward behind the mini-van. Dave blew out the van's headlight, barely missing the man. Was he trying to escape?

Not too far behind the mini-van the driveway angled upward and out of sight past the cop car. There was something about the driveway, he couldn't quite remember....Dave saw movement and blew out two of the mini-van's windows, but didn't think he hit anything. The guy was moving around to the rear of the van, closer to the slope of the driveway. Dave's eyes followed the lines of the van, and past it and not too far behind there was the bottom of the driveway slope and a big white rock. Almost a mini boulder, at the base of the ridge. Shit, there it was! He'd put the biggest one right there, to surprise unwanted visitors. Ten, fifteen pounds of it? Something like that.

The man popped out from behind the rear of the van and fired several times. Something tugged at his pantleg, and a bullet thudded into the hill behind him. Taking a breath, Dave steadied himself and fired at the white blob. Nothing. He fired again—

He saw the explosion before he heard or felt it. Saw the pressure wave speeding across the valley toward him, a distortion in the air, what windows were left in both vehicles blowing out, the van actually skidding several feet sideways into the Cherokee and rocking. Then the blast hit him and he found himself back against the slope, rifle still in his hands, breath knocked from his chest, head ringing. He was staring up at the sky, at grainy debris flying through the air, blinking in surprise. His legs hurt where they'd been peppered with rocks or something. Boom Goes the Dynamite.

Struggling back to a seated position, Dave let his tingling hand fall away from the trigger. The air was fuzzy with dust and smoke. He hoped that was the last guy, because he was just about out of fight. Could he just sit there on the slope a while, and rest? He was feeling a little lightheaded. It seemed really cloudy out. His eyes drifted around, and he saw that almost the entire roof of the house was in flames. The old dry wood of the house was perfect fuel for the fire. Thick smoke was spiraling into the air, puffing out every window and crack.

There was a very faint breeze, blowing in from the road. He saw the flag at the top of the pole, a few feet above the roof, teasing the flames, dodging here and there, waving through them it without being touched, until, finally, it caught.

Even on fire the flag fought, giving off black and acrid smoke, but the flames finally overwhelmed it. Dave watched the flag consumed by the flames; saw the fresh white paint on the flagpole start to change color from the heat.

He watched the house burn for a while, then heaved himself to his feet. That was a long way over there. Why did it have to be so far? Dave trudged down the short slope, focusing on putting one foot in front of the other as he walked across the hard-packed dirt and sand of the valley floor. Had to stop at the bottom of the slope, then again a little way later. His one pantleg was soaked in blood below the knee.

Halfway there he felt the heat of the fire on his skin. Closer and he saw the Turnerite had blown a crater three feet wide at the bottom of the driveway, and the big man looked like a pile of raw hamburger behind the mini-van's flat rear tire.

The flagpole was six feet from the front of the house, and before he ever reached it the heat became so intense it was like pushing against a physical barrier. Flames were roaring above his head, pushed by the wind to lick the flagpole. The white paint bubbled, turned black, caught fire. The front of the house was being engulfed by the flames now. He had to look down, the heat was so intense it was drying out his eyes.

Reaching the edge of the square concrete base, he dropped to his knees next to his father's initials. The rifle fell from his hands, and he turned them to stare at his fingertips through the air shimmering with heat. So much trouble. So much death for things he could hardly see, even squinting. It hardly seemed fair.

He grabbed the flagpole with both hands, and screamed.

"Man, this really is the middle of nowhere," Ringo said, holding onto the steering wheel as the rental car bounced over the uneven gravel road

"Yeah, isn't it great?" Aaron replied with a wide smile. "About a mile up, we're going to make a turn."

Ringo looked around at the brown landscape dotted with green, then did a doubletake. "Which direction?"

"What?"

"Which way are we going to turn?"

"Left, why?"

"Shit." Ringo floored the car even as he pointed out the window at the towering column of black smoke in the distance.

"Goddammit! Goddammit!" Aaron swore. He held on as the cop pushed the car hard, rocks clattering hard against the undercarriage. "Bet you wish your fucking gun was loaded now," he said through gritted teeth. Ringo didn't reply, but that was exactly what he was thinking.

Aaron then let go with one hand to point. "There, there's his driveway, turn there."

Ringo slammed on the brakes and took the corner in a bouncing power slide. As he straightened it out, they both looked up the driveway. There was something at the end of it, a car....Ringo slammed on the brakes halfway down the curving drive as the car revealed itself to be a Sheriff's cruiser, driver's door open, body on the ground next to it. Past the vehicle, out of sight, something was burning furiously, something big, the column of brown and black smoke at least ten feet across and hundreds of feet tall. "Fuck!" The trailing cloud of dust enveloped and then passed their rental car, and then Abruzzo was out of the car, crouching down, gun up.

"Now might be a good fucking time to get your gun out and load it."

"Yeah yeah yeah," Ringo said, bailing out of the car and then opening the rear door. He'd gone into hairy situations before, had to pull his gun on a lot of people, almost shot several of them, but he'd never had to *load* his damn gun while worrying if he was going to get shot.

Ringo had just gotten his gun loaded, a round chambered, when he jerked back as if shot. His head snapped around and he stared up the driveway. "What the hell was that?" It had been hideous, perhaps the tortured scream of a dying animal.

Aaron straightened up like a shot. "Dave," he said, and took off at a run.

Dave? Whatever that had been, it hadn't even sounded human. Ringo took off after Abruzzo, running up the driveway with his gun up. Abruzzo flew past the cop car but Ringo skidded to a stop before the body. The deputy in the brown uniform was on his back behind the open driver's door. There was blood on his hands, and a lot of it had soaked into the ground under him. Ringo knelt down, and saw the man's eyes were closed, but he was breathing raggedly. "Hang on buddy, help's coming," Ringo told him, reaching for the radio.

Aaron flew down the slope past the police cruiser. The house was engulfed in flames, the heat huge. If anybody had been inside, they were dead and cooked. Dammit, dammit. There was a mini-van parked in front of the house, and past it was Dave's Cherokee. Shit, had he been inside?

Aaron slowed his pace, held a hand up to protect his face from the heat, and jogged toward the vehicles. What the hell had happened? The mini-van looked like it had been in a demolition derby, and lost. Then he saw the first body, a big guy in a tac vest, blood everywhere. He moved around the vehicles and there was another body, so close to the house that the air around it was shimmering with heat. Peering past his raised arm, Aaron suddenly realized who it was.

"Dave!" he yelled. Moving forward against the heat was insane, but he did it, bending down. The flames were above and behind him, the house starting to collapse, when he reached Dave's feet. Moving his blocking arm down to grab Dave's ankle with two hands allowed the full intensity of the fire to batter his face, and Aaron's eyes teared up and clamped shut involuntarily. Blindly he dragged Dave back, back, until the heat was no longer malevolent, then back farther, until he tripped on something and fell down. Aaron opened his eyes to see he'd dragged his friend up against the facing slope, into a hole, fifty feet from the front of the inferno that had been a house, and still he could feel the heat.

"Fuck, dude!" he said, dropping to one knee. Dave's clothes were smoking, and half his hair had frizzled away from the heat. There was blood all over him, and he looked dead. Aaron put his fingers on Dave's neck to check for a pulse, and it was like touching a turkey in the oven. "Dave! Dave!" he yelled in his face.

CHAPTER TWENTY-NINE

Sheriff John Osterman woke up as he always did, instantly. It never took him more than a few seconds to become completely alert. He blinked his bleary eyes and through his glasses beheld the waiting room. It looked like a bomb had gone off, there were bodies everywhere, tipped this way and that on the chairs and curled up on the floor.

He righted himself and felt the sharp pain of a crick in his neck. He was too damn old to be sleeping in chairs, but he'd be damned if he was going to beg for a spare bed when there were sick and injured people who might need them. Never ask anybody to lift a hundred pounds if you aren't willing to lift a hundred and twenty-five first. His father had taught him that, and he'd lived by it his entire life.

In the dim light he checked his watch, but he didn't need to; he always woke within five minutes of 6 a.m. whether he had an alarm set or not. The glowing hands showed him it was 5:53. Okay, maybe within ten minutes of six a.m. There were two windows in the waiting room, and he could see the sun was thinking about coming up, but hadn't quite committed.

Standing up, gun belt creaking, he made his way out into the white corridor which seemed as bright as a runway. Ginny found him coming out of the bathroom two minutes later, her nurse's uniform nearly as bright as the corridor lights.

"Don't you know better'n to get in out of the rain, Sheriff?" she asked him. "We've got beds all over this hospital."

"One night sleeping in a chair won't kill me," he told her. Ginny was now the hospital's head nurse, and had more gray on her head than he did. "How long you known me, Ginny? Twenty years? You should know by now I'm too bullheaded to do things the smart way."

"Closer to thirty, John. Met you back before you were Sheriff. Do you want some coffee? I've got some brewing at the nurse's station."

Osterman checked his watch. "I'll let you know in two minutes," he told her. He looked around the floor, which was quiet and empty in both directions. "Anything since last night?"

"Doc Brennan's been doing the rounds tonight. Toby's still in intensive care. Too early to tell with him, but they tell me he's a fighter. The Anderson boy's in serious condition, and off the record the doc says he thinks he'll pull through fine, but he'll never tell you that. Nothing's changed since yesterday. The only thing he's really worried about are the burns, because of the chance of infection. Burns are just nasty things."

"Don't I know it." They heard the elevator ping, and looked toward it. "Ah, see?" he said to her. Sam Wheaton stepped off holding two tall cups of coffee and ambled toward them in his lazy cowboy walk. Between the walk and the bushy moustache liberally shot through with gray he looked like a cowboy in the wrong uniform, even though Wheaton hated horses.

"Mornin'," Wheaton said to Ginny, touching the brim of his hat with one of the cups before handing it to the Sheriff. Osterman took a long pull at the strong black coffee and sighed. Ginny headed back to the nurse's station.

"The older I get, the more I enjoy the one vice I have," Osterman observed. He looked at his second-in-command. "How's your girlie drink?" Wheaton dared to put both cream and sugar in his coffee, which as far as the Sheriff was concerned showed questionable moral character.

Sam Wheaton smiled behind his moustache and took a sip of his own coffee through the slotted lid. The two men stood in the middle of the corridor silently, just sipping their coffees and enjoying the silence. They'd known each other far too long to have to fill the air with conversation.

"Any change?" Wheaton asked.

The Sheriff shook his head. "Toby's still in ICU, and the kid's the same." He looked behind him toward the end of the hallway, at the door of Anderson's room. One of his deputies sat in a chair outside the door, awake but looking terminally bored. Osterman was glad to see he wasn't reading or texting on his phone. "Ginny said she had some coffee brewing, you want to get that man a cup?" he asked Sam.

"Yeah. Where's everybody else?"

"Passed out in the waiting room. Looks like a plague went through and dropped 'em where they stood." The Sheriff stood and sipped his coffee as his Captain brought a cup to the man pulling guard duty. They exchanged a few sentences, then Sam ambled back to his side. While his four Division Commanders technically outranked Wheaton, they all knew the Captain was the number two man in the department, flow charts be damned.

Osterman glanced back at the kid's closed hospital room door. "How long has he been in here now? A day?"

"Almost twenty-four hours. Brought him in yesterday morning by ten, I think. Why?"

The Sheriff pursed his lips. "I'm thinking if the feds do send somebody to snag him, there's a good chance they're going to come today. And if I was them, I'd come early, before everybody's awake and paying attention.

Before the news crews show up for the day. Better chance of getting in and out quickly with him, with no fuss."

"Me, I'm still trying to wrap my head around the why of it all."

"Don't you know better at your age than to ask why?" He glanced back at the hospital room again. "I want some more men up here. Some solid guys."

"All you've got is solid guys. I do the hiring, remember? How many do you want?"

"How many can you get?" he asked his Captain with a raised eyebrow, almost in challenge. He caught a glimpse of a smile under the hedgerow of a moustache. Wheaton took two long strides toward the elevators when the Sheriff called out to him. "And Sam? Bring me my shotgun."

The plague victims in the waiting room were looking more like the walking wounded half an hour later as the sun peeked in through the windows and started waking them up. "Can I get a refill?" the Sheriff asked Ginny, hoisting his empty cup.

"Sure." She filled it up for him then replaced the lid, then walked out from behind the counter. She watched him look back and forth down the hall. "What is it, John?"

He'd had the boy placed at the end of the hallway. The nurse's station was in the middle of the floor. The stairwell was nearly at the nurse's station, and the elevators were just beyond. "How many rooms are there from here to the end of the hall?" he asked her, nodding his head in that direction.

"Patient rooms? Um, eight, plus a storage room and a visitor/family bathroom."

"How many of them are occupied? Apart from the boy's room at the end."

"Just two. Why?"

He inclined his head toward her, and she followed him down the corridor most of the way to the boy's room and the bored deputy in the chair. The Sheriff stopped, and then looked back down the direction they'd walked. The hospital corridor was a study in whites—white floor, white ceiling, white walls, with only a few lines of color and small prints on the walls to break up the monotone.

"You know what this reminds me of?" he asked her, gesturing with his coffee down the white hall.

She shook her head. "No."

"The opening scene of Star Wars," he told her. "The rebel ship. After it's captured by the big...whaddayacallit. Star Destroyer. They're hunkering down in a corridor just like this, all aiming their guns in one direction. They know the stormtroopers are coming, and they know they're probably going to die, that all they're doing is making a futile gesture. The Empire's going to win, the Empire always wins, but they're doing it anyway."

She tilted her head and squinted. "Yeah, I guess so."

"You remember what the corridor of that ship looked like after the stormtroopers showed up?" Ginny looked at him, and he waved a finger around. "Those two patients on this end? I think you should move them. I think you should move them *now*."

The head nurse looked at him for a second, looked him straight in the eye as they were almost the same height, then nodded. "I'll call my girls up here. Shouldn't take us more than ten, fifteen minutes."

By a little after seven a.m. the other two patients at that end of the floor had been moved, and the groggiest waiting room occupant had been enlivened with coffee or donuts or both. For a hospital floor with only one patient there were a lot of people standing around.

Coffee in hand, wearing the same suit he'd had on for now the third day in a row, Ringo approached the Sheriff.

"How much of your work are you ignoring to be here?" he asked.

Osterman shrugged. "Got nothing more important to do than this." He glanced at his watch. "The doc is supposed to do his morning rounds at seven thirty. Then we'll see if he thinks it's okay to wake up Mr. Anderson." He glanced at the Detroit detective. "Anything else pop into your head last night about this live grenade you tossed into my lap?"

A Detroit mobster buying off an FBI agent or two to get at the person he thought killed his only son was completely believable. Half a dozen armed men in full raid gear—with no IDs—assaulting that person's house, however, was not the work of the mob, Detroit or anywhere else. Something else was going on. Something big, and the Sheriff agreed. Ringo had been at the scene for all of forty-five minutes when the Sheriff had shown up, exuding quiet confidence and barking orders to get his people moving in the right directions.

Twenty minutes after the Sheriff arrived, Ringo had been uncuffed and was standing next to him. They watched the ambulance scream off, loaded with Anderson and the severely wounded deputy. "Follow me," Osterman had said. He walked back to his Suburban with Ringo in tow, and they'd sat in the front seat. Very calmly he asked, "Would you care to explain to me that butcher's bill I've got sitting out there?" Osterman gestured out the windshield. He still had men combing the area, looking for more bodies. They were scattered around the property like confetti.

Osterman looked exactly like he did on TV, but by then Ringo had observed that he wasn't all show, the man actually knew what he was doing, and cared about his people. Add that to what Ringo knew of his politics, and guts....."Let me play you a recording," Ringo told him. He didn't regret the decision.

Standing in the hospital corridor, Ringo just looked at him, took a sip of his coffee, and shook his head. "You know everything I do." Anderson's partner Abruzzo was sleepily eating a donut in the waiting room, but otherwise all the bodies were deputies. A lot of deputies. He looked around and counted them. Eight, not including the one posted by Anderson's door, or the Sheriff, most armed with shotguns or AR-15s.

They all looked rather intense for this early in the morning, but then John Osterman seemed to attract the intense types, whether they loved him or hated him. Man his age, his reputation, he could wear whatever he wanted to work each day, suit and tie or a polo and khakis, but he insisted on wearing a full uniform including gun belt, radio, and Kevlar vest. That said something about him, as did the shotgun he was carrying with him, an old wood-stocked Remington semi-auto. With a buttstock shell carrier stuffed with Hornady buckshot. Ringo wouldn't have been surprised if there were notches carved into the stock somewhere. He wasn't called "Shotgun John" for nothing.

"Anything back yet on the prints?" Ringo asked the Sheriff.

Osterman looked at him, and a vertical line appeared between his eyebrows. "I've got seven dead and two wounded, including one of my deputies. Two of the dead are burned so bad the only way we're going to ID them is through dental records. That's the biggest crime scene I've seen in years, people burned, blown up, and shot. Our entire forensics unit is working in shifts at the scene, tracking footprints and photographing shell casings and trying to figure out just what the hell happened out there. We had to stop for six hours and call in the bomb squad because of all the unexploded bombs we found laying around like Easter eggs. So no. I don't even know if the prints have been submitted yet."

"Serial numbers on the weapons?" Ringo asked. And got a flat stare in response.

Just then Osterman's radio crackled. "Sheriff, I've got some guys heading up to you. This might be who you're expecting."

The Sheriff grabbed his mike handset attached to his epaulet. "'Guys'?"

"One guy in a suit, with a briefcase, and four trigger pullers, guys fully tricked out in tactical gear. Slung M4s. Feds. They see me. I'm coming up with them."

The Sheriff's men instinctively lined both sides of the corridor, standing near doorways. Wheaton stood next to him in the center of the corridor, not far from the nurse's station where Ginny and one of her young nurses waited nervously. Ringo stood at the entrance to the waiting room, Aaron coming to stand at his elbow. After a second, Ringo walked over to the Sheriff, and stood behind him. He'd started the party, after all, by calling the Sheriff's department, asking them to check on Anderson.

The elevator dinged, and off stepped a neat bureaucratic type in a gray suit accompanied by four large men in full kit—tan military-style body armor with rifle magazine pouches across their chests, multi-pocketed pants, and rifles slung diagonally across their chests. The Sheriff observed the DHS patches on their tactical vests.

"Ah, I recognize you from Fox News!" said the bureaucrat. "What did *60 Minutes* call you? 'America's Sheriff'? Agent Colman, Department of Homeland Security," he announced himself, and dug out credentials from an inside pocket of his suitcoat. If he was surprised to see so many deputies in the hospital he didn't show it, and radiated cheerfulness, but the tactical team members sure seemed unprepared to be outnumbered. They were looking all around, but Agent Colman had eyes only for the Sheriff. He glanced down at the shotgun in the Sheriff's hands.

"Shotgun John, if I remember correctly. Unless you don't like the nickname?" He glanced at the older deputy standing next to John who looked like a retired cowboy, and then at the pale tired man in a wrinkled suit right behind them. Detective? He looked like a cop. The Sheriff in person looked pretty much like he did on TV. Colman was surprised to see that his hair wasn't dyed, it was just surprisingly dark for a man his age—but this close, he could see the gray hairs running through it, like pieces of steel wire.

The Sheriff took the proffered credentials and glanced at them. They looked authentic, and probably were, for whatever that mattered. "I earned it," he replied noncommittally. He handed Colman his credentials. "Can I help you?"

"Yes! We're here for David Anderson. To take him into custody. I have a federal warrant, here, signed last night by the AUSA in—" As he was speaking, Colman set his briefcase on the counter at the nurse's station and popped the locks.

"You can't have him," the Sheriff told him quietly.

"Yes, well, I'm sure you have a lot of investigating to still do. I hear the scene was a bit of a mess, but Mr. Anderson was involved in something a little bit more important, and—"

"I don't care."

The Sheriff's immediate and blunt reply put Colman off his rhythm. "I'm sorry?"

"You can't have him."

"Sheriff Osterman, I understand there is a whole local law enforcement versus federal animosity in many areas of this country, but I assure you we are not doing this because of any perceived lack of effectiveness on your part. There are just other things in play, which is why—"

"You're doing an awful lot of talking, but not much listening," the Sheriff said to him. "I am not going to release him into your custody. You can't have him."

Colman stopped and looked down at the Sheriff—amazing how much smaller people were in person than they seemed on TV—then withdrew some papers from his briefcase. "Um, I'm sorry Sheriff, I don't want to upset you, but it's really not up to you. The Assistant U.S. Attorney—"

"He's not here. And if he was, I'd be telling him the same thing I'm telling you. We are not giving him to you."

Colman stopped. Okay, this wasn't just pigheadedness on the part of local law enforcement, which he'd experienced more than a few times. This was something else. *Did they know something? How could they?* He normally knew more than everybody else in the room, and didn't like this feeling one bit. He glanced from the detective to the old cowboy deputy and back to the sheriff.

"Ah, I confess, I'm at a little bit of a loss at your lack of cooperation, Sheriff. But," and he waved a hand over his shoulder, "I did bring some gentlemen to help move Mr. Anderson to our holding facility. These men are agents with the Department of Homeland Security, and if you get in their way you will be interfering with federal officers. If your men interfere with these agents trying to do what we came here to do they will be arrested. I didn't want this to be confrontational, but...."

The Sheriff eyed the bulky men with their armor and slung carbines. He imagined that they would have already pushed past him if they weren't outnumbered better than two-to-one. "If your men try to take Anderson I will have them arrested," he said flatly. "They seem rather heavily armed for guys just here to take an injured kid into custody. Sam, what do you think?" he said, turning to his second.

"Maybe trying for a bit of shock and awe," Wheaton said, sounding neither shocked nor awed.

"All right, I've had about enough of this shit," Colman said, finally reaching the end of his rope. It had been a long goddamn week. "We're taking the kid. We've got the warrant, so I'll politely ask you to get out of the way. I'll leave a copy of the warrant for you, don't worry."

"Your men try to get anywhere near Mr. Anderson and I will have them killed where they stand."

That brought everybody up short. The four tactical agents had been standing there looking variously threatening and annoyed, with their hands leisurely resting on or near the rifles slung across their chests, but after the Sheriff made that statement everyone in the corridor went still. The men on the DHS team moved their hands back to their rifles. Not ready to shoot, they didn't really think that would happen, but....

Colman chose his words carefully. "Sheriff, do you really want to start a gunfight with federal agents in the hallway of a hospital? Are you looking for an excuse to go out in a blaze of glory, put that cherry on the top of your very public career? Are you dying of an inoperable brain tumor and want to hasten the end? I must admit your sense of humor is lost on me." The detective behind the Sheriff looked surprised by the threat as well.

"You're right, I have been very lucky in my life," the Sheriff admitted. "And I have become a very public figure, even though I never wanted that. But because of that, most everyone here I'm assuming has heard the story of how I found Jesus Christ and came to the Lord in Vietnam. Shot six times, laying there on that riverbank in the A Shau, waiting to die. Surrounded by the dead, by the bodies of the men I'd come to know as my brothers. And those we'd killed. Laying on their intestines, watching fish eat their eyes. I waited to die. And waited.

"For two days I was in agonizing pain, and kept expecting for the end to come. But it never happened. In fact, my pain grew less. And I came to realize that was because the Lord had saved me. And if he saved me, it goes to follow he must have a purpose for me. He has a purpose for all of us, but I never realized that fact before that moment. I vowed to myself on that day that if I lived, I would be a good Christian for the rest of my mortal life, and I would treat every day above ground as if it was my last day on earth. Make every decision as if my life depended on it and God was looking over my shoulder, judging me. And somehow He gave me the strength to walk out of there, to walk miles to my unit, through jungle infested with the enemy, with wounds that should have killed me.

"Every day since then I have strived to do my best. While I know that the eternal reward is waiting for me, every day above ground, Mr. Colman, is a good day. Since that day I lay on that riverbank and waited to die, I have had fifteen thousand days above ground, and every one of them has been a good day. A glorious day. Not roughly fifteen thousand, mind you; I've been keeping count. Counting every day. Yesterday it was fourteen thousand, nine hundred and ninety-nine. Today, today I have received the gift of fifteen thousand days that I would not otherwise have had were it not for the Lord. Fifteen thousand is a good round number, a miraculous number for a man who should have died forty years ago but was saved by the hand of God. So if today is my day to die, sir, then it is a good day to die, and I go forth with a light heart."

Colman heard the click as the Sheriff disengaged the safety of his shotgun. It was perhaps the loudest sound he had ever heard, echoing up and down the hospital corridor. "Sam," Osterman said, "will you sing at my funeral?"

"It would be my honor," the cowboy beside the Sheriff drawled, his hand on his holstered pistol. "If I ain't layin' dead beside you." He popped the thumb-break on his holster with a thumb that looked like it was made of aged and stained walnut. The sound of safeties going off up and down the hallway was ominous.

Jesus Christ, thought Colman, blinking rapidly. *The hell did I fucking walk into?* The deputies were lined up along the walls, in open doorways, in a defensive formation, hands on their guns. Colman realized just how many of the Sheriff's men were carrying shotguns and rifles.

Shotgun John...how many men had the Sheriff himself killed? Something like six or seven, most of them with a shotgun. Maybe the same battered one he was holding now, which wasn't quite pointed at anyone. Colman could sense the DHS agents behind him, getting squirrelly, and they were all combat vets. Shit, *he* was getting squirrelly. "Look," Colman said, raising his open hands, hoping they couldn't see him sweating, "I know you might think he is, but he's not safe here."

"Even if I believed you," the Sheriff said, "you can't move him. He's been shot three times and has bad burns on his hands. He can't be moved for days, if not weeks. He still hasn't regained consciousness from the surgery yesterday."

Bad burns on his hands? That was news. That was......"Can I see him and speak to his doctor?" Colman asked, still keeping his hands raised in a gesture of surrender. "My men can wait here."

Without taking his eyes off Colman, Osterman said "Ginny? You want to call Doc Brennan?"

The nurse released the breath she didn't realize she'd been holding and paged Dr. Brennan. "He shouldn't be much more than a minute or two," she told them nervously.

"We'll wait right here," he told Colman. And then just stared at him, not saying anything, not fidgeting, just holding the shotgun. Safety still off, finger alongside the trigger guard.

It was closer to five minutes later when they all heard the ding of the elevator. When the doctor stepped out he stopped at the sight of so many men and guns in the hallway of his hospital. "What's going on?" he demanded.

"This gentleman from Homeland Security would like an update on Mr. Anderson," the Sheriff told him, holding out a hand for him to lead the way to the young man's room. "If you wouldn't mind, Doctor. Sam," he said, giving his second a pointed look, "keep the rest of these gentlemen entertained."

As the Sheriff, the detective from Detroit, and the suit from Washington walked down the hall behind him, Sam Wheaton smiled grimly behind his moustache, then stomped his boot on the floor. Then again. And again. By the third stomp every deputy on the floor was stomping their feet in time to his. The beat was slow, foreboding. The DHS guys looked at each other. They were already rattled...now what the hell was happening?

Outside the door to Anderson's room, Colman turned and stared back down the hall at the deputies stomping their feet solemnly, and then of all things the cowboy deputy began singing slowly, in a classical, trained baritone—

> *"You can run on, for a long time*
> *Run on, for a long time,*
> *Run on, for a long time,*
> *Sooner or later gotta cut you down*
> *Sooner or later gotta cut you down."*

It was eerie, the other deputies were stomping their feet, keeping time for the mustachioed old deputy. He stared directly at the DHS agents with their guns as he sung in a deep, gravelly voice, and every other deputy in the hall stared at them expressionlessly as they stomped. Every one of them had their hand on their gun.

"Shall we?" the Sheriff said to the distracted Colman outside the room.

"Um, uh..."

> *"Go tell that long-tongued liar,*
> *Go and tell that midnight rider,*
> *Tell the rambler, the gambler, the back-biter,*
> *Tell them that God's gonna cut 'em down,*
> *Tell them that God's gonna cut 'em down."*

The Sheriff pushed open the door to Anderson's room and Doc Brennan entered, followed by Colman, who seemed distracted. He suddenly turned to the Sheriff and said, "This is what you sang to the man on death row. You taunted him."

"If you mean Henry Lee Miller, who killed a woman, her child, and two of my men, and laughed about it all through his trial, then yes. He was a cop killer, and my men sang to him as he was led into the execution chamber," the Sheriff corrected him. "We weren't taunting him, we were educating him, lettin' him know what he had to look forward to."

"And the Attorney General sent you a letter of condemnation," Colman said. "Signed by the Governor as well. I remember. Demanding an apology to the family of the convict. Citing cruel and unusual punishment. You think you're a king down here?"

"I am no king. I was duly elected by the people of this county. Six times, now. And the Attorney General of the United States is a tool of Satan, of that I have no doubt," the Sheriff told him. "The only question I have is whether or not he is a *willing* tool."

Colman could feel the stomping in his feet, it was coming up through the floor. He stared out the door at the deputies staring at his men like zombies, stomping their feet like robots as the cowboy sang about death. Jesus fuck, it was creepy as hell. What was it Time Magazine had said? Oh yeah, his men displayed "an almost cult-like devotion" to their Sheriff. Colman felt sweat break out all over his body.

> "..I've been down on bended knee,
> Talking to the man from Galilee
> He spoke to me in a voice so sweet
> I thought I heard the shuffle of angels' feet
> He called my name and my heart stood still,

When he said 'John, go do my will!'"

The old deputy could sing, that was for sure, and his steady voice was echoing down the corridor eerily. Colman had apparently stepped into a Twilight Zone episode, and had completely lost control of the situation. Not that he'd ever really had it…which wasn't like him, not at all.

"How many lawsuits has the Justice Department filed against you and your department?" he asked the Sheriff, trying to regain lost ground.

"Nearly as many as we've filed against it."

Colman stopped at the foot of Anderson's bed and looked down at him. He was unconscious, an IV in one arm, sheet up around his waist. There was a large square bandage on his upper right arm, near his shoulder, and his hands were thickly wrapped. One side of his head was bright red and shiny, hair burned short and completely missing in patches. A large rectangular bandage covered the other side of his head from ear to neck.

"Give him the Cliff's Notes version, doc," the Sheriff said, shotgun still in hand and, perhaps not unintentionally, pointing at the open doorway.

Dr. Ethan Brennan looked at the Sheriff and the man in the suit, not liking the tension in the room, but said, "The patient had surgery yesterday, and is currently in serious condition. None of his injuries are immediately life threatening, but he's got a lot of them. He lost a lot of blood. He suffered a gunshot wound to the right upper arm which required a number of stitches to repair. He was also shot in the left thigh, I believe with a rifle bullet, which passed through-and-through and somehow did not hit bone or any major blood vessels.

"He was also shot in the face. The bullet skimmed along the jawbone, breaking it, and took a piece out of his neck. Very painful, I imagine, and ugly, but no major blood vessels were hit. Setting his jaw and stitching that up took us the most time yesterday. We've got an oral surgeon coming in tomorrow to look at that, because of the way the jaw was cracked. He also suffered first- and second-degree burns to the other side of his face which, compared to his other wounds, is a minor issue. The injury that has me the most concerned are the burns to his hands. His fingertips, to be more precise." Brennan didn't even mention the piece of drywall screw he'd found embedded in Anderson's left shin.

"His fingertips are burned? How many?" Colman said. "How did that happen?"

The doctor shook his head. "All his fingers. I've no clue how it happened, although if I remember correctly from the news reports his house did burn down. They're bad burns, at least third degree. As if he was holding onto something that was on fire and couldn't let go. He was semi-conscious when they found him, but non-responsive. There's a burn specialist coming up from Phoenix today to look at him. I wouldn't be surprised if he needed skin grafts."

"That bad? So there will be...scarring?" Colman asked.

"Scarring? I'd be surprised if he doesn't have range of motion issues. We might have to amputate the ends of some of his fingers, I don't know. It's really outside my area of expertise. This boy's fingers have been cooked, literally."

Colman stood there staring at Anderson for almost a full minute, thinking. "But he'll live," he said finally.

"There are no guarantees in life, but yes, unless he gets some sort of nasty infection, there is no reason why he shouldn't completely recover from his wounds."

"Minus his fingertips."

"Yes. Well, he might not lose them, but his fingers will be scarred for life."

Colman stood there and stared at the young man for a few more minutes, looking thoughtful, then turned to Osterman. "Okay, he's yours, you can keep him here. But I might want to interview him in the future. I'm not done with him."

"I would recommend calling ahead of time," the Sheriff said drily.

The DHS agents were soaked in sweat when he rejoined them, which was perfectly understandable. They'd been surrounded by stone-faced cops stomping their feet while another cop with the voice of a cowboy poet sang about how God was gonna cut them down. Nobody saying a word, everybody's hands on their rifles and shotguns.

"Let's go," Colman said to them, pulling his phone out of his pocket. He waited to make a call until he was back out in the parking lot, standing away from the tactical agents who stood beside their black Tahoe. They were trying to look like it was just another day on the job, but they looked as freaked out as he felt. He was pretty sure the Sheriff's deputies would have been happy to slaughter all of them in that hospital corridor. Probably while singing gospels. God and guns and mental illness—he hated Arizona so very fucking much.

"I don't think our issue is an issue any more," he told the person who answered the phone. "It seems to have resolved itself."

"Really? How did that happen?"

"Burns," Colman said. "Bad burns. Self-inflicted, I think. He did a John Dillinger. Wasn't it Dillinger who removed his fingerprints with acid?"

"I wouldn't know," said the voice on the other end. "I'm not quite that old. So are we done with this?"

"Not quite. They seemed to know I was coming. I'm not sure how. The fact that he did a Dillinger tells me that he knew exactly what his problem was, and I'm not sure how he came into that information either. And since I don't know, I'd feel better if we cleaned as much of this mess up as possible. The people who caused this mess are still out there....."

"And are not grocers, or truck drivers." He heard a deep sigh. "You'll need to be circumspect. Subtle. *Accidental*, given their occupations."

Colman smiled past the phone at the parking lot and the waiting tactical team. Shows of force were not his usual style, but you did what the job called for. He'd be happy to go back to being the gray man. "Accidents, as you know, are my specialty."

"I need to move out here," Aaron muttered to himself, staring at the departing backs of the DHS agents. The thumping beat of the deputies' boots and haunting words were making a few of them visibly twitch. He glanced over at Sheriff 'Shotgun John' Osterman, who as soon as the elevator door closed looked much more tired. Ringo was there standing next to him. "Right the hell now." He flicked the safety back on his Colt, and removed his hand from the stainless steel grip. His hand was shaking. And sweating. He'd thought for sure that standoff was going to end in a whole lotta dead bodies. At least EMS would be close......

"Well, that was something," Ringo told Osterman. His shirt felt soaked through. He glanced at the old deputy who'd been singing, who now resnapped his holster and then pulled out a toothpick and went to work with it. "I don't even know...." He stared down the empty hallway toward the elevator.

"I've known Sam here for almost thirty years," the sheriff said almost absently. "Ran into him at college. He'd just gotten out of high school, and I'd been out of the army for a few years, trying to figure out what I wanted to do with my life. We both ended up going into law enforcement." The Sheriff paused. "Although we both minored in Theater."

That made Ringo's head snap around. "Geez. Theater? I....uh.....wow. You really had me going there."

"Oh, I meant every word I said," the Sheriff let him know. "I'm a true believer. I would have blown him out of his socks right there and been happy to go meet the Lord, if that's how it worked out. The problem is making the *other fellow* believe. Sometimes, for that, you need a little.....showmanship. Warriors have been chanting to unnerve the enemy for millennia. War paint, battle cries, and chanting. It's one of those proven, old-fashioned things I've been trying to bring back into fashion, like actually punishing criminals."

Ringo stared at him. "And 'fifteen thousand days'?"

Osterman shrugged. "It's somewhere around there." He looked at the Detroit detective. "So, what do you think? Do you think he'll be back? Try it again?"

Ringo shook his head. "I don't know. I'd hate to guess, but it sure seemed like something in there flipped his switch to Off."

"Hmmf." The Sheriff had noticed the same thing, the DHS agent had gone from night to day almost instantly. He looked to his second. "Sam, I want round-the-clock protection on this kid while he's here. Three up here, and one in the parking lot to call anybody out. Long guns. Fifteen minute check-ins. And I don't care who shows up, with what paperwork, even if they're accompanied by the Governor, that boy goes nowhere. Understood?"

"You got it."

"For how long?" Ringo asked him.

The Sheriff looked back at the open door of the kid's room, then down the hallway where his men were waiting for further instructions. "I guess we'll see," he answered. He thought of the digital recording Detective George had brought him. There were right ways and wrong ways of doing certain things, but sometimes you just had to make shit up as you went. Improvise, adapt, and overcome, as his brethren in the Marine Corps liked to say. He looked back at

Sam. "Call Mindy Tonaka at Fox. Tell her I've got an exclusive for her."

AUTHOR'S NOTE

The details in this book concerning Supervisory Special Agent Dr. Frederick Whitehurst's ultimately contentious relationship with the FBI Lab, and its procedures, are accurate. Also accurate are all the details I have mentioned concerning the mis-identification and arrest of Brandon Mayfield by the FBI for the 2004 Madrid train bombings, because his fingerprints were a "100 percent positive match" with the suspect's. Exactly how much money the FBI was forced to pay Mayfield because of this error on their part has not been made public, but guesses put it upwards of $2 million.

In fact, all the technical information in this novel concerning how fingerprints are categorized, examined, and compared by law enforcement agencies (including the FBI), to the extent that I have described them in this book, is accurate. There is human input at nearly every stage of the process, and errors can and often do occur whenever you get people involved in anything. Many true "scientists" don't think much of fingerprinting as a science.

I would like to thank many people who helped me with this book, especially FBI Special Agent "Bart". He valiantly attempted to correct the errors I made, and any inaccuracies in this book concerning the FBI are solely on my shoulders, not his. Anyone familiar with the FBI Lab at Quantico or its in-house procedures might note that I have taken a few liberties, as is my right as the author of a fiction novel. That said, Special Agent Bart would like me to point out that as far as he knows, no two people have ever been known to have identical fingerprints, and the FBI does not make a habit of assassinating its own employees.

Darcy Leutzinger, John Rock, Greg Williams, and Bill Koenig were better Warren police officers than I ever was, and the time I spent working with them made this a better book. I'd also like to thank Ric Gallaway for the best one-liner about divorce I've ever heard, which I stole for this book.

If you ever decide driving an armored car around Detroit for little more than minimum wage would be a good career move, you could not have a better partner watching your back than Darrin Anselm.

Taran Butler is everything he is in this book and much, much more.

My depiction of Detroit may get a few area residents angry with me. I've spent almost my entire life living in the suburbs around Detroit, and nearly twenty years working in and around the city as a private investigator, among other jobs. Vacant overgrown land, burned-out buildings, corrupt mayors, packs of wild dogs roaming the streets....every ugly detail of the city that has made it into this novel I have seen with my own eyes. Including the racial polarization. Detroit was once a great city, and one day it may be again, but right now it is in serious trouble. Pretending otherwise does not do the city or anyone in it any good.

Mark Messens, Jeff Dickison, and Jason Murray, three of the best PIs I've ever worked with, helped fill in some local color. The incident in the book with Marsh and the young man with the screwdriver actually happened to a PI we know, but the most interesting stories we have about the job we can never tell.

ABOUT THE AUTHOR

James Tarr is the author of several novels, and co-authored Dillard Johnson's Iraq War memoir, CARNIVORE. A regular contributor to many outdoor enthusiast magazines, he also appears on the Guns & Ammo television show. Tarr lives in Michigan with his fiancée, two sons, and a dog named Fish.

60859545R00273

Made in the USA
Lexington, KY
20 February 2017